Angela Huth has written three collections of short stories, and seven novels – *Nowhere Girl*, *Virginia Fly is Drowning*, *Sun Child*, *South of the Lights*, *Wanting*, *Invitation to the Married Life* and *Land Girls*. She also writes plays for radio, television and stage, and is a well-known freelance journalist, critic and broadcaster. She is married to a don, lives in Oxford, and has two daughters.

ANGELA HUTH

South of the Lights

An *Abacus* Book

First published in Great Britain by Collins 1977
This edition published in 1994 by Abacus
Reprinted 1994, 1995, 1996

Copyright © Angela Huth 1977

The moral right of the author has been asserted.

A CIP catalogue record for this book
is available from the British Library.

ISBN 0 349 10554 5

Printed in England by Clays Ltd, St Ives plc

Abacus
A Division of
Little, Brown and Company (UK)
Brettenham House
Lancaster Place
London WC2E 7EN

'I did not know
That heydays fade and go,
But deemed that what was would be always so.'
                                        Thomas Hardy

PART I

Chickens, thought Evans. Bloody chickens. Their pernickety clucking had become a background to his life. Sometimes, good days, he could tolerate them. They reminded him of the years ahead, the house he and Brenda would have, the strip of garden at the back, the hen-house and run he would make for them. They would be free-range birds, of course, and lay brown eggs which Brenda would gather in a basket. Other times, in the dim smelly shed where he and Brenda seemed to spend so much of their time, he felt like putting a bomb to the place. He felt like blasting for ever their mouldy feathers and indignant red eyes and peevish chatter. Oh, he was sorry for them all right. But God, he hated them too. Today, he'd make sure to stay outside the shed. Today they'd get on his nerves.

Evans walked through the farmyard, May sun hot through his shirt. It hadn't rained for two weeks. His feet made small clouds of dust rise from the dry dirt track. He sniffed the rank smell of animals and manure. Brenda would like an hour off for lunch, he thought. Or perhaps she wouldn't. She was unpredictable like that. But just in case, he had bought two pork pies and cans of beer. It would be nice to sit in the field behind the sheds and eat in the sun. There, the farmyard smells were less strong.

He turned the corner. A hundred yards ahead stood the familiar hulk of tarred sheds where Wilberforce's chickens lived, laid and died. Brenda's territory. She leaned against the door, one knee bent, heel lodged behind it on some rough piece of wood. Her head was tilted towards the sun, eyes closed. A lighted cigarette drooped between her fingers. She raised her hand slowly to her mouth and inhaled, without opening her eyes.

Evans felt a swarm of love for her, giddying his head. He moved faster. She would not hear his step in the soft earth.

9

He would surprise her. She might be pleased. A few feet away from her he stopped to anticipate her pleasure, and to enjoy the sight of her before she became aware of his presence. She was wearing his favourite shirt: cream cotton covered with a pattern of chicks breaking out of their shells. Beneath the crowd of chicks her breasts rose and fell with her slow, even breathing. Last night they had overflowed from Evans's hands. She had shouted to him to be careful: the straw was scratching her something awful, she had said, and he had silenced her shouts with his mouth. Evans swallowed. No matter how good the night had been, he always felt uncertain how to approach her in the morning.

'Brenda,' he said.

She opened her eyes, turned her head slowly towards him, leaving it tipped towards the sun so that her chin was a defiant point.

'Oh, it's you.' No surprise in her voice. She puffed at her cigarette again. Evans allowed himself to be dazzled for a moment by the sparkling ring on her fourth finger, a small pink stone which, on less bright days, faded disappointingly.

'You smoking again,' he said. 'You'll cop it if Wilberforce catches you.'

'Wilberforce can't tell me what to do. I've got the sense to be careful, haven't I? Not likely I'm going to set his bloody ricks on fire.'

'But he said you'd get the push next time.'

'What would I care about that?'

'You'd miss the hens.'

Brenda flung her cigarette stub on to the ground. It landed beside Evans. He squashed it with his foot, buried it with the dusty earth.

'There are plenty of other hens.'

Evans felt an explosion of gunshot beneath his ribs. Its reverberations quickened the pace of his heart. He stepped towards her, roughly pulled down her chin between his thumb and finger, and kissed her.

'Don't be daft,' he said, the words smudged by her lips. She smelt of corn. Sometimes, evenings, when they went to the cinema, she would dab herself with lavender water or essence of bluebell, which her mother sent from Birmingham every Christmas. But the scent always wore off very quickly and gave way to the essential corn smell of her skin which, as Evans often said, made him feel drunker than a dozen double whiskies.

'Leave off,' said Brenda, pushing him away. 'It's too hot.'

'Just feel my heart.'

Brenda put her hand to his heart.

'You and your heart. You might as well give up if your heart didn't beat faster sometimes.'

Evans smiled, causing his drooping left eyelid to sag until it almost covered his eyeball. Moonlight nights in the barn, Brenda said it was his funny eye that made her feel sexy. In bright sun, he noticed, she often looked away from him, or concentrated on his mouth or other eye. So by day he had learnt to restrict his smiles.

'I brought us a bite to eat,' he said, flourishing the paper bag. 'I thought we might need it after . . .'

'After what?' Brenda was in a teasing mood.

'After all that. I'm shagged, myself.'

'Are you? I'm fine. Quite hungry.'

'We could go and sit in the field.'

'I like it just standing here.'

'We can't eat just standing here.'

'Don't see why not, pork pies.'

'How d'you know I've brought pork pies?'

'You always do, don't you?'

Evans's voice dropped.

'Sometimes I bring the steak and kidney, don't I? They were out of them today.' He handed her the bag. She took one of the pies. Its greasy pastry had a whitish sheen. They ate standing up.

'How's the post office, then?'

Every day, Evans dreaded the question. Manager of the

village's sub post office had not, in three years, turned out to be the job he had once expected. It was devoid of both interest and excitement. Promotion had not come his way and indeed, now Brenda was his life, in some ways he would not relish it: to be transferred to the local town would add to complications. Privately, Evans went so far as to pray for a hold-up. If such a thing took place he would act with commendable cool and bravery. He had rehearsed it many times in his mind, and he longed for it with a force that surprised him. For nothing less than a masked gunman would flame Brenda's interest in his job. Nothing less than near death would transform Evans into her hero.

'Quite a few parcels for the time of year.'

'Perhaps they're posting early for Christmas.' She said it in a lifeless tone. Only twelve hours ago, Evans found himself thinking, her voice had been husky, musical with desire. The remembrance brought a chill to his brow.

'Perhaps they are,' he said. 'But I wish there was more exciting news for you. I just seem to sit behind the grille, day after day, waiting for the next centenary stamp to brighten my life.'

Brenda shrugged, smiling. Sometimes, when he didn't try, the most unexpected things would make her smile.

'Elizabeth's not laying,' she said. 'Would you like to take a look at her? She looks right down.'

'No, I wouldn't, really. Not if you don't mind.'

'I told Wilberforce last week she was seedy, but he said don't be so stupid, he could tell a mile off when a bird was seedy. So now this afternoon I'll have to tell him she's not laying and he'll say: so what? The bird's not laying. Floribunda's going to be the next one. But I shan't say anything. He can find out for himself if he knows so much.'

'Wilberforce got a birthday coming up soon?'

'Not that I know of. Why?'

'Mrs Wilberforce was in this morning. Took twenty minutes choosing a card. Landed up with a picture of a bowl of hyacinths, a bit of real satin ribbon round the bowl and

Happy Birthday Dearest Love inside. Been in the place six months. Thought I'd never get rid of it.'

'Now that *is* news.' Brenda shifted her position. 'That wouldn't be for Wilberforce. That would be for the man she's seeing in Luton. Sees him every week, says she's visiting her cousin.'

'You know everything,' said Evans.

'I just hear without meaning to. Doesn't mean anything to me.' Brenda sighed, put her hands in the pockets of her jeans, stood with legs astride. Evans found the stance irresistibly provocative. He looked away.

'Come on,' Brenda sighed. 'Let's have the beer then I can get back to grading the eggs.' She had a curious way, on occasions, of sounding dismissive. Evans opened a can. The froth spurted out, spilling on to the ground, splattering the dark earth with deeper spots. He handed it to her, the liquid running over his wrists, his hand shaking.

'Wilberforce not bothering you any more, is he?'

'Wouldn't be worth his while, again, would it? I keep out of his way. He makes me sick.'

'I'd kill him if he laid a hand on you,' said Evans.

'No you wouldn't. You wouldn't kill a worm.'

'He's a bastard.'

'He's not worth bothering yourself about. He knows he doesn't stand a chance with me.'

'He better not try.'

'Oh, he *won't*, Evans. Do stop going on about Wilberforce.'

Evans watched the beer running down Brenda's chin. She had never learnt to drink properly from a can. He passed her his handkerchief.

'What would you like to do tonight?'

'Tonight?'

'You could come over to my place.'

'Not if it's your Dad's night in. I couldn't face your Dad, not tonight I couldn't. Besides, I want to wash my hair. Lark said she'd do it for me.' She put her hand behind her back and opened the door to the shed. At once the clatter of hens, which until now had been a subdued murmur, swelled to irritate Evans's ears.

'It's all very unsatisfactory,' he said, 'this not having anywhere to go.'

'Well, we're saving, aren't we?'

'We've been saving two bloody years, and we don't seem much nearer. If we had somewhere of our own, it'd be easier.'

'I'm not complaining.'

'Sometimes you sound as if you don't care.'

'No point in being impatient, is there?'

She pushed the shed door further open. Through the mottled light inside Evans could just discern the stacked coops, the pathetic heads and claw-like beaks that jerked from each one of them. If he stayed one moment longer Brenda would persuade him in to see Elizabeth.

'I'll pick you up this evening, then,' he said.

'I told you I was washing my hair, didn't I?'

'I'll pick you up and run you home in the car.'

Brenda took a packet of Woodbines from the pocket of her jeans. 'And shut up your nagging, Evans, will you?'

'I didn't say a thing.' His hands tightly clenched, one on each empty beer can.

'You get at me with your looks as bad as words. You'd better get back to sorting your parcels.' She turned and went into the shed. Her body at once shed its skin of light, became submerged in shadow, speckled and untenable as a trout under water. Evans walked back up the dirt track, uneasy in the heat. Three and a half stifling hours behind the post office grille before he could return to her, and, in the brief drive to her flat, try to find out what he had done wrong.

Rosie Evans pushed her wheel basket of groceries up the mild hill to the cottage in which she and Henry had lived all their married life, thirty-eight years. It was one of a row of thatched and beamed cottages adjacent to the church, the last remaining part of the original village. Since Rosie's childhood some fifty similar dwellings had fallen into a state of irreparable decay and been pulled down. They were replaced by a growth of ill-conceived contemporary houses which architects wrongly imagine are desirable: sour red brick, identical bubble-glass front doors and cement front paths. The kind of houses Rosie supposed might be all very well in a New Town, but were quite out of place in what once had been a small and pretty village. Even the old vicarage had been demolished. (No one could claim it was the best of Victorian architecture, but it had had thick Virginia creeper, and a lovely front porch, as Rosie and Henry knew from experience, for courting.) It had been replaced by a flat-roofed brick box, whose windows, which flowed from roof to ground, seemed to have been designed to expose the vicar's entire private life. His wife, although supporting her husband in the theory that a shepherd should always be available to his sheep, felt that this kind of availability was going too far. Her first week at the new vicarage was spent sewing old surplices together to form some measure of protection. These, she explained, would be no ordinary curtains: more, a kind of religious mist clinging permanently to the windows. The vicar saw light. They would add a mystical air to his movements, he thought, and he was able to rejoice.

Rosie, whose eyes could never be intent upon so ugly a building as the vicarage, glanced instead up at the three tall elms which grew in a triangle where the lane to the church and cottages petered out. They were still healthy. One day, no doubt, they would be stricken by the fatal disease, and have to be pulled down. Rosie hoped they would last her lifetime. She knew them well, in all seasons, and loved them. Every new demolition in the village had saddened her. Had it been ruined twenty years ago, she and Henry might have considered moving away. But its final devastation had only taken place within the last few years, and now they were too old to move. Besides, from the rooms of the cottage their small views had not changed: at the back, the graveyard, at the front the elms and the mossy green fence that surrounded the grounds of Wroughton House. So they were lucky, really. Lucky compared with Evans and Brenda, who would be forced to the wicked expense of buying a new place. Still, according to Brenda – and Rosie could understand – young people preferred bland walls with no beams, and all the conveniences of a modern building. She and Henry would leave the cottage to Evans, of course, but he wouldn't want it. He would sell it and spend the money improving his own house – if by then he had managed to buy one. She hoped he would be happy.

Rosie, whose sympathies were universally available, spent a considerable part of her life wishing for other people's happiness. She herself was embalmed in a contentment she had woven for herself, and made inextricable. Her own pleasures were simple, added to almost daily, while the pleasures of people around her, and people on television, added to the web of satisfaction. But she was not complacent. Aware that happiness is inevitably a precipice at the edge of an abyss, she regarded the good fortune of her life as something to be banked, and called upon to fortify if and when the fall came. She had a recurring nightmare that Henry, whose only skittishness became apparent in his fourteen-year-old Morris Minor, would one day be mangled in a car crash. She had been prepared for the tragedy for years. When it came she would be able to cope. She would recall that she had had thirty-eight loving years with Henry, more than the fair share of most human beings, and surely the grateful knowledge of that would help ameliorate the loss.

Meantime, the act of loving her husband had its positive rewards, even if they were not always in abundance. He had never been the easiest of men, but in him Rosie recognized a challenge to which she rose with most persistent enjoyment. She had learnt two very good tips from her own mother on how to provide a husband's pleasure: always have something warm in the oven, and never cease to welcome him. Lately, since the stability of Henry's teeth had been causing some concern, his unexpected appetites for a hot pie at odd times of the day had declined. Now, he was happier to suck gently at a ginger biscuit and, accordingly, Rosie had cut down on her baking. But in relinquishing one of her stable methods of assuring love, Rosie found herself doubling her efforts when it came to the other. In this, their peaceful retirement, her welcomes to Henry flourished. Even now, as she paused to enjoy the great yellow-green spread of the elms' branches, Rosie chided herself. She had been dawdling. Henry, sitting by the small coal fire, would have finished the *Daily Mirror*. He would be wondering where she was, missing her. She pushed at the handle of her wicker basket, impatient with herself. In the few yards left to the front door she pondered upon today's greeting, a fresh way to assure Henry that all was well, that here she was, back again.

Henry Evans was exhausted by his wife's welcomes. He sat in his armchair by the fire bracing himself for Rosie's return, relishing the last few moments of peace. Any moment these would be shattered by her kind smiles and eager questions and hopes for his well-being. Over the years he had learnt that to respond to her benevolence merely led to further, wearying counter-response. In self-defence he had become a taciturn man, only speaking if it became necessary to further the plot of his life. Which was not, as he had been reflecting this afternoon behind the *Daily Mirror*, a very exciting life. Nor had it ever been. In sixty-five years nothing surprising had happened: except for one wild storm in the Bay of Biscay, in his Navy days, he had known neither drama nor fear. He could have done with a few more storms. The murderous waves had raced his blood, somehow, giving him energy and adrenalin which had lasted for a year or so, then faded, leaving him dull to himself again. It was in his year of exuberance that he had married Rosie, a pretty young thing then, in spite of her hands. In those days he had been equal to her energy. But as the benefits of the storm receded, he found himself no match for her. She had been a tiringly good wife for thirty-eight years, and wasn't likely to change her loving ways now. In retirement, her cocoon of benevolence was particularly claustrophobic. There were so few chances, or reasons, to get out. Saturdays and Tuesdays he went to the pub, alone, because Rosie was of the opinion beer and darts were men's things, and she'd want no one to accuse her of pushing herself into a man's world, making a nuisance of herself where she might not be wanted. Mondays and Fridays he went to the local ironmonger for a couple of hours to look through the books. He'd always been good with figures, and he liked the small, stuffy back office where he was put to work with a mug of strong tea. He liked the smell of nails and potash and rubber plugs, and the half-dozen inevitable interruptions from Mr Daly, his boss, who had a lively line in complaints about what the Government was doing to his shop. In spring, Henry would sometimes try to escape for a walk in the bluebell woods, up on the hill, where he would listen to the thrushes and smoke his pipe. But however unadventurous he tried to make his proposed walk sound, Rosie would not be taken in. Undaunted by his warnings of wasps, stinging nettles and all manner of unexpected hazards, she would often insist on coming too. She would enjoy the walk with an energy that made Henry's heart retract into an impenetrable shell, and he would make no word of response to her reminiscences of times past when in their youth they had picnicked – and more – beneath these very trees.

'Do you remember, Henry, love? You in your uniform and I said take off your cap before you do anything like that to me.'

Her incessant jabbering drowned the birdsong – she drained the woods of all their peace. Lately, Henry had given up. He went for no more walks. He had grown fatter, slower, with resignation. He anticipated no excitements or changes before his death, and accepted the realisation as quite bearable. It was therefore with some surprise that he had found himself enjoying this afternoon more than he had enjoyed an afternoon for many a year. It was with even more surprise that he had discovered precisely what had caused the pleasure.

As it was a Tuesday he had gone to the Star for his usual pint at lunchtime. He had taken his drink to his accustomed table and was looking about him, in his quiet way, thinking they'd have to invest in a new carpet soon, judging by the fraying at his feet, when a woman came into the pub. This was not an unusual event: women in the pub caused no comment in spite of Rosie's beliefs – but this was a strange woman, one Henry had not seen before. She was not an old woman, nor a young one, and yet the term middle-aged, with all its implications, seemed most unsuited to her. She wore a fur coat, extravagantly dotted with leopard spots, and gripped round her small waist by a broad leather belt. Her short hair was blonde and curly and she had a freshness about her, a confident gaiety that caught the attention of everyone in the room. At her entrance the clink of glasses, the small sounds of low talk and shifting feet, seemed to diminish. Everyone could hear her order. A double Dubonnet with a twist of lemon, please, she said. Bill, the landlord, apologised, but he had run out of lemons. In response she turned away from him. Her eye fell upon Henry and she smiled an uncontainable smile, as if something within her could be withheld no longer.

'No lemon? How about that?' she said.

Henry, feeling her direct address to him must have been a mistake, hurriedly covered his face with his beer mug and drank too fast, making himself hiccough loudly. The woman turned back to the bar, drank her lemon-less Dubonnet, and paid for it all in a moment. Then she left in a hurry, smiling round the room as she went. Henry, his confusion still upon him, glanced at his fellow drinkers. He perceived that each one of them, behind his gesture of apparent indifference, was likewise a little shaken. Although an intangible thing, impossible to discuss, the strange lady's brief visitation seemed in some way to have ungrounded the secure, unexciting structure of an ordinary Tuesday. Henry could tell by the flush on the landlord's cheeks, and the way that old Jo let his moustache become confused with the froth of his beer – a thing that would never normally happen. For his own part, Henry felt unusual weakness in his knees. He walked home carefully, wondering. He tried to place the feeling: something long past, almost forgotten. Then, at the elm trees, very bright in the sun, it came to him. The storm. All those years ago, landing in Spain when the waves had subsided, realising he was both alive and safe, the combined sensations of exhilaration and weakness had struck him: and here they were again. Henry paused, letting his eyes wander up through the great blur of leaves, and he sighed with great contentment. Incredulous, he felt. Almost forty unfluttering years, and here was some new irrational flame, some pretty hope. He might never re-encounter the nymph in the leopard coat who had caused it, but that was no matter. He would feed upon what she had left behind for his own private pleasure: he would eke out the goodness, and when the bloom wilted at the end of some season, he would remember with gladness.

'Henry! You're back early. That's lovely. I'll be dishing up in just a moment!' Rosie was calling to him from the front door. Rosie was always bloody calling to him in her cheerful voice, but he was doubly protected from her beneficence now.

On his own, in the afternoon, Henry put aside his *Daily Mirror* as soon as his wife had gone. Legs stretched out before him, the warmth of the fire gentle upon his shins, he let the smile of the strange lady return to him. It was very bright in his mind. In fact, he could almost imagine her sitting there opposite him, smiling away, the afternoon light through the small window making her hair greenish, like a plant. Of course, in real life she'd be most uncomfortable, in her smart coat, on the old leather chair. Her polished shoes would skitter about on the tiled floor, and perhaps she would smoke, and need an ashtray, and there were no ashtrays in the room. On the other hand, she might just be the sort to curl up, knees under her, and listen.

If she would care to listen then Henry would like to tell her things, he thought. He would like to tell her how cumbersome he found his retirement, and with what nostalgia he looked back upon his working days. He had been a loader at the brick fields. In thirty years some hundreds of thousands – perhaps even millions – of bricks had passed through his hands. He knew the feel of them as well as he knew the feel of any part of his own body: the weight, the texture, the even dip of their spines, their raw reddish colour that looked quite sore on bright days, but mellowed under cloud. Henry could load up a lorry of bricks quicker than anyone: over the years he became known for his agility, his precision in stacking, his strength and tirelessness. What he never displayed was the pleasure a well-loaded lorry gave him. The satisfaction of the neatly piled structure – to last merely for the journey, then to be demolished by less loving hands – never decreased. He was offered many other jobs in the works, and he tried some of them, but always returned to loading. Indeed, as an unsurpassable loader he became something of a legend. (For all his modesty he was prepared to admit this.) The day of his retirement he had a friendly talk with Mr Dingley, the young manager, in the small office awash with all the paperwork of the business. Mr Dingley said Henry was the kind of man England needed to get industry back on its feet, and he would be sorry to see him go. Then he gave him an inscribed watch. Rosie had said it would be a gold, after thirty years. In fact it was silver, with a soft stretchy strap that felt comfortable on Henry's wrist. His mates had bought him more beers than he could drink that night, and slapped him on the back and said they hoped he'd come back to see them often – make sure they were doing things right. Henry said of course he would. But he never returned: he meant to, one day, but so far he had not been able to bring himself to do so. Besides the watch, he also took home a single brick. (He did not ask Mr Dingley's permission but felt that, in the circumstances, it would not be

21

considered stealing.) The brick sat on the window sill in the kitchen. Gathering dust, Rosie said. But Henry refused to move it. Sometimes, alone, he would hold it in his hands, feeling its familiar weight, reminding himself.

If the lady with the gay smile was here now and asked him about the brick, and she cared to listen, he would tell her the truth. He would tell her that most people in these parts resented the brick fields, scooped as they were out of the countryside, ugly, clustered with rail-tracks for the trucks, and the humped buildings where the bricks were baked. But Henry liked them. He liked the vast chimneys that speared the sky like masts, the sour sulphury smell their smoke sent into the murky clouds. Henry supposed he must have known hundreds of sunny times at the brickworks, but in retrospect the days he pictured were the ones he liked best: yellowish skies dappled with cloud. It may have been his imagination, but small clouds often seemed to gather round the chimneys in a busy, protective way. Sometimes there was a whole cluster of them over the brick fields, while not far away the sky was quite clear.

Winter was the time Henry liked best of all. Fraw, sullen, the bricks themselves the only bright things, gusts of warmth from the baking ovens as you walked past, the sulphur smell very keen on a frosty morning, stirred by an east wind. One year Henry had volunteered to guard the works on Christmas Day. He told Rosie and the Boy it was his turn: they had believed him, and sympathised. He arrived at the watchman's small office at five in the morning to relieve the man on night-duty. He stoked up the fire, boiled the black kettle and made himself a cup of tea. He walked round the works once or twice, checking all was well; but most of the day he sat in that small office drinking tea, listening to music on the radio, studying the picture of the Queen on the wall calendar, very demure in all her jewels. And when he listened to her speech in the afternoon he felt it as if it was to him alone she spoke, from the dingy wall. Impressed, he stood up and saluted her. Then he ate his cold mince pies, looked out at the high chimneys and their everlasting puffs of dun smoke, and felt glad not to be round the Christmas tree with Rosie's relations. It grew cold in spite of the fire, and was quite dark at four. He left much later, bicycling slowly through the night frost, past lighted trees in small windows, and was happy to be outside it all. At home, Rosie welcomed him with hot cherry brandy and much sympathy and concern. But he had needed no one's sympathy: it had been the best Christmas Day he could remember, though he could not tell them that. Pity: because he would have liked to have explained about it to just one person before he died, and the lady with the curly hair, he had a strange feeling, might have been a little interested. Something in the lively way she had said, 'A double Dubonnet with a twist of *lemon*, please.' Silly of Bill to have run out of lemon.

'Henry? Here I am back again. Sorry to have been so long.' The clatter of Rosie coming through the front door. 'Hope you haven't been missing me, love ... Now, what can I get you for your tea?'

She might have learnt by now Henry never answered such questions. Tea, more than ever this afternoon, held no interest for him. He gathered up his paper.

Brenda sat on an upturned box in the chicken house smoking the last of her Woodbines. She had fed the hens and there was nothing further for her to do. It was the time of day she liked best: evening sun coming quite sharply through the high cobwebby skylights – which it never managed to do earlier in the day – the smell of chickens, sweet and fusty. When she came in at eight-thirty in the morning, after a night of messing, the smell was more pungent, almost stifling. By midday she had grown accustomed to it and by evening, as now, it filled all her senses with well-being.

Brenda was worried about Elizabeth. Elizabeth's eyes had settled into an unbroken stare during the afternoon and the lashless yellow lids, shaped like small petals but rough with pimples, drooped almost to closing. Elizabeth was queen of the shed – Brenda had made her so – and she was going to die. This time tomorrow she might well be dead. Brenda wondered who should succeed her: Clarissa, by rights. Clarissa was an old bird who laid more and bigger eggs than any of the others. She emitted terrible squawks of triumph each time she did so and the other birds, judging by their clucking protests, resented her boastfulness. Besides, she was not glamorous. Roberta had pecked great lumps out of the left-hand side of her neck, and no new feathers seemed likely to sprout over the patch of raw pink skin. She was a bird of strength, but no dignity, not ideally suited to be queen. Marilyn (after Monroe) would perhaps be better. Marilyn, had fate made her a free-range bird, would have been sex-mad, taxing the most virile cock with her demands. As it was, from the confines of her cooped-up life, she brooded with particular frustration. Brenda could tell from the sad, coquettish way she bent her head against the bars, murmuring to herself in a husky voice. Perhaps, though, she was more of a sex queen than a real queen and Daisy, a duller, more upright bird, would be a better leader. Daisy's comb was certainly the brightest in the shed: upstanding, a fiery red, a real crown. Daisy it would have to be, though the appointment would cause terrible jealousy in Floribunda's heart. But Floribunda, for all her fine show of feathers, was ailing. One of her legs seemed to be paralysed. She would probably die soon, too, and Brenda wished to be practical. No point in changing queens every few weeks.

Her cigarette finished, Brenda began to fold and unfold the piece of foil paper from out of the carton. She dreaded Elizabeth's death. Well, she wouldn't be there. Wilberforce could deal with the whole thing. She'd go out. Where? Anywhere. Walk about, walk about fast in the fields trying not to think of Wilberforce's hands round Elizabeth's neck. She knew what a man's hands looked like on a chicken's neck, twisting. That time Uncle Jim had killed Hen – she would never forget that. She wasn't supposed to be around, but she had peeped out of her bedroom window and seen the whole thing. It was the afternoon she had bought her new green shoes, the ones with high heels and bows on the front. Uncle Sam had given her the money for them on condition she promised not to mention to Uncle Jim he'd been visiting her mother. Of course she wouldn't have mentioned any of the uncles to any of the other uncles. For a start there were so many of them she got them confused. Uncle Sam must have been daft to think she'd tell on him. She took the money gladly. She didn't care what any of them did so long as they didn't bother her. The only one who bothered her up till now was Uncle Ernest, whose whisky breath smelt right down the street. He beat up her Mum once so she had a black eye for weeks. And then Mum got the sack from the café as the stinking old manager said he couldn't have a waitress looking as if she'd been through a mangle, it was bad for business. She and Mum had eaten bread and cheese and tinned soup for a week. She didn't mind for herself: food didn't matter to her. But Mum got a thin greenish look around her mouth, and her headaches came on so bad she hadn't got the energy to go and look for another job. It was then that Uncle Jim, who had been around for a few weeks, suggested he kill Hen, and make her into a nice chicken casserole. Brenda had cried: broken down right there, banging her head against the kitchen table, till her own sobs and screams became a cloudy dome about her head from which she could see no escape. Then she heard Mum shouting to her to stop making such a bloody racket. She stopped at once, a sudden silence: and in the quiet she saw Mum's own eyes were skinned with tears.

'No use being sentimental,' Uncle Jim had said, cramming sliced cheese into his mouth. He was always eating sliced cheese, letting tongues of it hang out of his mouth, waiting for the inner bits to melt before sucking up the rest. At least he bought his own, but it was one of his habits that Mum said drove her mad. She said she doubted she could live with a man who had such a thing about sliced cheese, although Uncle Jim seemed pretty well installed already.

'It's no use being sentimental,' said Uncle Jim again, who believed repetition made for greater truth, 'the fucking bird hasn't laid for a year, and she doesn't have much of a fucking life in the backyard, does she?'

Brenda didn't answer. It was true, Hen hadn't laid for a year and some of her old vitality – her very thorough pecking for scraps in the concrete strip of backyard – seemed to have dwindled. But Uncle Jim hadn't seen her as a chick mewling in a cardboard box in the kitchen. Uncle Jim hadn't eaten dozens of her speckled eggs and been lulled by the sound of her clucking, lonely evenings, while Brenda sat in the kitchen waiting for her mother to come home.

'Uncle Jim's right, of course,' Mum said, who was afraid of the man. Brenda saw a look pass between them and she knew the hours were closing in on Hen.

'I hate you, that's all,' she said quietly to Uncle Jim, and ran out of the house. It was down the road she met Uncle Sam who had given her the money for her shoes, and tweaked the skin of her arm under the elbow. She ran straight on down to the shop, not caring about the mess she looked, dried tears blotching her face, and bought the shoes right away. They had been in the window for weeks. They fitted perfectly. She looked in the mirror a long time, incredulous. They were hers. Her first pair of grown-up shoes. The bows made her ankles look skinnier than ever, but they were so pretty. Her friend Lindy Badger, who had tons of money for shoes, would be right jealous. She ran home wearing them, ran straight up to her room to have another look in her own mirror. Then she heard the squawking, the bird screams of fear. She rushed to the window. Uncle Jim's hands were round Hen's neck. They gave a small sharp twist. Hen's head flopped over his wrist, beak opened mid-cry. He turned to the kitchen, walked towards it, swinging her limp body.

'That's finished the fucker,' Brenda heard him shout to Mum. Brenda expected to cry again, but she felt no tears. She sat down, took off the green shoes, put them in their box

26

and shoved it under the bed. She would never wear them, now.

Brenda did not discover whether or not Mum made a casserole of Hen. If she did, then she and Uncle Jim must have eaten it at dinner-time, while she was still at school, and hidden the bones. A few days later Mum got a job cleaning up at the local cinema, and they ate better again, though every time there was frozen chicken Brenda refused it. She thought she could probably never eat chicken again.

A year later Uncle Jim was still living with them, though sometimes, when he was on night shift, other Uncles would come round for a while, and without being asked Brenda would go up to her room. On those occasions Mum would dab behind her ears with a bit of Essence of Gardenia (which Uncle Fred brought from Manchester) that she kept hidden behind the tinned food in the kitchen cupboard. She would brush her hair and take off her apron and undo two buttons of her dress, and look quite pretty, for all the mottled tiredness of her face. On those occasions Brenda would think that if only Mum had had the chance she could have made something of her life, and they could have had a nice house in the country, perhaps, instead of years in bloody Birmingham. But Mum hadn't had the chance, and she hadn't the strength to make one. Everything had gone against her, in spite of her generosity. Men, she said, were all shits with magic wands, and once they'd shoved their wands up you all the magic went, and off they'd go to try their tricks elsewhere. She said this quite often; she'd been saying it for as long as Brenda could remember – long before she knew what it meant, and she could see that Mum believed it. But one day, Mum said, you might find a man who wanted to keep all his magic for you, if you were lucky. But that was a chance in a million and meantime, well, you had to keep believing, trying out new magic, just in case. When Mum said things like that she looked so sad Brenda felt an ache go all through her own body, and she didn't know what to do or say. But Mum was very brave: that was the wonderful thing

27

about her. The next moment she'd be laughing – some silly thing she'd seen on one of the films up at the cinema – and telling Brenda to snap out of it and get on with her homework.

One day Mum was promoted to part-time usherette. She was very pleased about this, although it meant working late hours, leaving Brenda at home by herself a good part of the evening. Brenda did not mind. She was just sixteen and, on evenings she didn't go out with friends, unafraid of being alone. She'd sit looking at telly all evening, or read a magazine and smoke her Woodbines, quite happy. Sometimes she'd even try her hand at making something for Mum to eat when she came home, warming up a pie and boiling frozen vegetables. But usually she forgot and simply made herself cups of Nescafé into which she poured an extravagant amount of condensed milk.

One evening she was curled up on the sofa, watching a thriller on television, when Uncle Jim came in. His night shift had been changed, he said, and he hadn't gone down for a drink as he wanted to watch the football. Without asking Brenda's permission, he switched channels to the game, and flopped down on to the sofa beside her. He smelt of cheese and tobacco and sweat. He rarely washed. Brenda wrinkled her nose and watched the game. After a while she said:

'I was enjoying that thriller.'

'Poor little Brenda. Uncle Jim goes and spoils it all for her, doesn't he?' He put his hand on her knee. Brenda looked from the television screen to his hand. It was large and calloused, the nails black arcs, the knuckles chipped like dry wood. Heavy. She watched it slide up her thigh, over the flat plain of her stomach, and come to rest again on her breast.

'One day our little Brenda's going to have the prettiest boobs in Birmingham,' he said. 'Give them a year and they'll be hanging out.'

'Leave off,' said Brenda. The hand was a comfortable cage round her breast, but it made her angry.

'Just a feel. A feel doesn't do nobody any harm, does it?'
He squeezed her.

'I said take your filthy hands off me, Jim Roach.'

'They're bigger than your mother's already.'

Brenda slapped his face. He drew back, surprised.

'No need to get nasty, now, is there? Just a cuddle. Your age, I'd been screwing all over the city. They called me Jim the –'

'– I don't care what they called you! You lay a finger on me ever again and I'll tell Mum and you'll be out.'

'They knew they'd get it big and good,' he sneered.

'Mum'll put you straight out on the street.' Brenda stood up, shaking.

'She wouldn't dare. I give it to her too good.'

'Shut up! You pig!' Brenda turned to the door. At that moment her mother came in, scarf over her head, face shining with rain.

'What's all the shouting?' she asked.

'We was just having a little ding-dong.' Jim stood with his hands on his hips, thick legs apart, flushed. 'Brenda's getting temperamental now she's getting a big girl.'

Brenda ran from the room, not wanting Mum to see her distress.

The incident seemed to have spurred some kind of desire in Uncle Jim: Brenda grew to dread being in the house alone with him. He said he wasn't going to do night shifts any more, and came back to the house early most evenings. He did not try to touch her again, but lay slumped back in a chair, one hand rubbing his pelvis, the other stuffing his mouth with sliced cheese. His eyes crawled over Brenda, his cheeks a solid crimson. He said just to watch her made him feel good. He said if only she wasn't her Mum's daughter he knew what he'd like to do to her. He'd pinch her tits, all nice, so's she'd cry to him not to stop. Brenda, hot, weak and frightened, would go to her room and lock the door. Sometimes she would cry. She couldn't tell Mum, because Mum would be wild and want Jim to go: though in her heart she would want

29

Jim to stay. In a way he was good to her: gave her several pounds a week and took her out for a drink Saturdays. No: it would be unfair to Mum to say anything. Brenda kept silence for several weeks.

Then one Sunday morning she was drying her hair in the kitchen. As it straggled wetly over her back she had pulled down the neck of her tee-shirt, and undone several buttons. She sat in a shaft of sun rubbing at her head with a towel, thinking of the afternoon she was going to spend with Robert, with the beautiful face, who seemed to be her boyfriend now. All the girls wanted Robert and she'd been out with him three times. Last time he'd kissed her. He'd kiss her again this afternoon, for sure. At the thought Brenda rubbed her hair harder, full of energy and excitement.

Uncle Jim came in. He'd been down to the pub for an early beer. There was white foam at the corners of his mouth. He was full of menace, sweaty. Brenda looked up from her towel, afraid. Instinctively she did up the buttons of her shirt. Uncle Jim laughed, and tugged at the belt of his trousers, began to unbutton his flies. Then he started saying filthy things, very fast, the words stumbling over one another. Brenda flung her towel at him with a scream, got up and ran. She ran to her friend Lindy's house and told her all about it. Lindy was barely sympathetic. So what? she said. At least it was Brenda's *uncle*. In her house it was their Dad who was always begging them to have a look every time their Mum's back was turned. For some reason this made Brenda laugh. It gave her strength, to think she wasn't the only one being pursued by filthy middle-aged men. It also gave her resolve. She dried her hair and went to the cinema with Robert. He kissed her again, very gently, and she felt a wild elation that was quite new to her. She told Robert she was going to run away. He said that was a good idea, and if she sent him her address he'd come and visit her.

That evening Brenda told her mother she was leaving. She wanted to see the world, she said. She'd be all right, easy enough to get a job somewhere. Perhaps in the country, she was sick of cities. Her mother gave her a funny look, didn't ask any questions. Instead she went to her savings – a tin of canned peaches which didn't look as if it had been opened – and took out all the money: £20.

'I been saving it for emergencies,' she said. 'Here, you take it. It's probably time you left home. But let me know you're all right, and come back sometimes.'

Brenda took the money and briefly touched her mother's scratchy hair, not quite knowing what sort of gesture she should make in the circumstances. Uncle Jim didn't come home that night. She and Mum opened a tin of rock salmon which they spread thickly with salad dressing and made it into great oozy sandwiches. They drank whisky from the small bottle that was kept for other kind of emergencies and, in front of the small fire, both admitted to feeling a bit spinny. Brenda promised she'd keep in touch, and Mum said don't get pregnant if you can help it.

Brenda left Birmingham next day. She travelled south of the lights in a meat lorry which she hitched in the suburbs. The driver told her he was going to London. Brenda thought she might as well go too, unless she saw somewhere that caught her fancy on the way. Two hours down the motorway she saw the chimneys of the brick works looming in the sky. It was still early morning. Brenda liked the way they made a tall, precise pattern against the saffron clouds. They seemed to be protecting the country behind them.

'I fancy it here rather than going to London,' she said. The driver obligingly pulled up on to the hard shoulder. He said the local town wasn't much, full of Italians, but there was a nice bit of country roundabout.

Brenda thanked him and jumped down from the high seat. From then on, as she wrote and told Mum, she fell on her feet in the funniest way. She hitched another lift to the local town and, hungry, went straight to a coffee shop. She hadn't been there five minutes when a thin, sad-looking girl sat down opposite her, and asked if she knew anyone who'd like to share a flat. Brenda said yes straight away. The girl was called Lark, a typist for a firm of engineers. She said there was plenty of work in the town, especially in shops. Brenda shouldn't worry. Brenda didn't worry. She was so excited by her good fortune her breath came in uneven gusts. She and Lark went directly to the flat: two small rooms, a stove in a cupboard, and a bathroom on a landing upstairs. It overlooked a jumble of dark buildings, beyond which rose the high walls of the prison. Brenda cried out with delight. The peeling wallpaper and gloomy paint meant nothing to her. It was her own flat – well, hers and Lark's. She was to sleep in the living-room: by day the bed was covered with an Indian cotton cover, excitingly patterned. Lark had made everything very clean and neat. A smell of polish came from somewhere, though Brenda could see nothing that was actually in need of polish.

'It's *lovely*,' said Brenda. 'Are you sure I can come?'

'I've been looking for the right person for two weeks,' said Lark. 'I'm sure you're her.'

'What makes you sure?'

'I'm just sure. And don't worry about the money for a week or two till you get a job. I can tide us over easily and you can pay me back. I've nothing but rent to spend my money on.'

'I got plenty, all me Mum's savings.' Brenda tapped her bag.

'You get settled in, then, and I'll be back this evening. There's plenty to eat, nothing to worry about.' Lark wore a grey jersey stretched down over her flat chest. She had yellow-green eyes, cat-shaped, the saddest Brenda had ever seen.

Alone, Brenda unpacked her small case. On the shelf above the gas fire she propped up an old Polyfoto of Mum, and an even more faded print of the man Mum had always claimed was her Dad. He was a Polish sailor with a long blond beard and wonderful eyes: even through the dimness of the photograph you could tell they must have shone more brightly than other men's. He had come into the café where Mum was working in the war in Solihull, and they had taken an immediate fancy to each other. He had taken her out dancing when the café closed – there had been no time for Mum to change, she had gone in her working clothes. Zeus, as he was called, said he didn't care. He gave her two pairs of nylon stockings, a great luxury in those days, and spent the night with her. Then he had to be on his way, but said he would come back. Mum, pregnant, waited. Although she hardly knew him, she felt he would have been pleased about the baby – she was positive it was his. He'd had the deepest kindest voice she'd ever heard. Yes, he'd be pleased all right and give her more stockings, perhaps. But the months passed and he never came. The night Brenda was born Mum prayed especially hard, through all the pains, that Zeus would come: all she had of him was the one photograph (the stockings were long since worn out). He had taken it from his wallet and told her to keep it till he returned: he had said it as if he meant it. Brenda knew the story off by heart. Every time Mum told it, even now, her voice went all low and a small pulse in her neck began to tick, and she'd be forced to sip at the emergency whisky. Brenda liked the idea of having a Dad called Zeus who was a brave Polish sailor. (She had no doubts as to his bravery.) She supposed he was probably an admiral by now, clanking with gold on his uniform and very important. She took particular interest in pictures in the newspapers that were anything to do with the Navy. One day she might spot him. She was proud of her unknown father.

When Lark came back she took great interest in the photographs, and asked many questions. Brenda told her a lot about Mum, and gave the merest hints about her father. Within an hour she liked Lark more than she had ever liked Lindy or Sybil or any of her Birmingham friends. Lark was marvellous, all drawn into herself, somehow, and yet seemingly full of interest in outside things. They ate egg and chips, then took a bus to the local village. Lark said there was a nice pub there called the Star, and on the way they'd see a bit of the countryside. They saw fields of kale. Brenda said they were a lovely green, and Lark said what got her was the red of geraniums.

They met a friend of Lark's in the bar, a fat man who bred pigs. He was talking to a tall young man with a droopy eye-lid, introduced as plain Evans. Lark started talking most earnestly to her friend about pigs: Brenda was left to Evans. He didn't seem to have much to say. She asked him about jobs, and at once he perked up. When he was able to be help-ful, she discovered later, he became his most vivacious. Yes, he knew of a job, if it was the sort of thing she might consider. Wilberforce, the poultry farmer, needed someone to look after his chickens. Not bad wages, though of course Brenda would have to come out on the bus every day if she was living in the town. Brenda was warm from the two whiskies Evans had bought her. She thought back, first time for two years, to Hen. Silly tears came to her eyes. Evans said he'd arrange an interview with Wilberforce.

He drove Lark and Brenda back to their flat in his white Mini with the posh red seats, and promised to be in touch next day. By now Brenda was tired, but too excited to sleep. When Lark had gone to her room, she sat at the small table and wrote a letter to Mum. Then, taking more time, she wrote to Robert. He could come at once, she said. Every-thing had happened smashing. There was plenty of room for him, Lark wouldn't mind. She must leave off now but she loved him, she really loved him, and she hoped he loved her. In the weeks to come she wrote again and again to Robert, but no reply. Now, she could scarcely remember the colour of his hair.

Now, three years later, people said Brenda had changed out of all recognition. She was both buxom and lithe, long legs topped with a high small bottom, luminous skin, shining hair the colour of conkers. She was quite aware of the fact that men fancied her no end. They made all sorts of sug-gestions and sometimes she was tempted to let them try out their skills, without going too far. For basically she felt quite an affection for Evans, and trying to remain faithful to him was something of a masochistic pleasure. He was no Gary Cooper, as her Mum had said on their first visit to Birmingham: but he was a good man, kind and loyal, solid, and willing to please. Brenda appreciated these things; for the time being they were good substitutes to the unreliable excitements that Robert had wrought in her. She could rely on Evans. If she wanted, she could have him just where she wanted for the rest of her life. The very realisation of this filled her with guilty unease. For the most part she put such thoughts from her mind.

Brenda rubbed her pink ring on the knee of her jeans. She reflected that it seemed to grow smaller every day, but it was pretty in the sunlight. People remarked upon it – at least they used to. In two years the wonder of it had somewhat decreased. In two years the excitement of the whole engagement had dimmed alarmingly: not even on the day Evans had given her the ring, here in this very shed with all the birds looking on, had Brenda felt the kind of ecstasy she had assumed might grip her. No wonder, really. It was with reluctance she had agreed to the arrangement at all. Engagement didn't mean much to her: both Lindy and Sybil had written from Birmingham to say they were having babies and might get married later. They had no rings, but they lived with their boyfriends. Here, Mr and Mrs Evans and, surprisingly, even Lark, would have been upset by that sort of thing. So after Brenda had been going out with Evans for a year – yacketing on about marriage and security for most of the time, he was – Brenda finally gave in. She said yes to please him and shut him up. She did please him but he didn't shut up. Every day he'd come up with some new idea about the prospective kitchen or fireplace or life assurance, till she thought he'd drive her bloody mad. Sometimes she shouted at him, sometimes she didn't listen. Either way he didn't stop producing his plans, but inflation swiped at his savings and meant their fruition was still a long way off. Privately (something Brenda wouldn't even tell Lark) the distance of the marriage gave Brenda a feeling of curious, pleasurable safety.

Evans was in the doorway, evening sun behind him. He'd put on a clean shirt, rolled up the sleeves in the way Brenda said she liked. Only he should have rolled them up a bit further. He had no natural style, though he did try. He was big-boned, clumsy, awkward about his funny eye. He began to walk down the passage between the cages, pushing through the sunbeams as if they didn't exist. The chickens flicked their heads at him with no pretence at interest: nothing could stir the apathy of their lives. Evans reached Brenda, looked down at her. She covered her cigarette stub with her shoe. Evans flushed. The blood surged right across his chest, clashing with the lemon of his shirt. Irritation pricked Brenda's skin. She'd wanted a quiet time with Elizabeth.

'All afternoon I've been thinking,' said Evans. The chickens continued their purring with no respect for his coming thoughts. He had on his quiet voice, the one he used at more appropriate times, when Brenda was past minding what he said. Now, she sighed. Tried for patience. 'All afternoon I've been thinking that it's the tilt of your eyes makes you seem nearer to smiling than other girls, even when you aren't feeling like smiling at all.'

Brenda glanced up at his red face. She wanted to laugh, but saw his seriousness.

'Quite the poet, aren't we? What's that supposed to mean?' She stood up. Evans kissed her, roughly squashing her breasts against his crisp shirt. She could feel the heat of his chest.

'It's not supposed to mean anything. You just get to thinking, sitting in a post office all afternoon.'

'I told you, Lark's doing my hair tonight.'

Evans stepped back. His arms drooped, weighted by sad hands.

'I told you I was coming to give you a lift home.'

'You didn't need to change your shirt for a lift.'

'You could always change your mind, I thought.'

36

'No. I'm not changing my mind.'

'When we're married, we'll be together every evening.'

'Well, we're not married yet, are we?'

The flush which had cleared from Evans's face returned. The crooning of the chickens seemed to swell a little as if in renewed and united indignation.

'How's Elizabeth?' Evans asked quietly.

'She's very bad. She's got worse all afternoon. She'll be dead by this time tomorrow.'

'Wilberforce can cope with that, can't he?'

'He can cope, but he'll despise me for it. He'll say if you take on a job looking after chickens, you should kill them like a man.'

'Bastard,' said Evans. 'Tell you what. I'll have a word with him if you like. After dropping you home. Save you having to be insulted. I'll tell him to . . . finish her.'

Brenda was grateful.

'Tell him top row, third from the end. He doesn't even accept they have names. They're just egg machines to him.'

'All right.'

'I don't fancy her empty cage tomorrow morning.'

'It'll soon be filled.'

'It won't be Elizabeth.'

'Come on. Let's go.'

'I'll have to make Daisy queen.'

'I'm sure she'll be a good queen.' One side of Evans's mouth curled slightly.

'Don't laugh at me.'

'I'm not laughing at you.'

Brenda followed Evans down the aisle of the shed. He had a narrow back, sloping shoulders. He dodged very slightly from side to side (hoping that Brenda wouldn't notice) to make sure the heads that darted from the cages would not touch him. Brenda did notice.

'They wouldn't bother to peck *you*.' She stopped at Elizabeth's cage. 'Look at her.' Evans turned, noted the dying eyes. 'You better say goodbye to her.' Brenda waited, staring at him. 'Go on. Say goodbye. Or can't you bring yourself to that?'

For the third time Evans blushed.

'Goodbye, Elizabeth,' he said. His voice was foolish.

'Goodbye *Queen* Elizabeth,' Brenda repeated. 'Though goodness knows you're not much of a queen now.' She tapped the bird's beak with her nail. The head swung a little to one side, too weak to return to its former position.

Outside the light was blindingly gold after the shadows of the shed. There was a distant smell of fresh manure, a slight breeze.

'You're insensitive to death, plainly,' said Brenda.

'I'm not insensitive to death.'

'It doesn't matter to you if an animal you love dies.'

'Of course it does.'

'You think I'm just sentimental, feeling like this about Elizabeth.'

'I don't. You know I've always been impressed, such affection for hens.' Brenda glanced at him, moving a little way from him in case he should take her arm. He walked looking at the ground, frowning. 'Anyhow, when we're .. . when we've got our own place and you have all the hens you want, we'll see to it they have a good life. We'll see to it they live a long time.'

Brenda shrugged. So often, in his well meaning way, Evans was nothing but irritating. He could not see that the thought of future hens was no consolation for Elizabeth's death. He could not understand the ache of an empty cage. By day, it seemed, Evans could understand practically nothing. Only at night, in the dark, in the hay, he instinctively knew what she wanted. Then, they didn't have to talk, and that was best. One day she would have to sit down and think, really think, whether she could continue her life with Evans for the sake of the nights. Lark would advise. Lark was good with advice. For the moment, all that mattered was that the next time she walked down this path, early tomorrow morning, the dry smell of pig feed in the air,

Elizabeth would be dead. She said nothing. To Evans, there was nothing further to say.

Brenda hurried straight into Lark's room without knocking. Lark was lying on her bed, newly painted geranium nails pointing to the ceiling. The wallpaper was dense trellis-work through which trailed scarlet and pink flowers, mostly geraniums. The window ledge was crowded with pots of the real thing. On the small table by Lark's bed stood a dozen small, spiteful cacti. 'My protection,' she called them. Summer evenings, warm with western sun, the room felt like an indoor garden, though it smelt of nail polish.

'The queen's dying,' said Brenda.

Lark sat up at once.

'Oh, Lord. Don't look so tragic. Wilberforce'll see to it, like he did to the others, won't he?'

'But he doesn't even *know* she's queen.'

Lark shrugged.

'Some people are that callous. Well, we must do something to take your mind off it.' Lark was practical about happiness. 'We'll have a nice supper of poached eggs on sweet corn, your favourite, and gin. There's half a bottle, so we won't need to stint ourselves. Then we'll get on with the patchwork.' They were making a patchwork tablecloth, all red materials, for Lark's widowed mother who lived with her arthritis in Westgate-on-Sea. 'There's Mahler on Radio 3, so we can listen to that and put brandy in our cocoa.'

Brenda had never heard of Mahler and was unskilled at sewing: Lark completed three hexagonals to her one. But the positive suggestions calmed her. She only had to knock at the door of Lark's small red world to be let in, comforted, eased.

'Come on,' said Lark, going to the door. 'First things first. Gin.' There was a ladder in her tights, a hole in the elbow of her grey jersey, her greasy hair fell into partitions. She bounced. If Brenda could have thought of a good way to put it she would have liked to have told her, to have paid her a compliment: Lark, you're strong, she would have liked to have said.

Rosie divided the bacon and egg pie in her mind. She calculated that if she took a smallish piece herself – and she never liked to appear a greedy eater in public, though one of her secret foibles was to pick at things in the larder – then they would just manage. It was really most difficult of Evans, being so vague about his evening plans. If only he had said yes quite definitely, then Rosie could have made a stew: but if he was going to be out, then it would be silly, all that meat and potatoes just for Henry and her. Rosie didn't like waste, but she also didn't like to inflict such worries upon her family. Therefore she struggled by herself, measuring out the pie with a knife, the inspiration of a tin of new potatoes in the back of her mind in case Evans *did* return. Would he, wouldn't he? The question rattled at her. He had come in and put on a clean shirt – she had only pressed it that morning, was worried whether it might not still be damp – and hurried out saying he might be back and he might not. The trouble was, and Rosie would admit this to no one in the world, Brenda had a terrible hold on Evans. He ran round her in circles, doing everything she required and more. He wouldn't hear a word against her: she was his life. Rosie had thought that once they were engaged, officially, things might have been different. But they weren't. Brenda continued to have the upper hand, anyone could see that. What's more, she had no sense of romance. Conversations about their new home seemed to bore her. Everything seemed to bore her except her blooming chickens, and they were a funny hobby for a girl, weren't they? In her heart, Rosie worried for her son. Even now, as she took the risk and opened the tin of potatoes, she felt a twist of anxiety in her stomach. Don't be a fool, Rosie Evans, she said to herself at once. Many's the time you've seen them go out together in the Mini, all smiling, off for a picnic somewhere, taking the rug and the basket of sandwiches in the back seat. Maybe alone they were all right. They must be, or Evans wouldn't stick around so long, would he? Not her Evans. He'd have more sense.

Rosie took a bunch of knives and forks to the table. She smoothed the white damask cloth just for the pleasure of feeling the silky knots of delphiniums, embroidered by her mother fifty years ago, beneath her hands. In the summer evening light that made their kitchen a smaller, huskier room, Rosie noticed her hands didn't look so bad, vulnerable though they were on the whiteness of the cloth. Nothing could take away from their shape – huge boxes, they were, Henry had once said, daft at the end of small arms like hers – but the warmth of the day had muted their colour. They were still a reddish mauve – nothing on earth would pale their skin to the white of the rest of the body – but at least the ugly mottles, so sharp in winter that the skin resembled tortoiseshell, had subsided for a few months. Rosie would have liked to call Henry's attention to the fact they were better today: funny how he only commented on them when they were at their worst. But Henry was deep in his paper again. Henry was a very thorough reader of papers, though usually he didn't spend quite so many hours over the *Daily Mirror* as today. Rosie thought it must be the heat playing havoc with his concentration. She herself had to read more slowly in the heat, so she understood. She kept her silence, and moved the egg cup, holding its one iris, a fraction of an inch nearer the centre of the table. Odd how one bloom could give so much pleasure. Evans often criticised her for being so mean with flowers, in the friendliest possible way, of course, just teasing. What she couldn't make him understand was the lesson she herself had learnt from a calendar of Japanese flower arrangements: how beautiful are just one or two blooms rather than a whole lot bunched together. Admittedly, she didn't have the right kind of vases, the kind in the colour photographs. And there were no exotic lilies in these parts, not even in the local florist's, to work with. So Rosie adapted in her own way: a single iris, a bunch of fuschia and two buttercups, a strand of ivy or honeysuckle bending wispily from a milk bottle.

Strange, really, how her arrangements had never achieved so much as a highly commended in the local flower show. But she understood why it was. Even in the world of flowers, the British were so insular: they would never look to arrangements beyond their own shores. Still, now we were in the Common Market, there was some hope. Now we had accepted Europe we might be persuaded to open our eyes further east and glance upon, and one day even seize upon, the Japanese way with apple blossom. That would be the day. For the moment, Rosie's arrangements were too far ahead of their time for the village. But, with faith in her theory, she was prepared to wait, quite patiently. She touched the blue petals with a gentle finger, and smiled to herself.

Evans came in. Henry turned a page of his paper.

They sat at the table, eating. As Rosie always helped the men to their food she had managed to divide the pie fairly between them, and disguise her own narrow wedge with a margin of potatoes. Henry held his knife like a hammer. Rosie could never feel quite happy about this particular habit of his, but in weighing it up over the years she had decided it was one of those things not worth mentioning. Even after three decades of love there are areas which must be left untouched, protected by silence. Evans ate with more refinement than his father, but drank his tea fast and noisily, treating it like beer. Rosie wondered how he managed not to burn his mouth, and what had happened between him and Brenda to cause his return. He had obviously been to see her down at the sheds, judging by the faint smell of chickens.

'Busy day?' she asked.

'Fairly. A lot of parcels.'

'People must be posting early for Christmas, thinking it's going up again.'

'That's what Brenda said.'

'Brenda all right?'

'Fine.'

42

'I thought she looked very nice, Sunday, that skirt.'

'Yes.'

'Perhaps you'd both like to bring Lark with you to tea this Sunday? I always think she has such a quiet life, Lark.'

'She's happy enough. I'll ask her. She's washing Brenda's hair tonight.'

Any news of Brenda's innocence in Evans's absence filled Rosie with a sense of private relief. Relief that made her almost skittish.

'Henry, love, you funny old thing, you've left all your nice pie,' she observed.

'Not hungry.' Henry was scratching his neck, all around the inside of his collar. In an ideal world, the sort of gesture that Rosie would have preferred him to carry out in the privacy of the bathroom rather than at table.

'But you always have an appetite for your tea.'

Henry stood up.

'I'm off down to the Star for an hour.'

'But it isn't your night for –' Rosie stopped herself. She would never wish to be accused of criticism. She watched him go, decided not to shout out to him he'd forgotten his jacket.

'The heat doesn't suit your father,' she said to Evans when Henry had slammed the door.

'Dad's never liked the heat.'

Evans helped Rosie clear away the plates. Then he, too, more gently, said he was going out. Once again Rosie controlled herself not to ask questions. The odd departures of the men in your family, with no explanations, was part of the lot a wife and mother should bear without apparent worry. She managed a smile.

'Have a nice time.'

But she did wish Evans wasn't so weak where Brenda was concerned. He should leave her alone, hair-washing nights. Not always be after her, always there. A small dose of doubt would do a girl like her a power of good. If she didn't have it all quite so easy she might be inclined to come running. That

43

would be much better than things as they were now – Evans, in his kindness, always the one chasing after her.

After a small battle with himself Evans came to a decision: he would not go to Brenda. The firmness of his purpose made him free to leave the house. He was in no mood tonight to be left alone with his mother's subtle sympathy. He wanted merely to walk, he needed air. Space, he required, in which to think. Quietness, to quell the turmoil in his blood.

He looked up at the elms, a deeper evening green now, and then towards the ugly shape of the vicarage. Behind their surplice curtains Evans could make out the shapes of the vicar and his wife at supper. Then the church bells began to ring: choir practice night. With a reverent little jump the vicar rose from the table, mistily as the Holy Ghost. In a moment he would be at the front door, hurrying with shining face to the church. Evans had no wish to meet him. Rather than turn back into the kitchen, he quickly crossed the small patch of common land between the cottages and vicarage and went through the front gates of Wroughton House. There, he hid behind the fence.

From his protected position he watched the vicar make his eager way to the graveyard. An encounter had been missed by seconds. Evans's heart beat fast with unholy gratitude. He leaned against the trunk of one of the elms – they grew both sides of the fence – feeling the deep ridges of its bark cutting into his back. The four desolate bells repeated over and over again their monotonous descending scale. He was vaguely aware that technically he was trespassing, that he was on private property, but he didn't care.

Moments went by. Evans edged round the trunk of the tree, looked up the drive towards the house. Elms grew each side of the drive. They protected the church on the right, fields on the left. In the distance Evans could see a small part of the façade of the house.

There was no one about. He began to walk, stopping only when he came to the large pond at the end of the front lawn.

44

It was a man-made pond, perfectly round and lined with cement, crowded with water-lilies and bulrushes. Behind it, dividing the lawn from the fields, grew a vast willow tree whose meandering boughs dipped and swayed almost continuously. Some of its lower fronds ruffled the brown pond water. Suddenly aware of his exposed position in the drive, Evans went to hide again, behind the willow tree. There, hands in pockets, legs set apart in a comfortable position, he contemplated the house once more. His heart had resumed its normal beating, the church bells had stopped ringing. They left a profound silence in their wake. A silence which dissolved his guilt at trespassing. Hidden as he was, he felt at peace in the garden.

In all his life in the village Evans had never really looked at Wroughton House before. It was protected from the rest of the community by its fences and tall trees, an impenetrable oasis among the new houses surrounding it. The only previous times he had walked up the drive had been to accompany Rosie to the annual summer fete on the lawn. Those occasions Evans remembered with little pleasure. Rosie insisted he toured the rose garden with her, and he could never think of any compliments to pay flowers, especially with the British Legion silver band blasting in his ears. He could never understand Rosie's awe of the place; but then he supposed it was to do with the fact that her mother had been a housemaid there after the First World War, and had married the under gardener. It was his own grandfather who had planted most of the bloody roses – a fact which left Evans quite unmoved, year after year, as Rosie repeated the story. She herself had never worked permanently in the house, though up until last year she was often called upon to help out at weekends. These invitations caused her a dither of excitement and pleasure. She would come back with stories of parties which held so little interest for Evans he scarcely listened and, now he tried to remember, he could recall no details. But he was aware that things had changed: that Mrs Browne, the owner, lived by herself now because Mr Browne had left. There were no more parties. Evans overheard gossip in the pub, but did not take it in. He had only seen Mrs Browne on a few occasions, darting about in a silver car. Smallish, not his sort of woman. For one who had lived all his life so near the house and its inhabitants, he was curiously uninformed.

Evans, who would never call himself a keen observer of fine buildings, continued to stare at the house. He supposed it was what people who knew about architecture would call beautiful – built in the time of William and Mary, he remembered his mother saying. It was very grand by his standards, the grandest house he had ever seen. But not intimidating. He would not be afraid to knock at the front door. He liked the way its tall windows reflected the pale flecks of late evening sky; the way its roots were settled in a wave of bushy lavender. He liked the colour of its walls – an irregular ochre, something like a winter beach he had once visited, buffetted to varying shades by the wind. A strange excitement came upon him. He was aware he was experiencing one of those moments that make an ordinary day a memorable one. He would have liked to wander round the rest of the garden and take a look at the sides and the back of the building. But the church bells started up again, reminding him he should not be there at all, jarring his conscience. Reluctant to move, he cast his eyes to the pond, where the water image of the façade hung absolutely still. A light went on in one reflected window. Glancing back at the house, Evans saw a woman standing there. She pulled down a blind. It was then he remembered: the house was for sale. His mother had been talking about it only yesterday. Mrs Browne was staying on alone until it was sold. The woman at the window must have been Mrs Browne.

Evans left his place behind the willow tree. It was almost dark. He walked without caution back down the drive. His excitement had crystallised into an idea, an idea that needed much attention. He would slip upstairs, avoiding his parents, and go to his room. There he would think it all out, calmly as he was able, and make up his mind before the night was through.

Gin, Lark always said, silvered the mind. By eleven at night both she and Brenda had achieved the silvery state they desired, and were happy. Lark was drying Brenda's hair with a hand dryer, its engine buzzing like a swarm of summer flies. Mahler had been turned down to a background hum to make talking possible. There was brandy in their cocoa.

'What's the betting he comes up here wanting his oats?' Lark asked.

'Don't think he will tonight. I said I wanted some sleep.'

'D'you think he's crying his heart out for you?'

'Expect so.'

'Perhaps you should try being nicer to him. Or he should try being nastier to you.'

'Let him try.' Brenda giggled. 'I'd be off. I'd be all right, wouldn't I?'

'You'd be all right.'

'Lark, how come you're all right, without any men? Without anyone, really?'

Lark pulled at a strand of coppery hair, tugging Brenda's head back, and pushed the hot nozzle of the dryer into the gaping scalp. Brenda grimaced in silence.

'Haven't the time,' said Lark.

'Haven't the time? You've got tons of time. You're in this flat night after night painting your nails and listening to your music. Think of all the other things you could be doing.'

'You've got to have your pride as a typist, even if it's only keeping your nails nice.'

'Haven't time! You're barmy, Lark. If you washed your own hair more often, and bought some decent clothes, you'd have them all after you.'

'What for?'

'Don't be so daft: what for? For a bit of fun, of course. Better than sitting in your room humming to yourself.'

47

'Singing. If I could find a choir near here I'd join it, then you wouldn't worry so.'

Brenda shrugged.

'Oh, I don't really worry. Don't think that. Did you really want to be a singer, thrilling away on a platform all by yourself?'

'All those bunches of flowers they throw up to you at the end. I could imagine it.'

'Hey, don't leave my hair.'

'It's finished.'

'Why didn't you go on with it?'

'They said I wasn't up to the training. My lungs.'

Brenda stood up. She turned round to see Lark, holding the hair dryer away from her like a conductor's baton. Her face seemed to have parted a little to match her hair.

'Why don't you try it?' asked Brenda.

'I tell you, I tried to persuade them to let me –'

'I don't mean singing.'

A pink flush seeped up through the grey skin of Lark's face. She snapped off the dryer. The Mahler was distinct.

'Don't go on, Bren. I tell you, I haven't the time.'

Through the silver of her mood Brenda recognised this to be one of Lark's mysterious remarks, but with the gin spreading like mercury through her veins the effort to ask Lark what she meant eluded her.

'Well, Evans isn't coming,' she said. 'I was right. I'm going to bed.'

'Sweet dreams and God bless.'

'You're not going through your whole blinking rosary *tonight*, are you?'

' 'Course I am. God forgive me for the gin, I'll say.'

'Crikey,' said Brenda. She pulled at her cotton bedspread. Its patterns seemed to have run into one another with bright confusion.

Rosie lay in bed looking at the dark shape of her husband's shoulders beside her. He was deeply asleep, she could tell by the way he kept quite still. Under the sheets her hands were clasped in a large knot on her chest. She moved them gently, so as not to disturb Henry, and rubbed the tops of her arms. In their fine lawn mittens they felt wonderfully smooth. She had started wearing night mittens seventeen years ago when Henry had said her knuckles scratched his chest. After the announcement he had gone straight to sleep, easy as if it hadn't been an accusation, as if he'd meant it as a friendly remark. Rosie had lain awake listening to rain against their window. It was a warm night but she felt cold. She wondered what to do, if there was a doctor she could consult about the terrible ailment of her hands. She would pay any money to improve them, but probably a doctor would merely laugh. By dawn she had had the idea about the mittens. The next day she had set about making them, and had worn them every night since. In seventeen years she had been through eleven pairs. After the first few nights of shyness – Henry had made no remarks – she had dared to stroke his shoulder with a covered finger. Then his back, his neck. But Henry remained silent. 'Don't they feel better, love?' she had eventually asked. Henry stiffened – she could just feel the muscles trying to disguise their contraction, and did not answer. Nor did he turn over, pulling the bed-clothes from under the mattress, which always seemed to happen when he felt desirous. He went quickly to sleep. Since then, on special occasions, New Year's Eve and birthdays, Rosie still stroked his shoulder blades tentatively with her muslin fingers, but he did not respond. She had given up, really. She realised that when that side of married life dies you cannot bring it back, and must make the best of other, more important things. Still, she had her regrets: one of the most profound was that she had ever started wearing the mittens. It had occurred to her some time ago that *they* were what had dampened Henry's urges. They were the culprits. In trying to disguise the burden of her hands she had inadvertently emphasised them. And on nights like these Rosie was haunted with new resolve: when she dared, she would throw away the wretched

49

things. There were still a few years left in which they would make up for lost opportunities, she and Henry. 'Oh, there are, my love,' she said to herself.

Henry lay wide awake looking at the moon perched on the elms like an owl. The Leopard, as she had become in his mind, had not been in the pub. He had drunk three beers and two double whiskies, something he was quite unused to at night. Still, the alcohol had inspired him. On his walk home he had had a brainwave. Tomorrow he would go and see his old friend Mackay. Mackay ran a small market garden a mile out of the village. He was known for his prize vegetables, in particular his cauliflowers. Henry didn't know why, but he had a strange strong feeling that the Leopard, sophisticated creature though she was, would appreciate good things straight from the earth. She was the kind of woman, he felt, who would go out of her way to attend a Harvest Festival Service. Now, if he could talk Mackay into it, he would persuade him to have one or two of his best cauliflowers constantly at the ready. He would have to be careful how he put this, of course, or Mackay, a sly old dog, would know something was up. But that was no real problem. The next part of the plan was less clear, he would have to work upon it. Roughly, it was this: the next time he saw the Leopard in the pub he would slip quickly out, muttering some excuse if anyone was interfering enough to draw attention to his departure. He would hurry along to Mackay – which would probably mean coming home to fetch the car, so an explanation to Rosie would have to be thought up – buy a couple of cauliflowers, and hurry back to the Star. There, he would hang about outside. He might even light his pipe, to look more casual. When the Leopard emerged he would wish her the time of day and fall into casual conversation, bringing the talk, of course, round to the magnificent cauliflower he was holding, which she would be bound to remark upon. Then he would say, 'Well, a beautiful cauliflower for a beautiful lady,' or something like that.

The precise words he would think out more carefully to-morrow. He might even write them down, trying out different things. The main thing was to hand her the cauli-flowers with a small, old-fashioned bow. It would be such a surprising gesture, so much more subtle than flowers, she could hardly refuse them. After that, it would be easy enough to ask if she would care to have a drink with him one day, next time she was passing through the village. After *that* . . . well, anything could happen.

The idea of playing with such fire burnt into Henry with a thrill that made him want to roar out loud like a forest animal, and clap his hands, and kick his feet in the air. As it was, he lay clenched into stillness, grateful for the self-control taught him by the Navy. Now all he had to get to grips with was patience. *Patience, patience, Henry old fellow.* The whisky was a sour pain in his chest. He would have liked to have moved his position. But it was never worth moving before Rosie was asleep. The smallest heave to greater comfort and she would start up with her confounded tick-ling. Henry shut his eyes.

Augusta Browne clung to her house. It was inevitable that it should be sold, now Hugh had gone, but she was doing her best to delay the sale. She had had her latest success this morning. A furrier and his wife from Hampstead had arrived in their Rolls and Persian lamb collars. She had let them carry on with their insults for quite some time (strange how rude are prospective buyers in front of owners, as if selling was a complete protection from hurt), smiling at their suggestions. 'We'd have to change the dining-room, of course,' said the woman. 'Terra cotta hurts my eyes. We could do it in a nice brocade paper and put beading on the shelves, like at home.' The man ran a fat hand down the walls which had undulated gently for 300 years. 'We'd have to smooth out these,' he said. 'It's all very well emulsioning walls like this, but you'd never get a decent paper to stick.'

Augusta waited until they reached her bedroom. The time

had come for her triumph. The small couple stood at one of the soaring windows looking out at the lime-coloured lawn, the ponds, the vast elm, polluting the view with their gaze. The man screwed up his nasty eyes into the distance.

'Are those the chimneys we saw from the motorway?'

'Yes. The brickworks.'

'Do they give you any trouble?'

Augusta paused.

'As a matter of fact they do.' She watched the woman, sniffing, judge the Williamsburg cotton of the blind between her fingers. 'When there's an east wind the smell is pretty bad.'

'What kind of smell?' The man was almost prurient.

'Rotten eggs. To be honest, it stinks.'

The man pursed his bulbous lips.

'Well, we'd be in Town a good deal, you see. I dare say the smell wouldn't worry us too much, once or twice a year. We could be away those days.'

'Well, on average, there's an east wind at least three times a week,' said Augusta.

They didn't bother to see the rest of the house after that, but hurried back to Hampstead muttering about a wasted journey. As soon as they had gone Augusta went to her study. It overlooked the walled garden – the wall was built of soft mellow stone. Augusta leant back in her comfortable, high-backed chair, lay her arms along its arms, conscious of their support. She watched a couple of blue-tits pecking at the bricks. Over the years they had chipped out several caves in the wall where they sometimes huddled, as if in a nest. This morning the birds were bright, elated. Augusta telephoned Hugh.

'Those people the agents said were very keen – they've just gone. They weren't at all interested.'

'Oh.'

In the silence Augusta sensed her husband was in a hurry.

'Hugh, if I came up next week, could we have lunch? We could talk about things.'

'No.'

Another pause. Augusta's voice trembled.

'If you won't have lunch with me, I'll never marry you again.' She slammed down the receiver before she could become any more ridiculous.

Now, the evening of that day, it rained for the first time in two weeks. The rain glittered down over the garden making sparks on the emerald of the May grass. The pond water, paled by the sky's reflected clouds, was pocked with rain-drops, suddenly alive beneath the weight of its water-lilies. Augusta stretched up her arms among the branches of the lilac bush, struggling for the purple cones. It was the nature of the best lilac blooms always to be out of reach. She stood on tip-toe, rain from the leaves pouring down her arms. Her light shoes were soaked in the long grass, she could hear the squeak of her toes as she moved them. She reached the branches, snapped them off, buried her head in the tight buds, aware for a moment only of their intense scent, of their wetness against the wetness of her face. She moved away, then. Walked across the wide lawn that sloped from the side of the house down to another, natural pond. There at its banks grew cow parsley shoulder-high, heads white as summer clouds. Augusta pushed her way through the frail jungle, listening to the quiet clatter of the shower. She picked the odd stalk, then bent to gather a bunch of cowslips. The rain had intensified their yellowness, their honey smell.

The ritual of the flower-gathering over, Augusta walked slowly back to the house. Her long cotton skirt clung about her ankles, she was suddenly cold. A fire, she decided. When she had put the flowers in water she would light the fire in the hall. And then . . . what would she do for the long evening? Oh, there was plenty of time to think. She would get warm first. Have a bath. Finish that half-bottle of Hugh's Sancerre. Some idea would come to her.

Evans, who had been cogitating upon his plan all day in the Post Office, was disturbed by the wet evening. He had not reckoned with rain. Now Rosie's fussing about his mackintosh would have to come into his calculations – easy enough to deal with, but a possible risk to his firmness of purpose. As it turned out, he need not have worried. Soon as she had cleared the tea, Rosie hurried off under her umbrella to a Mothers' Union meeting. At her exit Henry emerged from behind his paper, stood up and scratched at his ribs luxuriously.

'Well, Boy, don't know about you but I'm slipping down for a quick one.'

'Second night this week, Dad. Becoming quite the alcoholic.'

Henry, through lack of practice, was as diffident as his son about smiling. But Evans observed a tilt of humour flare at the corners of his father's tight mouth.

'A man's got to have some vices in his old age, Boy.' Then, in silent recognition of the other's private intentions, they put on their mackintoshes and parted at the front door.

Evans waited until Henry was out of sight before he crossed the strip of common grass and slipped through the gates of the house. He walked up the middle of the drive, hands in pockets, rain sloping pleasantly against him. He liked the gravel crunch under his feet, the swiftness of the clouds above him. The nervousness of the day had gone. Chances were his plan would fail, but he was no longer afraid to try.

He paused when he reached the part of the drive that unfurled into a broad sweep directly before the house. He moved his head from side to side, taking in the two rows of tall windows, feeling the rain running down his neck. He went to the porch, rang the door bell. Two minutes' wait. No answer. He rang again. Still nothing. He peered through the glass panes of the door: another glass door. Beyond it, murkily, the impression of a large hall and the flames of a huge fire. Eventually Evans opened the doors and went in.

As soon as he had done so he realised his mistake. This was

quite the wrong night to have come. The place was set for a party.

The hall was filled with music. The tunes seemed vaguely familiar to Evans, the sort of thing that accompanied old thirties films he watched on television. There was lilac everywhere: a pyramid set upon an oak chest, another one on the round centre table. The smell of the wet blooms, combined with the winter smell of the fire, almost stifled Evans. He put a hand over his nose, confused for a moment by the sweet power of the scents. *I must go*, he thought. *Quickly, before anyone knows I've been.* Reluctance was embedded in the thought. He made no move, but remained where he was, conscious that raindrops from his mackintosh fell on to the stone-flagged floor, encircling him in a grey ring of water. He looked about. Like church, and the gym at his old school, the place gave him a comfortable feeling of being a normal size. Here no one could accuse him of being clumsy, too big.

There were archways each side of the fireplace. Beyond one of them rose a pine staircase, shining with polish. As its half-landing was a magnificent arched window, an echo of the inside shapes, its panes blurred with rain. Evans, still motionless, was wondering about the practical problems of window-cleaners, when a woman he supposed to be Mrs Browne appeared on the stairs. From where he stood he had not seen her coming down the upper flight. She appeared as if from nowhere, startling. Evans saw her before she saw him. He had a few seconds in which to observe her unseen. She seemed to glide down the staircase, in time to the music, head high, one hand just brushing the wood banister. It was as if she supposed a hundred people to be gathered in the hall below, and was making a grand entrance, expecting their appraisal. She wore a long, soft skirt, same colour as the pine, so that half her body merged in with the backdrop; and a pinkish cardigan, cobwebby stuff, its sleeves pushed up her arms.

Halfway down the lower flight of the stairs she noticed Evans, and paused. She was dwarfed by the high window behind her. Its light made a subdued halo of her hair.

'Hello,' she said.

Then she descended the rest of the stairs very fast, not looking at her feet, one hand holding up her skirt. Evans felt a brief sensation that this was all theatre: that in some mysterious way he was inextricably involved in the action on a stage. A waking dream.

She stood before him, surprisingly small now she was on the ground.

'Who are you?'

'Evans. Er, Evans Evans.' The absurdity of his own name, when he was forced to give it, still caused Evans embarrassment. He clutched at the pockets of his raincoat. A small shower of water ran over his hands and added to the dark ring on the floor. 'You know my mother, Rosie.'

'Of course I know Rosie. She's always talking about you. How can I help you?'

'Well, as a matter of fact . . .'

'The cricket match, the Boy Scouts or some sort of raffle? Let me guess.'

She moved over to the fire, smiling. Stood with her back to the flames, arms folded under her small breasts, clutching to herself a small shiver.

'None of those things.' Evans had to speak loudly against the music.

'Then for goodness sake get rid of that soaking mackintosh and we'll go next door and have a drink.'

'Are you sure?' Evans was already struggling out of the mackintosh. 'I mean, it looks as if you're expecting company. I'm sorry, I didn't . . . a party?'

'A party?' Mrs Browne smiled again. Wistful this time. 'Oh, no. I just like to keep things going. Come on.'

She went to a door at the corner of the hallway. Evans followed her. The room they entered at once infused him with an unfamiliar sense of warmth, of caring. He had no eye for detail, was only aware of impressions: high windows in two of the coral walls: round the fire a gathering of sofas and chairs that seemed to have been built for large people; ancestral portraits and spring flowers. The music was quieter in here.

'Now, what will you have? Whisky? Let's both have whisky, all this rain . . .' She was moving about against the windows, swaying to the frail voice of the olden-days singer. *Love me or leave me* . . . Made bold by his part in the play, Evans sat down by the fire without asking. The well-stuffed back of the sofa eased him as no sofa had ever done before. He crossed his legs and stared at the oblong chunk of his thigh. In this radiant world of make-believe he felt curiously at home.

Mrs Browne handed him a drink. She sat opposite him, huddled into the corner of an armchair that was much too big for her, legs drawn up beneath her. Again the light from the windows behind her made her turbulent hair an almost colourless mass. Evans judged her to be about ten years older than Brenda. For her age, she wasn't at all bad. Come to think of it, he remembered his mother having said just that on several occasions. He sipped the whisky. It was strong.

'You've a very nice place, here,' he said. Mrs Browne looked down into her drink. Pale eyelids. In a lull in the singing they could hear the splatter of rain on the windows. 'I understand it's all going to be sold,' went on Evans. 'That seems a pity.'

'It's on the market, but it will take a long time. Not many people want a house of this size these days.' Something about the flatness of her voice made Evans realise the selling of the house was not a subject she wished to continue. 'What is it that I can do for you?'

'I had this funny plan. It came to me, sudden like, last night.' Evans wondered if Mrs Browne was aware of the fact that she was making the unfolding of his plan surprisingly easy. Her very position among the cushions seemed sympathetic. 'You see, it's like this. I've got this girl, Brenda. Mum may have told you we're engaged.'

'Yes.'

57

'Well, Brenda and me have been together two years now. We're saving up for one of those houses on the new estate so that we can start our marriage in a decent place, as it were. Well, we've still got some time to go before we can manage the down payment. And as you can imagine, waiting, like, a long time, has its problems.' Evans took another sip of the whisky, shifted his look from Mrs Browne to the rain beyond the windows. The warm room, with its outdoor smell of flowers, was protective in a way he had never previously experienced. Perhaps Mrs Browne had conjured this protection for herself, and was innocent of the effect it had upon her visitors. 'The thing is, we've never had anywhere to go. To be alone, I mean. Brenda shares this flat with a friend called Lark. She's a nice enough girl, but not a one for going out. She's always there. She stays in her own room, very tactful, but it's not the same as being alone, is it? Then of course at home – well, the house being that small, it's always crowded with Mum and Dad.'

'I see. So where do you go?'

'Fields, barns. It gets on your nerves.' Evans put his hand over his right eye, pretending to scratch his forehead. Then he allowed himself a slight smile. 'It's not what you'd call most comfortable, either.'

'Quite.' Mrs Browne smiled in return.

'So this is what I was wondering. You here in this big house all alone, I thought. Maybe, I thought, you'd have a room, somewhere in the attics, we could rent . . . until the place was sold.'

Mrs Browne nodded immediately.

'Of course,' she said, quietly. 'Of course. What a good idea.'

Evans noticed that the flames were growing brighter then, and his hand shook a little round his icy glass.

'I could pay you a month's rent in advance. We'd take good care of it, I can assure you that. We wouldn't disturb you.'

Mrs Browne swung her legs to the ground with a quick, determined gesture. She was suddenly vivacious.

'Of course you can have a room, but only on one condition: no money is involved.'

'But, in that case, we couldn't . . .'

'You could. Don't you see? No, I don't see why you should.' She stood up. 'The thing is, I'd *like* to feel someone was in the house, upstairs, having . . . nice times again.'

Evans stood too. There was something about Mrs Browne that made him realise it was pointless to argue further now. He was determined to bring the subject up again, later; but at this moment of the charade it all seemed irrelevant.

'Let's go up there right now,' said Mrs Browne. 'I can show you what there is.'

Evans followed her upstairs to the attic floor. She led him along a dusky passage.

'We ran out of money before we could do much up here,' she was saying. 'But at least it's warm. You could have any of the rooms, but I think this one is best.' She opened a door.

The room, by the standards of the Evans house, was large. It had a sloping ceiling and two casement windows. There was an ink-stained rug on the wooden floor, a brass double bed, and the shapes of other furniture under dust sheets.

'There's masses of stuff up here,' said Mrs Browne. 'You can have what you like.'

'No, really, we could –'

'Please. It would do the things good to be used again.' She went to one of the casement windows. This time the rainy light caught her face, threw a violet shadow from her chin on to her neck. Again she hunched her shoulders and folded her arms beneath her breasts, a gesture that seemed to be a habit with her. The position of her small body, as she stood like that, indicated a melancholy that was not betrayed by her voice.

'The garden is perfect for parties,' she said. For a moment Evans was confused, wondering whether she assumed he and Brenda were the kind of people to throw garden parties. 'We always planned to have one on this lawn. I'd had it all arranged to the last detail. We were going to have a merry-

59

go-round down there, look – and gondolas on the pond by the field, and fireworks over the round pond, and a marquee covering the rose garden at the back. But it didn't ever happen, of course. We hadn't the money. And now it never will.'

Evans was aware of the stuffiness of the room. It was evident that the windows had not been opened for some time. Mrs Browne had the same thought: she struggled with the catch.

'Here, let me.' Evans was beside her. He opened the window with a strong push and a small flight of rain instantly blew in on them. Mrs Browne laughed.

'That's lovely! We'll leave it open for a few days to air the place. It smells of dust.'

They remained by the window looking out at the dappled garden, the blossom on the bushes of May very white, the distant trees blousy with rain, the brickworks' chimneys half-hidden in a tangle of cloud and smoke. Evans sensed that the end of the charade was near. He felt suddenly compelled to be inquisitive, even if his question might jeopardise the arrangements that had already been made.

'Did you spend your life here giving parties, then?'

Mrs Browne disguised a sigh.

'Oh, no. Nothing like that. I must be giving a very flippant impression. Most of the time both of us were working very hard. But we did like having lots of people here: they seemed to enjoy it. We had wonderful nights, dancing, singing, playing silly games – I expect Rosie may have told you. But that was only a small part of our lives, until the money ran out. Then it had to stop.' She wiped a streak of rain from her cheek. 'But I do *remember* the parties, I have to admit. I remember them, perhaps better than anything else, partly because of the peace when they were over. We loved it when the house was full of people and music and things. But then we loved it even better when it went back to being quiet, like this.'

She put her hand on the window ledge, wiped dust from it

with her finger. They listened to rain on the roof. Near as he stood to her, Evans felt Mrs Browne was very remote. Not in a week in this room, imprisoned with her, could he touch her: she inspired in him no desire. He saw that some people might find her beautiful, but for him she was too self-contained. Everything about her suggested she needed nothing more than her house. She was friendly enough, generous, kind, but something of an enigma. And Evans had no time for enigmas. He preferred the instant, animal appeal of Brenda with her great warm body and wicked eyes. At the thought of Brenda, here in this room in that bed, the spell of Mrs Browne was broken for Evans. But as he followed her back downstairs to the drawing-room, he realised that in some curious way, as strangers sometimes are, he had been very close to her for a short while. The visit to her house, her private world in which ordinary things seemed to have been infused with some of her spirit, left him feeling that the indefinable magic he sometimes imagined could exist, *did* exist. It was a possibility. Mrs Browne had proved it.

Back in their seats by the fire she made practical suggestions.

'You can have a key to the back door, and if you use the back stairs I'll never know when you're coming and going, which I'm sure you'd like best. You must let me know if there's anything you want. In the meantime come up any time you want and get it all arranged. I'm here all the time.'

Evans had finished his whisky. Judging by the darkening windows it was getting late. He felt he ought to go.

'Don't you mind living in this huge house all by yourself?' he asked.

'Never for one moment. I like aloneness and it's never lonely. Besides, I have to keep it going in case . . . Well, no, I suppose Hugh will never change his mind about selling it, or coming back. But I like to keep it as it was . . . until it finally goes.'

'I'd go out of my mind,' said Evans, 'all alone in a place like this. I couldn't take the silence.' The unusually strong drink had speeded his words. 'I wouldn't know what to do with myself. It'd be quite spooky, I'd think, especially when those bloody church bells get going. If you don't mind me asking, Mrs Browne, what do you do with yourself all day?'

'Keep guard.' She smiled.

'I've never met a woman like you before. I mean, not even a *type* of woman.'

'Would you like another drink?'

'Don't know whether I should. I ought to be getting back, oughtn't I?'

Mrs Browne was a little hazy before him now, flitting about with glasses and ice. The room seemed full of shadows too hazardous to cross on his weak legs. He had never had a strong head when it came to drink.

'Not unless there's something special you have to do. And anyway, I'd like to hear a bit about Brenda.'

In the next two hours Mrs Browne listened almost without interruption to the frustrations of Evans's life, his hopes, his ambitions, his love for Brenda. When he left, much confused by the act of putting on his damp mackintosh, he heard her urging him to return soon, too. As he walked unsteadily back down the drive he reflected, in a confused way, that his plan had gone better than he could ever have anticipated. A room at last, and a smashing room at that. It was nothing less than a triumph. Evans gave a celebratory leap over a shallow puddle which quivered with moonlight. Unnerved, he almost fell. Recovering himself, he set about thinking how and when to break the news to Brenda. First he needed sleep, time to recover his calm. Then, in the morning, if he woke to find it had not been a dream, he would make more plans. Probably it would be best to keep it from her until the room was quite ready. Then he would take her there – she'd never believe him till she saw it – and they would celebrate in the way they both liked best.

There were times, not more than twice a year, that Rosie and Henry had a row. In retrospect Rosie could never be certain of the superficial reason for these rows. For all the love, it seemed that some friction which they could never discuss cumulated over the months and burst out in a guise that was little to do with the real cause. The guise, in fact, was nearly always the same: the name of their son. This was a subject that had meant anguish from the time he had been conceived, and they had had their ritual fights about it ever since. These fights had never shifted their own particular convictions that the other one was wrong. When over, each went their own way, nurturing his own inarticulate hurt. For her part, Rosie would clutch at the physical pain in her ribs with her clumsy hands, shed a few quiet tears under the sheets, and begin the next day as if nothing had happened. This was not entirely due to stoicism. She believed that rows were something everyone had to go through, once in a while, and, like childbirth, when they were over their pain was impossible to recall. They did nothing to clear the air because the air, she believed, in the case of she and Henry, was devoid of tension, full of love, *daily* love. The occasional outbursts were no more serious than a rare storm, Rosie told herself, natural to the rhythm of things. They were of so little consequence that she divulged them to no one, did not muse upon them herself. She simply made sure they never took place when Evans was there.

But for all their unimportance, the unease of an impending row twisted into Rosie's gut in a way that made her hands tremble and her mouth stiffen. She often thought that if it wasn't for the rigidity of her mouth she could smile at Henry and thereby dissolve the situation before it really began: but the paralysis made this impossible. Impeded as she was, there was no alternative but to endure the fray, trying to remember it was not the real Henry and Rosie taking part, but devils within them temporarily escaped.

Back from her meeting, as soon as she opened the front door, Rosie knew what was going to happen. Henry's mackintosh, hanging in its usual place, was wet. He had been out. It wasn't his night for going to the Star, but she would

63

make no issue of that. It was, however, a climax to the oppressive silence that he had lately inflicted upon them. As Rosie went into the kitchen a spasm drilled within her, and she saw her hands quiver with their own angry life.

'Evans not back?' she said. Henry put down his paper. He had guessed from her footsteps – they became staccato with an approaching storm – what was in store. Her tight face proved him right. In no mood for words tonight, the Leopard prancing in his mind, he made an effort to be flat.

'It's not late,' he said. Then he made his mistake. 'The Boy can come in when he likes, can't he?'

Rosie slammed a string bag full of papers on to the table.

'*Evans*!' she shouted. 'His name is Evans! For twenty-seven years – do I have to keep on telling you? I registered him as Evans. He *is* Evans. It's registered as Evans, do you understand?' Henry saw the metallic sky through the window behind her. He heard the rain against the small panes, a gentle backing to her voice. 'All his life you've referred to him as the Boy. He's had to put up with it. I've had to put up with it. What sort of father are you, Henry Evans?'

'I wanted my son to be Sinbad. I told you I wanted that, I told you at the time.'

'Sinbad! Pah! You and your fancy notions about sailors, the Navy, the sea. What did you ever do at sea to make us proud?'

Rosie knew how best to goad her husband. Chide him about his naval career, and there was no hope of his remaining calm. He threw his paper to the ground, stood up.

'Shut up, woman, will you? I want none of this tonight. What do you know about the Navy? What do you know about anything but keeping your petty little house?' Rosie sat down, flayed. Henry had gone too far, attacking her house. 'You're the one who's done the damage, take it from me. Lumbering the Boy with a name like that, making his life a bloody nightmare of embarrassment. How's that for motherly love?'

He was shouting so loud the people next door would hear.

On the white tablecloth Rosie's great boxy hands lay flushed and swollen.

'If he'd hated it so much, he could have asked us to call him something else.'

'I suppose you've forgotten he did ask you, many times, when he was a kid? I suppose you've forgotten what a scene you made? I suppose you've forgotten that. I suppose you've forgotten the days he'd come home from school upset by the teasing? I suppose —'

'Oh, stop repeating yourself, Henry Evans. I haven't forgotten.' In truth, she had, almost. In these ritual shouting matches Henry always reminded her. But the times in between the facts dissolved in her mind. 'Please don't shout any more.'

Tonight, more quickly than usual, her anger withered. She felt merely drained, limp. These fights would get them nowhere. Nothing now would ever change the only thing that came between them: the name of their son. Looking up at her husband, his great craggy face looming oddly from such a narrow head of grey hair, she saw that he, too, had exhausted his anger sooner than was customary.

'I'll go back out, get a breath of wind on me,' he said.

'Very well. I'll put the kettle on for when you come back.'

When he had gone Rosie continued to sit at the table without moving. She felt about her the profound silence that Henry had left behind: a silence polluted with dissatisfaction that was almost tangible. Her mind, as it always did after such upheavals, went back twenty-seven years ago, when it had all begun. For most of her pregnancy she and Henry had argued about whether or not the child should be called Sinbad. Rosie had always been adamantly against the idea, but could not think of an alternative name that appealed to Henry. Then, that wintry afternoon, when the baby was three days old, milk-smelling, sucking at her breast, it had come to her: Evans Evans. In her mind's eye she could see the words in gold paint on the side of a smart navy blue lorry. *Evans Evans*: it would be a most distinguished name for a contracting firm, an engineering firm – almost any sort of firm. With a name like that her son would start off with an advantage. He would go far. She would see to it he would go far. When Henry came back from work he cradled the baby in his big arms and she had told him her idea. He would be pleased at last, she had thought. He would see the point.

'Never,' he had said, quietly.

Rosie had not thought it worth arguing. Normally, throughout their married life, she wanted whatever Henry wanted. This time, her own desire was all that mattered. She did not contemplate changing her mind. She registered the child's name and told Henry later. He said nothing at the time, just refused ever to call the child anything but Boy. The contention between them became part of their lives. They scarcely acknowledged its existence and continued in their pattern of apparent happiness. Only infrequently, like to-night, did they give vent to their resentment. Such rare occasions, they hardly counted, thought Rosie, and chided herself for having been overcome by the silly rage that had spurred her when she walked through the door. She sighed, got up to put on the kettle. When Henry came back she would apologise: that was part of the ritual pattern. She would say sorry, love, and mean it; hand him his tea and rub briefly at his shoulder with the back of her cupped hand. In anticipation of peace, the horror of the past scene vanished as quickly as it had come. The nasty silence evaporated, too. Rain on windows, hum of steaming kettle, normality returned. Rosie's smile came back; she tried it out on herself in the small mirror above the fire. She would smile at Henry when he came back, welcome him: and all would be well again for months to come.

A pale night, the moon a scavenger among shifting clouds. Warm. Evans made his way along the edge of a wheat field to the barn. There was a smell of wet earth and hedgerows, a profoundly English smell that suffuses summer nights after rain. He felt good. All day he had been savouring the

thought of the attic room, tempted to tell Brenda but determined not to. Brenda waited for him in the barn. Its dark
shape was solid and comfortable against the rags of sky and
trees. Evans smiled to himself, trying to remember when it
was he had first called the barn the Hilton, and Brenda had
laughed.

She was standing at the door. She held a rug, a Thermos,
and a packet of Woodbines. Her shirt was undone almost to
the waist, revealing the melon shapes of her breasts. Evans
was surprised. Usually, she hid. He had to find her. It was
one of their nocturnal games. By the time he had chased her
voice in the dark, pretending to miss her whereabouts several
times, and then fell upon her, poorly hidden between bales of
straw, he could wait no longer. He would take her quickly,
that first time. Later, they would make the rug comfortable
and start all over again, more slowly.

'Why aren't you hiding?'

'Don't know.' Her mouth drooped. Evans remembered.

'Did Wilberforce –?' He had not thought about Wilberforce, or Elizabeth, all day. Lucky he remembered now.

'Yes.'

'Good.'

'He must have done it before I got there this morning.
Lark gave me a medicine bottle of gin for my elevenses to
get over it.'

'You mustn't think of Elizabeth any more.'

'I don't.'

'Let's lay out the rug.' They moved into the barn, climbed
three steep steps made by bales of straw to the first flat floor.
'Shall we stay here, or go on up to the penthouse?'

'Stay here.'

They spread the rug and lay down. Evans put a hand on
Brenda's denim thigh. His fingers kneaded a seam.

'Your hair smells nice.'

'So it ought.'

'Good thing the rain's come.'

'Lark's herb shampoo.'

67

'Shall I call for room service?'

Brenda tapped the Thermos.

'After.' Pause. 'What are you waiting for?'

'Just taking my time. I like looking up into the roof, don't you? Reckon I know those rafters better than any rafters in the whole bloody world.'

'Evans . . . get on with it.'

Denim thighs spread like a water diviner's stick. Free hand rumbling under the shirt, ripping buttons. Breasts warm round swirls of flesh. Nipples hard as corks.

'Go on,' she said, 'touch me.'

'Patience.'

'No.'

'Patience, I say.'

'Go on, Evans. Hurry.'

'Where?'

'You know where.'

'All right?'

'Um. Quick. Oh, that bloody light.'

'Like it. Can see you now.'

Silver moon prying through the great doorway. Dew glisten of flesh. Clothes flung away, limp corpses, aping stillness before this desire. Corn smell, hair smell, dust smell.

'Evans, do everything to me Evans. Anything you like.' She squelched beneath him. He sucked her. Mouth, throat, nipple, stomach. 'Go on.' Decent cloud, suddenly, to frustrate the moon's prurience. Only the feel, the taste, in darkness. Mutual churning world, making ready. Then the taking. Quiet groans, squeak of straw, arms slippery with sweat, biscuit-smelling rug.

'Oh, Evans.'

'Bren.'

'Don't move.'

'Christ, I like fucking you, Bren. Christ, I love you.'

'Shut up.'

Mood already sliding out of reach. Compliance gone. She'd be wanting a cigarette any minute. Or maybe she

68

wouldn't. She went back to being unpredictable, after. After a night without it, he'd like her again at once.

'Ready?'

'Course.'

They moved.

Eventually they lay quite still, listened to the small sounds of mice, the shuffle of a bird in the rafters. They watched the clouds skirmish across the doorway, heard the church clock strike two.

'Lark should try it,' said Brenda. 'I keep telling her.'

'She'd be crushed to death, her little bones.' They both laughed.

'It's lovely at the Hilton nights like this, isn't it?' In mourning for a dead chicken Brenda was always at her most gentle. Evans loved her best after a hen had died.

'Lovely.'

'I wouldn't mind, really, if we never managed to find a real bed. We could go on staying at the Hilton all our lives.'

She pushed herself up on to one elbow, stretched a hand into the folds of the rug for cigarettes. Evans thought of the attic room, curtains from somewhere at the windows, a bowl of Mrs Browne's lilac by the bed. He kept his silence.

'Don't be daft.'

'I mean it.'

'One day you're going to set this place on fire, then we'll be done for.'

'Promise I won't.' Her hip bone was a small sharp hill against the sky. She blew a puff of white smoke that filtered up into the darkness of the rafters. Then lay back close to Evans.

'What do you like best about me, Bren?' These sort of times, he often dared ask her silly things.

'What you've just done to me, 'course.'

'Don't you like me for my good looks, my money, my car, my bloody faithfulness?'

Brenda giggled:

'You're a silly sod.'

69

'You're not so bad yourself. Here.'

'Hey, wait. I haven't finished it.'

'Well, there's one way to stop you.' He took the cigarette from her, stubbed it out on the Thermos.

'Waste of money. Want some tea?'

'Tea can wait.'

'You're a rare one, you are.'

'Kiss me. Go on. I'm going to lie here.' He pushed her coppery head on to his chest, continued to push it. Here in the barn there was no doubt who was master. Here she'd do anything he wanted, beg for more, be the one to ask. Here she was his, completely.

His girl. Brenda. Brenda Evans one day. His girl. There was her mouth at last. Funny how she could make the moon writhe like that, the clouds jumble about his eyes, private summer snow falling from the sky . . .

His girl Brenda.

The next prospective buyer to see Wroughton House was disturbingly keen. His enthusiasm for every detail filled Augusta with dread. He would change nothing, he said. He liked it all just as it was and would be willing to buy the furniture and pictures as well. The smell of the chimneys would not offend him – seeing his seriousness, Augusta made more of this than usual – because he had lost his sense of smell when he was blown up in the war. In desperation, Augusta was driven to decrying the garden: it was much too big for one man to cope with and no one else in the village was available to come even part-time; it was an endless expense and a perpetual worry. The elms were strangled with disease, he'd have to cut them all down, Augusta said. But the buyer was still undaunted. He waved his hand and mentioned contract gardeners: didn't matter how far they had to come. It wasn't till they reached the stable block Augusta discovered his Achilles heel. The old building, of historic interest, was in truth in the last stages of decay, its beams and bricks crumbling, its garage roof unsafe. To renovate it would cost many thousand pounds.

'At the moment,' said Augusta, 'the local pop group rehearse every evening in one of the loose boxes. But I told them they can only use it at their own risk. The roof may fall on top of them *at any moment*.' She avoided showing the man that particular loose box, whose roof was in fine order, and was rewarded to see the blood drain from his face. It seemed he was not interested in the bother of any kind of renovation. He liked to move into a place that needed no changes whatsoever. Responsibility for the stables would cause him more worry than he was prepared to take on. A pity, for he had so liked the house. He apologised for having taken so much of Augusta's time and left – as do all disappointed house hunters – very quickly.

The danger temporarily over once again, a little more time in hand, Augusta wondered where to glut her pleasure. She decided to go up to Evans's room in the attic, which she was preparing with much energy. To do something positive again, for someone else, had filled the last few days with great delight. She had found curtains, more rugs for the floor, a table and two armchairs. She had polished, dusted and swept, given a coat of white paint to the small fireplace and window sills. Evans had returned on a couple of occasions. He had stood about awkwardly, wondering what he could do to help, and had seemed relieved to find Augusta organising it all with such efficiency. She had made up the bed yesterday, and promised it would all be finished by the weekend. Now she fetched a pile of things she had collected from all parts of the house with which to finally bring the room alive: books, pictures, ashtrays, mugs and candles, bowls of cowslips. She busied about trying out the things in different places, and at last there was nothing further left to do. She sat in one of the armchairs, creaky but comfortable and looked about her.

Hugh would have been pleased, could he see the room now. He had always regretted they had not been able to finish the attics, and rarely visited them. She had told him about the transformation on the telephone. He had tried not to sound

71

interested, and had asked if all the effort wasn't a bit silly for so short a time? Augusta had assured him it was most sensible, quite apart from being nice for Evans, and Hugh had said, 'Well, you'll do whatever you want, as usual.' 'I *can't* be as foolish as you say I am,' she had replied, and put down the telephone. Their conversations always seemed to end on a fatuous level, these days. It was no good on the telephone. If only Hugh would come down, just for one day. They could talk properly, then. But he refused. He said there was no more talking to be done.

Perhaps he was right. Going round in circles was merely destructive. There was nothing new to add. She had repeated so many times that she knew it to be almost entirely her fault, this catastrophe, and asked to be forgiven and to be granted one more chance. He had equally repeated that he forgave her: of course he forgave her, but she had killed something within him (and it was not the first time she had killed the thing she loved, remember) that could never be resuscitated. A substitute arrangement would be no good. He would rather go. And so he had gone.

Oh, Hugh, thought Augusta. What have I done?

This was their house. Other people haunted it, slightly, but she could scarcely remember them. In this very room, one chilly afternoon, she had spent an hour with a lover, for whom she cared nothing, uncomfortable on the bare prickly mattress. Hugh had never found out, but it had been a mistake. When it was over she was glad the man had gone quickly, leaving the house alone for her and Hugh again. A sentimental old film on television, that particular evening, she remembered; she had cried at the end, using it as a front to her terrible deception, the thing that in truth was the cause of her crying.

Now there was no possibility of more years together. She had destroyed all that and had to accept the consequences. While despising self-pity, and indeed never allowing herself to indulge in it, Augusta accepted the fact that regret was something she would have to live for the rest of her life. She reflected that regret is an indestructible weed that can exist among fine emotions; not a killer, just a strangler that can exhaust its victim.

She looked at her watch: four o'clock. Always the worst time of day, for her. Since Hugh had gone, Augusta was tempted to sleep much more in the daytime. She half-relished this easy way to traverse the hours, but at the same time cursed herself for losing precious time in the house. Now, faced with the long evening, she was suddenly depressed by the thought of the ashes in the fire downstairs. Conscious of her guilt, she went to the bed she had caringly prepared for Evans and Brenda. She lay down on the quilted cover, and slept there till next morning.

Henry Evans stood at his front door, looked at the sky above the elms, and made his judgement. It wasn't going to rain. He pulled the door shut behind him, buttoned up his jacket, and started off down the road.

Rows always released in him a new silence, and after the little upheaval last night, though all of course was calm now, he did not see fit to tell Rosie where he was going. He walked fast, just in case she should shout after him, striding widely over the puddles rather than skirting them, to help release the stiffness in his legs that had come from a morning of sitting in his chair. He enjoyed the sound of his own footsteps on the wet road, the wind against his face, the bright green of the hedgerows. Mackay lived a mile outside the village, in a pre-war bungalow. He and Evans had been to school together. A wiry little sandy-haired thing he was, then: not up to much as far as books went, but a good fighter. Henry could remember being flayed by Mackay's inky fists in the playground one day, thoroughly beaten. The cause for the row he could not recall, but in the end Mackay had passed his handkerchief for Henry to wipe his bloody lip, and they had become friends. Mackay had been a pilot in the war, but returned to the village; one of the few from their school-days to do so. Unmarried, he kept to himself, making annual appearances at local horticultural shows, where he consistently won all the big prizes for vegetables. He and Henry had little in common these days, and never intruded upon their sparse relationship by making plans to meet. But Henry counted Mackay among his friends. On rare occasions when they ran into each other in the Star, where Mackay celebrated his victories, they exchanged the odd word, shorthand acknowledgement of days past spent blowing robins' eggs and poaching pheasants in the bluebell woods.

Henry pictured Mackay's surprise. He would not, he knew, be asked into the house. Mackay was not an inhospitable man – it simply never occurred to him anyone would care to pass through his front door. As on the only other two occasions Henry had come to visit him, they would doubtless stand one each side of the wrought iron gate at the end of the front path.

Mackay's bungalow stood close to the road. Behind it rose an impressive amount of greenhouses. In front, the small patch of ground that divided it from the road, which most proud gardeners would have crammed with flowers, was completely cemented over. Not a blade of grass, not a ruffle of aubretia to soften the back-yard appearance. Only a miniature windmill, broken arms whirling in the wind, and a single stone gnome hunched over his fishing line, were rooted in the hard ground. Henry always wondered why Mackay, whose pleasure in life was to care for prize vegetables in the soft earth at the back of his house, should create such bleakness in the front. He could only conclude that the contrast was the thing that appealed to Mackay. Dead ground in one place, young shoots in another – perhaps Mackay had intended a constant surprise for himself.

His face was at the window. Henry stopped at the road side of the gate, not presuming to enter the cement territory. Mackay hurried out lest his friend should do so. His boots made an urban clatter in his garden. He was bent, old-looking, soil engrained in his hands, black nails.

'There, Evans, I was just giving myself a cup of tea.'

'Hope I'm not at an inconvenient time?'

'Not at all, not at all. I'm my own master, master of my own hours.' They looked at each other. Henry had imagined the encounter taking place on a sunny day. This greyness, all his rehearsed words seemed to have fled.

'Vegetables coming on all right, are they?'

'Lovely, just as ever.'

'Ah.'

'You keeping all right? And the wife?'

'Very nicely, thanks.' Henry put a hand on the curly top of the iron gate. Mackay backed away a pace, fear of entry by his friend clear on his face.

'Ah, Evans, you were just passing by, then?'

'Just passing. I'll be on my way. Though I was wondering . . .' The sky seemed darker, the wind pecked about his trousers. But it was Mackay who noticed the rain first. Alert of hearing, he heard a drop fall behind him.

'There, I knew we'd have another shower.'

'We could do with a drop. Do you ever sell your stuff, Mackay? Privately, I mean.'

'Take a load to the market couple of times a week.'

'Privately, though? Cauliflowers in particular, I mean. I was referring to cauliflowers in particular.'

'Cauliflowers in particular?' Mackay scratched the back of his neck. Rain was splattering down on the cement quite fast by now. 'Can't say I've ever really thought about it.'

Henry removed his hand from the gate. The gesture caused Mackay some relief: he folded his arms to think, unaware of the increasing damp of his shirt. Henry was grateful for Mackay's apparent oblivion to so heavy a shower. If he hurried away now there would be no chance to settle the matter.

'It's like this, Mackay.' He heard a note of confidence in his own voice. 'Some time soon, in the near future, like, there might be an emergency situation. Not to trouble you with details, I might find myself in a position when I should like to drive here, no notice, and buy a couple of cauliflowers off

75

of you. How would that strike you?'

Mackay shrugged.

'Easy. Why not? You'll always find me out the back.'

'But prize cauliflowers, Mackay. I'd want a couple of the
prize jobs. You know, make a person sit up when they saw
them.'

Sudden comprehension swarmed over Mackay's wet face.
He narrowed his eyes, making rain fall faster down his
cheeks. He licked some of it away with his tongue.

'Would I be right in thinking you'd want them for someone in hospital?'

Henry paused only an instant.

'That sort of thing. For someone in hospital, in a manner of
speaking, yes.'

'I took tons of green stuff up to my mother when she was
dying in the Royal, you know. She said take away your
blooming gladioli, Jack, she said: you can keep your blooming flowers. What I want is nice spring greens.'

'That's why I want the cauliflowers.'

'I never took her caulis, come to think of it.'

Henry felt the rain pouring down his neck.

'Would that be all right, then, Mackay – Jack? If I just
came sudden like and got a couple of cauliflowers?'

'Dare say. Though I couldn't promise you the real prize
stuff, could I? The second best would have to do you. Don't
suppose many people could tell it was second best. Lovely
heads.'

'Wonderful, how many prizes you get, you know, Jack.'
His mission happily accomplished, Henry felt it easy to be
complimentary. Mackay shrugged again.

'Got a few in my time.'

'Well, I'd best be getting back. The rain. You'll be expecting me when you see me, then?'

Mackay nodded.

'Mind, you'll have to twist their arms up at the hospital
kitchens,' he said. 'They're devils about cooking brought-in
greens.'

76

Henry turned his face into the slant of the shower, head held high. The rain soaked his feet and splashed his trousers, but he had no care. If the sparkling hedges had been covered in diamonds he could not have felt more excitement: never had he imagined his little transaction could have been so easy. He felt a warmth of gratitude to Mackay and all such uncurious men in the world, men with an instinct for making things easy. Now all he had to do was wait. Soon, the time would come. There he'd be, the two heads of cauliflowers in his hands, their pale crumbly flowers bursting from their leaves, huge, huge. The Leopard would be amazed.

The Leopard. His dear Leopard. There were tears among the rain in his eyes.

Henry's blood pumped fast with the joy of having achieved something that was linked with the woman who consumed his thoughts. The fact that she was unaware not only of his existence, but also of the surprise he was preparing for her, made no difference to his elation. He would feed off the pleasure for weeks, if necessary, trying to be patient, keeping a constant watch on the Star. He would be protected from the irritations of every-day life by his private anticipation. In such high spirits, even Rosie's concern about his wet condition, her chivvying about with hot drinks and dry clothes, could not touch him. The success of his cauliflower plan had brought the Leopard wonderfully close. No one would guess, from looking at him, he was alone with her in his heart.

It was still raining at nine that night when Evans drove along the same road towards Brenda's flat. The room in Wroughton House had been ready for a week now. For some reason which he could not decipher, even to himself, he had preserved the news all this time. Tonight, irritated by his father's sniffing by the fire, Evans had on impulse decided to get out of the house, and tell Brenda. It was not one of their regular nights. She would not be expecting him – she would be washing her hair, probably, having one of her gossipy evenings with Lark. Still, armed as he was with good news,

Evans imagined he would be welcome.

Lark answered the door. Surprise clouded her small face. Brenda was out, she said. Just gone down to the Air Base for a drink. Some party, she thought it was; why didn't he come in and wait? Brenda was bound not to be late.

Evans followed Lark into the sitting-room. The remains of a solitary supper lay on the table: half a piece of burnt toast, a jar of salmon fish paste, a bottle of tomato ketchup. Lark switched on the gas fire. The room was always dank.

'So who's she gone with?' Evans managed to sit himself quite jovially in the chair by the fire.

'That I don't know exactly,' said Lark, carefully. 'Some bloke she met somewhere, I think. Quite harmless.' She glanced at Evans's face. 'Like a gin?'

'Thanks.'

'I've eaten, but I could get you something.'

'No thanks, just a drink. She never mentioned this bloke to me.'

'No, well, she probably didn't think it important. Some men aren't important, are they, after all? Not worth mentioning, really.' Lark gave a small laugh, handed Evans a glass half full of neat gin.

'You've given me a whopper, Lark.'

'Go on. Drink it slowly.'

Evans took a gulp of the drink.

'We are engaged, you know,' he said, 'Brenda and me.'

'Well, that's very old news.' Lark smiled kindly.

'And would you consider, seeing as we're engaged – would you consider, in the circumstances, it's right that my fiancée should go gallivanting off to some party at the Air Base with another bloke, without so much as a word to me?'

'Well,' said Lark, 'depends.'

'Depends on what?'

Lark searched her mind for a word Evans had recently used.

'Circumstances,' she said.

'Ah, circumstances.' The gas fire's blue flames were

78

rubbing heat into Evans's shins. For a moment he experienced the dream-like feeling of running fast and yet not moving from the same spot: help from Lark seemed a long way off. 'In which circumstances would all this be correct?' he asked.

'Well,' said Lark, pouring herself a large measure of gin to give herself time, 'I think if you've been engaged to someone for a long time, like you and Brenda, and you trust each other, like you two do – well, then, there's no harm in it, is there? I mean going to a dance with someone else will only make her *appreciate* you much more. Don't you think?'

Evans looked at her. There was no doubt in her eyes.

'I don't know,' he said. 'Perhaps I'm being ungenerous.'

'I think perhaps you are. A bit, anyway.'

'I wouldn't have minded if she had told me. I would have understood, wouldn't I?'

'Oh, Evans, stop worrying. It's nothing to worry about, honestly. She'll explain all right. She'll be back soon. You just wait here by the fire. But if you don't mind –' she went to the door ' – I'll get back to my room. I was just in the middle of doing my nails.' She held up a hand. Three nails were scarlet, two were still unpainted.

'Who are you tarting yourself up for, then?' Lark liked to be teased.

'Just keeping my hands nice. You never know what to expect round the next corner, do you?'

'You're a funny girl, Lark.'

'You keep helping yourself to gin. It silvers the mind, you know.' She shut the door behind her.

Evans drank the first glass slowly. It was not a taste he liked, but it did indeed silver the mind. He listened happily enough to the small wheeze of the gas fire, and let his eyes curl about the twisted flames. He thought of silver birches, for some reason, their leaves up-brushed by the wind. He thought of his collection of sixpences: as a child, he had dropped them in the snow. They had made small glinting holes, like the beginnings of a thaw. Picking them up, the cold had bitten into his fingers, making them clumsy as he

79

tried to stuff them back into the jar. Perhaps Lark was right, he thought, and there was no need to worry. In all this time Brenda had not betrayed him. Why should she now? Probably, as Lark said, she was just enjoying the dancing. There'd be nothing funny, no funny business. Brenda would never allow that, would she? But then why had she said nothing? Why hadn't she said there's this bloke, Evans, who wants to take me dancing?

He finished the last of his drink. No one ever wanted just to take a girl dancing these days, did they? Especially a girl like Brenda.

The realisation broke savagely within Evans. He stood, poured more gin from the bottle on the table, conscious that his head, chest and shoulders were all hurting, a physical pain. Away from the fire, the heat of his legs began to fade: a chill, as if he'd been caught in a sudden wind, lashed over his body. The small, ordinary things in the room, the plain furniture and thin curtains, trembled as if they too were affected by the wind. Evans picked up the piece of burnt toast, ate it. It was bitter on his tongue, but food would steady him, he thought. He would ask Lark if he could help himself to a piece of bread and butter.

Carrying his drink he left the room, hesitated on the dark landing, then knocked at her door. She called to him to come in. He opened the door, quickly shut it behind him lest the stuffy warmth, which flowed up to him like the corner of a summer afternoon, should escape.

'All this gin,' he said, 'could you let me have some bread and butter, Lark?'

Lark was lying back on her bed in her dressing-gown. Barefoot, her scarlet toe nails plucked at the candlewick bedspread, making it writhe between them. She held her hands above her head, the nails flashing at Evans like a procession of ladybirds.

'Oh, dear, of course,' she said. 'Give us a minute and I'll get it for you.'

'Thanks.'

Lark smiled at him.

'I can see you're not a gin drinker,' she said.

'No.'

'I like it. It makes me feel happy.' She sat up, swinging her legs on to the wool rug beside the bed. There was a long silence between them. Then Evans said:

'One thing I've always meant to ask you, Lark: I've never understood about your name. I suppose your Mum said to you one day, when you were a kid, "you sing like a lark". And it stuck.'

Lark laughed.

'Yes, she did, as a matter of fact.'

'Funny how names stick.'

'Funny, yes.' She put her hands to her waist to tighten the cord of her dressing-gown.

An absurd pleasure at having made Lark laugh, at having guessed correctly the reason for her name, caused Evans to sway a little on his feet. Then the vision of Brenda, obliterated briefly by the gin, came back to him. She was dancing close to some man. Close to him and wanting him.

'Take that thing off,' Evans said. He was surprised, considering the fuzzy condition of his head, at the harshness of his own voice. With an economic gesture that conveyed a life of response to duty, Lark undid the dressing-gown. She threw it to the bottom of her bed. Then she lay back, eyes wide but showing no surprise.

Evans looked at her. The small fierce light that hung from the ceiling glared on to the flat white surfaces of her body, reminding him of snow. Her nipples were black chips, hard as charcoal: her limbs, scattered in awkward shapes, thin as winter branches. From her breastbone to her naval ran a jagged scar, its ruckled join a shining silver membrane. Each side of the scar, pink dots dimpled the flat white skin. Evans licked at the corners of his mouth, tasting the gin.

'You know what I'm going to do to you?' he said.

Lark lowered her eyes to look at him. She put one hand on the scar, feeling down its ridge with a scarlet fingernail.

81

'Yes.'

'What do you think about that?'

'Oh, get on with it, Evans.' Her voice was weary, impatient, without care.

Evans struggled to undo his belt, his trousers, his shirt. His hands were clumsy. Lark's eyes, very bleak, remained upon him. In his impatience, he shuffled himself awkwardly to the bed, trousers round his ankles. He crashed down upon her, felt her small bones writhe beneath him, the helpless flutter of a dying bird. He smelt nail polish – her fingers were clattering about his ears – and the sickly smell of hairspray as his nose dug about the brittle, frosty mesh of her hair. He felt himself to be lying on cold flat earth, enraged by the lack of undulations beneath him, but too desirous of release to get up.

It was over in a moment. Evans cried out, Lark remained silent. She pushed at his shoulders, eager for him to be gone. He sat up, swung his legs on to the floor, pulled his trousers up over his knees.

'Do you often do that?' he asked.

'Time to time. Not here. I wouldn't like men in my room, except you.'

'Brenda and me have often wondered if you had a boyfriend. Where do you do it, then?'

Lark, eyes shut, shrugged her bony shoulders.

'There are people at the office. Randy men. Lunchtime. Here, give me that.' Evans threw the dressing-gown over her. 'There's a room where they keep the files. Airless in summer, freezing cold in winter.'

Evans stood up, pulling his clothes together. Lark was a childlike mound on the bed. Impossible to imagine her, grey jersey and skirt pulled up, giving pleasure to some randy clerk who had backed her up against the files.

'Can't be much fun, like that,' he said.

'It isn't.'

'Well, it can be good.'

'Brenda says it's good with you.'

'Did you think so?'

Lark opened her eyes, cast upon him her usual consideration.

'Well, you didn't try with me, did you? I could hardly expect that, these conditions. Still, it was better with you than with the others. Don't worry though – I won't remember it.' She sat up, patting at her dead hair which, in the skirmish, had lost its temporary boost and had fallen back into its old partings. 'Now I'd like you to go, please, Evans. You can go back to the other room, help yourself to bread and butter, sit by the fire. You can wait there. Brenda shouldn't be long. I want to go to sleep.'

Evans took the remains of his drink from amongst the cacti on the bedside table. He felt in need of more alcohol. Deflated. His body still ached with an unfamiliar pain.

'You might tell me now, then, who she's with.'

'I won't, and I can't. I don't know his name and if I did I wouldn't tell you because she's my friend, Brenda.'

Evans laughed.

'Your friend? And you've just –'

'Go on, Evans, get out.'

'If I were you, I wouldn't tell her, for all she's your friend!'

'I wouldn't say too much about it either, if I were you.'

'You can trust me. But if she buggers off, some other bloke, I've every right to –'

'Go on, Evans. Please. I'm tired.' Lark stood up. In the moment before she succeeded in securing her dressing-gown Evans caught sight of red marks on her flat breasts, the beginnings of a bruise beneath a sharp hip bone. Perhaps he had hurt her. He could not remember how it had been. But her eyes were limp, in deep shadow despite the blaze of the overhead light. She seemed to be exhausted, very old.

'I'm going,' he said. 'You all right?' Lark nodded. 'I didn't intend, you know . . .'

'No need to explain.'

'Night, then, Lark.'

Back in the sitting-room he closed the door and sat at the

table. It was two-thirty by the clock on the fireplace. The bottle of gin was empty. The gas fire hissed and spluttered: there was a faint smell of gas. Evans felt both sick and hungry. He opened the jar of fish paste, scraped inside it with a knife. It had a sour, smooth taste, nothing to do with salmon, difficult to swallow. He heard Lark open her window and switch off her light. In a few moments, he hoped, poor battered scrap of a thing, she would be asleep. Perhaps by morning she would not remember much of tonight. Perhaps she would be able to cocoon herself back into the small scarlet world of her room unharmed, unresentful. She was a good friend, Lark. He would not want to hurt her.

Evans lay his head on his folded arms. He had no wish to think about it any more. He slept.

Two hours later he was woken by Brenda opening the door. In the stone-coloured dawn, increasing in the window, he saw that she wore a shawl over her shoulders – a shawl he had not seen before. Her hair was glossy as usual, but then it was the kind of hair that never tousled, no matter how energetic had been their love-making. Her face? How was her face? Through his aching eyes Evans found it hard to tell. Soft, somehow. The lines of defence, so familiar to him in daylight, evaporated. Sulky.

'What the hell are you doing here?'

She leant up against the door, head back, one knee bent, the pose she so often used against the chicken shed when she knew Evans was approaching. 'It wasn't your night for coming round. Spying on me?'

Evans picked up the empty fish paste jar, rolled it in his hands, feeling the ridged glass. Confused by sleep, head full of searing pains, he had to be careful. He had to take things slowly: not do or say anything reckless, or she'd go. She was in a mood, Brenda was, he could see. If he was too hard on her, she'd go for ever.

'It's half-past four,' he said, looking at the clock.

'So?'

'That's late to be out with another bloke when you're

engaged to be married to me.'

Brenda slouched towards the sofa, her bed, and slumped down upon it. She crossed her legs, pulled the shawl round her breasts, leaned against the wall. An uncomfortable, uncaring position.

'I haven't done nothing wrong,' she said.

'I don't know what you've done, do I?'

'I'm telling you.'

'Who was he? Why didn't you tell me?'

'He gave me a lift last week.'

'I've told you, Bren, you shouldn't go getting hitches any more, not looking like you do. You're asking for trouble.' In his effort to be calm, reasonable, Evans spoke very slowly.

'He was nice enough, works up at the Air Base. Said there was going to be this party, would I like to go? You know how you don't like parties. I didn't think there would be any harm.'

'Is this the first time you've done anything like this?'

'Like what? I haven't done nothing wrong.'

'Gone out with someone else, not telling me. I wouldn't have minded if you'd told me.'

'You would. Bet you would. You'd have got yourself so screwed up I wouldn't have been able to go.'

Evans sighed.

'Where'd you get that shawl?'

'Bought it.'

'What, for the party? Specially for the party?'

Brenda shrugged. She ran a finger round the outline of her lips, to test if they hurt, a thing she often did after Evans had kissed her fiercely.

'I needed a shawl.'

Evans felt his heart quicken. He rolled the jar faster in his hands. Brenda, defiant, was beautiful on the bed. Out to provoke him.

'We're engaged to be married, you know,' he said.

He had intended to say something quite different. Something witty and light, to make her laugh and ask forgiveness.

Then, in spite of the cruel headache, he would kiss her and take her, make her cry out she was sorry –

'So why did you come round? Spying?'

'I came round to give you some news.'

'Oh, yes.'

'Honestly.'

'Postage going up again, is it?'

'Bitch.'

Brenda laughed.

'You look quite furious, sitting there. Quite the furious fiancé. Here, come and sit down.' For a moment, patting the bed with a hand that slipped from out of the shawl, she was almost coquettish. Without giving himself time to think whether he did the right thing, Evans went to her. He too leant his head uncomfortably against the wall, stuffed his hands in his trouser pockets. They made ugly lumps, material growths, upon his solid thighs. Through the window he could see a strand of lemony light on the prison walls.

'I'm not yours, you know,' said Brenda. 'I'm not yours to possess, absolutely. Not now, or when we're married, or ever.'

'But we're engaged.' Frustrated to hear himself repeating this feeble protestation, Evans tried to scour the thumping mess of his head to find a more lucid reason for his distress. 'And when people are engaged, there are usually rules. Duties to each other.'

'So there may be,' said Brenda. 'But people make their own rules. So if yours are different from mine, well then, you have to live by yours and I have to live by mine.'

'That attitude takes no account of love.'

'Ah, love.' She pouted. 'If you really loved me you wouldn't be making this silly scene. You'd be letting me get to bed.'

With sudden relief, Evans took this as a hint. He leant towards her, fumbling at the shawl, aiming his mouth at hers. Brenda pulled back, grimacing.

'You smell horrible! You smell of gin. Take your hand *off*, Evans. You're hurting.'

Evans tightened his grip on her shoulder. The sudden energy of anger flowed through him, giving strength to his drained body, numbing the pain in his head. Incredulous, he kneaded her flesh. Brenda was rejecting him. Back from the Air Base with another man, she was rejecting him, her rightful fiancé.

'What did he do to you?'

'Leave . . . me . . . *alone*.' Brenda struggled. 'He didn't do anything.'

'Is that the truth?'

'That's the truth – you wouldn't know the truth.' She closed her eyes. Her mouth squirmed open in pain. Evans felt a smile spread across the stiff skin of his own mouth.

'I'd kill him if he touched you.'

'Bragger!' In spite of her discomfort Brenda managed to spit out the word. 'You wouldn't hurt a mouse.'

'That's what you think. Did he touch you?'

'No! You're hurting me, Evans! Let go.' She kicked uselessly at his shin. In her struggle to get away from him she slid to a lying position on the bed. Evans glared down at her, his breath fast.

'Did he touch you? Did he touch you?'

'No! Stop shouting. You'll wake – all right, in the car! In the car, if you must know, he put his hand on the back of my neck and I told him, I told him, Evans, *not to go on*!'

She was crying now. Evans gave her just one slap on the face. It stung his hand.

He stood up, examined his own palm and huge fingers in the light that was now pale and clear. Then he looked at Brenda, head in her shawl, whimpering. The sound bubbled in strange harmony with the hiss of the gas fire. One of her shoes had fallen off. Her bare foot, moving slightly, was blackish between the toes.

'I'll not be seeing you for a week or so, then,' Evans said. 'I'll have to be thinking things over.'

Outside, he was struck by the chill of dawn. He had

arrived, so long ago, without a coat. Now, in the car, he shivered.

Evans drove home but could not tolerate the idea of spending the two hours till breakfast in his room. Instead, he decided, he would go to the room awaiting him in Wroughton House. He had the key to the back door. He would not wake Mrs Browne.

He walked slowly up the front drive, no longer aware of the cold. Ground mists were rising from the lawns and distant fields. They frothed, too, about the base of the house, confusing the more solid lines of lavender. Evans felt stiffness in his legs. He moved from the drive, whose scrunch broke the silence, to the grass. He took long strides across to the natural pond, dew soaking his shoes. The air was soft with promise of a fine day, but no mere panacea of early morning could quell the feelings insurgent within him. When madness settles upon men's minds, the madness of lust or rage or jealousy, the path to reason is quite lost: the desire to find it, even, obliterated. Thus it was that Evans strode almost blindly about the gardens, the bright trees, the white of hawthorn flower and brown glint of water hurting, rather than healing, his eyes. One thing only was clear to him: Brenda, always so elusive, was now quite lost to him. Knowing little of her Birmingham childhood, Evans judged her to be a girl unused to violence: they had had rows before, but never like this. She would have every right to leave him, now. His reckless behaviour had not 'accounted for love'. The irony of his own words, chiding words of just an hour or so ago, tightened the band of terrible pressure about his head.

He passed the kitchen window for the third time. A figure waved at him from within. The church clock struck six. He went inside.

Mrs Browne had made the kitchen warm. Coffee puckered on the stove. Evans sat down at the white table, chosen in the days when efficient cooking was required to fill the needs of constant guests. Mrs Browne, small as Lark, it occurred to Evans, was in a dressing-gown – pretty quilted cotton stuff, nothing like Lark's, *that*: he might have had the energy to admire it on a more ordinary occasion. There were shadows under her eyes: deep as evening shadows upon tired faces, strange so early in the morning. Taking a seat opposite Evans she poured two cups of coffee, pushed a bowl of sugar and jug of milk towards him.

'I was up early. I saw you wandering about,' she said.

'I've had a night.'

'Aren't you cold?'

'Warmer now, thanks.'

They sat in silence for a while, two people so deeply submerged in that state of preoccupation with their own thoughts that neither could summon the energy to enquire about the other. Eventually Evans said:

'I went to tell her the news about the room. I thought she'd be pleased, and I hit her.'

'She'd been out with someone else?' Evans nodded. One of several good things about Mrs Browne was that she understood things before there was need to explain.

'So I didn't tell her in the end. About the room, I mean. No use now, really. I mean, I suppose it's all over between us.'

Curiously, considering the seriousness of the situation, Mrs Browne smiled.

'Of course it's not! I should go and tell her tonight, if I were you. Bring her here.'

'I told her I wasn't going to see her again for a week or so. I told her I had to think things over.'

'Oh, I shouldn't do that.' Mrs Browne was almost gay. 'There's no point in thinking things over if you know what you ultimately want. Besides, leaving her for a week will give *her* time to think up all sorts of things against you. Stupid.'

'But I hit her.'

'Women can survive a few bashes.'

'Never imagined I could do such a thing, not in all my life.'

'I expect she provoked you.'

'She did. She provoked me all right.' He paused. 'The thing about Brenda, it's always been the same, I never know where I am with her. She's my fiancée. She's mine, isn't she? Yet I can't seem to . . . get a real hold of her. I can't seem to be sure of her, ever. I'm always scared she's just out of my reach.' He poured himself more coffee, warm now. The heaviness of his head was lifting. 'I don't know how to set about it, I've tried all different ways. I do everything I can for her, show her I love her. I'm always there when she needs me. She knows she can rely on me. We're marvellous in – well,' he managed to smile, 'in the barn. It's just this un-sureness. It unnerves me. I don't know if you can under-stand.'

'Perhaps it makes you too anxious, too clinging, too demanding. Perhaps it irritates her, your constantly wanting her reassurance and presence.' Mrs Browne looked at him. 'Perhaps you're claustrophobic.'

Evans looked back at her. Her eyes were humorous.

'Never thought of that,' he said. 'I thought women liked all the reassurance bit. Thought I was doing the right thing.'

'Some women do, same as some men. Others, only to a certain extent. But to a few people, I think, the confines of absolute security are inhibiting, imprisoning. To be escaped from. The clever thing, once you've judged your partner, is then to judge just how strong you should make your net of security. It must have some – ' she searched for the word ' – *slack*. It must have some slack which can be taken up. Cast it too tight and the natural reaction, to some people, will be to escape.'

They remained in further silence, Evans thinking about her words. He was not entirely clear what she meant, but he had caught her gist. Her understanding, anyhow, was a comfort: she had renewed in him an almost inevitable hope that perhaps after all the ghastly night was not the end with Brenda.

'That shows your education,' he said at last.

'Oh, I haven't much education. I don't know much.

Nothing of any consequence when it comes to . . .' Evans's problems seem to have faded from her.

'Why were you up so early?' he asked.

'There are more people coming today to see the house. There haven't been any for ages, but they're coming today. People who want it for an office.'

'Don't worry, it's no good as an office, is it?' Their roles suddenly reversed, strength gathered within Evans.

'Well, it might be. A *prestige* office they say they want, whatever that is.'

'You can go on to them about the chimneys, can't you? The smoke, the bloody awful smell.'

'Oh, I shall. I shall tell them the whole place is falling down.' She spoke like a defiant child.

'But you can't go on staying here for ever, can you? I mean, one day, someone's going to buy it whether you like it or not.'

'Of course I can't stay here for ever. That's quite impossible. Anyhow it would be ridiculous, wouldn't it? Just me all alone in a house like this, no money left? Oh, I quite see how ridiculous it would be. But I shan't go before the autumn. I can't go before the mulberries . . . I want another Christmas here. I must be here another Christmas.'

'What, alone?'

'I don't mind being alone.'

'Well, I don't suppose the office people will want it. It would be quite wrong for an office, wouldn't it? Lovely place like this.'

Evans got up. Mrs Browne remained where she was.

'Tell Brenda tonight,' she said. 'Bring her here.'

'Might,' said Evans. 'I'll think about it. I must go now. Thanks very much for the coffee.'

Outside the sun was high, the dew melted. He walked back down the drive elated by the rise of new optimism. Events of the night, unlike happy events which harden into reality in retrospect, had become insubstantial in the daylight. Their consequences no longer threatened.

Evans looked forward to a breakfast of eggs and bacon. He would relish, this morning, his father's taciturnity and his mother's cooking. Rosie met him as he opened the door.

'Good Lord, Evans,' she cried, 'and where have you been all night? Your father's ill. I've been up hours with him, and you not here. The doctor's on his way. I've not known what to think.'

Five miles away Brenda and Lark were also much preoccupied with their own thoughts. It was their custom to speak little in the morning, a habit which, properly observed between close friends, saves all the inaccuracy of recounting nocturnal events too soon. Later, an evening alone together, her opinions finally set, Brenda would reveal what had happened. (Lark, naturally, would be called upon to do no such thing: *her* night, as Brenda would suppose, as usual having been spent in dull solitary fashion.) For now, Lark kept to their arrangement of asking no question that strayed beyond politeness. As usual she had got up before Brenda and made breakfast. Baked beans, this morning: knowing them to be Brenda's favourite, she chose them, perhaps a silent apology.

'Marvellous,' said Brenda, sitting at the table. 'I'm ravenous.'

'Evans finished the gin and finished the fish paste waiting for you,' said Lark, 'so there's nothing to go on our toast.'

'He was in a right mood when I got back, I can tell you.'

'Thought he might be. Have a good time?'

'Not bad.' Brenda's mouth was full. 'You're a bloody marvellous cook.'

'Oh, I don't know.' Lark was naturally modest about her talents. 'Anyhow I've had this good idea. In the night – it came to me in the night.'

'What's that?'

'I've decided that I shall put it about that I'd be quite willing to sing for charity.'

'How do you mean, sing for charity?'

'Well, you know, if there's a do somewhere in aid of something, and they want a singer, I'd be quite prepared to do it for nothing. For just a drink and something to eat. For the experience.'

'Good idea,' said Brenda. Another morning she would have been more receptive to a new idea to further Lark's career. As it was, wiping up the last of her beans with a piece of toast, she lacked concentration.

'So that's what I'm going to do,' said Lark, 'let it be known I'm available – in that way.' She smiled at her own joke. 'And if you want to do me a great favour, you'd put it about a bit, too.'

'Put what about, Lark?' Brenda was blowing her tea.

'What I've just been saying. Weren't you *listening*?'

'Oh, that. The singing. Yes. All right. 'Course. I'll put it about a bit too.'

'Thanks very much.' Lark was gathering up the plates. 'Sometimes you don't know what a friend you are. I'll be sure to get you free tickets and seats in the front row.'

'That'd be wonderful, Lark. I'll look forward to that, really I will. Honestly,' said Brenda.

Henry Evans was not very ill, but the plight of his mind had exacerbated the condition of his body. A soaking in the rain, the excitement of anticipation – the combination had been too much for his normally stable equilibrium. His temperature soared. He had a feverish chill, Rosie said, and, spelt out like that, the courage Henry had shown among the waves gave way to alarm.

Soon as Evans had gone out (after Brenda, no doubt, foolish Boy, though now Henry felt a new sympathy) he had allowed himself to be put to bed. Rosie, naturally, put a good face on the whole matter: her stalwart smile, slightly askew with real concern, would have touched the heart of anyone who had not lived with her for thirty-eight years, and who knew how delighted she was at last to have found a good reason to exercise her love and caring to the full. She stuffed the pillows into new cases – the old ones had only been on two nights – took clean pyjamas from the airing cupboard, and filled three hot-water bottles. She put aspirin, water, and a single iris in a milk bottle by the bed, cluttering up the small table in a way that left Henry speechless with irritation. She brought him the *Daily Mirror*, newly folded, knowing he had already read it thoroughly, but wondering if he might like to go through it again. On the matter of whether or not the window should be open she was undecided for some time: but after a series of tests, darting her head in and out, licking a finger to find a breeze, she came to the conclusion that it should be shut now, while Henry warmed up, open for a while to air the room later, and finally shut when they put out the light. A moment later, having made this final decision, she snatched at the privilege of changing her mind: perhaps her plan was unwise after all. That way, she said cheerfully, Henry was bound to catch his death. No: the door should be left open, the window firmly shut. That was the solution. She herself, of course, was unable to sleep in a room without plenty of fresh air: but that was no matter because she would be quite comfortable downstairs in the armchair. Henry wasn't to worry about her at all. With a silent nod he agreed he would do no such thing, and at last she left the room.

Protected as he was from Rosie by the visions of his Leopard, the steely needle of real alarm, that punctured even this protective skin, concerned death: what if he should die, now, unable to see the Leopard again? That he should go to his grave without ever speaking of his love, without enriching her life with the knowledge of its existence, seemed to him a tragedy beyond contemplation. It also seemed quite likely. He felt very close to dying, at this moment: sweat seeping over his body, head thumping, eyes pricking, hands weak, three hot-water bottles scalding his shins. It would not be a dramatic death, a courageous death, his: it would be a mere death. There would be no reason for the Leopard to hear of his passing, unless she happened to be in the Star on the day of his funeral and someone mentioned it. There would be no possibility of her extending so much as a sigh of regret. In the circumstances, Henry reflected, perhaps it would be better to start wresting himself back from the gaping jaws – pull himself together, face the horizon, breast the waves: for where there was life, in his case, there was at least constant new hope of seeing the Leopard again.

The thought invigorated him. Almost at once he felt better. Unused to illness – not a day in bed for twenty years – Henry remembered it was a question of mind over body: think yourself well and the battle is half over.

During the night he braced himself to put his theory into practice and, in some measure, it worked. The fact that the swirling, sweaty sheets clung to him like tendrils, his damp pyjamas chafed, his head ached and his throat was a hollow cinder mattered to him not at all: such bodily discomforts were quite bearable. What he could not endure was the torment of his mind: mind over mind – there was the weakness. That was the part that did not work.

For no sooner had Henry re-established himself firmly upon the banks of life (a not ignoble feat which one day he would confide to the Leopard) he was at once beset by one of its tribulations: worry. Searing worry that increased its grip with every moment – the worry that the Leopard would return to the Star and here, in his prison bed, Henry would miss her. At the thought of such irony, having surreptitiously managed to visit the pub every day since her appearance, Henry groaned out loud. Rosie, wonderfully alert to any such signs of distress, came hurrying from her armchair downstairs.

'Oh, my poor love, what's the matter now?' she asked, in a voice appropriately low for a sick room. 'What can I do for you?'

As there was nothing Rosie could do to alleviate Henry's real suffering, but as he felt too weak to say so, he remained silent. Rosie took this to be serious. With great diligence she repeated all her useless ministrations – pumping pillows, straightening sheets, even blowing her warm tea-and-biscuits breath on to the burning skin of his forehead. Henry nodded ungratefully and finally, imagining that the information would put him at least partly at his ease, she said again how comfortable she had managed to make herself downstairs, considering.

Henry's night then bloomed with cauliflowers. Over and over again he imagined himself, the magnificent frothy white heads in his hands, placed auspiciously in the car park as the Leopard swung out of the pub door in her inimitable style. Over and over again he imagined his beautifully timed approach, the look of amazement and wonder in her blue (blue? blue-green, more) eyes, the grateful way with which she took the cauliflowers and clutched them to her breasts – a moment which inspired Henry with the new idea of how delightful it would have been to be born a vegetable, tendered by Jack Mackay. But once she had the cauliflowers firmly in her pretty hands, what happened next was a little confused in Henry's vision. He knew quite definitely they were suddenly in her Jaguar, speeding down a car-less motorway, the cauliflowers back on his lap as her hands were on the steering wheel. But when he went to return them to her she was mysteriously coming out of the pub again. They went through the whole process of the meeting once more, and the journey in the Jaguar. All this happened twenty, thirty times maybe, the non-fruition of the car drive, as each time it made a mysterious U-turn back to the pub, driving Henry to greater realms of frustration.

Wracked by such sudorific thoughts, he tossed noisily about, maddened, aching. As the church clock struck four, Rosie paid another of her regular visits, this time to say there was no need to worry, no need at all, but she thought he ought to know Evans was not home yet. Whatever could have happened? Whatever had happened, Henry brought himself to say, it was neither their business nor concern. The Boy was grown up now, and the sooner she got that into her head the happier her life would be. He spoke so sharply that Rosie hurried away, having only dabbed at a crumpled pillow, full of understanding about how in sickness people say things they do not really mean.

In the peace that followed her departure an idea then came to Henry that was to boost his low spirits for the rest of the night. The Boy: that was it, surely. Could not he be Henry's salvation? It could all be done so delicately, why, the Boy might never need to know just what act of goodness he was undertaking. Fired by his inspiration, the next part of the plan came easily to Henry's troubled head. He heard the conversation, loud voices in his ears, as it would be next morning.

Henry:	You going down to the pub, Boy, lunch-time?
Boy:	Yes, Dad. Why?
Henry:	You keep your ears open for any news, there's a good lad. Don't like to miss any-thing, stuck up here.
Boy:	'Course, Dad. But not that much happens down at the Star.
Henry:	Well, you never know. Old Joe might have a heart attack, a flighty Luton woman might do a striptease – wouldn't want to miss anything like that.
Boy: (laughs)	I'll keep an eye out, Dad, don't worry.

It was so easy. Why had he not thought of it before? That sense of tranquil pleasure, peculiar to times of sought-after solution, brought calm to Henry's fiery limbs and eventually, much to Rosie's disappointment, he slept. She would not, now, in truth, be able to say he had been awake *all* night. Nonetheless, they had been worrying hours which had caused a not unwelcome stir in the ordinary fabric of her life.

When Evans had gone Augusta Browne gathered herself together once more to protect her house. She wandered about from room to room, each one quiet and husky with early sunlight. She despised herself for these nostalgic pilgrimages, reminding her as they did of the bright times that were over: but she indulged in them all the same, ashamed of her weakness. Restless, afraid, she touched the pale wood of the panelled walls, she paced the stone flags of the hall, confining to memory for ever the places where they dipped unevenly. From her study she saw that the first roses were in bloom. Later, she would pick them. But not now: she must detract, somehow, not add, to the pleasures of the house, till the predators had gone. Mounting the stairs, dazzled by sunbeams, she prayed for vile skies, torrential rain and an east wind to inquinate the place with a sulphur smell unbearable to the noses of all prestigious office men.

In the upstairs room at home Evans felt particularly large. He stood at the end of his parents' bed, head bowed to avoid the ceiling. His father was propped up among an extravagance of pillows, uncomfortable, flushed. A crochet pattern of sun and shadow, made by the elm leaves outside, played upon the bed cover.

'You not so good, then, Dad?'

'Had a rough night, Boy.'

'Ah. I'm sorry. Mum says Doctor Kennet is on his way.'

'There was no need to fuss the doctor.'

'Well, anything I can do for you? Anything I can get?'

Henry swivelled his eyes towards the window. Their whites were strung with brown veins.

'Going down the pub, lunchtime, Boy, are you?'

'Yes, Dad. Why?'

There was a long silence. Henry continued to look out of the window.

'Well, you never know,' he said at last. He flung out his hand towards the bedside table, an indeterminate gesture, his mind fixed on the casual way he should say the next words. He knocked over the milk bottle that held the single iris. Water poured down the side of the bed. The iris head and small stump of stem lay on the table like some obscene purple organ, smile full of stamen dust, mocking.

'Dratted flower,' said Henry, 'throw the thing away, Boy.'

Evans was at the bedside, clumsily wringing part of the wet sheet.

'I'll get Mum. She'll soon clear this up.'

'Yes.' Henry picked up the iris, scrunched it up in his hand. He watched the slimy purple juices run into the lines of his palm.

'I must get to work, Dad. Sure there's nothing I can do for you?'

'No, Boy. Thank you.'

Evans waited a moment.

'Take care, then,' he said, and left.

With a clenched fist Henry wiped a trickle of saliva from his chin. There was a horrible sweet taste of tea in his mouth, but the thought of having to take out his teeth, put them in a glass of water and give them to Rosie to scrub, in order to get rid of it, was intolerable. She should not be allowed the pleasure of such intimacies, not Rosie. He would endure the tea-taste. Endure, somehow, the stifling day ahead. Already, at eight-thirty, Henry was beginning to realise he had taken the wrong decision: perhaps, after all, he should not have made so fine an effort to fight the lure of gentle death which had beckoned him last night.

By mid-afternoon Rosie was exhausted, what with all the running up and down stairs, changing the sheets, hurrying to the shop for instant coffee (Henry had suddenly taken against tea) filling hot-water bottles, making two lots of junket (the first hadn't set), emptying the chamber pot, opening and shutting the window – quite apart from all the usual housework. Doctor Kennet had pronounced the illness to be a slight chill, and even given that the doctor was a man of exaggerated understatement, Rosie could see Henry's condition could cause no alarm. But the way he was carrying on, just like a man, you'd think he was dying. Still, to be fair, it was the first time he had been ill in twenty years: he had every right to make the worst of it – and this gave Rosie a good opportunity to make the best of it, which she felt secretly she was doing, and was not displeased.

Now she sat in her small neat kitchen, slippered feet on a stool in front of the fire – an unaccustomed position, for her, mid-afternoon. The chair and stool were Henry's property, but in his absence she felt the rest was deserved. Besides, as he was too weak to come downstairs, he would never know of her laziness, and that was important because one of the things he loved her for was her energy. (Or so he once said, some thirty years ago.) He would also never know that at lunchtime, while he had been sipping at his junket upstairs, complaining it hurt his throat, she had stood in the larder, eating small slices of cold canary pudding. Solid and clammy, just as she liked it, it had stood in its plate of congealed treacle, wonderfully tempting. She had happily given way to temptation, running her finger through the treacle, slicing the sponge with a small knife. Picking, Henry would have called it: a habit he deplored – a habit, unable to relinquish, Rosie continued at subtly chosen times of day in the privacy of her larder. Oh, you've been playing truant today, Rosie Evans, she said to herself.

There was no need, of course, this time of year, to have a fire: it was a warm June afternoon. But Rosie liked a fire all year round. One of her little luxuries, she called it. An empty grate gave her the spooks, a strange feeling of hollowness in her stomach. And so she watched the small flames and the shifting sun patterns on the floor, and turned her mind to Evans. The look on his face when he had opened the door this morning had given her quite a turn. She would not like to think what he had been up to and tried to remember, in her anxiety, if she had plied him with the sort of questions a son prefers his mother not to ask. He had been very offhand and gruff, she thought, leaping upstairs to see his father without any kind of satisfactory explanation. Rosie had not wanted to know any details, naturally: but surely it was up to a son to put his mother's mind at rest after a whole night out?

Ah, the young. They were hard to understand, sometimes. Their lack of thought, their funny ideas about right and wrong. Not that she could complain in general. No, on the whole Evans was a good and kind son, a bit quiet, like his father, but diligent and appreciative, good-natured. It was only since Brenda had come into his life that Rosie had begun to worry about him. The merry dance she led him was quite a strain, sometimes, judging by the pallor of Evans's face. But still, there was a long time to go until the actual wedding day. Anything could happen before then. In fact in her most secret heart, as Rosie once confided to the vicar, she wouldn't be that surprised if anything *did* . . .

She looked at the lumps of her hands lying on her lap, their imperfections diminished in the speckled light, and smiled to herself. Part of her present contentment was due to the fact that she had decided, this afternoon, to put the first part of her plan into action. This afternoon she would burn her mittens. This afternoon would mark the passing of a seventeen-year phase which had, perhaps, been a mistake. Still, better late than never, and she was sure it was not *too* late.

When Henry was better, she had decided, and longing for exercise again, she would let him go off on a walk alone. She would then, taking a different route, hurry to the woods herself. It was lovely up there, this time of year, the place he would be bound to visit. He would come upon her in one of the glades, sitting in the long green grass, wearing her straw hat (she would get a new ribbon) and nice new seersucker blouse. Amazed, he would ask her what she was doing. She would be very careful what she said. Not talk too much. Just smile at him and say something like was that a missel-thrush or a song-thrush, Henry? I was wondering which it was. He would be delighted to tell her. He knew a lot about birds and warmed to people who shared his interest. Well, though she couldn't tell a hedge-sparrow from a female chaffinch herself, and didn't privately much care, from now on she would be interested. Henry, surprised and filled with pleasure, might then suggest she join him for a drink in the Star. Not that she liked pubs *in themselves*, but she liked to be in a public place with Henry. She liked to be beside him up at the bar, to hear him say, 'A shandy for the wife, please.'

If all this happened, as in her bones Rosie felt it might, she would further please him with steak-and-kidney pudding for supper, gentle on his teeth, and roly-poly pudding. She herself couldn't abide suet for two courses, but Henry could live on the stuff. If the plan was to work, of course, much sacrifice was required on her part, and she was prepared for that. Because in the end she would be rewarded. In the end, her unmittened hand on his shoulder, surprising him, moon in the window, window ajar as he liked it – he would turn to her.

At the thought of it, the heave of the bed as Henry rolled over, Rosie's heart gave a small flutter. She pulled the pair of white lawn mittens from the pocket of her apron and threw them on the fire. The flames quickly consumed them, leaving a small dust of ashes on a lump of coal.

'A good thing that's done, then, Rosie my girl,' she whispered out loud, 'it was about time.'

Leopard spots among the elm leaves in the window: damn leaves and their confounded bloody moving, never still for a moment, never possible to catch clear sight of her face, shifting sun and leopard spots always hiding it. My dearest Leopard keep still one moment dearest Leopard for me to see you. Smile upon me and I shall come to you and we shall go to a place which is quiet and still, no elm leaves, and you will take off your coat take off your Leopard spots and then be warm against me. Dearest Leopard what are you doing now? How cruel it is that you might be at the Star while I lie helpless here . . .

Towards evening Henry's temperature rose again. The one comforting thought was that the Boy would be bound to come and see him, soon as he got home, and mention he'd been at the Star. It shouldn't be too difficult to ask if there had been any new life down there, anything going on.

Oh, yes, that was certain: Henry could rely on the Boy to come back and tell him. Not long now. He tossed in the hot sheets. An hour or so. Impatiently, he waited.

Even without Augusta Browne's encouragement Evans would have found himself walking towards Wilberforce's farm when work was over. There was no possibility of his not seeing Brenda for a week, no matter what she had done. As the emerald rage diminished during the day his desire to be with her again had increased.

They met at the door of the chicken shed: Brenda was locking up for the night. She turned to him, head high, but docile eyes.

'I wasn't expecting you.'

'Thought I'd better come.'

'To apologise?'

'I'm sorry I hit you.'

'Well, I suppose I should have told you I was going out.'

'That's all right.'

'Where are we going?'

'I have a surprise for you.'

She walked with him quietly to Wroughton House, asking no questions, though she seemed surprised when they turned into the back drive. She was further amazed when Evans took a key from his pocket and unlocked the back door.

'Are we going to pay a social visit on Mrs Browne or do a burglary?' she giggled.

'Wait and see,' said Evans.

The house was quite silent. No sign of Augusta Browne. Evans led Brenda up the stairs to the attics, flung open the door of the furnished room. She stepped inside, looked about at the comfortable arrangement of things, the evening light on flowered curtains and patterned rug.

'Ours,' said Evans.

'Are you mad?'

'Ours till she sells the house.'

'I don't know what you mean, I really don't.'

Brenda sat on the double brass bed, testing the mattress. Evans would have liked to have sat next to her, but thought better of it. Instead, he paced up and down, hands in pockets, explaining how the whole idea had come about. Brenda seemed bemused.

'No more nights at the Hilton, then?' she said at last.

'Not unless we want them. Are you pleased?'

'I suppose I am. Here – let's look in the cupboard.'

She began to explore the room, opening drawers, counting hangers. 'There's everything here, isn't there? She's thought of everything. Quite luxurious, I must say.'

Evans attempted to contain his pleasure.

'Not too bad. Tide us over till we've got our own place.'

Brenda joined him standing at the casement window. They looked down on to the wide lawn. Four men wandered about. One of them made solemn gestures, casting his arms in various directions. Augusta stood a little apart from the men, arms folded under her breasts.

'Who are they?'

'She said people were coming to see the house today. Thought it might do as an office.'

'Never! Not a place like this. It'd be wicked.'

'Terrible. I don't suppose they'll want it.' Evans turned to her, remembering the time he had recently stood here next to Mrs Browne, her pale face all violet shadows. He had not had the slightest desire to touch *her*. It was only with a great strength of will he managed to keep his hands off Brenda. This close, he could smell strongly her peculiar scent of corn and lavender water, and the irresistible warmth of her skin seemed to roll off her, almost a tangible thing. They listened to the church clock strike six.

'What about your Dad, Evans? Is he any better?'

'He's all right. Just a bit of a chill.'

'Hadn't you better go and see him?'

'He won't want to see me. Reckon he likes being left alone, when he's ill.'

'What are we going to do, then?'

Evans thought for a while.

'Perhaps we should drive out for a bit of food somewhere, then come back here for a while.' He smiled. 'Try the place out.'

Brenda nodded, repentant eyes. Strange, thought Evans, how the terrible events of the night had made her to act just as she did when a chicken died: soft and malleable, looking to him for a lead, making him feel master. Long may it last, he said to himself. Gently he took the part of her arm he had hurt last night, in the fight that now seemed like a bad trick of the imagination.

They left the room.

When the office men had gone Augusta remained in the garden. They had said very little, but made copious notes in black note-books, each one stamped identically with a silver eagle. She had said a great deal: all her usual *spiel* about the enormous disadvantages of the place. But they had taken little notice of her, merely shrugged, and said things could be overcome. What most unnerved Augusta was the fact that they asked no questions. They seemed ominously uncurious, although they made their own small private investigations, digging their heels into the lawn and glancing at the turf as if they were experts in such matters; tapping with their hairy knuckles at the wood panelling in the hall. Augusta, trying to conceal her hostility as their hideous eyes travelled without appreciation over Hugh's pictures, felt a strength of hatred that chilled her skin in the warm air, and she clutched at herself to stop trembling.

In the rose garden, now, she fingered the first blooms, yellow petals that deepened imperceptibly into pink, and tried to wipe the memory of the last two hours from her mind. Unless she quickly engaged herself in some practical activity – she would pick and cook a bunch of asparagus, perhaps – there was danger on such an evening of falling into a state of inextricable melancholy. Turning towards the kitchen garden, clattering along the small paths between low box-hedges much in need of a trim, the wild thought then came to Augusta that she should telephone Hugh. Surely he would have some sympathy about the office men? After all, she was not alone in loving the house. Had things been different he would have wanted to keep it, too. Perhaps – she could make a sauce mousseline – he would drive down for dinner. Even stay.

But by the time she reached the asparagus Augusta admitted to the foolishness of her idea. He would never come. He would never change his mind, now. She started to pick the thin green spears, enough for one.

Later, awake in her bedroom, Augusta heard footsteps in the room above. Then the churning of the old bed. She was pleased to think someone was enjoying her house again: to guard its pleasures to herself, as she had been doing with reluctance for the last three months, was a terrible waste.

Rosie was sitting in Henry's chair in front of the fire when Evans got home soon after midnight. The disturbances of the past night had inflated the pouches of brownish skin beneath her eyes, but she was stoic, calm. She had determined, during the evening, to curb her curiosity and ask Evans no questions. He would no doubt tell her what was up all in good time.

'Your Dad was asking for you,' she said. 'He kept saying you'd be back for sure at six.'

'Oh, dear. I thought of coming but I reckoned he'd rather be left alone. How is he?'

'He seemed very restless. I expect it's the fever. Burning itself out, you know. I gave him a couple of pills. He's asleep now.'

'You're not going to spend another night down here, are you, Mum?'

'No. I'll come on up now. With those pills I'll not disturb him tonight.' She gave a small smile. 'I was just waiting up for you, see if you wanted anything.'

'You shouldn't have done that.' Evans bent down and

lightly kissed his mother's grey hair. 'You spend far too much time thinking of other people.' She smelt of oatmeal soap and knitting – grey wool, he recalled it had always seemed to be, as a child: she would put down her yards of grey knitting and clutch him to her oatmealy bosom, always pleased to see him, full of interest in the small events of his day.

'Nonsense. There's milk by your bed – you look as if you could do with a good night's sleep yourself.' The remonstrance, in Rosie's version of a brusque voice, was twofold: it spanned both his night out and the compliment he had paid her. Praise confused Rosie. Twisting her hands, she remembered she was about to spend her first mittenless night for seventeen years. It was a relief to think that Henry, knocked out by the pills, would not know. She would appreciate, just at first, getting used to the strange new feeling on her own.

A week later, better but thinner, his normal strength not wholly returned, Henry Evans went to the Star for his Tuesday drink. During the long boring days of his convalescence, body slumped in his chair, mind constantly beside the Leopard, the cauliflower plan had inexplicably turned sour on him. Cauliflowers, he had decided after all, were rarely associated with romance (though he did recall, one shore leave in Marseilles, having a very good French cauliflower cheese with a generous girl called Hélène). However magnificent a specimen, there was something a little absurd about a cauliflower: the originality of his plan, Henry saw in a moment of lucky revelation, might not be appreciated by one of the Leopard's sophistication. His next inspiration was a canary in a cage – a green canary in a pretty cage made of filigree stuff, like one he had once seen in a junk shop. But the practicalities of carrying out this plan soon killed that idea. Even if he bought the canary, supposedly for the pleasure of the Evans household (and Rosie hated birds) he could think of no way of explaining his snatching it up one day and hurrying it off to the Star. Finally, the perfect solution came to him: strawberries.

There were few women on earth who could not be won over by a punnet of hand-picked strawberries. For Henry, of course, would pick them himself. Only a mile from the village lay acres of strawberry fields. He would go there, as he had done so many summers, and collect the finest berries: hands rummaging expertly among the warm evening straw, parting the ferny green leaves, sucking at one or two to test their sweetness. The clear sky would be corded with smoke from the distant chimneys (Henry's post-fever mind automatically included references to happy days at work, along with his new romance) and he would feel strong with the satisfaction that this back-aching task was all for the possible love of his Leopard. Yes: that was it. Settled. Two or three times a week, strawberry season, off he would go. Only disadvantage would be Rosie's jangling delight at the harvest in the larder. But if he supplied enough strawberries it should be easy enough to steal a single punnet, come the time, without her ever knowing.

Henry arrived at the pub calmly pessimistic. The Leopard would not be there, of course; but if she was, it would be a surprise beyond all imagining. Henry pushed his way through the door. At once he stopped short, clutching at the back of a nearby chair. There, sitting up at the bar, back to him, alone, *was* the Leopard: spotted coat, beautiful haze of curly golden hair.

With incredible speed – Bill behind the bar scarcely had time to notice him – Henry stepped back outside, again. His heart thrashed so fast he felt close to fainting. He leant against the wall, dizzy and sweating.

In his preoccupation with the strawberry plan, Henry had not fully prepared himself for the shock of surprise: he had girded himself only for disappointment. This amazing turn of events, combined with his physical weakness, stunned him into helplessness.

In a timeless moment all the old ideas, scorched deeply into his brain during the last week, flashed in strobe lights before his eyes. Canaries? There were no canaries for miles

. . . Strawberries? Oh God, they were not ripe. Cauliflowers? The possibility of returning to his original plan brought Henry's first calm breath. But someone was speaking to him. It was the Boy. What was the Boy doing here?

'Coming in for a pint, Dad? Look as if you could do with one.'

'No, Boy, thanks. No, I –'

'You all right? You look pretty shagged.'

'I'm all right, just getting back on my feet. Takes a few days. First time out and all that.'

'Well, I'm just going to stand myself a quick one. See you later.' Evans went into the pub.

Henry continued to lean against the wall. His breathing was very fast and noisy. He looked wildly about. Precious moments were speeding past. If he didn't make a decision within seconds, his chance would be lost. But he was in no condition – weak, hollow legs – to hurry home and get the car. His eyes fell upon an old-fashioned bicycle propped up against the pavement, the property of old Joe. Henry made a lightning calculation. If he rode very fast to Mackay, snatched up the vegetables with the promise of payment tomorrow, he could be back here in a quarter of an hour at the most. Old Joe always spent two hours, midday, at his drink. He would never know his bicycle had been borrowed.

In a trembling rush Henry grabbed at the handle bars, huge hard rubber things – kicked the pedal away from the pavement. It was a heavy, ill-balanced machine, snatching at Henry's arms as he tried to guide. But the madness of love gave him energy to fight. He swung his leg over the seat, unsurprised at the easy way it soared. He raised his head, and pushed down upon the pedals with crazy strength. Suddenly, he was off.

Evans always felt a sense of well-being in the lounge of the Star. He liked the smell of hot sausage rolls and cool rubber flooring. He liked the thunk of darts on the cork board – there always seemed to be players – and the small open fire.

The beer was good, too: without asking, Bill pulled his pint at lunchtime, gave him a single whisky in the evening. He felt the privilege of being a regular: he knew everybody, everybody knew him.

Today, a rare thing, there was a stranger in the lounge – a blonde woman in a leopard skin coat, sitting up at the bar. Evans was instantly aware of the slight change of atmosphere her presence caused: voices were fractionally lower, silences between the sips of beer a little longer. It was as if the regulars, usually relaxed, were mutually alert to the possibility of something happening.

Evans took an empty stool beside her at the bar. Bill passed him his mug of beer. They exchanged a few comments, cricket scores and the miners' strike. Evans noticed the woman's drink was a small glass of Dubonnet with a twist of lemon peel. She smoked, holding her cigarette in a long ebony holder between her third and fourth finger. Both the way she drank – frequent tiny sips, and the way she smoked, pecking at the holder so that it clacked against her teeth, indicated she was in a state of some unrest. At one moment she twittered her fingers on the wood of the bar, making a mouse sound with her silver nails. Then she pushed back her fur cuff to glance at a gold watch.

'Do you suppose he's not coming?' she asked Bill.

'Couldn't tell you, madam. Couldn't tell you what he's up to.'

It was the first time Evans had ever heard Bill call anyone madam. He winked. Bill winked back. The woman missed the signal: her spikey black lashes were fluttering down at her drink. Evans realised that both he and Bill were struck by a powerful smell coming from the woman: nervous sweat undisguised by the sickly scent of some hot-house flower. Tuberoses, Evans thought. Bill sniffed.

'Well, I don't know,' said the woman, apparently to herself. 'Really.'

Evans asked Bill to give him a sausage roll. The woman shifted her position, leant a little further over the bar.

'Give me one of those, too, will you? And one more Dubonnet.' She pushed her glass forward and turned to Evans. Her eyes were matching starfish, the lashes of each one divided into not more than four or five jet points. 'Do you recommend them?'

'They're very good.'

The woman smiled. One of her middle teeth was chipped at the corner, the colour of a bruise. The skin round her mouth, heavily powdered, puckered into a network of small lines. Friendly.

'I'm famished,' she said. Then they ate sausage rolls in silence.

Evans had a further pint. The woman looked at her watch again and turned to him.

'Well, I might as well give up. I'm not waiting any longer. Could you tell me the bus situation in this place? I've got to get back to the station to catch the 3.30.'

Evans rubbed his chin. He was unacquainted with the local bus timetable, but the possibility of being helpful always spurred his adrenalin.

'Don't believe there's anything till four o'clock,' he said. The woman looked alarmed. 'Bill, when's the next bus?'

'Four-fifteen.' Bill was dusting the bottle of Dubonnet. It hadn't been called upon since the blonde lady's last visit.

'Oh, Lord. That's marvellous, that is,' she said. 'What the heck am I going to do?'

Evans had been brought up by Rosie to believe that practical help was often of more value than the sympathy of words. He replied by instinct.

'Well, I've got my car out the back. I could run you to the station.'

'You couldn't?' The starfish eyes dazzled with relief.

'No trouble. It's not far. I don't have to be anywhere till two-thirty.'

'That would be absolutely *marvellous*!' She was already slithering down from the stool, pointing her sandalled feet – thin straps round smashing ankles – towards the floor.

'Think nothing of it. Always pleased to help a lady in distress.'

The woman led the way to the door, head high, scarlet lips parted. Following her, Evans was aware that every eye in the place relished the scene. Christ, he'd be in for no end of a wigging tonight. His blush was uncontrollable.

In the car the smell of sweat and tuberoses was almost overpowering. Evans opened the window. She wouldn't think it rude, he thought, considering the warmth of the summer's day. Starting the engine, he wondered if she was aware of her own smell.

'If you don't mind my asking,' he said, 'why do you wear a great thick fur coat on a day like this?'

The woman pushed at the collar so that it stood up round her neck.

'I always feel the cold,' she said, 'all year round. Think I must have thin blood.' She gave a slight shiver and smiled her nice smile. Evans, with particular care, turned into the road.

In retrospect Henry could remember little of the journey to Mackay. The bicycle seemed to have a will of its own, shying at things in the hedgerows, jolting at the slightest touch of the brakes – on several occasions he was nearly thrown. But, half-blinded by the sweat in his eyes, scared by the loud wheezing noise in his throat, Henry kept up his manic speed. Although the road seemed interminable, he must have reached Mackay's house within seven or eight minutes.

Stopping with a jerk at the gate – almost falling once again – he flung the bicycle on to the verge and ran up the front path. The ring of his feet on the cement enhanced his own sense of urgency. He rang the bell, waited a few seconds, rang again. He heard its silly chimes echo within. No reply. He banged the door. Still nothing. God in heaven . .

Henry then noticed the blinds in both front windows were drawn. That meant Mackay must be out at the back: he was the sort of man who would draw the blinds if he was not actually in the room. Henry ran again, slamming his way through a series of small gates, a bursting feeling in his chest. But the market garden, its cloches and greenhouses and neat strips of vegetables, was plainly deserted. Henry called Mackay's name out loud several times, but there was a deadness about the place, a feeling of absolute desertion, and he knew there would be no answer. Tears mixed with the sweat round his eyes. He cursed Mackay out loud, spewing forth a jumble of obscenities unused since his days at sea.

Once again, he had to think quickly. There was no alternative but to hurry back to the Star, wipe the damp from his face, and join the Boy for a pint after all. From then on he would be in the hands of Fate. But surely, so near to the Leopard, it would not be untoward to offer her a drink?

He began the return journey, clumsy in his hurry. His previous energy was ebbing away. He tried to pedal fast, but his legs were useless. The ride was a nightmare of slowness.

Then, as the Star at last came into sight, Henry sighted a further setback to his plans: the Boy's white Mini was nosing out of the car park. Damn him! He must be stopped. He must return to the lounge *with* Henry to ease any possible awkwardness. Recklessly he let go of one handle and waved. The whole bicycle lurched as the front wheel swung from side to side, and Henry fought to regain his balance. The car was almost level with him now: in a split second he saw the Boy's face, smiling, his hand raised in a wave. He saw also, a one-dimensional vision behind the glare of sun on the windscreen, the blonde hair and smiling face of the Leopard, a small ridge of spotted fur round her neck. Then they were gone.

With the dazed movements of people who have been in an accident or earthquake, Henry dismounted the bicycle. He propped it up against the pavement, just as it had been before. Then he went to the slatted wooden table, with its two matching chairs, left on the pavement in summer in case anyone should feel like sitting outside.

Henry crashed down upon one of the chairs, instantly

conscious of pain as the slatted wood cut into his thighs. He felt his mouth fall open, sweat thick as rain running down his face. After a time the noise of his own groans subsided, and he listened to the silence of the afternoon which roared about him in great waves.

At first Evans hadn't recognised the old man, white hair blown stiffly out over his ears, wobbling about on the bicycle. When he saw it was Henry, he laughed.

'Good heavens, that's my old man! Whatever can he be doing?' In fact Evans did not stop to think what his father *was* doing. Uncurious by nature, the most unlikely sights held little wonder for him. If he had met his father in a Soho brothel he would have been neither surprised nor interested: their relationship had always thrived on their apparent mutual indifference.

'He looks pretty unsafe,' said the woman, and they both waved.

At the station, Evans got out and held open the car door for her. She was very grateful.

'That was really kind of you, dear. Honestly, if it hadn't been for you, I'd have been in terrible hot water, I can tell you. Well, so long, and perhaps we'll run into each other again one day in the Star. Nice knowing you.'

She smiled again, her chipped tooth blacker in the bright light and her hair a less delicate gold than it had seemed in the pub, dark at the roots. Back in the car Evans opened the other window: her smell was still thick and sickening in the air. He better get rid of it, he thought with a smile, before picking up Brenda tonight.

The show of mastery by Evans on the night of Brenda's excursion had induced in her a flutter of new respect. He had not hurt her physically, and the blow had been no surprise. She had often guessed, particularly on wild nights in the barn, violence rumbled within him. One day, provoked far enough, Brenda imagined Evans might lose control: she had speculated with interest on just how wild he would be when the time came. The events of that night had also made her feel unusually grateful to Evans. After his initial burst of jealousy he had chided her no further – indeed, he had made no further mention of the matter. This, Brenda considered privately, generous behaviour. For all her protestations to him about having done nothing wrong, she knew his reactions to her own behaviour were not unreasonable, and his outrage had caused a stimulating ripple in their uneventful days.

Also, the room at Wroughton House had done much to increase Brenda's inclination towards Evans in the past week. His idea, and its realisation, boosted her respect for his imagination (an element she previously felt he lacked). They had already spent many hours in the room: the barn and its discomforts were a thing of the past. Never lacking in concupiscence, Evans seemed to have been spurred by Brenda's night out to even further desire. She was temporarily sated. Her flesh felt mousse-like. Too dazed by love-making to think sharply, the feelings of dissatisfaction that so often haunted her daily life had temporarily vanished.

Benevolent inspirations come most easily to contented minds, and in her present sated state Brenda found herself thinking that it would be a good idea to reward Evans for his charity: she would, she decided with pleasure, turn up at the post office a few minutes before he was due to open it for the afternoon. He would be amazed and pleased: she had never made any such gesture before. It was always he who came to her, and was often barely welcomed. But this afternoon, in the warm still air, it would be no trouble to flatter him: to observe how nice and orderly his post office was, and to take an interest in his neat files. She would ask him to buy her an ice-cream on a stick – the sight of her licking an ice-cream always aroused him, and he would kiss her, the ice melting between their mouths, pressed up against the counter.

Full of such happy intentions Brenda locked the chicken shed behind her and walked up the dust path to Wilberforce's farmhouse. On her way to the post office she had to call in and ask him about a late delivery of grit. She had not spoken to Wilberforce for some time – since the death of Elizabeth – but the urgency of dwindling stocks forced her now to break her silence. She knocked at the back door, went in.

Wilberforce was sitting at the kitchen table. Unshaven, he held a half-eaten pork pie in one hand while he filled in his football coupons with the other. Steam rose from a mug of tea beside him and the table was littered with a mass of papers and unopened letters, unwashed dishes and unemptied ash-trays. The windows were shut. Brenda gasped as two smells, cramming the room, surrounded her: Wilberforce's sweat, and pigs' trotters boiling on the stove.

She closed the door behind her but remained standing close to it, hands behind her fingering the cracked paint. Wilberforce looked up at her briefly: his eyes flicked down to her breasts. In the greenish light of the room his skin had the glow of discoloured lard while his hair, smarmed down with grease, gave him the look of a third-rate gangster. He wiped his nose on the back of his hand.

'I know what you've come about, girlie, don't I?' he said. He spoke with his mouth full so that Brenda could see the mush of pork on his tongue. He reminded her of Uncle Jim.

'We're down to three more feeds. Four at the most.'

'Bugger. The order was in weeks ago.' He sniffed again. 'Care for a cup of tea, would you?' Brenda shook her head. 'I'm in a hurry, right now. But I'll phone them again this afternoon, put a bomb under them.'

He gave no appearance of a man in a hurry, chewing slowly on his pie, pushing at the litter around him to make more space for the pools coupon.

'Thanks.'

'Birds all right, are they?'

'Fine.'

'Laying good, I see.' He stood up, holding his belt with both hands. The position was menacing. From his side of the table he now looked down on Brenda.

'Boyfriend all right?'

'Evans is fine.'

'He's a lucky man.' Wilberforce licked a speck of pork jelly from the corner of his mouth. Brenda was unlatching the door.

'Well, I must be going,' she said. In the back of her mind she wondered, should she stay another moment or so, what might happen. Wilberforce took the slightest pause for encouragement, as she had learnt in the past.

'Honoured by the visit, believe me.' He smiled and came round to the door. Unnecessarily he held it open for her. So close, the stench of his sweat was foul. 'Sometimes, you know, I get the distinct impression you try to avoid me.'

'Do you really?' Brenda intended to sound hostile, but had a feeling she was friendly instead.

Wilberforce ran a hand round his scrubby jowl.

'Tell me this, anyhow,' he said, 'give us a piece of advice for old time's sake. Just supposing I was off to meet one of the opposite sex, as they say, man to woman. Just supposing that was the case . . .' Brenda, sun on her shoulders out here, the gate to the road only ten yards away, felt safe. 'Then would you say I needed a shave?'

He snatched at Brenda's hand, ran it over his prickling skin. Seeing that this was all he meant to do – safe as she was out here – Brenda did not try to pull it back.

'Yes,' she said. 'Definitely. You filthy old thing, you.'

Wilberforce pressed two of her fingers to the wet squelch of his mouth, dabbed at them with his tongue.

'Then that's what I'll have to be doing, my lovely girl,' he said, and let go of her hand. Brenda, not meaning to, smiled. Pathetic, Wilberforce was, really: always trying to make you think he was going off with a lorry-load of chorus girls, bragging he could have every girl in the village if he felt that way inclined. She ran from him, thinking she must be strangely content if even so revolting a man had no power to annoy her.

She walked the short distance down the road to the post

office, enjoying the sun. There was no one about except, in the far distance, an old man on a bicycle. He approached so slowly he seemed hardly to be moving. Brenda wondered if her own progress on a cumbersome bicycle in fifty years' time would be similar. But she had not much patience with visions of the future – herself as a sexless old woman was quite unimaginable, for a start – and quickened her pace at the thought of an ice-cream with Evans. She'd like him to lock the place, keep the customers waiting a while, let them bang on the door . . . She wondered if she could persuade him.

She turned right, hurried across the disused car park to the prefabricated post office building that had been 'temporary accommodation' for nine years now. It was still shut, the plastic blinds drawn. No sign of Evans. Brenda was annoyed. She disliked postponement of her plans: it was now or never, this particular kind of visit. What was Evans up to? He was never late.

She turned back to the road to see the white Mini passing, Evans driving, a woman beside him. In that fraction of a second Brenda was quite sure it was a woman. She ran to the pavement, looked up the road. The car was turning the corner, almost out of sight. But there were quite distinctly two heads. Incredulous, Brenda stood with legs apart. Then she heard a cry, a dreadful groan. She spun round the other way to see, on the opposite side of the road outside the Star, that the old man on the bicycle, trying to get off, had only just managed to stop himself falling. He staggered to the wooden chair, slumped down behind the table and beat his temples with his fists, just as Brenda had seen people acting in films. She was about to cross the road and go to him when she saw it was Henry Evans. She stopped herself. Henry Evans! She hadn't known he had a bicycle – surprising. But this was no time to wonder about *him*. Oh, no. It was his son who was going to have to answer the questions this afternoon. It was Evans Evans himself, the man so outraged by her little waltz down to the Air Base, who was going to have to face the music this time. Christ, he was.

She would wait for him. Hours and hours, if necessary – bugger the hens, this was an emergency. (They would understand.) Oh, she'd wait any amount of time, work out in her mind how best to begin. When Evans returned he'd be amazed to find her there. What you doing? he'd ask. She'd smile up at him, all innocence, watching his confusion. Waiting for you, course, she'd say. Where've you been, Evans?

Where've you been, Evans? she'd ask again.

Who was that blonde bit in your car, Evans?

Ah. He'd have some explaining to do. Brenda, by the post office wall, leant back her head, shutting her eyes. The sun dazzled behind the lids, two blots of shooting light. The concrete wall behind her was warm against her back. She began her wait.

Rosie happened to look out of the window just as Henry, on his way home, was a hundred yards from the door. It occurred to her – though perhaps this was her imagination playing her up – that since his illness his hair was whiter. Definitely whiter. Surely, only a fortnight ago, the back of his head was a deep steely grey, as it once had been all over? Now, there seemed to be nothing dark left. Also, he stooped. His gait was normally so upright and firm: today his manner of walking was that of an old man. Poor dear Henry, thought Rosie: shows that at our age a chill can take its toll. Still, a few weeks' convalescence, quiet days and early nights, plenty of good food, and he'd be back to his old self.

Rosie felt glad there was a cold rice pudding in the larder. Henry's favourite, she had cooked it for lunch but he had not come home. His first day back at the Star after a week's absence, she supposed, had meant a little celebrating. A few more drinks than usual with the boys. He had probably eaten a couple of their greasy sausage rolls (Rosie wouldn't touch them herself) and forgotten the time. That was unlike him, he was a punctual man – but, well, it was understandable. The way to keep a happy marriage going was to be understanding, even if it meant food was sometimes burnt or wasted and the person left at home was subjected to a deal of worry. She had always done her best to be understanding, Rosie, and she doubted if anyone could accuse her of failure on that score. So, today, she determined to put a cheerful face on the whole incident, to make no mention of the worry she had suffered when he still hadn't appeared at half-past one, and suggest he might like the rice pudding with a cup of tea.

Henry came through the door, leaving it open behind him so that he stood waist-deep in a ray of sun. The lower part of his body, dazzling, made his head and shoulders seem strangely shadowed and Rosie, looking hard at his face, was shocked. He appeared haggard and ill. Grey, drawn, vacant.

'Henry, love, it's gone three. Whatever –?'

'I'm all right. Sorry I'm late.' He went to his chair and sat down. The sunbeam, now a pure shaft, slanted through the door, making a yellow pool on the tiles at its base. Henry kicked at it. The toe of his shoe caught in the light and glinted.

'Let me get you – I was just thinking what you'd like was a cup of tea and a nice bit of rice pudding. It's all ready – '

'Don't want any rice pudding.'

'But Henry, it's your favourite – '

'Don't want any rice pudding at this time of the afternoon. Or any tea. Or anything. Least of all suggestions.' He gazed at the floor. Rosie, alarmed by his ferocity, kept her silence. At last she said,

'Well, I can't think how to help you.'

'You can't help me.'

In face of his dejection Rosie instinctively became more cheerful. If she could only make him realise that he had done too much too soon, that the reason for his present fatigue was nothing more than that – why, the simple facts would raise his spirits.

'You've been overdoing it, you know, love. First day out

you shouldn't have stayed so long. In bed all that time, quite low, you should have taken things more easily at first.'

Henry looked up at her: the lifting of his eyes seemed a great effort.

'I'm going out,' he said. 'It's too bloody hot in here. I'm going up the woods for a breath of fresh air.' He stood and went quickly – movements more like his old self – to the door.

'But Henry! That's very silly, overdoing it, love. Please – '

But Henry was gone. Rosie would not shout to him from the door, of course, and have all the neighbours thinking something was amiss. She stepped back into the kitchen, mind spinning, and went to the larder. There, spooning up small helpings of the rice pudding, things became instantly calm and clear. She had not had much warning, but here was her chance. The chance she had been waiting for, planning. Sucking the sweet, creamy grains of rice from her teeth she went upstairs to the bedroom. Quickly she took off her old cotton dress and replaced it with a navy gaberdine skirt, the one she wore summer Sundays, and her new seersucker blouse. That she had never worn. She had sent for it by mail order, having been attracted to its pin-tucked bodice in a newspaper. It wasn't, in reality, quite the elegant shirt the drawing had conveyed, but it was neat and handsome, suitable to Rosie's age, and a good clear blue. Then she put on her straw boater – a hat which years ago Henry once said he liked because it made nice shadows on her face. (They had been walking back from evensong at the time: he had said the shadows were full of holes and needed darning. She had laughed and he had said keep your laugh down, woman, we're still in the graveyard. At the same time he had taken her arm so she knew he wasn't really criticising her.) The straw had gone a bit droopy, and the striped ribbon was quite faded. Still, there was no time to change that now. Chances were Henry would never notice a ribbon: Rosie rammed the hat on the back of her head. Grey hair spurted out beneath it, making a fuzzy frame to her face. She looked in the mirror. There was not much light in the room through the small window – the elms so thick with leaves across the way – but, their shadows dancing about her cheeks, veiling the ruddy colour of her skin, it occurred to Rosie she didn't look too bad. She dabbed a puff of yellowish powder on her nose: a sudden small breeze spun a shower of molecules on to the walnut wood of the dressing-table, and on to her navy skirt. She wiped at the material, impatiently, making a pale smear: but decided there was no time to start messing about with damp cloths. Besides, her hands were trembling. You're all of a dither, Rosie my girl, she said to herself. Fancy that. Now, where was that rose water? She found it in its place in the drawer, quickly uncorked the pretty bottle. Evans had given it to her a couple of years ago for Christmas. He had said its scent was so subtle it was suitable only for her. In two years the subtlety seemed to have vanished altogether, but then Rosie had never had a sharp nose where commercial things were concerned, though she could tell you any flower by its smell in the dark.

She stabbed the neck of the bottle on to her own neck: the transparent liquid flowed down the gulleys of her throat and made damp patches on the collar of the seersucker blouse. Never mind, they would dry in a minute in the sun. The same thing had happened, once, when Henry had been courting. In the excitement of getting ready, she had spilled lavender water all over the bodice of her dress and hadn't known how to hide the damp patch from her mother, who considered perfume a vulgar habit of the upper classes, not to be copied by those of the lower orders. But Henry had loved it, nuzzling his nose into the fabric stretched across her chest until she had had to cry out to him to go no further . . . *Stop, Henry, love,* she had cried out, very feeble, and, because he was one of nature's gentlemen, Henry had stopped.

Rosie smiled at the thought of the incident, so long ago, and pulled herself back to reality. There was no time to lose. She hurried downstairs, pulled the door behind her. With a quick look at the neighbouring cottages, to see no one was about, she patted her hat more firmly on to her head and set off up the road towards the woods.

For the second time that afternoon Brenda's plans were foiled, this time by Wilberforce. He came striding across the waste ground towards the post office, a look of annoyance twisting his face. Brenda opened her eyes, angry at the disturbance.

'You're going to be late back, aren't you? What, waiting for the lover boy?' Brenda said nothing, kept her eyes on his newly shaven cheeks. He had cut himself twice. Two sparks of dark blood, not quite congealed, were forming into drops ready to start falling. He wore a clean checked shirt: sickly after-shave mingled with the old smell of sweat.

'He's not in the Star,' said Wilberforce, 'I just been there.'

'I know,' said Brenda.

'Something the matter?'

'No.' She shrugged.

'Daresay he's gone home for a bite.'

'Daresay he has.'

'Come on, or I'll be docking your wages, won't I? Extended dinner hours. I'll ring about the chicken food, tell you what they say.'

There was nothing Brenda could do. In silence she walked beside him back to the farmhouse. If she had insisted on staying at the post office for another five minutes he'd most likely have given her the sack then and there. She knew his moods: something had happened to annoy him and, in that state, he acted without thinking. On many occasions she had seen him lose his temper and sack employees with no explanation. It was lucky she had managed to last out so long, and she had no wish to lose her job. It suited her, the solitude, and she loved the chickens. She had a private and rewarding kind of communication with them, each one individually. In spite of what she had told Evans recently, about not caring if Wilberforce gave her the push, she knew in truth she would miss them if she had to go.

They returned to the kitchen. Wilberforce shut the door, pushed a few things from the table on to the floor to make himself enough space to sit, and lifted the dirty telephone on his lap. Brenda went over to the stove, sniffed at the pigs' trotters, turned out the flame beneath them.

'If I don't turn it off the water'll boil away,' she said. Her initiative seemed to please Wilberforce. He smiled.

'Anyhow where's Mrs Wilberforce – Eileen?' went on Brenda. 'Haven't seen her for days.'

Wilberforce picked something from between his teeth.

'She cleared out last week. Gone to London, I believe. I told her to go, mind, bloody trollop, carrying on like she was. Here – ' he inclined his head – 'come and listen to what they say while I give them a piece of my mind.'

Brenda went and stood by him. She leaned her head close to his, the telephone receiver at his ear between them. The various smells made her feel sick again, and the heat was something terrible. Evans was in his car with a blonde, first time he'd ever been unfaithful to her, she could swear, and Wilberforce was breathing noisily. When he put his free hand on her stomach, and ran it gently down to her thigh, Brenda felt an extraordinary sense of helplessness. Revenge was not precisely in her mind. But she had no more energy, no desire to move.

It was a particularly dull afternoon in the post office for Evans – scarcely a customer, two flies buzzing and flicking against the window panes. He busied himself with a sheaf of pink papers, but could not concentrate on the small print. He was trying to define for himself the line of demarcation between sexual attraction and sexual vulgarity. What imperceptible thread of gold divided one from the other? How was it that Brenda, for all her warm and vibrant sluttishness, could never be called vulgar? – While the fur-coated woman, she was quite a different matter. Neat, in a way: expensive clothes, shoes and hair. But coarse. Calculated. Hard. A lot of men, thought Evans, would find her sexy, couldn't wait to make her. But not him. He wrinkled his nose, remembering her smell. Not in a whole year, on a desert island, would he lay a finger on her. It was a dreadful thought, all that powder and lipstick. No. She was definitely the kind of woman, no matter what the circumstances, he would make a special effort to avoid.

The land surrounding the village was flattish, the fields unlush. They provided scant grazing for sheep and cattle or, when ploughed, dull earth. It was an unlovely part of the Midland countryside, scarred by the quarries and brick-works, untempting to the builders of suburban houses. Even the beauty of the elms would soon be a thing of the past: fast ravaged by the disease, they were being slaughtered by the hundred. Except from the lawns of Wroughton House, there were no pleasing views – and even from there, the detached observer might say, there was nothing much to fulfil the visual senses. At the foot of the great sweep of lawn to the west side of the house lay the natural pond: beyond it, fields inclined gently towards a minor peak. In these parts such a rise was considered a hill: a hill crested by the woods which had become Henry's refuge over the years.

They were owned by a local farmer who cared little for such an unproductive gathering of trees. His lack of attention had resulted in thick undergrowth and the general tangle of unpruned boughs. But still there remained a few paths through the rubble of foliage, worn down by generations of people from the village in search of privacy and shade. At bluebell time the ground was an almost solid, steamy haze of blue and later, in September, the place was rich with black-berries. Henry knew and loved every part of the woods: the sharp snapping sounds in winter, the softer summer noises, the spring birdsong. He liked, from one side of the trees, the distant view of Wroughton House, classic façade aloof above its bed of lavender. He liked even better, in the other direction, the sight of the tall, smoking chimneys, five times the height of trees, against changing skies.

But fond though he was of the woods, Henry doubted whether they could provide him with much solace this afternoon. The happenings of the last few hours, at the risk of being dramatic, formed the greatest catastrophe of his life. He was still stunned by incredulity, and yet he knew them to be true. He had had to believe his own eyes. The Boy and the Leopard driving off together – his son and the only woman he had ever loved, mightily, causing his blood to churn and his mind to writhe night and day – the two of them had disappeared before him. It was his own fault, what's more. Why had he been such a bloody fool as to make his decision with rash speed, dashing off to get the bloody cauliflowers? It wasn't as if she would have *wanted* the things, even had he been successful. What woman in her senses could be wooed with vegetables? He must have been out of his mind.

He must have been out of his mind, too, not to have accepted the Boy's invitation. Had he only said yes, and gone with him to the bar for a pint instead of darting away like a scared rabbit, it might be *him*, Henry, the Leopard was passing her afternoon with now, instead of with the Boy. At this very moment they might be gliding through the lanes in the Morris Minor (taking the corners at quite a speed, to impress) looking for a good field, or a small café, in which to have their first conversation. Whoever it was up there guiding our destinies – and surely God as Henry believed in Him could not be so unfair – had made a right balls-up. What, now, was to be done? Cursing himself, over and over again, whiplashes in his mind, Henry could see no solution.

But there was one thing he was quite positive could *not* be done: he could not question the Boy. They had always preserved between them a lack of interference and that, at all costs, should not be broken. The Boy was reserved about his own affairs, so it was unlikely he would drop any hints, even in jest. He might, of course, mention – when Rosie wasn't there – having seen his father on a bicycle: but even if he did, it would not be up to Henry to enquire who was with him in the car at the time, or why. That would be breaking the rules. No: the only thing he could do, without any intention of spying, was to watch the Boy carefully, and to spend every possible moment in the Star.

Henry tramped heavily up and down the same path: he had no energy to turn corners and find himself in a denser part of the wood. He sucked on his pipe and listened without pleasure to the thrushes. A horrible restlessness fluttered with him, sour as indigestion. His own son so near the Leopard, in a car with the Leopard, *touching* (most likely) the Leopard – regoaded by these thoughts, he stopped sharply. He leant against the trunk of a larch tree, needing physical support in his despair. Oh God, he thought, I am no match for the Boy. Really, I should be glad: this turn of events might take his mind off Brenda. And yet, I am not glad. I am twisted and ugly with regret. I want what he has. I love the Leopard. I want her for the rest of my life. I want someone to live for: she has inspired in me that need. I must have her, or I must die.

Henry blinked. Through a small space in the branches he could see two distant chimneys. In his vulnerable state, they increased his desolation. He thought, as he had on the day he first saw the Leopard, of his happy years among the bricks: of his good mates, and of the satisfaction of getting through the work. To Rosie, it had been no more than his job, not worth talking about. The Leopard, if and when he could explain, would understand it was more than that: the point of his existence. But it was no use thinking of such a luxury: the Leopard would never be his, now. He could never tell her the multitude of things piled up in his heart, and the burden of them was too great. Moving again, this time towards a small grassy clearing he often visited, furnished only with an old tree stump that made a comfortable seat, Henry made his decision to die.

But even in his raging gloom practicalities came bubbling to his mind. Out here, he was equipped with neither a gun nor pills. And as the woods were the only place he could find the courage to do it, there was but one alternative. Henry took a box of matches from his pocket. There were three left. Even if he lit three different parts of his clothing at once it would be a horrible death. Once on fire, it would be unlikely he could put out the flames should the agony of it force him to change his mind. However, he doubted he would do any such thing. Physical suffering would be trivial in comparison with his present feelings: it would be worth enduring the vilest death rather than continue to live a life without the Leopard, knowing his son was enjoying her. 'The only antidote to mental suffering is physical pain.' The words came back to Henry for the first time in thirty years: a friend in the Navy had tried to make him read Marx. It had not made much sense to him, except for that one message. An encouragement, now, he'd have Marx on his side. Shaking the matches, Henry reflected briefly on how he would be mourned: Rosie, knowing her, would have a search party out by evening and they, poor things, would experience the nasty shock of finding his charred body. Rosie would be hysterical, need tranquillising shots from the doctor. The Boy, well, he might be quite upset. They'd arrange a decent funeral, pile up the coffin with Rosie's favourite flowers, no doubt, and his friends at the Star would bend their heads in respect at the graveside. There might be a small paragraph about him in the local paper, if they were short of news this week, and he would be remembered as a loyal, happy husband and devoted father.

Henry reached the clearing. He stood looking at the tree stump, trying to choose his spot. There was an old straw boater on top of the stump. For a moment Henry presumed somebody had left the hat behind. Then he saw it move. His heart surged. One more twist in the bad dream of the afternoon, perhaps? Had the Leopard somehow arrived here?

Even as he contemplated such a thing Henry realised his own foolishness. The hat was a cruel trick. Someone from the village was here to usurp his privacy. He would have to go elsewhere, to the far end of the woods.

Quietly, not wanting to disturb whoever it was, Henry edged his way round the clearing, protected from sight by the trees. Then he saw that the hat belonged to Rosie. There she sat, dressed up in her Sunday clothes, looking about her in some kind of trance as if a choir of angels up in the trees, invisible to anyone else, sang her lullabys. She had thrown off her shoes and her stockinged toes wiggled in the grass. Every now and then she touched her hair, or patted the absurd hat, with one of her huge red hands. Henry, hardly breathing, stared.

His instant reaction was that she had gone mad and he would have to hurry off for help. She had been acting strangely, of late, since he had been ill: smiling constantly, filling the larder with small dishes of pudding, and brandishing her hands in the strangest manner at bedtime, as if she expected him to remark upon them. But now, here, there was no madness in her eyes – rather, a kind of waxy calm. Unfortunately, Henry coughed. Rosie instantly spun round, standing up. She spied him at once in the tangle of branches.

'Henry! Oh, Henry.'

She had trapped him. If he turned and ran away now she would come screeching after him. All he could do was to get rid of her as soon as possible.

'What the hell are you doing here?' he asked. His gruff voice in no way damaged her expression of beatitude. She merely smiled, an aged nymph daft as a button in her gaberdine skirt.

'I thought, like you, it would be nice up here,' she said. 'And of course it was – it is. I've been listening to the birds. They make quite a noise, don't they, when you're just sitting, listening, alone?'

'Not this time of the afternoon, they don't,' said Henry, but Rosie was still not snubbed.

'Anyhow, I've been enjoying myself and I hoped I might run into you so that we could walk back together for tea.'

'Not much chance of missing another person in woods of this size,' said Henry gloomily. 'Why don't you go off home and put on the kettle? Cut me a slice of rice pudding' (anything to get rid of her) 'and I'll be along later.'

'Henry! That's very unfriendly.' She moved towards him, stood very close so that he could count the bubbles of seersucker on her blouse – a dreadful blue. He looked at her eyes, remembering them as they had been forty years ago: clear and bright, not a line on the skin around them. She had had a fine pair of eyes when she was young, he had to admit. Now they were quite dim, trapped in a mesh of pouchy lines, small blood vessels wiggling across the whites like a continuation of the marks on the skin. At this very moment they were full of pleading. Henry's stomach heaved. The bravery of spurned women was only slightly less bad than their tears.

He sucked on his pipe and spat out a bitter piece of tobacco, a thing that always taxed Rosie's tolerance to its hilt. But she said nothing. Henry lit one of the matches, held it to the dying tobacco, then let it fall to the ground. With only two matches left, his problem increased.

'Do go on home, Rosie,' he said. 'Can't you understand a man likes a few moments' peace on his own sometimes?'

But on such occasions, when Rosie's will surged strongly within her, understanding evaporated. She took Henry's arm, laughed. She slid her feet into her shoes, and patted her hat.

'Oh, come *on*, you silly old thing. You've been quite ill, you know, and you need someone to take care of you. What's a wife for if it isn't to support a man when he's down?' She was horribly flirtatious, flapping her great hands perilously near to Henry's face. He kept his pipe firmly in his mouth to protect himself from her actual touch. And all the time he felt the strength of resolve draining from him. 'You spent far too long out at lunchtime – you looked quite done in when you came home. And I shouldn't wonder you've had nothing to eat since breakfast. There's a fruit cake in the tin, and a new pot of honey. So come on, my love, for I shan't go without you.'

In a reluctant daze Henry felt himself move forward, close

to her. They retraced his old steps down the path, Rosie keeping up her blinking chatter all the while. Henry remained silent. At least, he thought, the search party would be spared a gruesome time: that was the only good thing about Rosie's unwanted appearance. God, she was a nuisance, the woman. It was all he could do not to hit her. And yet, in the depths of his sad and empty stomach, he felt a pang of hunger. If she forced him, he wouldn't say no to a bit of fruit cake. It would give him the strength to work out what to do next.

They reached the edge of the woods, started down the gentle hill. The late afternoon sky was cloudless, the soft grass bent about their ankles. They moved slowly, locked into that uncomfortable position when one person clutches and the other leans. Augusta Browne, standing by the pond at the bottom of her lawn, looked up and saw them. She thought what a loving old couple they made, and reflected that her own chance of ever becoming one of such a partnership was now quite over.

Augusta, too, had had a disturbing afternoon. The agency had rung to say the office men were keen for the house, and would shortly return with their architect to discuss its possibilities. Its possibilities: Augusta tried to put from her mind all the ways in which such people could destroy the house. In great anguish she attempted to keep herself busy: picking flowers, dusting, sorting out a cupboard – all unnecessary things which did nothing to alleviate her gloom. She tried to think, as she had so many times in the past months, about her future. For there was no escaping the reality of the situation: eventually the house would be sold. And what then? A small flat in London? A country cottage? She would never mind the solitude: that would not perturb her. But she doubted she could find the strength ever to care about a house again, once Wroughton House had gone. She would have to work, of course. She would not expect Hugh to support her. In any case, she would enjoy working again.

But she could not, at this moment, contemplate looking for the kind of job she wanted any more than she could consider looking for somewhere new to live. The future was a murky space she had no energy to inspect. Only the present was vital: the savouring of each moment as time ran out. Lowered by such reflections, Augusta felt a sudden and rare longing for company. She hoped that Evans and Brenda would be coming to the room tonight. She would like to waylay them and invite them to supper. She would like to hear about *their* lives – and so put aside for a while the melancholies of her own.

That same day Lark, at work, felt ill. She had a sharp pain in her lungs – a familiar pain, it had often struck her in the past few years. She knew it to last a couple of days, then to vanish as fast as it came. Its cause she could not discover, hard though she tried to work out whether it was to do with something she had eaten or drunk. She had given up cheese at night and had cut down her smoking: but still the pain returned from time to time. The doctor – whom she hadn't thought worth consulting for a couple of years – said it was surely indigestion, and prescribed tablets. They did her no good. She was forced to the conclusion the mysterious pain was something she would have to put up with every now and then.

Today the pain had been stronger than she could remember: typing at her desk, she bent forward a little, hoping to release it, but hoping also that her boss would not notice there was anything wrong. She hated sympathy and she hated days off. With the help of aspirin and cups of tea she would make an effort to disguise the discomfort: the idea of a day in bed filled her with apprehension.

But by the time she got home Lark was bent almost double in her attempts to quell the pain. She filled a hot-water bottle and, falling back on to the bed, rested it against her aching ribs. She had discovered that on some occasions if she fixed her mind on pleasurable things, happy memories and small hopes, the pain subsided. But this evening there were few good things she could recall: in fact, in the last week she had had more than her share of problems for one who tried to maintain a quiet grey life.

For a start there had been no lucky break in her singing career: this puzzled her because she was, after all, offering her services for nothing. She had imagined that people would grab at anything for nothing. She had imagined that people would grab at anything free. This was not so in the case of her prospective performance. She had written out a dozen small cards claiming she would be willing to entertain any kind of gathering with a few songs – 'a vast repertoire' – she had called it, in return only for but expenses. These cards were prominently stuck in the windows of local shops. To add to the allure she had called herself, simply, Lark: by eliminating the plebeian Jackson she felt she increased her chances. But only one person had shown any kind of interest, and that turned out to be the wrong kind. A gentleman had telephoned explaining he'd like a private cabaret – if she liked to throw in a few songs, well, he wasn't fussy. The lack of response depressed Lark, but she knew the way to success was a long, hard, soul-destroying one, and there was nothing for it but to be patient.

Then there was the problem of Evans. She had broken her word to him – not that he was aware of this, or ever would be. But the private knowledge troubled Lark. She had told him she wouldn't remember their love-making – if you could call it that. And she *had* remembered it, too clearly. Far from being able to forget it, the memory clung to her all hours of the day. Not an unpleasant memory either – in truth, confusingly, an exciting one. She had never before been taken by a man so large and handsome as Evans. She had assumed such men were reserved for the likes of Brenda, but had always had a secret fancy for Evans, knowing him to be right out of her reach, and knowing he felt not the slightest desire for her. His seduction – and Lark was quite aware that in his anger about Brenda he had used her simply as accommodation

– was the surprise of her life. She hoped she had acted with appropriate cool: cool was not what she had felt.

They had not met since. Indeed, since the availability of the room in Wroughton House, Brenda had not been here much either. Lark missed her. She missed Evans: his heavy feet on the stairs, his friendly teasing, the evenings he came to fetch Brenda. They used to take her with them, sometimes, to Sunday lunch at the Evanses' cottage, or the occasional cinema. There had been no such outings for a long time. Not that they would be so enjoyable now, were they ever to happen again: Lark would be closely observing Evans's attentions to Brenda while longing for such attentions herself. Oh, Lordy, what a muddle. So much easier not to fancy anyone, ever, and avoid such confusions. She'd been pretty good at that to date. Perhaps it was now her turn for an era of amorous discomfort.

Lark shifted her position. The pain seemed no less bad in spite of the heat of the bottle. She wished very much Brenda was here, but supposed it was much nicer for her to be in Wroughton House. Still, when she did return, no matter how late, Lark would call her in. Brenda would be kind and worried – she was always at her best when worried. She would probably, as she had on other such occasions, suggest sending Evans along to cheer Lark up. 'He'll come and tell you a bit of post office news, get you laughing no end,' Brenda would be bound to say. 'You can trust Evans to take your mind off the pain.' In which case, Lark decided, she'd do well to stay right here where she was, in bed, tomorrow. Much though she disliked a day off from work, she would sacrifice anything if there was a chance of seeing Evans again, alone, for a few moments. The strength of these new feelings puzzled her a little, but the pain continued to grind too hard into her bones to concentrate upon them. Instead, she put her mind to anticipation. Evans would most likely come at lunchtime. The pain wouldn't be bad enough to stop anything – that is, if he wanted . . . With an effort she raised herself on one elbow and searched among the bedside cacti for a bottle of geranium nail polish. Can't let him catch me looking a real wreck, she thought. Nails first, this evening, then a nice glass of neat gin.

Brenda let Wilberforce kiss her once. As his sour tongue moved over her teeth she remained placid, hating his mouth. When his hands began to scrabble at her breasts she removed them firmly.

'Fucking teaser,' he said, 'you deserve a spanking. If you wasn't so good with the birds you'd be out on your arse.'

Brenda decided the best thing was to humour him.

'Oh, come on, now, Mr Wilberforce. Don't be like that. I give an inch and you want a yard. That's not right, with my boss, is it? You're lucky to have got anything at all.' She smiled at him, pushing out her bottom lip. 'And don't forget, I'm engaged. Other people's property. Evans would break my neck if he knew about this – and yours. First.' She smiled again, apologetically.

The threat of Evans quickly douched Wilberforce's present desire. He backed away from Brenda, resigned.

'Creates something terrible in a man's mind, having a girl like you around and not being able to touch her,' he said, quite amiably. 'You'd better be off for now. But bear in mind I'll not give up trying.'

'You'll never get me.' Brenda went to the door.

'Want a bet on it? Bit of persistence and they all give in in the end.'

'Not me, Mr Wilberforce. I'll be on my way.'

Brenda went to the chicken shed and the incident quickly left her mind. She had more important things to think about than sods like Wilberforce this afternoon: she had to think about what to do next. Maybe it was the time to make a major decision about her life. That she should go, for instance. Leave this whole crummy joint and go to London, and take a job as a model – so many people had told her she would be a smashing model, hadn't they? Live it up a bit. And yet, that idea held no great appeal. If luck wasn't with you, you could come an awful cropper in London, get into drugs and crime and even prison. She'd seen enough of Mum struggling to know that she wanted no kind of struggle herself – ever. Here, at least, was security. Evans might not be the most exciting man in the world, but he was solid and kind. Boring though he was about their future, it was the kind of future Brenda aspired to, (in some moods) so long as she was *someone* in the community. That was important to her. And which of course she was, and would be, as a couple, with Evans. Every girl in the village fancied him and he never gave them so much as a glance. Every man fancied her and she, well . . . She never quite said yes, put it like that. Certainly, as a couple in the village there would be nothing to touch them. They'd have chickens and children and a quiet life, envied for their looks, perhaps: no great ambitions and no great worries. She wouldn't be a bad wife, either, if she tried: cooking and dusting, and that. And should she suffer from a little human weakness over the years, not always able to manage to resist, she'd never in a million years spoil Evans's trust by telling him. That would be barmy. Sure way to upset the applecart.

Brenda walked up and down between the chickens. She let their clucking trickle over her, a strange sound, half restless, half content, rather like water jerking at irregular speeds over a pile of loose stones. (She must remember to put that in her book of Thoughts when she got home: a book she kept instead of a diary. It was full of the kind of silly thoughts that come to a person's mind during a day alone, far too stupid to tell anyone. For months now she had been trying to work out exactly what chicken clucking was like – how you could explain it, accurately, to anyone who had never heard it so they would get the sound in their ears. She had had several goes, none of which was any good. This water over loose stones idea was the best yet. Just the sort of thing that would have made Robert, had she told him, laugh at her and pinch her and tell her to shut up while he kissed her.) Robert! She hadn't thought of him for some months. She lit a Woodbine. His face was dim. How had it been, exactly? She had heard it said that faces you know really well never go from you. But they do. In the end they fade. Well, that was good to know, to have proved, anyway. Bugger Robert like bugger Evans. Everything Mum had said about men was true: even the faithful type like Evans. In the end they let you down.

Brenda stopped by Daisy, newly queen. She was a sulky bird, Brenda had concluded of late. Her honourable appointment had made no difference to her general apathy. She barely clucked, in the shadow of Brenda's attention: just lowered her gritty yellow eyelids and looked fed-up. Floribunda, next to her, was much livelier. Floribunda was sprucing herself up as if for a date, murmuring in useless anticipation. Floribunda would have sympathy, were she able to understand.

'Bloody mess,' Brenda said to her, out loud. 'This is one hell of a bloody mess, Florrie, isn't it? All because I go down to the Air Base for a bit of innocent fun, didn't I? Didn't do nothing wrong, did I? Well, not so's you'd notice. Not so anyone'd notice. Just a bit of a snog, nothing much, was it?' She blew a bulb of smoke through her nostrils. 'Sorry my love. Get in your eyes, did it? Well, I mean: I mean it's not my fault if a man gets a hard-on dancing, is it? Nothing I can do about it, don't you think, Florrie? And what's the price I have to pay? My faithful old fiancé whips round and gets himself a blonde not five hundred yards from here. Cheekiest thing I ever heard of.' She paused. The sympathetic chicken seemed to have lost interest, continuing to pluck at her own frayed breast. 'What am I to do, Florrie? I don't want him going off, really. Not in the end, I don't, all things being equal.'

Brenda let herself cry for a while. There seemed no point in making the effort to stop. The tears released her sadness, but stimulated her anger. She put out the cigarette and blew her nose. One thing for certain – she wasn't going to have Evans thinking she cared. Oh, no, the last thing she'd ever do was allow him the luxury of thinking she cared. He could go to hell, as far as she was concerned: if he wanted to play it that way, then so would she. There was another do down at the Air Base this evening. Well, she'd tell him. She'd tell him she was going. She'd have her good time while he was out with his fancy lady. That was only fair – if that was how it was going to be, they might as well start as soon as possible.

And so, determined upon war, Brenda left the chicken shed and crossed the yard to the small building which she liked to call her office. In fact it had been built as a place in which to sort, grade and stack the eggs before they were collected to be sold. Brenda had persuaded Wilberforce to let her install an old table and chair under the window. This, her 'desk', she kept tidily furnished with a few biros, the book in which she recorded the daily number of eggs, and an old jam jar filled with whatever flowering weeds were in season in the farm-yard.

Brenda guarded her office jealously. If she was in it when Evans came for her she would join him outside, never invite him in. Wilberforce had never set foot in the place: Brenda would take the book to him once a fortnight in the kitchen, where he made a perfunctory show of interest. When the van came to collect the eggs she handed the boxes to the driver from within. Mean sanctuary though it was, Brenda liked to feel it was a room uncontaminated by any other humans. While in the chicken shed itself she felt a sense of companion-ship, alone in the office among the eggs-scapes she revelled in a protective shell that she would not wish to be broken.

In winter the office was unbearably cold but, in her mittens and scarves, Brenda declined to ask Wilberforce for the luxury of an electric fire. In summer, as now, it was stuffy, airless. It smelt of grey cardboard egg boxes, and the groggy light meshed by cobwebs in the window gave no indication of the sunniest day outside. But Brenda liked the gloom. Having hurried through the brightness of the yard, she shut the door behind her, panting hard as if she had run a long way. When her eyes had grown accustomed to the dim light she raised her chin to the small piece of mirror fixed to the one free space on the wall – her only concession, in this place, to vanity. Her eyes and nose glistened with that scaly pinkness that comes after tears, her lips were dry. She licked them, and tossed her head. She'd get Lark to wash her hair tonight, before going down to the Air Base, and she'd try a little experiment with make-up. Give herself bright cheeks and emerald eyelids, perhaps – give them all something to think about. She'd wear her new white cotton shirt and leave most of the buttons undone, and swill the last of her bluebell essence everywhere, not just behind her ears . . . Brenda narrowed her eyes at herself. In a few hours' time she would look and feel smashing.

For the moment, there was nothing useful she could think of doing in the office. The eggs were all collected, washed, graded and stacked in their boxes for today. They filled the shelves, waiting for collection next morning.

Brenda sat down at the desk. The splintery edge of the chair, as usual, caught the back of her knees. Now would be the chance to sandpaper the wood, but she felt disinclined to do so. Instead, she opened the egg book and turned to a clean page at the back. She took up a wettish biro, chewed it for a moment, then began to write.

Dear Evans – I want you to know I'm going down to the Air Base this evening to another dance because its all over between us and there isnt any reason why I shouldnt do what I like now. Theres no use you thinking you can get away with it so easy going out with blondes because you cant. I saw you with her so theres no use denying it is there? Sorry in a way because it would have been nice being married to you tho I expect I would have made a bad wife and you with your fancy for blondes would have been a bad husband so we can spare ourselves a lot of rows this way. Sorry about this messy pen, I will return the ring if you like.   Bren.

She read it through. It lacked the note of firmness she had intended – but still, it would have to do. She had never been much of a one for letters. Tearing the page from the book Brenda looked around for a drawing-pin. She knew there was no such thing, here, but she meant to stick the note to the door and leave just before five-thirty, sure to miss Evans. The lack of a drawing-pin frustrated her unreasonably: what should she do? Helpless, suddenly, she felt near to tears again.

Increasingly, Evans found himself much affected by the boredom of his post office job. In the beginning, taking over from the previous postmaster, who had let the business decline into a dreadful muddle over the years, he had found it a challenge. With great energy (and inspired by some vague idea of being required for an interview on *Panorama* in ten years' time) he got the place on its feet again – sorted out the files, threw a mass of obsolete stuff away and, best idea of all, installed the deep-freeze full of ice-cream and lollipops. He also took pains with the choosing of the Christmas and birthday cards, and replaced the old-teeth colour of the walls with a wash of pale blue. He knew all his customers by name and made a point of being consistently cheerful, willing and friendly. As a result of his efforts, trade picked up – a little. Except in the few weeks before Christmas the place could never be called lively, and since the catastrophic rise in postal rates Evans had noticed a distinct decline in the sending of letters and parcels. Consequently the hours at work felt long and dull.

The afternoon Evans had given the Leopard a lift to the station had been particularly oppressive. Maybe this was in contrast to the small flutter of excitement he had felt in driving a strange woman, however undesirable to him, in his car. He couldn't wait to tell Brenda about the whole incident: they'd have a good laugh . . . As a matter of fact it would be no bad thing for her to realise that strange women in beautiful coats weren't averse to his offering them a lift . . . Sometimes, he thought, Brenda made out she had Evans exactly where she wanted him. This might give her a beneficial jolt. Teach her to go gallivanting off to the Air Base . . . Annoyed with himself, Evans put that thought from his mind.

He had forgiven her long ago, and disliked the nagging feeling of unquiet that rose within him every time he recalled the incident.

At five past five, having changed the blotting paper in the two blotters, and dampened the rubber sponges, Evans decided that, at the risk of being sacked, he would leave. He could no longer stand the buzzing flies and the warm stuffy smell of ink and linoleum. Soft evening air was what he longed for: a walk with Brenda round Mrs Browne's garden (she had given him permission to go where he liked, but so far he had not taken up her offer). They might go to the rose garden. Brenda, like Rosie, was a sucker for flowers. Then they would take a couple of cans of beer and a packet of crisps up to their room, open the window, lie on the bed, and see how things went from there. Evans, locking up, was pretty sure he knew how they'd go: since the famous night she'd been almost insatiable.

He swung his jacket over his shoulders and walked swiftly to Wilberforce's farm. Down through the yard, warm familiar manure smell all about him, Evans looked towards the shed for Brenda. No sign of her. Strange. Evenings like this, she usually stood about in the sun, smoking away at her bloody Woodbines in defiance of Wilberforce's threats. Evans poked his head round the chicken shed door: filthy stench, cluck cluck bloody cluck, but no Brenda. He couldn't think how she could stand the hens, day after day, let alone feel affection for them. He crossed the yard to her office, cautiously knocked on the door. No answer. He pushed the door ajar, looked in.

She was sitting at her table, shoulders hunched, back to him. She gave no sign of having heard him.

'It's me,' he said.

Brenda turned her head. Even in the etiolated light Evans could see there was a kind of silvery sheen over her face, perhaps sweat. It was so hot in here. Then he noticed two curling rims of what looked like fine sand at the corner of one of her eyes: the salt of dried tears.

'You can't come in here,' she said. 'You know you can't come in here.'

But Evans remembered the lesson he had learned that terrible night. Brenda responded best to mastery.

'I'm in here,' said Evans, half shutting the door behind him. 'Is anything the matter?' He could not be sure – this dimness was confusing after the bright sun outside, but he thought Brenda was regarding him with antagonism. He found it difficult to breathe in the close, grey cardboard air, and Brenda's silence was troubling. 'Anything the matter, Bren?' he said again, and let his eyes wander from her face over the small mountain ranges of eggs. Trays and trays of eggs, piled almost to the ceiling – brown ones, speckled ones, white ones, he wondered how many –?

'Get out,' said Brenda. 'Go on, get out.'

Evans stepped back, pushing the door completely shut behind him.

'Come on, Bren, don't be silly,' he said. 'Look, I got off early – risk the sack for that, you know. But I thought it was such a nice evening we could go up to the house and take a turn round the garden, take a sniff at the roses, you've been on about the roses, Bren, haven't you –?' Under her gaze he found himself running on, anything to break the silence, to appease her. In one movement she rose from the chair and sat on the table. This way she did not have to look so far up at him: her head was at his shoulder level. She folded her arms under her breasts, heaving them up, forcing a cleavage to show in the undone neck of her shirt. She swung one foot backwards and forwards, gently hitting the chair each time.

'I'm not coming up the house or anywhere else with you, Evans Evans, thank you very much. I'm going back down the Air Base. There's another dance on tonight.'

'What?' Evans could hear his own heart, its sudden booming thump.

'I'm going to a dance.'

Calm, Evans, calm, he said to himself. I'm not understanding right. There must be some mistake.

'I don't understand,' he said.

'Perhaps you'd understand if I told you I know all about you and your blonde.' Brenda gave her breasts an almost enjoyable heave.

'My blonde?' For a moment Evans could not think what she meant. His mind broke into a blinding white star of guilt, and yet he could not think why he was guilty. 'My blonde?' he said again, and he knew his mouth had fallen open and his bad eye was beginning to twitch.

'Oh, come off it, really! Don't waste my time with your pretended innocence. You know quite well what I'm talking about.' Her voice was nasty beyond recognition.

'I don't, Bren. I really don't know what you mean.' But even as he said it, he did. Even as he uttered the feeble denunciation, he knew what must have happened. She must have seen him, wondered, brooded all afternoon . . . Oh, really, it was laughable. His slow smile reflected the pace of his clearing thoughts. Brenda jumped down from the table. She faced him eye to eye. Christ, what a stupid drama all for nothing . . .

Evans stumbled back as Brenda hit him on the cheek. She was shrieking something about it being no laughing matter. What did he think he was? The shit, the swine, the deceiving bastard, getting at her like that the other night when she'd done nothing wrong, when all the time he'd been having it away with some filthy blonde tart – the words shot out, ricocheting off the darkness of Evans's comprehension. There was cuckoo spit at the corners of her mouth. Her hair was swinging about in heavy chunks, cider coloured, conker coloured, changing as she moved. As her hand rose to swipe him again Evans caught hold of her wrist.

But she twirled around, snakily escaping his grip, shouting all the while.

'Deny it, deny it, deny it!'

She's gone mad, thought Evans. Off her bloody head. He snatched her wrist again, missing it.

'And keep your fucking hands off me. Just you try denying

you were in a car with her this afternoon.' Brenda paused for a moment, backed up against the table, breasts quickly rising and falling as she panted.

'That's quite true,' said Evans, 'but keep calm a moment while I explain.'

'I knew it!' Brenda screamed, and suddenly her arms seemed to be flailing everywhere, filling the whole small mottled space. Vaguely, as he backed himself against the door, shielded his eyes with an arm, Evans saw her clutching at a tray of eggs. He saw the jolting of their neat mountain ranges as Brenda raised it above her head – he smelt a new whiff of cardboard. It bashed down upon him, a mad cloudburst. He heard the prickling sound of three dozen cracking shells, small explosions beneath the wild soprano screech of her voice.

Then he felt the mess. Slime among his fingers, threads of yolk, less rubbery, skulking through his hair, falling in a fringe over his bad eye. He saw an abstract pattern of yellow on the wall, a glinting pool of transparent slime on the floor. And Brenda's wide mouth, screaming screaming screaming unjust abuse.

He hit her. He left a mess of yolk on her face. She swung about, reaching for another tray of eggs, but slipped. Quickly Evans snatched the tray and saved it from falling: as Brenda tried to right herself, tried to stand, Evans crashed it down upon her head. It covered her hair with a web of yolks, whites and broken shells. He felt her fists in his stomach, his balls. He lashed back, enraged by the pain. They both reached for single eggs, clumsily hurled their ammunition at each other, screaming obscenities all the while. In the moments of timeless insanity Evans saw the raw eggs as injured eyes, the foul yellow of their pupils split and running into the liquid shapeless globs of their eyeballs. Christ, the bitch the bitch the bitch, he'd kill her.

Then Evans felt a searing pain in his own eyeball, the bad one. Cowering against the shelves he shouted to Brenda to stop, he had eggshell in his eye. He heard his own moan from a long way off, and felt a warm jet of tears stream from the eye.

Brenda stopped, sat back on the desk. Through his good eye, Evans focused on the absurd sight of her – hair, face, arms, breasts, legs, everything enskeined in dripping yellow, chips of shell, translucent slime.

'Help me,' he said.

Brenda came over to him. He dropped his hands, which he had made into a mask over his eye. Brenda gently lifted up the lid with trembling fingers that smelt of egg.

'I see it,' she said. Tears from the smarting eye ran among her fingers, ran over the egg whites like oil over water. 'Here, wait. My hanky.'

She pulled a handkerchief from the sleeve of her shirt. Part of its hem was stained yellow. She screwed up a corner and pulled Evans nearer to the dun light of the window. With her spear of white cotton she skimmed about his eyeball. Evans clenched his teeth and ground his fingers into his palms to stop himself screaming. It was as if she was nicking at him with a razor: he tried not to think what happens to a sliced eyeball.

'There.' Her head was bent over a tiny chip of shell on the handkerchief. 'It's out. Sorry if I hurt.'

Evans put out a hand to Brenda's shoulder. His eye still overflowed with water and he could not see her clearly. Her shoulder was covered in mess, gritty with broken shells. He felt the movement of a noiseless sob.

She moved away from him, sat back in her old position on the table.

'Glory be to God, Evans, I don't know what got into me.'

Evans ran a hand through his gluey hair, and round the back of his neck. He could feel trickles of liquid slobbering down his back.

'She wasn't my blonde,' he said quietly. 'You got it all wrong. She was a woman I never saw in my life before. And, good God, I never want to see her again. She was waiting for some fellow in the Star who didn't show up. She had no way of getting back to the station. I took her out of the goodness of my heart, otherwise she would have missed her train.'

'Oh,' said Brenda. She looked up. Her eyelashes were stuck together, yellow spikes blurred by fresh tears. Evans managed a smile.

'Don't think I've ever seen such a sight as you in all my life,' he said.

'You should take a look at yourself,' said Brenda. 'What are you going to do about all this?' She looked around.

'We'll think about that later.' Evans pulled her towards him. 'Here.' They kissed, tasting the raw egg splayed round each other's mouths.

'God, we're revolting,' said Brenda.

'I love you, girl,' said Evans. 'I love you, you silly jealous bitch. I wouldn't go out with a blonde. You know I wouldn't go out with a blonde, don't you?'

'Don't suppose you would, as a matter of fact.' With the useless handkerchief Brenda was trying to rub off some of the egg from her shirt.

'Lucky I got the car at the top of the yard,' said Evans. 'I daresay we can get there with no one seeing us, and slip in through the back of the house. Mrs Browne never seems to be around.'

'Just a minute. We'll go in a minute.' Brenda let the slimed handkerchief drop to the floor. She seemed quite exhausted, but her tears had stopped. They remained in silence for a while, looking round at the ludicrous mess left by their violence. 'What was all this about, Evans? What was all this about?' She reached behind her and picked up the folded note she had written two hours before. 'I wrote you this letter saying I was going because I saw you in the car with that woman.'

'You always act so hasty, Bren. Without thinking.'

'So do you. Who beat me up for going down to the Air Base?' She scrunched up the piece of paper and threw it on the floor.

'Let's talk about it later. Let's go. Come on. It stinks in

here. We'll come back later and clear up.'

Out in the yard, dazzling with evening sun, they laughed at the sight of each other. The egg whites were beginning to congeal, streaking their skin with silvery trails: splatterings of yellow yolk clung to them everywhere. They held sticky hands.

'I just saw red,' said Brenda.

'You drove me mad,' said Evans. 'So unreasonable.'

'A person has every right to be unreasonable sometimes.'

'Never knew you had it in you, jealousy.'

"'Course I wasn't jealous, silly. I was just angry at being deceived. That's quite different.'

'Ah,' said Evans, 'but you weren't being deceived.'

'Thought I was, so it comes to the same thing.'

'Bloody women,' said Evans.

They managed to get unseen in the car to the back drive of Wroughton House. They slipped through the back door and along the passage to the narrow flight of stairs that led directly to the attic. But halfway up they heard Mrs Browne below them, calling. It was almost as if she had been waiting for them. They stopped. They turned to her, noticing small blotches of egg yolk in their wake. For a moment Mrs Browne's eyes trembled with enquiry, then she smiled.

'You both look as if you could do with a bath,' she said. 'There are masses of spare bathrooms.' She sounded apologetic. 'Come on, I'll show you.'

She led Brenda to her own bathroom, Evans to one that overlooked the walled garden. She provided towels and soap and shampoo. She asked no questions and they volunteered no explanations. Later, she helped Brenda rub dry her hair. Brenda would only talk about the size of the bathroom, which impressed her.

'Twice as big as our living-room at home,' she said. 'If I had a place like this I'd lie in the bath hours and hours just looking at the view and thinking nice thoughts.'

'I do.' Augusta was being efficient, folding towels. 'As a matter of fact,' she said, 'I seem to have made myself far too much kedgeree, and there's lots of cheese and salad. Would you and Evans like to stay for supper?'

'That would be smashing.' Brenda, sitting on the mahogany lavatory seat, bare-breasted, was dabbing at her hair with a comb. 'Smashing, if it's not too much trouble.'

'Lovely. I'll go and get some wine. Help yourself to anything you want. There's make-up and stuff in the bedroom.'

She left the bathroom very quickly. Brenda, in a kind of day-dream, continued ineffectually to comb her hair, staring all the while out of the window at violaceous shadows fluttering over the lawn. She did not question the unreality of her present position just as, earlier, she had not questioned the unreality of the extraordinary fight. Sometimes, things just surged up, grasped you so tight you couldn't breathe or reason, swallowed you up, spat you out and left you sitting there, chewed, torn, exhausted. Then you recovered and went back to normal. Only when you looked back on the event could you see what it had all been about. Well, that's how she saw it, anyway. Meantime, this particular process of recovery, with a nice supper cooked by someone else in a posh kitchen to look forward to, was far from disagreeable.

Brenda and Evans changed into clothes they kept in their attic room, and joined Augusta Browne in the rose garden. She flitted from bush to bush, gently touching puffy blooms, bending her head sometimes to smell them, contradicting herself about her favourite – carrying on just like his mother, thought Evans. His eye still smarted and continued to spurt odd tears, blurring the rose colours in which he politely tried to show some interest. Brenda really did enjoy them: there was Mrs Browne telling her she should take as many as she liked, whenever she liked – it was a pity for them to be wasted. Women were a right soppy lot when it came to flowers: but still, it was pleasant out here, warm evening air and all that, and great slack feelings of release after all the tension and daft fighting.

Later, they ate in the kitchen. Mrs Browne had put a bowl of yellowish roses on the table, of course, and when Brenda had said they were the colour of egg yolks they had all laughed. There were a couple of lighted candles and three bottles of wine. Brenda, by candlelight, not quite dark sky in the window behind her, looked bloody marvellous, Evans thought. He had a good idea they would stay in the attic all night, tonight. So thinking, he scarcely concentrated on Mrs Browne's funny stories. She was making Brenda laugh a lot: oh yes, she seemed to be very gay, Mrs Browne, tonight. Her gaiety, it seemed to him after four glasses of iced dry white wine – went down easy as anything – was almost visible, spinning about the candle flame like a moth or something, rubbing up against them, affecting them – him and Brenda – too. Hell, he couldn't half be fanciful when he was a little drunk.

'Yes, just another glass, thanks.' He shouldn't have said yes, by rights, he'd have an awful head in the morning. But tonight, everything considered, seemed to be rather a special night: fight over, Brenda's flesh to look forward to – Christ, he'd show her how he loved her. Christ, he would. He picked up his glass.

A combination of gin and sleeping pills eventually eased Lark's pain. Weak with relief at its going, she struggled to keep awake, but hopelessly. The last real thing she remembered was ash coloured sky in her window. The last picture against her closed eyelids was of Evans bearing down upon her. She imagined his weight. She put a drowsy hand on her ribs, where he would lie. Painless, now. Pain gone. She remembered she would be fine in the morning. Have to go to work, after all.

For Rosie Evans it was another wakeful night in the bed beside Henry. She had much to reflect upon, much to sort out in her mind.

Already, eyes blinking at the summer stars twinkling through the elm leaves, she had been over the whole afternoon a hundred times. For all the rush, her plan had, surprisingly enough, gone almost perfectly. Henry had found her, and hadn't seemed to notice her slight limp caused by pins and needles sitting all that time on the tree stump. Judging by the look in his eyes he was nicely surprised by her appearance – hadn't gone so far to *comment* upon her romantic choice of clothes – but, then, he'd never been one for observations, and his very lack of comment was a compliment in itself. True, he had spoken a little gruffly, asked her to go away: but that was a natural reaction by anyone taken by surprise when they think they're on their own. And in the end, she'd won him over, of course. He came with her very meekly, biting on his pipe happily enough, listening to her reflections of the warmth of the evening and the blueness of the sky. At home, he'd settled down in his armchair and eaten three slices of newly baked bread spread thickly with honey, three chocolate biscuits and two lumps of fruit cake. Rosie hadn't seen him eat so much for weeks. The sight had overjoyed her. She had busied about, full of encouragement, trying to convince him he'd be quite better in no time if he kept eating like that. He'd refused the rice pudding, it had to be admitted, but that was quite understandable, considering the amount he had eaten before. When he'd finished, he got up and put on his coat, said he was going back down to the Star.

For a moment Rosie thought he meant her to go with him, like on Christmas Eve and her birthday, though he didn't go so far as to say that. 'Won't be long,' was all he said, and swung out of the door, wanting to be alone written all over his back.

Rosie was stung. Disappointment jabbed all through her, making her sniff and blow her nose loudly, as she would never have done in front of Henry or Evans. She was bemused. Her plan had gone so well till then. Why now had it failed?

Still, husbands were puzzling things and it was a wife's duty not to be got down by them. She tidied everything she could think of tidying, chose a tin of tomato soup to warm up when he came home, and sat down to read the paper. But she was restless. An uncomfortable feeling of nervousness jangled through her, stopping her concentration. She realised, suddenly, she was still wearing her boater. Well! In the excitement of Henry's large tea she must have forgotten to take it off. What a silly old thing she was. She must have looked ridiculous, serving him his tea in her hat. Why hadn't he said anything? Unlike Henry not to point out a mistake like that. She puffed up her hair and found herself making for the larder. It would be foolish to waste the end of the rice pudding, and it didn't look as if Evans was coming home. She scraped it up slowly with a small spoon, leaving the bits of gold skin till last, enjoying its sweetness. Then she went back to pace the kitchen.

Henry returned at eleven. He hadn't stayed out so late for years. Rosie quickly controlled the worry on her face, gave him a welcoming smile and suggested the tomato soup. But he wanted none of it. He seemed not to notice her, he seemed quite preoccupied. And then she understood. He had been drinking. Not just his normal two or three pints, mind. But real drinking. Whisky. She could smell it on his breath, see it in the liquid red-brown of his eyes. She did not manage quite to conceal a gasp, and then she saw, mounting the stairs, he was very unsteady. She had given him an arm, said there, there, you're all right, my love, Rosie's here – and helped him to bed.

He'd been asleep a couple of hours now. Snoring. Rosie sighed. Her plan had so nearly been entirely satisfactory. A pity . . . But still, you couldn't hope for everything. Not all at once. There was plenty of time.

Under the sheets Rosie rubbed her hands together, feeling the skin still greasy with tonight's helping of hand lotion. Oh, he would be amazed, Henry, when the time came.

He would not believe it, would he? She didn't mind waiting, really, of course. She was so sure all would be well at last. At the feel of her soft bare hand on his shoulder he would turn over, wouldn't he? Aroused, wanting . . . And all the old passion – no more than a memory for so long – would be upon them both again. Rosie Evans, she said to herself, squeezing her greasy fingers, you should have thrown away those mittens years ago. So much wasted time to be made up for: we must begin tomorrow night.

She heard the church clock strike three.

PART II

Summer expanded: hot, dry. Last year, Augusta remembered, was altogether more temperate. There had been a spate of light showers, sudden from a clear sky, catching them unawares. On several occasions they had had to run from tea in the garden – in those days Augusta still occupied herself with cucumber sandwiches of brown bread, honeycombs, and iced coffee swirling with whipped cream – anything, anything to delight Hugh, to deter his thoughts of leaving. With their guests they had had to pick up plates and glasses, run across the warm grass, the warm gravel, and into the sudden dimness of the hall whose flagstones, too, were warm beneath bare feet. Augusta recalled, in the present silence, the laughter of their friends: the released movements of people cooled by shadow when they have come in from the sun, cobwebs of rain on their hair, the high, irresponsible feeling they all shared of there being nothing to do but to please themselves till dinner. In fact the frail showers were a kind of bonus, making the view of lawn and trees a temporarily new place, a landscape of spun glass: then the sun would return to melt the sparkling, and on the barely dampened grass they would take up croquet mallets and continue their game. It was the laziest summer ever Augusta could remember, but, beneath the idleness, chimed reverberations of implacable fear.

To protect themselves from each other Augusta and Hugh surrounded themselves almost constantly with friends. Every weekend the house was full and it was not difficult to put discord aside. Hugh was wonderfully benign, proud of his house and exhilarated by the delight it gave other people. Augusta shared his feelings and, together among their friends, they were at their best. Funny, gay, they sparked off in each other ever more absurd plans which would never materialise, but the thought of them was nonetheless enjoyable. There was no time for dispute. In the pleasure of those armoured days there was no occasion for the deadening discussions of their own problems. High spirits would be the order of the weekend: not till Sunday afternoon did Augusta begin to feel the chill of an ebbing tide. It was the time of week she most dreaded: that peculiar sadness of an English Sunday afternoon, that long chilly slope that begins with the apple tart and cream and dwindles into the bleakness of cold meat for Sunday supper when everyone has left. This abhorrence, Augusta supposed, was inherited from her days at boarding school: the sickening feeling of imminent return to real life which no amount of jollity can disguise.

In happier days at Wroughton, Sunday afternoons had been less bad: while teasing her for neurosis Hugh had at the same time skilfully worked upon releasing her from it. Augusta, in retrospect, was unable to analyse just how he had done this: she simply recalled that, for several years, weeks of Sundays would go by with only an occasional lapse into familiar melancholy. But, their last summer, Hugh's magic worked no longer. The disintegration of Sunday symbolised the disintegration of their lives: the lamentable bells of evensong were a horrible cry. They would wander about their warm garden, soothed by the smell of tobacco plants quivering with their own scent, reluctant to face real issues and yet unable to avoid them. The problem of money increased daily, but they were united in their madness of overspending. Monday morning there would be more bills: Sunday evenings, discussions about how to pay them had an air of hopelessness. While butterflies flurried about the lavender, the reality of a vast overdraft seemed not quite to touch them with its deepest implications. But for all its moments of dread and fear, Augusta remembered last summer as gravid with idyllic days. It was a time not wasted, not regretted: for all its blemishes, it shone with that particular light that distinguishes a few seasons in a lifetime, and it would remain thus for ever in her mind.

This year it was harsher, starker. Lack of rain caused the

leaves to dry prematurely. Their crisp shapes, against blaring near-white skies, made eyes to ache with their brilliant green. Shade was anaemic: patches of lawn were burned yellow, birds were too parched to sing.

But the office men, impervious to heat, gleaming necks in nylon collars, returned with increasing frequency to survey the house and grounds. They became cockily familiar with the place, pouncing over and over again upon the same cracks, shouting possessively about the 'grand views' from the windows. Augusta came to recognise them as individuals: the strutting chairman; the managing director with his weird smile which looked as if his mouth, in reality very small, was permanently distorted by magnification; the fat spinster secretary whose plastic stilletos caused her to stumble uneasily across the lawns. She was unused to such spaces of grass, as she kept informing everyone in her Wimbledon voice, and was given to much panting when the chairman made her take notes while he traversed the garden in his puffed-up manner.

The seriousness of their intent was in no doubt, and they began to take dreadful liberties. One day they brought cans of beer and executive sandwiches – inappropriate Gentle-men's Relish – to eat in the shade of the elm tree for lunch: they did not bother to ask Augusta's permission until half-way through, and seemed insensitive to her disapproval. They merely tightened the laces of their suede shoes, as city office men find it necessary to do after a few hours in the country, and stubbed out their mini cigars among the daisies. They spoke of the possibility of the back drive becoming a car park, and enquired if domestic and secretarial help was readily available – they actually used the phrase readily available – in the village. Augusta assured them no one was in search of a job.

But she knew surrender would soon be forced upon her the day they brought the architect. A pale Mr Droby, of subur-ban inclinations, was the architect – a friend of the estate agent through whom the Brownes had originally found the house. Having accomplished his minor function of linking drains to new bathrooms, he had boldly suggested to Augusta and Hugh that he should then go on to improve the general architecture of the William and Mary building. His idea had been to embellish the place with archways, and alcoves of shelves lit with concealed bulbs. In his view it was advisable to flatten out the undulating walls, double glaze the windows and hide the beautiful pine stairs under a thick protection of Wilton carpet. Furthermore, he suggested, his wife could be very helpful when it came to interior design, as he grandly called it, should Augusta find herself with no ideas. He brought along snippets of man-made silk in 'various shades' to 'tone in' with unsubtle paints straight from a chart. He was sent away rebuffed, and disapproving of Augusta's plans. But he waited. Time would come for his revenge, and with the arrival of the office men, it did.

He was called upon for his valuable opinions and most vociferously he gave them. Augusta, in the background, over-heard his frightful suggestions with increasing horror. She understood that Droby realised here was a renewed chance to ruin something on a grand scale, and this time he was not going to let that chance elude him. With a sense of complete helplessness Augusta listened to him describing the mock Georgian porch with which he would 'make a feature of' the façade: in his hands, she realised, there would be no end to the ruination of the house. It was imperative the office men should be deterred. But, by now, nothing could stop them. A week after Droby's visit, inspired by his optimistic views of how the place could be much improved under his guidance, they made an offer. The price was disappointing, but it was the only offer in six months. The money was guaranteed: Hugh, with surprising sadness on the telephone to Augusta, explained they could not refuse it. 'Because once the house has gone, we can't really mind what happens to it,' he said. 'Oh, but we can, we will,' retorted August. 'We must save it.' 'No good being sentimental,' said Hugh, 'I've agreed they shall take possession in January.'

January. Four months.

The positive news blasted Augusta with what turned out to be a new series of acute sensations. The nature of uncertainty, in which she had been living for the last year, is some protection. Stripped of that, and faced with an inescapable ending, it is a strong mind and body that can survive intact. Augusta knew that she must be calm: frenzy would waste the days. All she could do was to make the most of the last weeks, living each day, in the biblical sense, as if it was her last: praying for slowness of the hours. Self-pity she had always abhorred and never indulged in: her new problem was how to deal with the physical symptoms of incredulity. As they crushed her, that first evening she heard the news, she found herself little equipped to resist them. With no heart to go into the garden, she stood in the brown light of her study, head resting against the warm glass of the window pane, and allowed herself to weep outrageously. Tears were a strange sensation, she was unused to crying. Their release did nothing to ameliorate the anguish, but the sound of her own moaning in the silence provoked a detached curiosity about herself. She was spurred by self impatience. What was the good, what was the good? Glutting sorrow upon roses, Keats's facile suggestion, was no help outside poetry. No: she must return to the normal habits of an evening, continue as naturally as possible. But what were those habits? Since Hugh's departure the rhythm of things had been upset. Most days she floundered, restless, unable to concentrate, only intent on constantly re-establishing by actual touch the existence of her territory. It occurred to her – she smiled to herself – that if anyone in the past few months had observed her pacing about touching flowers, walls, pictures, they would have thought her quite mad. She must pull herself together.

Augusta blew her nose, thinking how ugly she must look. She had a long, cool bath, watching the elms dissolve into cumbersome shapes as the sky faded. And, later, she did in fact achieve some kind of exhausted calm, although a strange pain began to drill her jaw. She was determined there should be no more private outbursts: they did nothing but enfeeble. The uselessness of tears was disillusioning. She did not cry again.

Rosie Evans was inclined to see omens in small things that might escape the notice of less observant people. The afternoon the Red Admiral flew through the kitchen door – trying to escape the ruddy heat, poor thing – she knew at once her luck had changed. Although almost two months had gone by since she had burned her mittens, she had not yet approached Henry. Why, she could not exactly explain to herself, but some instinct warned her to remain patient for a little while longer. The fact that Henry had made no comment on her hands, naked now every night, seemed to her a good sign. They cannot have repulsed him, or he would have broken his silence. Maybe he thought they had improved, and when the night to touch him finally came he might not be surprised. He might even be pleased.

But the Red Admiral signalled the end of all such hopes. Rosie watched it fluttering against the window pane, seeking escape. She put up her hands to catch it and return it to the door. It was then she noticed, in the fierce midday light, their sorry state. Overnight, it seemed, the soft greasiness of her skin, achieved by two months of rubbing in hand lotion, had vanished. Her fingers were wintry again, dark and swollen, scored with rough cracks. She uttered a low moan. Tears came to her eyes. It could only be some confounded allergy – but to what? The doctors had no idea: she had been asking them for years. Dear God, it was unfair. She had no spirit to sew herself more mittens and tonight, if he noticed her hands, Henry would turn away his head, barely hiding his disgust. He would heave himself away from her to the far corners of the bed.

Rosie caught the butterfly. She felt its wings flickering in the black cage of her palms, vile palms rough as sawdust, which Henry could never forgive. She kept it trapped for a moment longer than was necessary, its fear a wicked comfort. Then she let it go, dropping her hands heavily to her sides. It flew up towards the elms, dazzling as illusion, and disappeared. Rosie licked the corners of her mouth. She tasted salt. She looked at the dry earth, the dusty lane, the unbroken blue of the sky, and struggled to control a sob. The luxury of weakness, she contemplated, would suit her now. She would like to slip into the cemetry, unobserved, go to her mother's grave in its shady place under the hedge, lean her head against the rough stone cross and roar out loud against the unfairness of her inherited hands, till all her grief was exorcised. As it was, she saw Henry in the road. Even from this distance she could tell he was unsteady on his feet. Rosie returned to the kitchen: in all the upset she was late laying the table for his dinner. But would he eat it? For several weeks, now, he had done no more than pick at his food, complaining of the heat. Every afternoon he had slept in his chair, no pretence of looking at his paper, waking just in time to return to the Star when it opened at six. Through the tangle of her own preoccupations Rosie was aware that all was not well with Henry. She put it down to the sun – every blinking day, there hadn't been a cloud in the sky for two weeks – and the monotony of retirement. He wasn't a man to take to rest easily, not after a life of vigorous work. Rosie worried about him. Perhaps, she thought, they didn't go out enough. The Morris Minor sat under its plastic cover, untouched, for months on end. Silly waste, really. Rosie herself had no taste for pottering along lanes in a stuffy car, whose brakes she could not credit, but she knew it gave Henry pleasure. Perhaps she should suggest . . . a cinema, one evening. They hadn't seen a film in years. That would make a break, surely. Something to talk about for a week or so – something to take Henry's mind off his wretched bricks.

Rosie brightened at her idea. Going out, evening, there would be nothing unnatural about wearing her nice lace gloves, which would give her confidence. She needn't always be hiding her hands. Perhaps, if she was feeling very bold, she might even try *brushing Henry's knee*, in the safety of the dark, as she reached to get a toffee from the bag she would insist he bought on the way in. Ah, hope! There was remedy for all things in hope, Rosie knew, and she wasn't one to be dashed by a spell of bad luck. Besides, there was so much to be thankful for. A happy home, a faithful husband who needed her at this time. She began to slice the luncheon meat, and to arrange her smile of welcome.

'Henry, my love,' she said, hearing him outside. She looked up. He stood swaying in the door, averting his eyes from her face. With a great effort of will, Rosie continued to smile.

'And this,' said Evans, with a sweep of his arm, 'will be the lounge.'

He stood on one of its walls, three bricks high, surveying the foundations of their future house: his and Brenda's. Heat and pleasure had caused damp patches under the arms of his shirt, and he imagined the bathroom, where next summer he would wash every day. He fancied tiles, some pale colour chosen by Brenda, and a mirror high enough for him to shave into without having to stoop. He also had in mind an especial front door, one that would be a cut above the other front doors on the estate, with a brass knocker in the shape of a cockerel's head. He hadn't managed to find such a thing as yet, but if the worst came to the worst he would have one made. A silly extravagance, his mother would say, but it would please Brenda no end, and when it came to the house she would take a bit of pleasing.

He knew that in her heart she longed for it to be ready as much as he did: to be married, settled, chicken-breeding, decorating – to be safely cocooned by the gentle monotony of their own lives. But something perverse in Brenda – and after all it was her spirit he loved her for – caused her to complain. Not only to complain, but to be downright insulting about the whole place, the whole idea. Her lack of enthusiasm might have daunted a feebler man. To Evans, it merely spurred his determination to enchant her with visions of their future.

'And that, there, where you're standing, Lark, will be the front path. A nice fine gravel I'll get from a mate up the road.'

'Bet the regulations won't let us,' said Brenda.

'Bugger the regulations.' Evans jumped down from the lounge wall. At the back of his mind lurked something far more worrying than the regulations – the money. The house would be finished by Christmas. Evans had persuaded his friend in the agency selling the houses, for the price of a few drinks, to secure this particular house – the best site, on a corner, a patch of trees not far away. But for the moment he was still short of £200 on the deposit money. How he would find it in time was a problem that kept him awake at nights, Brenda asleep in his arms, exhausted by his love-making. (Worry, he'd noticed lately, was a strange aphrodisiac.) She never asked him about money – such things as deposits and mortgages were beyond her understanding and interest. Evans considered it wise to keep the problem to himself, disguising it with cheerful optimism. He tilted his head to the sky.

'Our bedroom,' he said. 'Picture window, according to the brochure, overlooking the garden here.'

'Don't know how you can imagine it all,' said Brenda. 'Walls and everything, conjuring them up in your mind.' She was pouting, face gleaming with sweat, bored.

'Lucky one of us can.' Evans turned to Lark. She squatted on the wall that was to divide the lounge from the kitchen. They had brought her along because she had looked depressed, nothing to do with her evening except drink gin while she painted her nails. 'What do you think of it, Lark? What's your professional opinion?'

'Marvellous.' Lark grinned. She liked to be flattered by Evans. She'd let him have her opinion by the hour, given half the chance. 'Bloody marvellous, you lucky sods.'

Her glance followed Evans's to the sky. She could see it all: the bedroom, a simple square. White paint, patchwork quilt

163

on the bed, the one she was making them for their wedding present: hexagonals all different reds. (She'd had the devil of a job finding enough different shades to make it dramatic.) A white dressing-table, kidney-shaped like she'd seen in a old Ginger Rogers film, its drawers hidden by frilled curtains: red roses would be nice, with curtains to match. One of those soft white carpets, of course, that tickle between your toes when you're bare-foot. Matching tables each side of the bed, piles of magazines. Pictures of flowers on the wall. Evans's clothes on a chair . . . Evans slumping down on to the bed, on top of the quilt, not bothering to draw it back. Work over, but no time to wash: the smell of ink and rubber stamps on his fingers, lunchtime pork pie still on his breath. Evans wanting her before supper.

And then the lazy straightening of things. Sated. The slow descending of the steep stairs, dressing-gown half undone, not bothering: the slumberous feeling of walking breast-high against a gentle current, limbs weak, eyes blurred as if with rain water. Here, where she was sitting, the kitchen neat and sparkling. A small roast in the oven, frozen sprouts in the freezer, toasted sliced bread and Cheddar cheese. Later, the television, there where Evans stood now in the lounge. His arm round her shoulder. His presence every day, every night. His weight on the sofa, his hand on her knee, wanting her again.

He was beside her on the low wall, thigh touching hers, clumsy fingers kneading the top of her spine.

'Glad you like it,' he said.

'Leave off, tickling,' she said. He removed his hand. Brenda was looking down at them.

'Can't keep his hands off anything in skirts, can he?'

'Piss off, woman.' He stood up, smiling good-naturedly, rubbed at one of Brenda's nipples. 'If you had as much imagination about what it's going to be like as you do about what I do with other women – you'd be better off.'

Placated, because she was never really alarmed by his flirting with Lark – he did it to be kind – Brenda gestured towards the invisible bedroom.

'Faces north,' she said. 'That's no good.'

'West, excuse me.' Evans was playing with the lobe of her ear, pressing it between thumb and finger. 'Sun in the evening.'

'Who wants sun in the evening?'

'Shut up being so difficult.' Evans leant over her to kiss her on the cheek, but Brenda, whole body stiffening, thrust her tongue into his mouth. From where Lark sat they looked tall as giants. She felt a sudden spasm of nausea and buried her head into the darkness of her arms folded on her knees. The familiar pain in her chest began to tick, rhythmically as a clock. Scarlet petals of a destroyed geranium swooped dizzily in her mind. She tried to shut out the voices from above her.

'First time you have me, it's got to be before we move in, right?'

'All right by me. November, some time.'

'On the bare floor.'

'Bloody hard, bloody cold.'

'I fancy that.'

'Bloody sex maniac, you are. Here, come on.'

When Lark opened her eyes they had parted. Evans looked down at her, gave her a hand, helped her to her feet.

'You all right? You're white as a sheet.'

'Fine.' Lark smiled. Even open-eyed the red petals still swam in her vision, but the sickness had gone.

'Look to me as if you could do with a drink. Coming?'

They left the outline of the future house, crossing a strip of bare earth that within months would be lawn. Evans walked between the two girls, an arm round each of their shoulders.

'You'll have to come and babysit, Lark,' said Brenda. Lark nodded. Her head was pushed forward by the weight of Evans's arm on the back of her neck. She relished her few moments of discomfort.

In the Star they found Henry sitting by himself, a double whisky on the table in front of him. At the sight of them he made some attempt to stir himself from his reverie: he invited them to sit down, and gave Evans a pound to buy a round of drinks. From his half-smile it might be guessed he listened to what they said, idle chat about the house: but a glance at his vacant eyes indicated his mind was on other things. Lark noticed that each time the door opened he shifted a little, as if expecting someone. His breath smelt quite strongly of whisky, and his hand shook when he raised his glass to his lips. Had there been a chance, Lark would have asked Evans if there was anything the matter with Henry: perhaps he had not fully recovered from his chill a couple of months back. But in front of Brenda she didn't like to appear inquisitive: Henry's well-being was none of her business, and Brenda never liked to discuss her future parents-in-law. She had little interest in them.

So Lark kept her queries to herself. At closing time, Brenda and Evans gave her a lift back to the flat, though she would have been quite happy to walk the two miles. They themselves were to spend the night at Wroughton House – it had become their habit. They were there most nights, now.

Evans saw Lark to the door. He kissed her on the cheek, as he sometimes did after a late evening, and said he was glad she liked the house, such as it was. She must come there often, he said. He and Brenda would like that. They'd be expecting her there most evenings, he and Brenda would, or there'd be trouble.

Henry resisted Rosie's dreadful idea for two weeks. Finally worn out by her enthusiasm he agreed to go.

The elusiveness of the Leopard was taking its toll and he no longer much cared what he did, where he went. The only thing he looked forward to was opening time at the Star. He sat there at a corner table for hours each day, refusing to be drawn into any kind of conversation, waiting. Each time the door opened a small pain of hope flickered within him, only to swell into a more universal ache as the new arrival turned out not to be the Leopard. Pain, ache: pain, ache: he was growing accustomed to the rhythm, and when it became too bad he ordered whiskies more quickly. Far from a complete remedy, at least they helped to blunt reality. And reality, this summer, was confusingly blank. No news, that was the worst of it. In all the hours he had sat in the Star listening for the smallest scrap of information about the glamorous stranger, Henry had heard no word of her. It was as if she had never existed, never sat at the bar asking for a Dubonnet with a twist of lemon, never cast her spell upon the place. The Boy had not mentioned her: that was the only minor consolation. Henry had observed him carefully over the last few weeks, and concluded that the Boy was as much infatuated by Brenda as ever, and that no other woman existed in his life. He must have been giving the Leopard a lift somewhere, to the bus, perhaps, out of kindness. If on that occasion Henry had gone ahead with his plans of suicide, he reflected, then his death would have been untimely. Not that he had saved himself for any rewards: his present life was an ordeal he doubted he could endure much longer.

The evening of the outing he fortified himself with three drinks before going home. He walked back from the pub slowly, reluctantly, the warm evening air irritating his eyes, making them water. He thought, as he always thought, that if the Leopard was here beside him, on his arm, that would be strong. Upright, firm. A man to be proud of, a man she could rely upon. As it was, lethargy dulled his limbs, making the act of moving at all difficult: the only release was to move his lips as silently he mouthed to himself her private name: *Leopard, my Leopard.*

On reaching home, Henry directed himself to his parked car. With great effort he took off its plastic cover. Folding this up seemed to take a very long time, longer than he ever remembered. It took his breath away, he needed to rest. He opened the driving door and sat in the small green seat: that, at least, was familiar, comfortable. He liked the smell of warm plastic and clean carpet: he noticed with pleasure the shining paint of the snub-nosed bonnet: he gripped the steering wheel with confidence. Then he let his hand pat the empty seat beside him. How many times, in his imagination, had it been filled by the Leopard! In his heart he was convinced she was a Jaguar lady, but she was no snob, his Leopard, and she would appreciate the feel of his car. She would wind down the windows and cry out for joy as they spun down the lanes, white with May, off to some-where . . . somewhere far away where they could drink a Thermos of tea in the shade and she would invite him to hold her hand.

Henry looked up to see a different hand waving at him through the windscreen: Rosie, anxious. He must come at once and wash, or they would be late. Rosie was wearing the absurd straw hat again, God knows why. It would only irritate people behind her in the cinema. But Henry could not find the energy to tell her so. He could feel a pulse thumping in his temples, and getting out of the car was a less simple matter than he might have supposed.

Twenty minutes later he was back in the driving seat, hair greased flat, Rosie beside him. She could never embark on an expedition with the kind of calm that Henry respected, and the thing that troubled her now was the question of the window on her side.

'How do you open it, Henry?'

'Turn it to the right.'

'There.'

Henry started the engine. They moved a yard or so. Rosie let out a little shriek.

'Oh, my! I'll have to close it again. My hat will blow off, won't it?'

'There's not a breath of wind.' Henry's mind was so far from the problem in hand his patience could not be ruffled.

'There will be once we get going. You know how you drive.'

'Well then, close it.'

After several attempts at turning the handle the wrong way, Rosie closed it. She folded her hands, gloved in nylon lace, on her lap. From the corner of his eye Henry saw her turn the colour of a beetroot. Such maroon flesh, he thought, was particularly nasty against the electric blue of her blouse.

'Oh, Henry love,' she said, 'I do believe I can't breathe, now, this dreadful heat.'

Henry wound down his own window a couple of inches. He wondered if he had the energy to request her not to speak again: it interrupted his concentration. Besides, her voice, sharp with its various worries, exacerbated the throbbing pain behind his eyes.

He guided the small car down the lane, swinging it a little from side to side as if to pay his respects to both pavements. He had not the slightest inclination to show his mastery of the car: it would all be wasted on Rosie. All he required from her was continuing silence, right up till the time they had to decide on the price of the seats. As a precaution, to keep her quiet, he drove at a shameful twenty-five miles an hour, a speed at which he hoped he would meet no one from the Star who had in the past heard tell of his acemanship at the wheel.

He might have known it, though: his cornering troubled Rosie, for all his care.

'Brakes, Henry love,' she screeched. 'Did you get them seen to?'

'No need.'

'Oh, I don't know about that. You can never trust brakes.'

'I can trust these brakes.'

'*Henry!*' She fell against him as they swerved round a bend: his judgement had not been as accurate as he calculated. '*Brake!* You'll have us in the ditch.'

'If you could keep your voice down, I could put my mind to concentrating more.' He glanced at her hideous fat fingers, gripping each other. He despised himself for ever having said he'd come. It would be the last time, positively the last. He'd sell the car, take the Leopard on holiday with the money and not tell Rosie where he was going. Probably he'd never come back, for that matter – not to all Rosie's pestering to spend good money on a film neither of them wanted to see: not to all this shouting. Full of such resolves Henry crushed his foot down on the accelerator, goading the old car into a burst of speed accompanied by much triumphant snorting of the engine.

It took Rosie quite some time, settled in her cinema seat, to recover from the journey. Not for worlds would she mention it to Henry, but her heart was thumping alarmingly fast. To add to her discomfort, her blouse was damp from nervous sweat, and her feet had swollen uncomfortably in her shoes. Henry had always been a terror in a car and this evening, Rosie couldn't help thinking, it was almost as if he had driven dangerously to provoke her: well, he had not succeeded. After her first few shouts, too spontaneous to control, she had sat quietly, gripping at the door handle for support as they lurched about, praying for God's mercy. And He had granted it, for miraculously they had arrived at the cinema car park intact. Once out of the car, of course, Henry reverted to his usual mild self. He had bought two expensive seats without quibbling, and also a bag of toffees, now wedged between his knees, when Rosie had made the suggestion. It was true he had snapped at the usherette when she made off too fast down the steps with her torch beam, leaving them in darkness: but now he seemed quite settled, content, staring with expressionless eyes at *Tom and Jerry*. In spite of the inauspicious beginning, Rosie's spirits recovered. She felt that after all they might achieve an enjoyable evening, if the Lord continued to watch over them on the journey back: and, who knows, things might even develop unexpectedly.

If they had come last week, or the week before, as Rosie had suggested, they would have been able to benefit from films of a romantic nature. As it was, by the time Henry had agreed, the Odeon had switched its programme to an adventurous film of bloodshed and violence, the kind of thing which held little appeal for Rosie. But she had said nothing, taken her chance while it was there: Henry might not let himself be persuaded

another time. Besides, there had been a picture of a battle-
ship on a stormy sea in the advertisement, and, as Rosie had
pointed out, it would do him the world of good to get a look
at the sea again. And what mattered most, this evening, was
Henry's pleasure.

Rosie sensed that this was unfortunately short-lived. The
director had used the sea merely for a series of dramatic
pictures before the titles, then had swung his attention to
shots of mountains and jungles, and Rosie felt Henry slump
beside her. She herself tried to concentrate, but within
moments violence prevailed, corpses spewing blood all over
the screen, which made her feel quite queasy even though
she'd heard tell it was only tomato ketchup. The last film
Rosie had seen was *Spring in Park Lane*. She let forth a sigh of
nostalgia for Michael Wilding's gentle manners, so much
more satisfactory than all this decapitation. What's more, it
was hardly the stuff of romance, hardly the kind of thing that
would encourage Henry to slip his arm round her shoulders
and remember his youth. To take her mind off the general
disappointemnt, Rosie reached for the bag of toffees. Henry,
she saw, was asleep. Snoring, slightly. She hoped he wouldn't
disturb the people nearby. She slipped a toffee into her mouth.
Its familiar sweetness was a wonderful comfort. In no time
she had finished the bag. Then, in spite of all the groaning
activity in front of her eyes, drowsiness came upon her. She
felt her eyelids droop, and a lovely confusion of food came to
her mind. Perhaps they could go out for a meal when the
film was over. It would make a change to eat in a restaurant
again: she could not remember how long it was since they had
last been out. Years. She'd like to try that new place – French,
she thought it was, with gingham curtains in the window. By
candlelight, she could look quite girlish, and surely there'd
be some things on the menu that wouldn't turn her stomach:
a nice fresh vegetable stew, perhaps, and French rice
pudding.

Rosie woke with a start to find people all round her

standing up. For a moment she was confused: the music certainly wasn't *God Save the Queen*. Then she saw the gold curtains falling over the screen and realised it was all over. She arranged her hat, which seemed to have slipped over one eye, and nudged Henry. She saw that on waking he, too, was confused, and a little guiltily found herself taking advantage of his befuddled state. Determinedly she guided him out through the crowds, across the street and through the doors of the small restaurant she had observed when she came in to do her weekly shopping.

At once Rosie realised the place was not all it might be when it came to hygiene. For a start, there was a strong smell of garlic in the air, and burnt cheese. The tablecloths were paper, splattered with grease from candles stuck in bottles. High fire risk, she thought. Funny people. No sense of order. Didn't look as if business was doing too well, either. There was only one customer, at a single table in a corner, dressed in a blue and white fisherman's jersey. He got up, wiping his mouth.

'Did you book?' he asked, in a heavy foreign accent.

'No,' said Rosie.

'Did you want a table?'

Insolent type: what else would they be here for?

'I don't know we do, we could get a bite at home if you like,' Henry said to the waiter, blinking his eyes fast, focusing. But Rosie was already sitting herself down at a table near the window. She could make herself quite clear when her mind was made up.

'You could sit there,' said the waiter, indicating the table Rosie already occupied.

'Ah,' said Henry, inner protest too strong for further words, and sat himself opposite his wife.

Rosie now had a view of him that sometimes she had dreamed of: a candle flame within inches of his nose, making his white hair sparkle, and deepening the lines on his dear handsome face. How she loved him, still. She could feel the love within her, bubbles racing through her veins so that suddenly her breath came quite fast and she found herself panting. Surely, tonight, reinvigorated by his long sleep in the cinema, Henry's fancy might turn to things that had been dormant between them for so long. Even now he was raising his hand towards her . . . But it stopped at the candle. He snuffed out the flame between thumb and finger. A brown thread of smoke twisted up into the air between them, and she could hardly see his face.

'Oh, Henry!'

'Bloody thing. What are we doing here, anyway?'

'I thought it would be nice to have a meal out, to round off the evening.'

'Better off at home.'

'Well, we can't judge till we see what they have to offer.' Rosie was determined to be cheerful. Henry swung round in his chair and beckoned the waiter.

'La menu,' he shouted, and Rosie beamed with pride.

'I didn't know you could speak French,' she said. 'Perhaps we could go for a holiday abroad one year.' The Eiffel Tower and fancy cakes spun before her eyes. With Henry's command of the language they could order anything they needed and they would be quite safe so long as they took their own lavatory paper and insisted their water was boiled . . . In truth, Rosie did know Henry had picked up a few words in Marseilles, but tonight was a good time to flatter him, and a less talented man might have forgotten things he learned in the war.

When the menu came Henry said, 'bon, bon,' several times, and 'tray bien'. Then he fell silent. He handed the grubby bit of paper to Rosie.

'Can't make this out,' he said. 'Think it must be bloody Italian.'

He was right, of course. In the smudged writing Rosie recognised the word 'spaghetti' several times. Neither of them had any great partiality for spaghetti, but Rosie was determined this should not spoil the final lap of the evening. Now was the time for her to come to Henry's rescue, to ease him from the awkward task of decision making. She took a wild shot in the dark, praying to God the Italians were acquainted with ordinary decent food.

'We'll have two lamb chops with a portion of peas and some plain spaghetti with tomato sauce, if you please,' she said to the waiter, adding the spaghetti purely out of politeness. For a fraction of a second his pencil hovered doubtfully above his pad. Rosie's heart thumped. She smiled authoritatively, won the waiter's respect.

'And drinks?' he asked.

One last hurdle. With some relief Rosie saw the words *Unlicensed to sell alcohol* at the bottom of the menu. She scanned the list of soft beverages.

'Two orangeades,' she said.

'Bloody hell. I want a proper drink.' Henry was scowling.

'I'm sorry, we have no licence. You could go down the road to the pub and buy a bottle of wine,' the waiter said.

'Catch me buying wine.' Henry turned in his chair again. 'What's that you're drinking, stuff in the glass on your table?'

The waiter paused.

'Scotch whisky,' he said at last. 'I own this place, you see. It's my private bottle.'

'You wouldn't, for a consideration . . .?' Henry smiled up at the proprietor, causing a snip of jealousy in Rosie's heart: she had not seen Henry so soft since their courting days when he had wanted, that first time in the bluebell woods, to undo the buttons of her blouse.

The waiter shrugged, scratched at his greasy hair.

'See what I can do, if you like,' he said, and went away.

'Very obliging fellow,' said Henry. 'They're all right, these foreigners, if you know how to deal with them.'

But Rosie felt no gratitude to the waiter. Rather, she was filled with dread. It would require all her tact to prevent the demon whisky coming between them. The night was now in danger.

*

In the dim light Henry was not able to see too clearly the horrible mess of Rosie's chin. It shone with a mixture of grease and tomato sauce, which she kept dabbing with her paper serviette. To make matters worse she seemed to think the whole procedure of eating the filthy stuff was funny. Laughing as she spooned the spaghetti into her mouth, half of it would spew out again and hang like worms over her bottom lip. These she would attempt to gather up with her fat grey tongue, thereby splattering her blouse with tomato sauce, and asking for the aid of Henry's handkerchief, which he refused. From time to time she lifted her glass of orangeade to her lips, bunching up her fingers still in their hideous lace gloves, and closed her eyes in some kind of private ecstasy. She was a disgusting sight and Henry hated her with his whole being.

With every drink – the proprietor had most kindly sold him all that remained in the whisky bottle – Henry's feelings of loathing increased. They became strangely tangible, insects crawling on the table between them. He wondered why Rosie could not see them. How could she live with someone so many years and not recognise hate that sprouted from him like a skin disease? How could she be so impervious to his suffering, to the daily torment of his mind?

'How about a sweet?' she was saying, and ignoring any opinion he might have had on the matter, given a chance, asked the waiter for a strawberry ice with chocolate sauce.

Henry decided to kill her.

It occurred to him that he was not by nature a violent man, but if murder was the only way to freedom, then murder it must be. The best way would be to take her up to the woods, mid-week, when no one was about. One bonk on the head and she'd be down on the ground like a jelly. Then it would be easy to strangle her, or suffocate her, whichever took his fancy that particular day. He'd dig a grave and bury her right there, and have all the pleasure of listening to the thrushes singing in celebration as he trod down the earth. He could smoke his pipe in peace, and go home to make his own tea: no more bloody welcomes. They'd come for him in the end of course, and lock him away. But nothing on earth would bring Rosie back to life, and that triumph would remain with him until his own death.

He swilled the last of the whisky round his mouth, trying to clear the taste of fried onions and tinned peas. His decision made, he felt curiously at peace. Once Rosie was dead, he could pursue the Leopard more openly. Put advertisements in papers. Make enquiries at the Star. In the end, if only for a short time before he went to prison, they would come together: spend a week in Blackpool, perhaps, seeing the shows and walking the pier arm in arm. They'd stay in a nice boarding house, sea views from the window of their room: huge double bed. And late every night, a few drinks inside them, they would make use of that bed: bloody hell they would. Henry would do things to the Leopard she would never have imagined. Things he'd done to that girl in Marseilles, which made her cry sometimes, but beg him for more.

He paid the bill, scattering pound notes clumsily. Outside, the street lights seemed to be swaying gently, giant fireflies. And the dark buildings were tumbling towards him, crashing down like card houses.

'Steady,' Rosie was saying. He felt her appalling hand on his arm. Glancing down, he saw she was afraid. Stupid bloody woman. All her fault for making him come out on this daft expedition in the first place.

Somehow he managed to start the car. They lurched out of the gates of the car park. Rosie screamed, hurting his ears. Henry slammed on the brakes. They missed a passing lorry by a few inches. Swearing, Henry turned to Rosie, shouting it was all her fault. But Rosie merely smiled up at him, eyes full of fear, mouth askew in a courageous smile.

'That was the best evening I've had in years, love,' was all she said, and patted him on the arm.

Henry could have coped with anything but forgiveness. He felt the swift nausea of guilt, the stab of contrition. Only moments before he had been planning to kill her, now here she was declaring her pathetic pleasure in the evening. Well, he would make it up to her in his private way: he supposed she deserved that. He would drive as carefully as he was able, and buy her a drink in the Star on the way home. Thus killing two stones ...

The view before him had disintegrated into separate scraps, flakes of solid snow. But he tried. He gripped the steering wheel with rigid hands, barely touched the accelerator. Rosie was humming. *The Last Rose of Summer*, Henry thought it was.

He managed to negotiate the journey without mishap, but was in no condition to survive the weakness of anticipation that struck him as he entered the saloon bar. He felt his legs unsteady beneath him, and was grateful for Rosie's arm. Bill, alert to his condition, at once handed him a double whisky, and a shandy for Rosie. Henry swallowed it in two gulps, and felt an unnerving mixture of dizziness and strength.

He managed to keep his eyes quite steadily on the door. It swung open and shut many times, but the Leopard did not come. On the few occasions that he glanced at her, Henry noticed Rosie looked unhappy. Her face had the same kind of puffed up indignation as when, once long ago, they had gone down to the beach and misjudged the tide. She had scowled at the approaching water, powerless as King Canute to insist on its retreat. The whisky was making his memory wonderfully clear, Henry realised, and smiled to himself, knowing any indication of enjoyment in a pub would annoy.

They stayed till closing time. The tricky business of negotiating their way to the door was not helped by Henry having to bend himself almost double to ease the burn of disappointment in his chest. Rosie took his arm again, and outside the warm night air struck him savagely, renewing his weakness.

'Shall we walk, love?'

Rosie's voice echoed through a tunnel. Henry shook his head. He could never make it, walking.

Somehow he managed to get into the car. And there, the steering wheel between his hands, a wonderful sense of peace, or rescue, came upon him. This was no Morris Minor, but a ship of war, a destroyer. The kind of vehicle he was used to. If they went with the waves, kept to the swell, they would make it to port without mishap. Through the windscreen the full moon spun like a coin: heads, and he would win the Leopard. Tails, and they would drown. He started the engine.

But forces of gravity pulled against his ship in a way that was quite surprising. And this particular sea was cluttered with strange hazards he was not prepared for: mighty trees and solid shapes, like houses. He wrenched the steering wheel from left to right, so hard he could feel the pull of muscles in his shoulders. But instead of the sough of well navigated waves, horrible moans came from his left, Rosie's voice contorted with silly fear. There was a fleeting sensation of having come to rest, of poising on the edge of a wave before it sent them spinning. Henry wondered if they were home. He heard Rosie whimper. Then silence. Something warm gushed out of his ear, tickled his neck. He opened his mouth to apologise to the Leopard, but no words came. A bloody great wave crashed over him, submerging him in its blackness.

When Henry came round he was instantly aware of the familiar bustle of his wife beside him. She was struggling to open the door. The whole weight of her seemed to have covered his knees, and was uncomfortable. They were in a strange position. Slipped sideways, he thought. Must have been a dreadful storm.

Rosie turned to him. In the tremulous moonlight Henry could see blood on her cheek and an absurd smile of welcome.

'You all right, love?' she asked. 'I think you went out for a moment. We're in a ditch.'

Closing his eyes, no will to answer, Henry felt this to be an unnecessary statement of fact. There was nothing wrong with a ditch. The liquid on his neck was warm, and he was quite comfortable if he didn't move his shoulder. The noise of Rosie banging at the door to open it – stupid woman, she'd never had the knack – was rhythmic and comforting.

'Good thing we're insured,' she was saying, 'there's bound to be a bit of damage. Blood everywhere.'

Some time later Henry answered, 'Don't worry, it's all tomato ketchup.' But by then he was talking to himself. Rosie had managed to scramble out of the car, and was stumbling towards the nearest house for help.

It came very quickly, or it may have been a long time. Henry neither knew nor cared. All he wished was that people would stop interrupting his thoughts. He heard the whispers of rescuers, and saw faces cracked like mosaics by the moonlight. He felt himself being carried, he felt a searing pain in his shoulder. Then he recognised the steadiness of his own bed beneath him. Safely at anchor at last, he thought. Time now to dream, to tell the Leopard how he had braved the storm, brought them all back to land. She would be quite proud of him, he had no doubt of that.

'My Leopard,' he muttered out loud. And in the last seconds before sleep he saw not the Leopard's eyes, but Rosie's – wide, troubled. Uncomprehending, as always, the silly cow.

Brenda had had a rough night. It had begun well enough by she and Evans taking their supper on to the lawn of Wroughton House. Mrs Browne had said she would join them, but then she declared she had a headache and was going to bed early. She had given them a bottle of white wine, very cold and tasting of grapes. They drank it in paper cups. Evans said Mrs Browne looked white as a sheet, didn't she? He wondered if anything was the matter. His note of concern annoyed Brenda: but she kept her silence, not wanting an argument on an evening like this.

She lay on her back on the grass, smoking Woodbines. She liked the smell of the dry lawn, the boughs of the trees above them moving lazily in the sky, as if some invisible puppet man had little energy left to pull their strings. She liked pushing her hard-boiled egg into a mound of pepper, and sneezing at its sharpness; she liked the warmth in her limbs caused by the wine.

Evans lay close to her. The church clock struck nine, the sky deepened into shadow colours. Brenda found her thoughts wandering in their usual direction.

'Shall we?' she asked. Evans's fingers massaged through her hair, soothing, arousing.

'Not here,' he said. 'Not tonight.'

'Why ever not?'

'If Mrs Browne looked out of the window, she'd see us.'

'So?'

'I wouldn't like that.'

Brenda drew deeply on her cigarette. She quite liked the idea of Mrs Browne seeing them at it, herself.

'Prude,' she said. 'It wouldn't exactly surprise her.'

'Nor it would. But it would be unnecessary.'

Brenda could see he was trying to be patient, not to cross her. He suggested they went in. It was getting cool.

But in the bedroom the mood of excitement between them, frustrated by Evans's refusal to make love outside, vanished. Brenda was left full of resentment: she hated her romantic ideas to be quashed. Instead of undressing she sat in the only armchair and began to chide Evans for the inadequacies of their own house. The subject, she knew, was a red rag to a bull.

'It's going to have poky rooms, no room to swing a cat. No feeling of country, either, looking outside just to see a lot of other identical houses. No privacy. Prying neighbours, complaining about our hens. And there's no space on the plan for a washing machine. Where will we put the washing machine? If you think I'm going to spend my life doing all your bloody shirts by hand . . .' She went on and on, her voice harsh. Evans, at the window, back to her, said nothing.

Suddenly – she did not notice any precise moment when it

180

happened – the room was dark. She paused. Evans turned to her.

'If you don't like it,' he said quietly, 'if it's going to be as bloody awful as you make out, you can go.'

Brenda registered the menace in his voice. She stood up. Perhaps she *had* gone a bit far, all that wine.

'Oh, come on,' she said, 'you don't want to take me too seriously.' She touched his arm, tried to drag him towards the bed. But he would not move.

'I do, you know,' he said.

'Come *on*!' She was being endearing now. She gave him one of her desirous looks: that always won him over.

'No!' he shouted, and shook off her arm. Brenda recognised his anger, and was annoyed. She could bait him too easily.

'Shut up! You'll wake Mrs Browne.'

'Maybe.'

In the dim light from the window Brenda could see him smile, and the smile made her stiffen with misgivings.

'Take me, Evans,' she said, unbuttoning her shirt.

'I don't want you, not tonight.'

'You do.'

'I tell you, you bitch, I don't.'

Brenda buttoned up her shirt again. He was stubborn as they come, sometimes.

'I do believe it's Mrs Browne you fancy,' she said, mocking. 'You seem all concern for her, these days. Don't know why I didn't think of it before.'

'That's an idea,' said Evans, 'the beautiful Mrs Browne.' His calm was maddening.

'She's got no tits,' said Brenda. 'She's not your type.'

'Look, would you mind going now? I'd like a peaceful night's sleep.' He turned his back again, leaning his elbows on the high window ledge.

'And how am I supposed to get home, may I ask?'

'Walk.'

'While you screw Mrs Browne?'

'While I screw Mrs Browne, if that's what you like to think.'

'Christ, I despise you, Evans Evans. Fucking sod.'

She stumbled to the bedside table, picked up a vase of roses and threw it at him. Inaccurate with rage, her aim was wild. It hit a wall, broke on the bare boards round the edge of the carpet. In a shaft of moonlight Brenda could see three yellow blooms in a pool of water. Still Evans did not move.

'Get out before you smash the whole place up,' he said, and Brenda went to the door. She slammed it behind her.

Outside, shaking, she was grateful for the coolness of the night air. By the light of the full moon it was easy enough to see her way. She began to walk down the lane. Just outside the village she saw the shape of a car lying on its side in a ditch. As she came close to it she saw it was a Morris Minor, pale green, the same as Henry Evans's. She wondered if it could be his: he hardly ever went out in it, she knew, but perhaps he had taken it somewhere this evening and had had an accident. It was said in the village Henry was drinking a lot these days, though Evans had never mentioned it. At the sight of the car Brenda felt all her anger spent. Weariness, suddenly. What had it all been about? Should she turn back, climb into the double bed, ask to be forgiven? Should she tell Evans his parents' car was in a ditch?

Brenda hesitated. To go back and find the room empty would be unbearable, and judging by Evans's coldness tonight she had no doubt there was a good chance he would try his luck with Mrs Browne . . . who could not, of course, refuse him. No one in their right minds could refuse Evans, the irresistible sod. Oh God, in all her confusion, in all her regret at having behaved so stupidly, she wanted him. It took uncommon strength to keep walking in the direction of the flat.

Augusta Browne went to bed at eight o'clock. She drew the blinds, but the evening sky seeped through the lilac cotton making the room an aquarium of mauve shadowed light. She stretched a leg into the cool empty area of linen where Hugh should have been. The sheets hurt her skin. She shut her eyes and probed at the flesh of her cheeks with her fingers. Pain rankled far beneath, gnawing through the bone. The doctor had said she was suffering from migraineous neuralgia, and there was little he could do to help. Against the pain she was conscious of the smell of lavender and roses by her bed. After a while she slept, deeply.

Two hours later Augusta woke to exploding pains in the bones under her eyes, and in her jaw. The room was still not quite dark. She reached for two more pills and a glass of water. Above her she heard angry footsteps, then the slam of a door. She switched on her light and picked up her book, *Swann's Way*. She had intended this to be her Proustian summer, but reading increasingly hurt her eyes, and progress was slow. Now, the print blurred. Her eyes were filled with neuralgic tears – a common symptom, the doctor said – and she knew if she looked at them they would be hideously bloodshot. She closed the book and lay quite still, for any movement made the sheets prickle like thistles.

More footsteps. Evans was coming down the stairs from the attic. Augusta wondered if he was going after Brenda. They led a hopelessly dramatic life, as far as she could tell. Perhaps it stimulated them. It would exhaust her: all *she* required was interesting peace. The footsteps crossed the landing outside her bedroom, came right up to the door, then stopped. Silence. Augusta raised herself upon one elbow. There was a soft knock.

'Evans? Is that you? Come in.' Through the hammering of pain in her face she found it difficult to muster her voice.

The door opened. Evans came in. He stood just inside the huge room, sleeves rolled up, a V of reddish skin in the open collar of his shirt. His face was pale and hard. Augusta realised he could see her breasts. He was looking at them without shame. She switched off the light.

'Sorry,' she said, 'my head. It makes everything dazzle.'

'That's all right,' Evans replied, and in that moment August understood why Brenda loved him. His voice was infinitely caring. 'I saw your light and wondered how you were.'

'Not too bad.' There was no point in trying to explain the peculiar condition of the sheets.

'Nothing I can get you?'

'No, really, thank you.' Pause. 'Brenda's gone?'

'She went off in some kind of state.'

'It'll be better when everything's settled, perhaps. When you're in the house.' Augusta was aware of the futility of her observation.

'Daresay it will.' Evans rubbed at his eyes with a large hand. 'Well then, I'll leave you if you're sure there's nothing I can get you.' His voice was quiet, his shirt almost luminous, his kindness a distant balm. Augusta recognised it beyond the pain.

'Thank you, Evans,' she said.

'Goodnight, Mrs Browne.'

'Goodnight.'

He left the room, closing the door gently behind him. His formality in the dark made her feel quite stupid with gratitude. She closed her eyes and tried to sleep again.

It had been a sleepless night, bright with visions of Evans and Augusta Browne. Now, at seven-thirty in the morning, Brenda was light-headed and restless. She dressed and made a pot of tea, wondering how best to patch things up with Evans. There was a small fear within her, not consciously felt before, that one day soon she would provoke him too far. He would feel there was no safety in their future, and cast her out for good. Someone else would be mistress of the house, someone else might even breed chickens in the garden. The thought was intolerable. Brenda dug a spoon into a tea bag, watching its brown liquid spiral into the water.

Lark came into the room, waving a letter. Face like a ghost, she had: thumping dark shadows under her eyes.

Brenda could never understand Lark's perpetual tiredness. She went to bed early most nights, and slept long hours, and yet every morning she looked like death. Today she smiled an uncontainable smile. Brenda scowled back. She was in no mood for anyone else's good spirits. Whatever joy Lark wished to share she should not count on Brenda to be responsive, not this morning.

'It's come,' Lark said, rather breathlessly, sitting at the table. 'It's come at last! My first proposal!' She flapped the letter in Brenda's face.

Brenda reacted slowly. As far as she knew Lark had not been going out with anyone, and it seemed a funny way to propose, by letter.

'When's the happy day?' she asked.

'December the thirteenth. How about that?' Lark was reading the letter again, incredulous.

'Who's the lucky man?' Any other time Brenda might have cared. The flatness of her voice indicated that, this morning, she could not. Lark looked up.

'The what?'

'The man. You said a proposal.'

Lark laughed. 'That's all you ever think of, Bren. Not a *man*, idiot. Not that kind of proposal. Something much more exciting – the real thing. My first concert. They've asked me to sing.' She flushed a little, her voice unsteady.

'December the thirteenth? That's a long way ahead.'

Lark giggled. She seemed to be quite weak with pleasure.

'Perhaps,' she said, 'they thought I might be booked up if they left it any later.'

Brenda couldn't help smiling.

'Where is it? Albert Hall?'

'Not exactly.'

'They paying you a huge fee?'

Lark hesitated.

'They're not really paying me anything, in cash, like. But they're giving me supper, and as many drinks as I like. And they're paying me expenses. You know, a taxi.'

'A *taxi*? To London and back? Or Luton, or wherever?' Lark said nothing. 'I think that's bloody mean,' went on Brenda. 'Ridiculous. A person's got to earn their living. I should say no.'

'I've already written to say yes. It would be stupid to turn down my first chance, wouldn't it? I don't care about the money. Really I don't.'

Brenda sighed impatiently.

'Who are these people you're to sing for?' she asked.

'I'm not telling you. Please don't make me tell you. I want it to be a surprise. I'll send you complimentary tickets, of course. I'll see to it you and Evans get complimentary tickets.'

'Thanks,' said Brenda. 'And we'll throw flowers on to the stage and shout for an encore. Why don't we celebrate with bacon and eggs? I'm ravenous.'

'Couldn't eat a thing, myself, the excitement,' said Lark, 'but I'll get you some.' She went to the stove and broke two eggs into a frying pan.

Brenda's interest in Lark's concert expired. Her head was now aching: she needed comfort. She stirred her tea.

'Lark,' she said, 'what would you say were Evans's chances with Augusta Browne?'

Lark looked up from her cooking, puzzled.

'I should say absolutely none. Why?'

'Supposing Evans and I had had a bit of a ding-dong. Would he go off screwing her to spite me?'

''Course he wouldn't, silly. He's the faithful type.' She sounded quite certain, Brenda thought. But then Lark couldn't really know. She wasn't the type Evans would be attracted to, ever. 'Well, I mean,' Lark went on, 'I don't know Mrs Browne, do I? I've only seen her once or twice. But she doesn't look the sort to me who spreads it about.'

'You can never tell,' said Brenda. Lark put a plate of eggs and bacon down in front of her. 'Thanks. I'll never be able to do breakfasts like this for Evans. You'll have to come round every morning, once we're in the house.'

'Delighted, except after late night singing engagements.' Lark's merriment this morning was almost more than Brenda could take, but she supposed it would be mean to make a sarcastic remark. Instead she asked,

'If he succeeded, if he had her, do you think he'd tell me?'

''Course he wouldn't, idiot. What a daft idea. Men don't tell about the odd screw if it's going to get them into trouble.' She sounded quite definite again.

'Well, then, do you suppose I'd *know*? By instinct?' Brenda wiped her plate with a piece of bread and sucked up the runny egg yolk, in imitation of her Birmingham friends in roadside cafés. It was a habit which had always annoyed Evans but she made no effort to give up.

''Course you wouldn't. People are good at disguising things.'

'Then I shall make it my business to find out.'

'Come on, Bren. What's *up*?' Lark was a bit impatient.

'We had a row last night. All my fault, I suppose. He turned me out. He hinted he was going downstairs for a bit of comfort.'

'Nonsense!'

'So I think the thing to do is to go and see Mrs Browne today. Find out the truth from her. I'll take her some eggs, six large brown. If it turns out I'm wrong I won't say a word to Evans, and I don't imagine she will either.'

'I'm all for leaving the truth alone, myself, cases like that,' said Lark, 'but if you've got to go nosing about, that sounds like quite a good plan.'

'You've got to get at the truth if things are going to work for ever,' said Brenda. 'There's not many things I believe, but that's one of them.' She noticed there was sun on the red rooftops outside. Breakfast had calmed her. Lark filled both their cups with tea. Poor old Lark, she was good in a crisis. You could depend on her for support. She deserved a nice man to look after her, one day. She deserved someone who would make her understand the disadvantages of independence.

'Where do you think I should go for a dress?' Lark was saying.

'For a dress?'

'For the concert.'

'Oh, for the concert.'

'I was thinking of a pale grey, almost a white.'

'Tea-time, I think I'll go.'

'Go where?'

'Up to the house with the eggs.'

'You could ask her, perhaps, if she'd be interested in coming.'

'What to?'

'The concert, of course. I'm sure I could get her a complimentary ticket, too. I mean, seeing as they're not paying me.'

'I'll take her six of the big speckled ones,' said Brenda. 'Hope Wilberforce won't catch me.'

Lark got up and began to clear the table. For all their tiredness, her eyes were sparkling in the light of the September morning.

'Perhaps I'll go for a silver,' she said. 'Christmas time, that would be appropriate, I think.'

By dawn the worst of the pain had receded, leaving Augusta's face merely a dull ache, and a pulse beating in her temple. She got up and dressed, went outside, and breathed deeply. The lawns shimmered with dew. Spider webs spun like Catherine wheels among leaves, and the bulrushes by the pond were parted from their roots by a ground mist.

Augusta went to the walled garden at the back of the house. The mulberry tree, a wizened old thing when stripped of its foliage in winter, was now rich with geometric leaves. Among them clustered dark red berries, more than ever this year. Augusta picked one and ate it. Sour, still, and quite hard. The juice ran from the corner of her mouth. She dabbed at it, and it came off on her finger like blood. The colour of their mulberry mousses – how many had they eaten in four summers? – had been altogether paler. A creamy pink. Swaying, fragile things, surprisingly sharp. Hugh was very fond of mulberry mousse. (He considered the mulberry far superior to the strawberry.) This year, there had been no mousses. *Oh God, I'm in mourning for the best puddings of my life* . . . Augusta leant against the striated bark of the tree's trunk. Its leaves made a low canopy all about her, variegated greens. The private acts of solitary behaviour were beginning to interest her. A year ago, had anyone suggested she would one day rise at dawn and stand in melancholy fashion under the mulberry tree meditating upon puddings – why, she would have laughed them to scorn. Now, it seemed quite natural. Now, it was no longer shocking to contemplate burning down the house. She had thought about it several times during the past few days. She would set light to it, then go up to the woods and look back at the flames. There would be no saving it. Its old panelling would be devoured in a moment, but it would never know the indignity of being altered by the office men. That, at least, it would be spared.

Christ, though Augusta, am I now deranged? (The last owner of the house, soon after she left, was sent to an asylum.) But there is a talent in endings. Some people have it: she felt she was not one of them. Some people can love, and leave without regret. Some people can achieve flights into the void: others fear swift grounding. If parting is a smaller death, there are few adequately equipped for that kind of dying. Augusta knew herself to be unprepared, and feared her own weakness. For a start, she could not persuade herself to accept the facts. The steady progress towards the precipice remained unbelievable, a nightmare from which she expected to wake every morning. And yet it *was* true. The contract was signed. Hugh had telephoned to break the news yesterday.

Augusta slipped to the ground, sat on the soft earth, supporting her back against the tree's trunk. She was weak from lack of food, yet eating nauseated her. She was drained by the storms of neuralgia which, on occasions, made her groan out loud: and as one unused to pain or illness of any kind, she was angered by their force, and by her inability to cast them out. Now, even as she sat beneath the mulberry tree listening to the church clock strike seven, Augusta felt the absurdity of her own position. But she was powerless to change it. To remain where she was, undisturbed, the tree's prisoner, was her only inclination. She would be quite happy to die there . . .

> *And mourn not me*
> *Beneath the yellowing tree*
> *For I shall mind not, slumbering peacefully.*

As it was, she remained there all day. Sometimes she dozed. Sometimes, quite awake, she rubbed at the grass with her hand, and made small holes in the earth with her finger. At midday she felt the heat beneath the leaf canopy grow denser, and needles of sunlight penetrated here and there, making speckled shadows on her legs. By late afternoon it was quite cool. Augusta got up at last. Stiffly, she returned to the house. Swallows were gathering on the telephone wires and pigeons, their iridescent breasts puffed up in competition with the pinkish sky, preened themselves on the roof. She marvelled at the benevolence of God, or whoever, providing such an evening at the end of a lost day. Now, all she required was someone to talk to for an hour or so – someone to exorcise, temporarily, the useless ravings of her mind. She settled on a window seat in the bathroom. Outside, the distant chimneys of the brickworks sent spires of white smoke into the sky. The lawn was the lavender colour that grass becomes to indicate autumn. Augusta concentrated on willing someone to arrive. Anyone would do.

Brenda had no trouble in making off with the six largest, brownest eggs she could find. Wilberforce was not about. She had seen him little of late. In fact, his interest in his farm seemed to have declined. Weeds grew in profusion in the yard. Buildings rotted, hinges grew stiff with rust. There were several holes in the roof of the chicken house – Brenda's only concern. She would have to persuade Wilberforce to mend them before winter, but felt disinclined to approach him. She had decided to put off the tiresome day until the weather changed.

Brenda walked up the back drive of Wroughton House, carrying her carton of eggs, pleased to think that no one she knew had seen her on the way. She wanted this meeting with Mrs Browne to be private: above all it was essential Evans never discovered her plan.

She noticed the sickly smell of roses – hundreds of them tumbled over the wall that divided the drive from the kitchen garden – and the buzz of swallows on the telephone wires. Both things annoyed her. Irritation prickled along her spine. She was on edge: had been all day. The mental pictures of Evans having it off with Mrs Browne last night, just because of a bit of a disagreement, were enough to get anyone down. Not that she was of a jealous nature. Jealousy was not a thing she would succumb to, it made everyone so ugly. Though, to be truthful, when it came to Evans, a weird anger sometimes overcame her at the thought of his fancying anyone else.

Inside the house it was wonderfully cool. Brenda shouted to Mrs Browne. No answer. Silence. She went through the door that led to the front hall, clogs clicking on the flagstone floor. There, from the drawing-room, she could hear the melancholy whine of old dance music. Awful thirties stuff. Almost gave her the spooks, music like that playing in an empty house.

There was no one in the drawing-room. It looked as if it had been deserted all day. The other downstairs rooms were empty, too: each one smelling of roses. In Mrs Browne's study the windows were open and an ostrich-feather quill pen on the desk fluttered in a small breeze. Creepy as anything, thought Brenda, shutting the door quickly behind her. She was glad she would never be able to afford such a house herself. Thank heavens for the inventors of the ordinary estate.

She went upstairs, saw the bathroom door open, and crossed the landing. Mrs Browne was huddled up on the window seat, a silhouette against the huge window. Brenda knocked at the open door and went in. She held out the carton, aware that she trespassed upon some kind of private reflection.

'I've brought a few eggs,' she said. 'Large brown.'

Augusta turned towards her, her face conveying complete amazement. In spite of its suntanned skin, Brenda observed it was horribly pale. Unhealthy. Remindful of Lark.

'How kind, Brenda . . . I'm quite out of eggs, too, and somehow I didn't manage to go shopping today.' She smiled.

Now she was here Brenda wondered how best to get round to the subject that had brought her. The words she had been rehearsing all day to herself in the chicken house seemed to have fled her mind. There was a long silence while Mrs Browne opened the carton and looked at the eggs.

'Thank you so much,' she said. 'I shall boil two for supper.'

There were built-in cupboards all along one wall of the bathroom, and one of the doors was open. Brenda could see a mass of dresses squashed together: pale colours, mostly. Summer cottons and winter velvets, all muddled. She sighed. Some people had all the luck.

'Are you feeling better?' she asked at last. 'I mean, your headache, last night . . .? It must have been bad to go to bed so early.'

'Oh, yes, thank you. It's much better today.'

'You look a bit tired.'

'Do I?'

Brenda wondered why she didn't get up – normally she was so full of energy – and suggest they go downstairs.

'Evans and I had a lovely picnic supper on your lawn,' she said, 'but then we ended up rowing.' Augusta looked surprised. 'It's often like that,' Brenda went on. 'I don't know what gets into us, really. Anyhow, I hope it didn't wake you.

I made rather a noise, leaving.'

'I heard something, I think,' said Augusta. 'But I was awake anyway. Evans saw my light on, actually, and came and asked me if there was anything he could do, which was kind of him. Then the second lot of pills knocked me out.'

Her resounding truthfulness left Brenda weak and foolish. Well! All that daft worry for nothing. She might have known it, had she thought less hastily. Evans, for all his silly threats, was too decent a man to lay a finger on someone else. And Mrs Browne, of course, was not the type to entertain passes from those outside her own world, even if Evans had been so unwise as to approach her. She felt herself blushing.

A breeze came through the open window, stirring Mrs Browne's long hair and making the skirts of some of the dresses in the cupboard to dance a little.

'Lordy,' said Brenda, to change the subject and disguise her confusion, 'you've got enough in there for a film star, haven't you?'

Mrs Browne got up, then. She went to the cupboard and opened the door wider. Several of the lighter materials fluttered quite hard.

'Far too many,' said Augusta. 'I never throw anything away. They go back years . . . Goodness knows what I shall do with them when we leave. Give them away, I suppose.' She took a dress down from the rail and held it out – a chiffon gathering of indeterminate greys: a lot of pretty rags, it looked like, to Brenda. Augusta was swishing it about like a feather duster. '*A Midsummer Night's Dream* sort of dress, I think, don't you? It might have been worn by Peaseblossom or Cobweb or Moth . . . better than by me.'

'Oh, no,' said Brenda, 'it would look lovely on you, I can imagine.' She wondered if after all this time alone Mrs Browne had gone a bit funny in the head. Her eyes seemed very large, distant, as if she was addressing William bloody Shakespeare himself instead of her, Brenda.

'It was Hugh's favourite of them all,' Augusta was saying, holding it up, unmoving now, in front of her. 'Where on earth would I ever wear it again?'

At that moment inspiration struck Brenda blindingly.

'My friend Lark,' she said, 'you know about Lark? Well, she's my friend.' The impact of her own idea confused her. 'She's a singer, a marvellous singer. She's going to do her first concert in December, some huge hall somewhere, and she's looking for a silvery dress. I wonder if I could buy it for her? She's just your size.'

'Give it to her,' said Augusta, at once.

'No really . . .'

'Go on, please.' Quite firm, she handed the dress to Brenda.

'That's terribly kind of you. You can't imagine how pleased Lark will be. She'll get you tickets, of course, for the concert.'

'I should like that,' said Augusta. 'December . . . I leave in January.'

Brenda followed her out of the room and downstairs. Enfeebled for a moment by relief at the news about Evans, she was now exhilarated by her gesture towards Lark. Also, she felt that her short encounter with Mrs Browne in the bathroom had established an especial bond between them Evans could never achieve. Boldness overcame her.

'If you don't mind me asking, I don't like to be nosey, but all those parties you used to have . . . all those people here. Why don't you have them down any more? It would be more cheerful, like. This big house.'

'Ah,' said Augusta. She stood quite still in the hall, listening to the music from the drawing room. 'I suppose it's because I'd like them to remember it as it was.'

'There's something in that,' said Brenda, privately thinking the idea was barmy, 'though how you stick this place all alone I don't know. I'd go potty.'

Augusta smiled, and opened the front door. Beside her Brenda was conscious of feeling very large, big breasted, clumsy, too healthy. She understood there was no point in trying to prolong the visit, much though she would have liked to carry on chatting: she'd never met anyone so peculiar as Mrs Browne in all her life. But she looked very tired, and clearly wanted to be alone again with her boiled eggs. They said goodbye and Brenda left. Her plan was to return to the flat and lay the dress on Lark's bed. She would then go out somewhere for a while, and return later to find Evans waiting for her, a bit anxious, perhaps. It would be no bad thing to make him suffer a little. Then they would have a nice evening to make up for last night. They would take Lark with them – she'd be all of an excited dither about the dress – for a drink in the Star. Later, Evans might be persuaded to go back to the Hilton. They hadn't been there for weeks, and soon it would be too cold. And tonight she particularly fancied the barn, more than their bed in the attic. She felt randy as a cat. She'd give Evans his money's worth tonight, if she could keep her hands off him till closing time.

The bus arrived with lucky timing. Brenda sat on a warm seat whose stuff scratched the back of her thighs, the filmy dress flung over her knees. She lit a Woodbine, blew the smoke slowly out of her nostrils. She felt upon her the admiring gaze of other passengers – warming, to be honest, as she anticipated the pleasures of the evening ahead.

Lark had not felt so well for weeks. All morning she had hummed at her typewriter, counting the minutes till the lunch hour. Then she had made a dash round the shops in a preliminary search. It was disappointing, as she had told herself it would be. Not the right time of year for silver dresses, they all said. Come back nearer Christmas. But Lark knew she could not wait that long. She decided to go to Luton on her next Saturday off. Or, if that failed, to London.

She walked back to the flat, singing all the way, the only pain in her stomach caused by hunger. There had been no time to eat anything since breakfast. She planned her evening: a toasted Marmite sandwich and a glass of gin while watching *Coronation Street*. Then the Elgar concert on Radio 3 while she did her nails and thought more about the dress. She would also make a new list of songs to sing – she had already made three and discarded them. Oh, there was much to do. With a real concert ahead, the tempo of the hours was marvellously changed.

After the glare of the sun outside it took Lark some moments to accustom her eyes to the dimness of her room. Its shadows were split by the Venetian blinds. Only the massed geraniums shone scarlet as ever. On the bed lay a scant little dress, limp, bedraggled, reminding Lark of a dead bird left out in the rain.

She paused, blinked – it was still there, no hallucination. She picked it up, not understanding. Wisps of chiffon fluttered about, different tones of silvery grey. Without thinking, as if in a dream, Lark ripped off her skirt and shirt, and pulled it over her head. There was a faint smell of expensive scent, the cool swish of the silk lining on her bare breasts. She went to the mirror: face, neck and arms all horribly white and thin, she thought, but the dress fitted perfectly. She stroked its skirt gently with both hands, to check its existence, expecting it to expire like a puff of smoke. But still it remained. Incredulous, she stood without moving for a long time.

Then, footsteps outside. Brenda! Of course, Brenda. Who else could have done such a thing? Brenda was the dearest sweetest girl alive. She had always known it from the moment she had met her in that café two years ago. For all her funny gruff ways, her forgetfulness and dreadful untidiness, she was the kindest girl in the world

'Oh, *Brenda*!' she cried, and flung open the door. Evans stood there, worried face.

There was no time for Lark to rechannel her delight, to reach for calm. She threw herself upon Evans, clinging to his neck like a small monkey. She kissed his cheeks, his mouth, uttering incomprehensible explanations. For a second she felt him catch his breath, harden. Then, roughly, he pushed her from him.

'What's up?' he said. 'What are you all dressed up like a dog's dinner for, then?' His eyes went all over her, puzzled.

He followed her into the bedroom and shut the door behind him.

'Brenda gave it to me,' she said. 'It must have been Brenda, it can't have been anyone else. For my concert. They've asked me to sing, you see.' She blushed under his look.

'It's beautiful, Lark,' he said, eventually. 'You look smashing, really. Never seen you look like that before.'

Then Lark was sitting on the bed crying. The surprising tears had come too quickly to check: they dripped on to the dress spotting it like rain. Brenda's kindness, Evans's approval -- it was all too much. Evans sat on the bed beside her, put an arm round her shoulder.

'Now leave off that noise,' he said, 'for heaven's sake. You'll spoil your looks.'

Lark managed a smile, felt her tears wetting Evans's shirt. *I love you, I love you, I love you. Oh, Evans, I don't half love you.*

'Can you get a couple of glasses?' was all she sobbed, 'and we'll have some celebration gin.'

Evans gave her his handkerchief and went off to the other room. Lark stayed in her dress, and they sat watching television, drinking their gin neat in respect of the occasion. Brenda arrived back some time later and admitted to being fairy godmother, but would not say where she had found the dress. She was surprised Lark did not guess, though her delight was so abundant all rational thought was impossible. Lark agreed to come with them for a drink at the Star. It was only with great difficulty they persuaded her to change back into her old clothes. She would try the dress on for an hour or two every night until the concert, she said, to keep proving its existence. Reluctantly she slipped out of it, head beautifully silvered by gin, now: the best evening for years.

Much later Evans and Brenda lay at the top of the Hilton. The harvest long over, the barn was almost full of bales of straw. They had had to climb high to find a suitable platform: the rafters of the roof were only a few feet above them.

Cobwebs, they could see by the light of the moon, dangled close. The occasional scuffle of mice was the only noise.

Brenda had been at her most insatiable. Evans had often thought it was not worth letting her have a night off: it resulted in such demands when they met again. But he was proud always to be able to quell her desires in the end. She lay quietly now in his arms, naked, coppery head on his chest, smelling of chicken feed and essence of bluebell, the two scents most dear to him in the world. He hoped she would not draw away just yet and reach for her cigarettes. There were things to tell her.

'Good news and bad news,' he said.

'Oh?'

'Mum and Dad had an accident last night. Dad put the car in the ditch.'

'I thought it might have been theirs I saw,' said Brenda. 'Are they all right? Why didn't you tell me before?'

'Didn't want to. You weren't in the mood, and Lark full of beans and that. They're not too bad. Dad bruised, and a cracked rib. He'll have to be in bed a few days. Mum's a bit shaken, but that's all.'

'How did it happen?'

Evans paused.

'I didn't like to ask. Dad's been a bit under the weather just lately.' So disloyal a confession he would confide to no one but Brenda.

'I heard.'

'What did you hear?'

'That . . . like you said. He's been a bit under the weather.'

'Don't let anyone tell you anything else.'

'No.'

'Promise, Bren?'

'Promise.'

Evans drew her closer to him and kissed her hair.

'Funny thing,' he said. 'I was in with them a while, this evening, before coming over to fetch you. I was standing by Dad's bed, Mum was downstairs. He didn't say much. Well, he never does. Then he takes this fob-watch from the table, a bloody great gold fob-watch, been in the family years, and he says he wants me to have it. He says it's no use to him any more. It goes all right, right as rain. But he doesn't want it any more. So I pick it up, listen to its tick, admire it, say that's very kind, Dad. He looks at me in a funny way, almost as if he can't see me. Then – you might not like this bit – I don't want you to leave it to Brenda, he says, or to your son if you have one. I want you to leave it to someone else. A very remarkable woman. You'll know who I mean if you think about it hard.'

'Who did he mean?'

'Don't ask me. Couldn't think for the life of me. Still can't.'

'Why didn't you ask him?'

'I did. But he didn't seem to hear. He seemed to fall asleep. Maybe he was asleep all the time, talking in his sleep. Suffering from shock, perhaps.'

'You know what I think? I think he means your Mum.'

Evans laughed. Suddenly the mystery cleared.

''Course he does! That's what he means. Don't know why I didn't get it at once. He finds it so difficult saying things straight, Dad. He's sometimes very puzzling. Anyhow . . .' He paused to kiss Brenda again. 'Know what I'm going to do with it?'

'No. What? Go on. Stop . . . all that and tell me.'

'I'm going to sell it.'

'Never!' Brenda stiffened with shock.

'I'm going to sell it, I tell you. What does my mother want with a man's watch? What do I want with it? I could get £300 for that watch tomorrow. With £300 . . . Get my meaning?'

'The deposit?'

'The deposit and a bit to spare. What do you think?'

The very idea was an aphrodisiac to Brenda. She ran a hand over Evans's cold buttocks, and along his thigh.

'Marvellous. No more worry.'

'So we can be in by January if they keep to schedule.'

'In January . . . That's lovely. But stop talking about the house just now.' Brenda sighed.

Evans raised himself upon one elbow and looked down at her. He picked up a single piece of straw from her stomach and threw it away. She had the largest darkest eyes he'd ever seen, a beautiful shining mouth that teased even in repose. He put a hand over one of her breasts, flicked at the nipple in the way she liked. He had no thoughts now but his love for her, no sensations other than an exuberant calm, knowing he could now provide for her. He would not let her down. She could do what she liked: rant at him, throw things, slam doors, quibble. But she would not shake him off. Never.

'Sorry about last night,' she was saying, voice husky as when in mourning for a dead chicken.

'Oh, that,' he said. 'That was last night, wasn't it?'

They quickened simultaneously, as was their way. Their flesh had cooled in the night air. Summer was over.

'I love you, you minx,' said Evans.

'So you bloody should,' said Brenda. 'Now shut up talking, will you, and get on with it.'

Henry stayed in bed for two days, then, against the doctor's orders, got up. He ached all over. His ribs were strapped with bandages, one eye was badly bruised, and there were cuts on his hands. It hurt to move. But Henry saw no chance of recovery in the claustrophobic atmosphere of his bedroom, Rosie fussing in every few minutes to rearrange things that were perfectly all right as they were, and being a general nuisance. Besides, the last of the whisky had gone, and Rosie refused to buy more. And what Henry needed, he knew, to get himself back on the road, was a good stiff drink.

He left the house when Rosie was out shopping. It was painful to walk, and his progress was slow, but he was glad to be out again. It was early October by now: leaves turning, sun still bright in the hard air. Good time, October. Best time of year, autumn. Going to the brickworks, early mornings on his bicycle, Henry remembered enjoying the sharpness of the countryside for a few weeks before the clamminess of November set in. He used to note with some satisfaction the progress in the fields he passed on his journey: Long Corner, a broad sweep of stubble that led up to its barn stuffed with hay, held particular memories that sometimes came dancing back on an October morning. The barn had been built when he was a lad, and had housed many a secret exploration between his friends and their pubescent girls. He himself had lain in the hay with one Lily, a girl of blubbery flesh and breath that smelt of acid drops. She had shrivelled into a mangey spinster, Lily: Henry saw her collecting her pension sometimes. But she kept their secret well, it had to be said. Her watery eyes gave no indication that she remembered those Sunday afternoons when they were both fourteen: but then perhaps she didn't.

Lily had given pleasure to half a dozen boys before Henry came along: for him it was the first time, too quick, but unforgettable. With Rosie, of course, it had been quite different. He had always fancied Rosie for her gentle mind rather than her polite body. He had scarcely touched her before they married for fear of ruffling her religious beliefs. She used to whimper, slightly, lying on the ground in the bluebell woods, but if Henry made to reward her desire she would smack at his hand as if it was an insect, chiding at him for being too fresh in their engaged state. He would lie back and think wistfully of the way Lily used to squirm in the barn, and of the passionate girl in Marseilles. Sometimes, home from the brickworks, he would report to Rosie the state of the fields: Long Corner was under plough, he would say, or they'd planted wheat in Bray's Field. But she never seemed interested: earth, sea, bricks, held no pleasure for her, as Henry learnt over the years, and so had given up encouraging her to understand them.

As it was too early for the Star to be open, Henry went to Mr Daly's office behind the ironmonger's shop. It was a private place, the office. Crammed with old papers and bits and pieces, a terrible mess, quite unlike home. Above the desk hung a 1954 calendar, a picture of ducks on the Cam. Cambridge, Henry had thought lately, would be a good place to take the Leopard – probably she would prefer it to Blackpool. There was a train timetable somewhere . . . he might look up a train. The Morris Minor was in no condition to make the journey to Cambridge, or indeed anywhere else.

Henry shuffled among the papers, pushing aside a bottle of dried ink, an assortment of pens with rusty nibs, a bag of screws and some lengths of fine chain. It pleased him to be back. No one could worry him here, he could do things in his own time. Daly would be in with a mug of tea, shortly, then he would go through the books before opening time. Regret-fully – for he liked to do things that had some small con-nection with the Leopard, even though she was unaware of his existence – Henry gave up his search for the railway timetable, and turned to the first of the accounts books. In his absence Mr Daly had been filling them in each night. They were, Henry noticed at once, quite illegible. The writing was blurred, as if it had been left out in the rain. Henry rubbed his eyes. There was no improvement. The figures remained unclear to him. He remembered, then, he had had difficulty reading the paper yesterday. Come to think of it, ever since the accident his eyes had been giving him trouble. At this rate he'd have to arrange a private visit to an optician: one thing he couldn't tolerate would be Rosie's concern.

The door opened. Daly stood there, two mugs of tea in his hands. Their steam had misted his glasses.

'Back on the road, then? Better, are you? I reckoned you'd be away a week or so.'

'Mending nicely,' said Henry. Daly put one of the mugs on the desk, scattering a clump of drawing-pins. 'Thanks. Things all right here?'

'So so. Can't hope for too much seeing as the country's in the hands of the Unions.'

'No,' said Henry. The tea scalded his aching ribs, but

there was comfort in the beginnings of their ritual conversation.

'Small shopholder's bloody strangled.'

'He is, too,' agreed Henry.

'This rate, I'll be putting up the shutters within the next year or so.'

Henry looked up, surprised. It had always been Daly's habit to declare he would not be beaten by the system.

'As a matter of a fact,' Daly went on, 'while on that subject, there's something I shall have to speak of . . . to you, personally,' he added. He took off his glasses and polished the steam from them with a handkerchief streaked with grease. Henry sensed his awkwardness.

'Oh, yes?'

'It's the books, Henry.'

'The books?'

'There've been mistakes. A lot of mistakes.'

'Mistakes?'

'Errors. Call them what you will.' There was a silence between the two men. They sipped their tea, then, simultaneously breaking it. 'You've always been so accurate, you see. I was surprised. But these last weeks, there's no doubt, there've been bad mistakes.'

'It's been my eyes,' said Henry, at last. 'They've been giving trouble.'

'Ah,' said Daly. 'You should get them seen to.'

Henry ran a finger round his collar. The tea was unusually bitter. The smell of paraffin in the room almost stifled him. The words on the piles of papers all about him were a jumble. But clear in his mind was the picture of someone else checking his books. Someone else sneaking in, after hours, double-checking his calculations at Daly's request. Some noseyparker accountant disputing his sums, criticising the impeccable neatness of the figures he had taken much pride in for the last few years.

'Why didn't you say something about this before?' he asked, at last. 'Why didn't you come to me, direct like, instead of checking up behind my back?'

'It wasn't a matter of checking up behind your back . . .'

'It bloody was.'

'Now look here, Henry. No need to take offence. We've had a good working partnership these last years, and I wouldn't like us to fall out. I'd be very sad about that, very sad indeed. I mean, we've always understood each other. But lately, common knowledge, you've been under the weather. Not your former self –'

'Common knowledge?' Henry felt weakness splinter his ribs.

'Well, people have been saying this and that.'

'What manner of things have they been saying?'

'Nothing offensive, mark my word. Nothing offensive. You're a well respected member of the community, take it from me. But it's been noted you've been spending a lot more time than usual at the Star. And on some occasions . . .'

'Ah, I understand,' said Henry.

'Well, any of us, some occasions, human weakness . . . I know how it is. Used to drink a bit too much myself, years ago.'

'Did you.' Henry's answer was too flat to be called a question. Daly gripped his mug with both hands, as if to brace himself.

'And the long and the short of it is this, Henry,' he said, 'I am terminating your job.'

Terminating. Terminal. A word from the world of trains and fatal illness. A chilly word. A word that pushed you outside, gave you the sack, said you'd lost your chance. Meant the end. No more peaceful mornings in the unruly office, – walls the colour of dead skin, as they sometimes seemed to Henry – crouched happily over the lined paper, ballpoint pressing into the spongey texture, adding up out loud, tongue slipping over dry lips between each column . . .

'I understand,' said Henry. When the end of something came, there was no point in hanging about. When he'd left the girl in Marseilles, he remembered, she'd stood on the jetty, waving her handkerchief, wiping her eyes: but he had turned away quickly, gone below decks. No use prolonging such moments. He stood up, put out a hand to Daly. They shook, quite friendly.

'Goes without saying, I'm very sorry about this,' said Daly.

'Quite,' said Henry.

'And I shall of course be sending you a suitable cheque – a small golden handshake, you might call it. A token of my appreciation.' He smiled slightly: teeth all shades of brown and black. 'Expect, anyway, you'll have no difficulty, man of your qualifications, finding another little job. Must be awkward, retirement, for someone like you.'

Henry attempted a return smile, but it turned out to be a grimace against the pain in his ribs.

'I shall do very nicely, I've no doubt,' he said, and glanced finally at the ducks on the Cam. 'Might even find time to visit Cambridge. A thing I've always had in mind.'

'Ah, Cambridge, now,' said Daly, and opened the door for Henry to pass through into the shop.

Outside, the air was invigorating, the sky still blue. He'd been worried for some time, of course, that calculating hadn't come so easily to him, that on certain days VAT confused his head considerably. But he had hoped Daly would not notice, would not catch him out. He had hoped he could have hung on, struggling through the figures, somehow, until the day of the Leopard, when everything in the world would be clear again. Well, luck had turned against him. It was a blow, but what was one more blow? Only problem was what to tell Rosie. The last thing he wanted was her sympathy. He'd have to make sure to avoid that. Think up some story over a drink.

Henry looked at his watch. Opening time. A double Scotch, he needed, to dull the bloody ache in his ribs, and to clear the water in his eyes. Slowly, he set off in the direction of the Star.

That afternoon it was Rosie's turn to do the church flowers.

This was a duty shared by three ladies of the village, and Rosie, allowing herself the small vanity, had always felt herself to be the superior arranger. Today she had picked a bunch of shaggy-headed chrysanthemums from her own garden, bronze and claret, and a few yellows, as bright as sunflowers. There was in fact a small supply of petty cash available to buy the altar flowers, but Rosie felt it a matter of pride never to use it. When there were no flowers in her own garden she made do with hedgerow things and, at rose time, she took advantage of Mr Browne's kind offer, when he moved to the house some years ago, to help herself from the garden of Wroughton House.

She stretched up now, patting the flowers into place, balancing their stems in the tall vases of golden china bequeathed to the church by a former vicar's wife. A shaft of late sun came through the stained glass window, fretting her bare hands and arms with blues and reds and greens. It was a peaceful place, and she liked to be there alone. She liked to run her hands along the altar cloth, feel the softness of its satin, and the sudden hard ridges of embroidery; arum lilies beautifully depicted in gold thread some hundred years ago. It had been just such an afternoon, she recalled, that she and Henry had stood looking up at the lighted candles on the altar, promising they would stick to each other for better or for worse, and Rosie had had no doubts in her heart that any event could change their resolution. Oh, it had been a happy day. Friends and relations squashed into the house for sherry and beer and sausages and wedding cake: the taste of her mother's powdery tears as they had kissed each other goodbye. And all the village, it seemed, had turned out to wave goodbye.

They had been driven away in an old upright taxi, its windscreen so thick with confetti the driver had had to use the wipers to clear his view, to a small village not far from Wroughton. They spent the weekend in a simple hotel run by a distant aunt: it stood on the banks of a river, and there seemed to be the permanent noise of river birds outside their window. What a night that had been! Rosie on her knees at the altar, sweeping up fallen leaves, felt herself blush. Such memories were out of place in church, she told herself, but, and may the Lord forgive her, Henry had done such wonderful things. She paused in her sweeping, newly aware of the hideous shapes of the hands that held the dustpan and brush. What had she done to be so cursed? Had it not been for *them*, there might have been years of wonderful nights. As it was, once she had become pregnant, Henry's interest in any kind of night-time activity began to wane. Rosie had never liked to ask him what was the matter, of course, and tried to believe him when he pleaded tiredness at the end of a long day in the brickworks. But sometimes she caught him looking at her hands, as she sat by the fire sewing or knitting. He never said anything, but Rosie knew. She could tell by his look he regretted having married a woman with such ugly hands, however much, in those early years, he claimed he loved her (which, in truth, was not very often).

Rosie walked down the altar steps and closed the wooden gate behind her. Now, there was little hope. She might persevere – indeed, nothing would stop her determined perseverance – but there was no real hope. And faith without hope was of little value. This afternoon, forcing herself to face the reality of the situation, Rosie felt a heaviness of step. Her feet were clumsy, unusually noisy in the quiet of the aisle. There seemed to be a weight in her stomach. Neither the thought of God's great love, nor of the jam sponge she had made for tea, could lighten her darkness. She contemplated kneeling for a moment and praying for strength. But there was a danger that Mrs Jackson would come in to neaten the prayer books, as she bossily took it upon herself to do most afternoons, and catch Rosie at it. Well, to Rosie's mind prayer was a private matter, except when you were part of a congregation, and she didn't wish Mrs Jackson or even the vicar himself to see her down on her knees: knowing their minds, they'd instantly suspect she was in some kind of trouble and, God forgive her, she'd do anything to avoid *that*.

She returned the dust-pan and brush to the cupboard in the vestry, and threw away the bunch of dead flowers which Bridget Goff, bless her heart, had made a real mess of last week. Then she walked home to get the tea.

She found Henry asleep in his chair, mouth open, spittle running down his chin. Rosie uttered a small cry of relief: at least he was safely home. When she had returned from shopping this morning and found him gone, and then he had not appeared for lunch, she had guessed where he could be found and had steeled herself not to go in search of him. But it had been a worrying time because he was still in a shocked condition. The doctor said he should have had a week in bed before trying to resume normal life. And there he was, obstinate old thing, plain defying the doctor's orders. Though of course it was his spirit Rosie loved him for. All she could wish . . . and, apart from that, that he would let her know his movements, sometimes, to save her so much worry.

Rosie knelt on the floor beside him and gently dabbed at his chin with her handkerchief. He stirred abruptly, then swiped at her with his arm, pushing her roughly away.

'Bloody woman!' she heard him mutter. He moaned, as if the gesture had hurt his ribs.

Rosie gasped. She stood up, backing away from him. He opened his eyes. They were bloodshot, watering. His mouth moved, but whatever he said was incomprehensible. A terrible word came to Rosie, then: a word which had been trying to press its way through to her consciousness for weeks, and which she had kept rejecting. But now it screamed through her mind, wild, frightening: *drunk*.

Henry was absolutely drunk.

The heaviness Rosie had felt in church fled from her. Scarcely knowing what she did, she ran from the kitchen, coatless, slamming the door behind her. She hurried back to the churchyard, made her way to the dark corner where her mother was buried between two yew trees. Rosie flung herself down upon the tombstone. The chill of its marble flared through her thin skirt and blouse, and stung her forehead. She wept for a while, not knowing whether to call upon God or her dead mother: feeling neither would understand her horror. Henry seemed to be set upon a course from which there was no turning back. She doubted all the love she could give him could save him now. She should have faced the truth sooner, months ago: consulted the doctor, tried to talk to Henry. What had led him to this? It was as if there was some canker within him, consuming him, taking him further and further from the one who loved him with her whole being . . .

After some time Rosie dragged herself into a sitting position, and rested her head and hands upon the headstone. It was a bulky cross made of rough granite, and hurt her skin. Feeling the pain, Rosie dragged her hands along its arms till the pain increased. Then she turned her hands and scraped their backs along the cross, drawing blood. They looked as if they had been dragged through brambles, the blood a pattern of small dots. Rosie gazed unbelieving at what she had done. Then she stood up, noticing a ladder in her stocking. It was quite cold by now. The sun was setting behind the church. She shivered, wondering at her own behaviour. The strain, she thought, these weeks, had been too much: she must take a hold on herself. Never again would she give in to such a display of hysteria. Disgraceful, Rosie, her mother would have said. Quite disgraceful. She'd be turning in her grave.

Rosie walked back along the church path, calmed by her own shame. She would wash the blood from her hands and get Henry's tea as if nothing had happened: the weak moment would be banished from her mind. And this evening, when Henry returned to the Star, she would cut herself a new pair of mittens. Now, she was quite resigned.

By November the office men were taking further dreadful liberties. They sent men to measure up the rose garden, where they planned to build a prefabricated extension to house the typists. They sent men to judge the state of the elms, and the brick walls round the kitchen garden, and the ailing fig tree. They would stand in the sweep of drive by the front door, scratching at their nylon collars, envisaging the neo-Georgian porch with which the architect planned to improve it. Augusta, from an upstairs window, would watch them. They took no notice of her.

She would watch them and remember the day of the move to the house: it was May, very warm, white butterflies hovering like occasional snowflakes about the lavender, the village grocer bringing loaves, assuming they would need bread. In and out of the house she and Hugh went, directing where the furniture should be placed, always seeming to agree.

By evening the rooms were furnished though there were no curtains and many of the walls were still shabby with old paint. Among the piles of unsorted stuff in the hall Augusta found vases, and instantly arranged bunches of lilac: so that her earliest memory of the house included the smell of flowers. Hugh, she observed that night, already wore the face of a squire: he had laughed, said what nonsense, she was the grand one. They had wandered about till it was quite dark, carrying candles into unlighted rooms, making their endless plans; it had taken a long search to find this house, and buying it, they both knew, was probably financially irresponsible. But they were full of mutual optimism. Something would happen. Money would come from somewhere. They would do things slowly. After all, there were unlimited years.

But Augusta was of an impatient nature and organised the decorating, as economically as she was able, quickly. Within months, all but the attics were ready for living. And then came the friends, for weekends, for parties: so much pleasure. But, at quieter times, the problems: the rotting stables, leaking roof, new machinery needed by the gardener . . . Demands that seemed endless, but for a while, surmountable.

And now that Hugh was gone, and the house was almost gone, the weakness of nostalgia left her without defence. Despising her own frailty, she tried to fight the invious sorrow from hour to hour. But the empty house, the empty rooms, the empty garden crowded with happy recollections, made mockery of her battle.

She stood in the hall listening to the crackle of the fire behind her, smelling the smoke of apple boughs. Her problem this morning was whether or not to buy a Christmas tree. Every other year they had had one which reached the ceiling, frosted with firefly lights and glinting with glass balls. This year, she told herself, to decorate a tree would be absurd, a further mockery. And yet she was tempted. With only a few weeks to go, she might as well keep up the old standards, if only for her own benefit. But her thoughts were interrupted by the sight of an old woman walking up the drive, head swathed in a long scarf to protect her from strands of melting fog. Augusta opened the front door. The dank air slapped against her, at once causing the now familiar neuralgic pain to start up in her jaw.

It was Lily Beal. She had speckled skin and a distinct beard. She lived by herself in an old cottage by the post office, and was the village expert at laying out the dead. This was a task she willingly undertook in return for a cup of mournful tea. Until her eyes had become too bad she had earned her living making lace. Last winter her coal store had been raided and she had nearly died of hypothermia.

The warmth of the hall made Miss Beal shiver with relief. She clutched at her arms with bony hands. Augusta drew two chairs up to the fire. Miss Beal seemed nervous.

'Terrible out,' she said. 'Fog gets into your lungs. They say Harry Andrews has only got a few more days. So I expect they'll be calling me up in the middle of the night. They always seem to die at night, men. Women, now, are more considerate.' She gave a little sniff, and unwrapped her scarf. The face was still heart-shaped, the dim eyes set wide apart. Augusta saw that once she must have been pretty.

'Ah, yes,' she went on, 'I knew Harry Andrews as a young man. Fine young man, he was, then, too. You'd never have supposed . . . to look at him now. Well, that's how it goes, Mrs Browne. One day there's your man all strong. The next you're laying him out.' She gazed into the flames, apparently seeing the dying Mr Andrews as she had known him all those years ago. 'Anyhow, what I've come for, not to waste your time, is a request on behalf of the Darby and Joan Club.' She paused, took courage. 'Seeing as your husband is away, we were wondering if you might be so kind as to represent him at our Chrismas party this year?'

'I don't go out much, these days,' said Augusta. A mass of irrelevant thoughts came to mind: what if her face hurt as it did now? How could she bear to come back to the house, late, by herself?

'It would just be of an evening,' went on Miss Beal. 'We're laying on an entertainment, and everybody would be most obliged if you could come.'

Augusta smiled. It was impossible to refuse. Lily Beal stood up, triumphant. She promised Augusta it would be a good evening, and returned to the front to depart efficiently now that her mission was over.

'I see the swans are still with you,' she said, looking towards the pond. 'They've nested there every year since I was a child. We used to sneak into the garden and climb the willow tree to watch them. Those were the days I liked.'

When she had gone Augusta felt a small surge of energy. The Darby and Joan Club's Christmas party was a single date to look forward to in the decreasing days. Determined to take her chance, to make use of the energy while it lasted, she went to her study. She would begin the job she had been putting off for days: sorting out, throwing away, putting into boxes, dividing. That would be the worst part – the division of things.

She sat at her desk and opened the first drawer. It was filled with old letters from Hugh. She began to re-read them, knowing her own foolishness. But in moments of despair, when the essence of the past is distorted by present doubts, evidence of the truth brings some comfort. The irony of such evidence may mean renewed regret: but just to be reminded is an indulgence few can resist. Augusta, that November morning, gave way to temptation, and was able to postpone for another day the ordeal of packing up.

It was both cold and stuffy in the chicken house. Brenda sat on an upturned box smoking a Woodbine. She listened to the banging on the roof – Wilberforce was mending the leak at last. The noise disturbed the chickens. They shuffled from claw to claw, irritated: the noise of their clucking increased. For the last week, in fact, they had seemed generally unhappy. Perhaps it was the cold: they liked neither the intense heat of summer, nor this dankness of November. Spring and autumn was their best time. Well, it was hers, too, thought Brenda. Next spring would be a good one. Settled in the new house by then, maybe her own chickens at the bottom of the garden. Maybe pregnant. Of late, surprising herself, she hadn't half fancied having a baby. But doubtless the mood would wear off.

Brenda stood up, stamped to warm her feet, moved off down the rows of chickens. Some of them worried her. Some of them seemed really under the weather, and no one to care a damn about them except her. She couldn't tell what exactly it was to worry about. But she was aware of a general feeling of discontent, hostility. When she came into the shed, early mornings, they no longer set up their cluck of welcome. It was as if they'd ceased to care, as if they were exhausted by all the eggs they had laid and waited, apathetic about their fate, to die. Clarissa, for instance – Clarissa who laid the biggest eggs of all. She hardly laid at all now, and when she did the eggs were mean specimens, not much larger than a bantam's eggs. She no longer squawked boastfully as she laid, either, but kept her silence, ashamed, as she watched her tiny product slip through the grille for Brenda to collect. Roberta, most jealous bird in the shed, no longer considered it worth pecking at Clarissa: but still the patch of raw skin on her neck remained, implumed, a raw and shining pink. Brenda had a nasty feeling Clarissa would be next to die. She doubted if she could last the winter. She pushed her finger through the wire and stroked the bird's head. In the old days, Clarissa would have been proud of such a privilege, reacted with a murmurous purr. Now, she merely half-opened her pithy eyelids for a moment, dim acknowledgement of Brenda's concern, and let them fall again.

Marilyn, sex queen of all the birds, was brooding too. Spring was far off, and perhaps she knew it would bring no rewards of the kind she desired. She sat in her coop mourning her frustrated past, a streak of blonde feathers curling down one side of her head. Brenda had a plan for Marilyn: when her own chickens were established at the bottom of her garden, she would ask Wilberforce to sell her. Brenda would turn her into a free-range bird, give her a chance to strut the earth with puffed-up breast, and cast her coquettish eye towards the cockerel . . . But even as she reflected, Brenda knew that the plan was no more than a dream. After so long in her battery, Marilyn would be in no condition to withstand the rigours of an ordinary chicken run. She would be cast out by the other birds, the last of her sexuality demolished by their scorn. She would choke upon a cabbage stalk and die. It would be kindest to leave her where she was, an old flirt with no one to flirt for, rather than to know the bitterness of disillusion.

Brenda moved on to Floribunda, most faithfully affectionate of all the birds. Floribunda had acted with great dignity when Brenda had not made her queen. She had understood you could not have a queen of the shed with a paralysed leg. Quietly, she had clucked about the matter to herself, but otherwise gave every appearance of welcoming Brenda's decision. Each time Brenda passed her coop, Floribunda stirred herself on her good leg and murmured appreciation. Flattered, Brenda paid Floribunda more attention than the other birds in return. In fact, since the death of Elizabeth, Floribunda had become her favourite. She tried to fight against her feelings because she knew that for Floribunda, too, the days were numbered, and she did not look forward to all the distress of another bird's death. As for Daisy, next door to Floribunda, she hadn't turned out to be a very prepossessing queen. She was a dull bird, reliable in the matter of eggs, but with little charm. Responsibilities of her position had taken their toll, it seemed, too: her comb, once brightest in the shed, now drooped, an undistinguished red, symbolising a slipping crown.

'Poor old Queen Daisy,' whispered Brenda, 'you weren't really cut out for the job, were you?'

Lack of spirits in the chicken shed this morning had affected Brenda. She relied on her birds for understanding all her moods, and when they did not give it she felt at a loss. The dank air was particularly depressing, the stench of bird muck sour, and Wilberforce's perpetual banging jangled Brenda's nerves. She would have liked to have left the shed for the office, but a feeling of protection towards the hens kept her where she was. Should Wilberforce's confounded banging cause too much alarm, she wished to be there to comfort. Cold fingers shaking, she lit another Woodbine.

The door suddenly opened. Wilberforce stood there, massive, wisps of fog clinging to his hair and legs. He came in, swinging a hammer, pulled the door shut behind him.

'That's done,' he said.

'Good,' said Brenda.

'Thought I told you not to smoke in the sheds.'

'So you did.'

Brenda saw him loom towards her, unshaven face dark in the poor light. He snatched the cigarette from her mouth, threw it on the ground, crushed it with his foot. Brenda did not move.

'Bloody cheek,' he said, 'you deserve the sack. Anyone else, I'd tell them to go within the hour.'

'Sack me if you like,' said Brenda. Wilberforce looked at her in silence, eyes sneering all over her, prying through the thick wool of her jersey.

'No,' he said.

Brenda shrugged.

'It's up to you,' she said, 'I don't care one way or the other.'

Wilberforce leant up against the coops, blocking Clarissa's view. She gave a cluck of protest.

'That's what's the matter with women. They don't care a damn, one way or another. Treat you like dirt. They're all the same.'

Brenda smiled slightly.

'You having trouble?' she asked.

'You could put it that way. City women lead you a merry dance, judging by my experience.'

'Bad luck,' said Brenda.

'You don't sound very sorry.'

'I'm not, very. I daresay you give them as good as you get.'

'Unfeeling bitch, you are. I'd like to get my hands on you, one day. Teach you a thing or two.'

Brenda looked at him with defiance. She opened and shut her eyes very slowly.

'You'll never succeed there,' she said.

'We'll see about that,' said Wilberforce. He ran his hammer backwards and forwards across the wire of Clarissa's coop. She moved nervously. 'How's it you got such bloody long eyelashes?'

When it came to compliments, Brenda knew herself to be weak. She felt a shimmer of reluctant pleasure. To disguise it, she tried to look scornful.

'Don't do that, if you don't mind. You'll frighten Clarissa.'

Wilberforce laughed.

'That her name, is it? Pretty name for an ugly old bird, I'd say. What, you spend all your time thinking up names for the chickens, do you?' He bent down, peering into Clarissa's coop. 'Doesn't look to me as if she's much longer for this world, anyhow.'

'She's past her prime,' said Brenda. Wilberforce's callousness suddenly alarmed her.

'Better put my hands round her neck, perhaps. Replace her with a new one.'

'No!'

'What's the matter?' Wilberforce straightened up again, moved nearer to Brenda. He looked her in the eye, mocking. 'Got to be business-like, you know, in chicken farming, haven't we?'

'Clarissa's all right,' Brenda shouted, 'I'll let you know when she needs to be . . .'

Wilberforce held up his hand. He ground his fingers into his palm, twisted his wrist, in imitation of strangling an imaginary bird. The hand was huge and cruel as Uncle Jim's. It all came back in a flash, then, that loathsome day, the killing of Hen. Brenda screamed. Then the hand was upon her, its weight over her mouth, smelling of tar.

'Shut up, you bitch.' Wilberforce was shouting, too. The hens began an outraged cackling. Brenda struggled. She felt herself pushed against the coops. Wilberforce's hand slid away from her mouth, gripped her shoulder. His other hand caged her breast. His lips were on hers, tongue deep in her mouth. She could taste onions, and salt.

Brenda had no idea how long it was before she felt her body slacken. Opening her eyes, she saw Wilberforce's eyes were shut. She saw a great chunk of greasy hair had fallen over his forehead. She saw a net of cobwebs across the grey skylight. The officious chatter of the birds filled her ears, familiar music. One of Wilberforce's hands had left her breast, was sliding down her stomach, causing a spiral of vile desire for this man who repulsed her, leaving her weak.

Suddenly Wilberforce pushed her away. She almost lost her balance, grabbed at the wire of Clarissa's coop to stop herself falling. Perhaps Wilberforce had been aware of her reaction, and to spurn her now was his punishment for her rejections in the past.

217

He stood looking down at her, licking his lips, smiling, horrible.

'I'm giving you the sack,' he said. 'Do you want it?'

Brenda was panting. She tried to control herself. Anger, fear, frustration, tears – they all fought within her.

'Who would mind the birds?' she asked, eventually. She had intended her voice to be strong, but it came out feebly.

'No trouble in getting someone,' said Wilberforce, 'don't you worry.'

'You shit,' said Brenda.

'There's a word for you, too,' said Wilberforce. He banged at Clarissa's coop with a clenched fist. 'You won't go, then?'

'I didn't say that. I haven't had a rise in eighteen months . . .'

'I could give you another couple of pounds a week, daresay. That'd be fair enough.' The voice, for Wilberforce, was gentle.

'I could tell Evans about all this,' Brenda replied, 'and he'd knock the living daylights out of you.'

'I could tell him a thing or two as well. The way you carried on.'

'He wouldn't believe you.'

'Daresay he wouldn't. But it'd liven up his mind with a few suspicions, make him think twice about making you Mrs Evans, perhaps. Well, are you going or staying?'

'I'll think about it,' said Brenda. She knew she ought to go, right now, run from the shed, through the farmyard, and never speak to the bastard Wilberforce again. But then he would wring Clarissa's neck before she was due to die. He wouldn't care a bugger about any of the hens, just treat them as egg-laying machines. No, she couldn't leave them, not just yet. 'I'll let you know this afternoon,' she said.

'No word by two o'clock, then, and I'll assume you're staying.'

'Assume what you like,' said Brenda, 'but for Christ's sake fuck off out of here now . . . before I spit.'

Wilberforce smiled again.

'That's not the prettiest language I ever heard from the mouth of a beautiful girl,' he said, and left the shed.

When he had gone Brenda allowed herself to cry for a while. They were tears of anger. It was ridiculous that any-one despicable as Wilberforce could so affect her, but he was a cruel man and his cruelty frightened her. She shivered: revulsion. It occurred to her that the feeling she most dreaded, and she had suffered it many times in her life, was animal desire for a man who repelled her. Such perversity was beyond her understanding. On the occasions it happened it left her full of confusion, self-hatred and shame. That night at the Air Base it had been just the same . . . But she had no desire to start recalling all the occasions. She would leave the shed, walk to the house and see how it was getting on. Maybe she could concentrate on nice domestic things, like what colour they should paint the kitchen. Such problems would at least take her mind off Wilberforce, and the fate of his wretched hens.

That same morning Lark suffered such bad indigestion she had to leave the office. At home she took a clutch of pills and lay down for a while, but the pain was relentless. She decided that movement would be better. Walking, she was forced to bend almost double. But the concentration required to move at all, she felt, might alleviate the agony. She wrapped a long mohair scarf round her neck and went out.

On the bus to the village, perhaps dulled by the mass of pills or dislodged by the movement of the vehicle, the pain began to subside. The relief brought transitory happiness. Lark felt herself smiling at the fog out of the windows, at the occasional lighted window, and the bear shapes of the people on the pavements. She was a little amazed to find herself on this journey. There had been no conscious thought of going to Evans's and Brenda's house, but now she found herself making her way there the idea of wandering through the empty rooms, imagining them as she would make them, was exciting.

She arrived at the estate – walking in more upright fashion now the pain had almost gone – as the church clock struck eleven-thirty. Builders, fuzzy shaped in the fog, were working on several other half-finished houses: in the dank air chipping noises of hammer on stone sounded like tuneless bells. There was no one in the Evans house. Lark walked through the front entrance which still lacked a door. She saw at once there had been much progress since her last visit. The floors had been laid with concrete. The windows were in, the smooth plaster walls almost dry.

Lark went to the kitchen. There, the sink unit had been fixed under the window. She leant against it, feeling the hard ridge dig into the skin of her ribs where, much deeper, a different kind of pain had so lately seared her guts. She looked through the small square window, half-veiled with condensation. The garden was a narrow stretch of bald earth. At the end was the indefinite shape of a tree. Brenda would get to know this view so well she would no longer notice it. For years and years she would stand here, hands among the plates in soapy water seeing the tree in a haze of young green, or autumn gold, or with its bare winter arms: while behind her she would listen to the sound of Evans eating at the Formica table, and to the chatter of her children. Lark sighed. She knew it was not her fate ever to be part of so desirable a scene. This did not make for bitterness, but for a resigned sadness. For it was impossible not to think that if it had been *her* Evans had loved, instead of merely wanting to crush in a fit of lust, she would have made him so much more suitable a wife. She would have seen to his daily needs in a way that would never interest Brenda. Even now, Brenda couldn't fry a decent egg, let alone iron a shirt. It was unlikely she would ever master Queen of Puddings, Evans's favourite, and yet Brenda was the one he had chosen to stand at his kitchen window for all the years to come . . .

Lark looked up to see Evans standing in the doorway. From his stance she judged he might have been contemplating her silently for some moments. She was confused.

'Oh, Evans, I'm sorry,' she said. 'I hope you don't mind. I hadn't been over for a week or so, was wondering how progress –?'

'You look white as a ghost,' he interrupted. 'Anything the matter?'

'No.' Lark thrust back a long end of scarf over her shoulder.

'Then how come you're not at work?'

'One of my attacks of indigestion. They let me home but I thought it would be better to move about than to lie down and think about it.'

'I see.' Evans moved into the bare room. Lark thought he looked concerned. She had no wish for him to worry about her. She wanted simply to please him by showing the kind of enthusiasm for his new house that did not come automatically to Brenda. Evans stroked one of the smooth walls.

'We'll be in by New Year,' he said.

'It'll be lovely. I can just imagine it all.'

Evans smiled.

'Can you really? That's a talent, you know, being able to stand in a bare room and see it all furnished. I can't do that, nor can Bren. Tell me then, how d'you see it?'

Lark gave a wave of her hand. She described a pine dresser and table, a cork floor, gingham curtains, yellow walls, baskets of brown eggs.

'Really cosy, like a farmhouse kitchen,' she added.

Evans scratched his chin.

'But this isn't a farmhouse. This is a bloody housing estate!'

''Course it is, you nit, but that doesn't mean you have to make it look like a housing estate inside.' Seeing his smile of agreement, she felt quite bold. 'Besides, you'll have the chickens at the bottom of the garden.'

'Ah, yes, the chickens.' Evans ran a finger round the sink unit. 'First house, first sink,' he said. 'That must prove something, doesn't it?'

'It means you've come a long way, Evans Evans. Postmaster, after all. There's not many as can claim to be the good postmaster you are – everyone says.' She herself felt warm with the praise she dispensed with the intention of warming him. Evans smiled at her, tweaked her scarf, sighed.

'That's as maybe,' he said, 'but it's all a long way off, isn't it, to Postmaster-General?'

'Is that what you really want to be?'

'Postmaster-General no less. I'll tell you a secret, Lark. I've always fancied myself on *Panorama*. I've always had this conviction that given the chance I could make sense to the people. I speak their language, don't I?'

Lark, shaken by having been taken into his confidence, honoured with his greatest secret, could think of no immediately wise answer.

'Oh, yes,' she said eventually, 'you *do*, Evans. I think you do. But are you quite sure you're going about it the right way, the job of Postmaster-General, I mean, stuck out here?'

Evans frowned.

'Now, that's something I've often wondered, I have to admit. It's the right thing, of course, to start on the shop floor and work your way up. But take this morning. Practically no business, in spite of the time of year. People complaining they can't send Christmas cards any more. I ask you, will there ever be any Christmas trade again? Anyhow, there I sit, bored out of my mind, everything in order, everything done, staring at the bloody fog, hoping for a break. But when and how's my break going to come, I ask myself? When are the powers that be going to wake up one morning and say to themselves, bugger it, Evans Evans is due for promotion? I ask you, Lark, when is anything going to *happen* to the master of a sub post office?'

Lark could not resist laughing at his expression. She felt the warmth come back to her body, colour return to her face. She felt herself reeling a little on the concrete floor, giddily, happily.

'I don't know,' she said. 'I know you're being serious, very serious – it's all a serious matter. But oh your face! Worse than a funeral.' She stopped to take in his smile, far nearer to him than that time he had mashed her bones. She leant up against the sink unit again, where Evans too was standing.

'How would you like to live in a place like this?' he asked.

Lark made herself sound full of gaiety.

'Terrible,' she said. 'Wouldn't suit me at all. No, when I find the man of my dreams we'll live in a city attic and listen to the rain and the cats clattering on the roof. And breathe the permanent smell of cabbage from the communal hall.'

'Sometimes, Lark, I never know whether to take you seriously.'

'You must never take too seriously anyone who's searching.'

'Bet you'd fill the place up with bloody geraniums.'

'You bet I would.'

'All the same, it's a good place, here, for Bren and me.'

'It's a lovely place you've got, even though it wouldn't suit me.'

Evans looked at his watch.

'I might suggest the yellow walls,' he said, 'only I'd have to be careful. Bren would know I'd never have an idea like that myself.' He gave Lark a conspiratorial smile. 'Well, like a drink to warm you up? I was on my way to the Star.'

As Lark turned to Evans to accept, a sudden gust of weakness blew through her, rocking her on her feet again. She gripped his arm for support. Behind him the pink of the plaster walls divided into shapes like interlocking snakes.

'Lark, you all right?' Evans clutched both her shoulders with his hands. She nodded.

'The pills take away the pain and leave me a bit funny, that's all.' She leant against him, head on his chest, feeling the damp shiny stuff of his anorak. Shutting her eyes she craved to be a small animal who could cling to him for a while, undisturbed, letting him rub her head, as he did now, for a long time.

Then suddenly he was pushing her away from him,

talking to someone over her head.

'Hello, Bren! Surprise, surprise! I just found Lark up here.'

Lark turned to face Brenda, wondering at the insubstantial quality of the walls behind her. Through her own confusion she heard the mocking of Brenda's voice.

'Surprise, surprise indeed! Never thought I'd see the day when I'd catch you two at it!'

'Now look here, Bren, Lark's ill.' Evans's voice was wonderfully authoritative. He pushed Lark back to the sink unit so that she could lean there again. 'Take a look at her face! White as a sheet, in terrible pain. Indigestion. They let her off work and she thought a walk would make it settle.' He reached out a hand and rubbed at her hair again. Lark could feel his fingers shaking. 'Don't worry, love,' he said, 'Bren's only joking, aren't you Bren?'

There was silence. They all listened to the chip-chip of hammers on stone somewhere beyond the doorway. Lark's eyes met Brenda's. Things were no longer out of focus. Brenda's eyes were fierce as a tiger's, tawny in the flat light. Her thick black lashes were stuck together in clumps caused by the damp. Then quite suddenly they were no longer angry or suspicious, but worried.

'You all right, Lark?' she asked. 'You look awful.'

'I'm all right, blinking attacks. I'm off now, leave you two to a bit of deciding. A quick gin at the Star and I'll be as right as rain. Really.' She moved towards the door. They stretched out hands towards her. 'No, leave me.'

'We'll join you for a drink in half an hour,' said Evans.

'Wait for us, mind,' said Brenda.

Lark, nodding, buried her chin deeper in her scarf and set off down the road whose curbs were still merely indicated by lines of string.

When she had gone Brenda and Evans stood at opposite sides of the kitchen looking at each other.

'She looks ghastly,' said Brenda. 'I've never heard of such indigestion.'

'Still, if she hadn't looked so ghastly you might not have thought I was just supporting her.'

'You lay a finger on Lark?' Brenda laughed with confidence. 'Never. Not if she was the last girl on earth. She'd kill you if you tried – she's that loyal to me.'

'I believe she is, too,' said Evans.

Brenda fluttered her damp eyelashes.

'Come on,' she said. 'Something I've always promised myself. There's time.'

'What for?'

'Oh, come *on*, Evans Evans. You're a slow one, sometimes. Let's take a look at the view from the bedroom.'

She led the way upstairs. The small square room, pink plaster walls as downstairs, was floored with pale boards. It was both cold and airless. The high window was meshed with fog.

'It's bloody freezing,' said Evans. 'It'll be bloody uncomfortable.'

But Brenda was easing him out of his anorak, throwing it on to the floor. Then she grasped his belt, the neck of his shirt. All the while she panted, as if suppressing some far greater kind of groaning, and fluttered her eyes. Evans, despite dullness inflicted upon him by the tedium of the morning, despite his sharp hunger for something to eat, and despite the dreadful cold, felt himself quicken. Decades to come passed before him in a flash – years of love in some soft bed in this room, painted and carpeted. But perhaps this would be the only chance of the particular excitement of the room as it was now, stark.

Now Brenda, on a mattress of anorak and trousers on the floor, was ripping off her clothes. With one eye Evans saw a pattern of small bubbles swoop like half a necklace across the window: with the other he saw Brenda's breasts quiver beneath the cold as she thrust her arms above her head and called to him.

He lowered himself cautiously on to his knees, alert to splinters. The boards beneath his elbows were hard as stone.

Then the whole floor, proving it cheap as it looked, began to shake and squeak.

'Bloody lived-in, at last,' murmured Brenda.

After three measures of neat gin Lark regained her strength. She guessed that Evans and Brenda might be detained, and decided not to wait for them. She could go for a walk, and when she was far from any habitation she would sing out loud to practise for the concert. It was only two weeks away now.

She made her way to the bluebell woods. There would be no one there at this time of year: she could feel quite free to try out her repertoire.

Patches of fog moved in an indeterminate way, bustled about by a thin cold wind. Vapours trailed from branches and trunks of trees, and hid the skeleton shapes of dead teazles, tall as Lark, until she was almost upon them, so that she shrank back as they brushed by her, for a moment scared by their anorexic appearance. Dead branches and twigs were soggy underfoot. There were none of the crackling noises of a dry winter's day. No birds sang. The sky above the trees was flat as still water. It was impossible to imagine that spring would ever confuse ground and branches with a multitude of greens again. Or, summer, needles of sun would pick out lovers on the mossy ground. For now it was a place for ghosts, or for the old, to whom winter was an enemy and to whom, when they limped up winter Sunday afternoons to try to remember, the naked trees made mockery of a lifetime of remembered summer foliage. For to the solitary, like Lark, the sepulchral feeling of the woods was remindful of the state of complete aloneness which in winter can bring chill to the bones. She was not afraid, but devoid of any false hopes, such as can trick a single person beneath a blue sky. She knew without question that there was to be some important interruption in her life in the near future, and she waited for it with patience. She could not decipher what shape it would take, but assumed it must be some man, second best to Evans, who would love her enough to take her away from the typist's job and her geranium room. She looked forward to the prospect with no excitement. The only thing that warmed her in this wet air was the thought of the concert.

Lark came to rest by a silver birch tree. She lifted a hand to its trunk to support herself, for the shrouded undergrowth confused her vision – the pills were playing terrible tricks on her again. She determined to take no more. Her white hand, bones like small taut strings, lay against the silver brown bark. Her scarlet nails were arranged in a fan pattern, ladybirds stripped of their spots, horribly bright in all the gloom. Lark thought that if she could be granted a wish, she would request the silver birch to be transported to the concert hall. There, on the platform, in her wispy grey dress, she would lean against it for support, as she did now, and it would give her strength. She would sing better. As it was, she would have to stand alone on the stage, arms by her sides. Arms by her sides? What did singers do with their hands? The questions, which had not occurred to her before, suddenly worried her.

She began to sing, quietly at first, then pushing out her chest so that it rubbed against the scratchy wool of her jersey, and the sound poured clear and hollow through the mists. Lark was exhilarated by the contained power of her own voice. It had the quality of an echo. It haunted. She felt herself trembling, red nails clutching harder at the silver birch. She wondered that so pure a note could come from her own frail chest, and as she took a new breath of foggy air into her lungs she felt an icy sweat on her back, and sweat, or tears, scratch at her eyes.

Since the difficult afternoon when Henry had broken the news to Rosie that he had been sacked, he had felt more than ever debilitated by her welcomes, and went to great lengths to avoid them. On that particular afternoon she had not said much, but sat by the fire, sniffing, cutting out some fine white stuff with a pair of small scissors. Although he looked at her unflinchingly all the while he explained what had happened, she had not raised her eyes and met his. He had had the impression she was in an unusually untidy state: stockings wrinkled round the ankle, a smear of mud on her arm, revolting hands grazed as if by brambles. But he had lacked the energy to enquire whether any mishap had befallen her when she had run screaming from the house earlier, and, as she made no mention of the matter, he let it rest. She had not chided him for losing the job, of course: but she had not abused Mr Daly for his untoward action, either, which Henry felt would have been the loyal thing to do. No: she simply continued daily life with her usual calm, though it sometimes occurred to Henry from the pitch of her voice that cheerfulness caused her more effort than usual. She had doubled her efforts to welcome him on every homecoming, even on the occasions (and they were most occasions) she was forced to turn her head to avoid the smell of whisky on his breath, and to give an arm to support him to his chair. She constantly provided him with the kind of surprises he could not abide, and Henry knew himself to be surly in his lack of appreciation. Once he had found a lump of tissue paper on his chair. It contained a tie made of porridgy tweed, Woven by Countryfolk, it said on the label, which Henry would not have cast upon his worst enemy. She had bought it from the Boy who, in his misguided fashion, had started a small line in ties in the post office, supposing this might bring a little excitement to trade, and act as a small step in the direction of Postmaster-General. Henry had made no pretence at politeness or false gratitude, and had fallen asleep with the dreadful thing slung across his knees.

So lately it had become his habit to walk about for an hour or so after the Star closed, trying to summon the strength and the steadiness to face Rosie's welcoming tea. Most afternoons he went to the woods, knowing quite surely there would be no one else there: Rosie, he was convinced, would never visit them again. They were his protection from her and he needed their solace as much as he needed the increasing amounts of whisky he consumed every day.

It had become his custom to sit on the uprooted tree, the damp bark soft against his thighs, and let the silence lap about him while he contemplated the winter sky. On the bitterest days he would take off his tie and undo the top buttons of his shirt, and relish the cold against his chest. This way, he felt, he would be sure to die of pneumonia quite soon, which wouldn't be a bad death. But although he had continued this ritual for several weeks, so far he had not been assaulted by the mildest sniffle. Today's fog, therefore, filled Henry with hope. Surely the wet vapours would scorch his innards with some wicked disease, and he would pass away in the night. He breathed in deeply, mouth open, making a sucking noise, then spewed the air out again. He watched the small grey bulbs expand from his mouth and merge into the greater grey, which now, in the mid-afternoon light, was turning dun: and he felt the cold swipe through his lungs, stinging like smoke. His legs were no less confused by the fog than his eyes. At moments, stumbling over the soggy ground, Henry was near to falling. He decided to pause for a while, to try to consolidate the spinning greyness both within his head and all around him. He held on to the trunk of a larch tree, unsure where he was. He knew every inch of the woods but was unnerved to find his sense of direction had suddenly gone. Was he south or west? Screwing up his eyes, he peered through the trees attempting to see the brickwork chimneys on the horizon. But all was obscured. The fog seemed to be thickening. Perhaps he should not have come, but he liked to clear his head in the afternoon air. Even rainy days he enjoyed his pipe under the dripping trees, chewing at its stem, and hawking in a manner that was not permissible at home. On many an afternoon here, lately, he had found some kind of comfort among the trees: he had known the freedom to shout his sourest thoughts out loud, and to listen to them smash against the impervious silence, undisputed.

With his free hand Henry felt in his pocket for his pipe and matches. The simple job of lighting up seemed particularly confusing, but at last he had the stem between his teeth, could taste the tobacco on his tongue. He cocked his head on one side, straining for the sound of birds. Silence swirled round him for a while. It was broken by a thin piping of a clear voice, some tune Henry thought he recognised: more like a human than a bloody thrush. He moved a few paces, trying to decipher where the voice came from. Very puzzling. Who besides himself would want to be here on a day like this? The song took him back to some long forgotten childhood evening, haymaking in a Welsh valley one summer, years before the family had moved here: his mother used to sing that song as she lifted the bales, easily as a man with her strong arms.

Then the answer came to him. It resounded through his head with the force of a shot, clearing all inebriation, inspiring the kind of courage that spurned the confusions of mere fog. Fate, acting in its devious way, had sent her. For some reasons Henry did not bother to work out, the Leopard, on one of her visits to the village, had been drawn to the woods on the hill, and alone on her walk was singing to herself with uninhibited joy. So near at last, all he had to do was to find her.

In frantic anticipation Henry began to move between the trees, too fast to make a way for himself between the branches, so that they scratched wildly at the skin of his face and hands. The voice eluded him in a tantalising way. One moment he felt he was almost upon it, then it seemed to shift direction and he plunged again into maddening obscurity. After stumbling about for a long time, Henry stood still, heart racing: there, in what he dimly saw to be the familiar clearing, he saw the indistinct shape of a small figure. It seemed to be wearing something yellowish, though in the poor light no identifying spots were visible.

'Oh, my God, my Leopard,' he said out loud, and found himself running.

Within a few yards he realised his mistake. This was not the Leopard, or anyone at all like her. It was Lark, Brenda's friend, muffled in a yellow scarf, one hand at her throat, the other swiping vaguely at the fog in a helpless manner. As soon as she saw Henry she stopped singing. He realised he must have frightened her. He could see her hair was quite damp, as if she had been out in the rain, and her eyes were startled smudges in a white face.

'Sorry if I interrupted you,' he said. 'I couldn't think who it could be, up here in this weather.' He gave a small bow, remembering that once, years ago, some girl had told him he could be quite gallant if he put his mind to it. Somehow he managed to charm Lark.

'That's all right, Mr Evans. I was just practising for the concert – you know, they've asked me to sing.' She smiled. 'It's quite ghostly up here, isn't it? I was beginning to think I'd never find my way back, and it's coming down thicker, I think.'

Henry looked around. The spongey greyness of the air seemed to be closing about them. He wanted very much to spit, but Lark's presence inhibited him. Instead he cleared his throat, and rubbed at his chest, where a gash of disappointment lacerated his skin.

'It does indeed,' he said, 'but I know these parts pretty well. I can guide you back, if you like. You must be cold.'

Lark shivered.

'I suppose I am,' she said, 'and I could eat a horse.'

'You follow me, then, and come back to our place for tea. My wife would love to see you, you haven't been over in a long while.' Something about returning home with this waifish creature appealed to Henry: her presence would protect him from Rosie's enquiring looks. He told her to follow him, and turned back into the trees.

In some incomprehensible way Henry's instinct now acted like a laser beam through the fog: the path seemed clear to him as if it was a bright day, and in a short while they reached the gate that led to the field. From then on there were no problems. They descended the mild slope towards the garden of Wroughton House, which loomed in the mist, one lighted window upstairs, bleached to the colour of moon-light through the fog.

'You sing very prettily,' Henry said eventually. He had never thought of himself as a conversational man, but to pay a compliment was no bad thing, and it would give him a little practice for the day of the Leopard. 'Just like a choirboy I once heard. You must be happy to sing like that.'

'Oh, I am. Very.'

A few yards later Henry found himself overcome with indiscretion.

'I'm going to Cambridge, as a matter of fact,' he said. 'In the spring. To see the Cam.'

'That should be lovely. The daffodils.'

Something about her understanding increased his reck-lessness.

'With a companion,' he added. And the relief of having confided to one other human being in the world left him light-hearted as he had not been for weeks.

'Well, that's quite right,' said Lark. 'I mean, it would be a pity for anyone to have Cambridge in the spring all to them-selves, wouldn't it?'

Henry agreed with her most emphatically, but in his temporarily cheerful state he was too overcome to say so. Instead he took Lark's arm and helped her climb the fence into the garden of Wroughton House where, in the new thickness of the fog, the one lighted window hung suspended, unsupported by walls, and casting an etiolated reflection into the waters of the pond.

As the church clock struck four-thirty Rosie opened the door to look out for Henry. She had resisted doing this for some time, but worry had finally overcome her. To her relief she saw him coming up the road, very hazy in the fog, but apparently quite steady on his feet. By his side was the small shape of a girl, muffled in a scarf, features impossible to recognise.

Rosie clapped her hand to her mouth to stifle a scream. Of

course! That was it. In a flash she blamed herself for not having understood before. It was another woman who had been causing all this trouble, and here he was, coming to explain at last. Coming to have it out. Well, at least the truth you know . . .

Fighting tears, Rosie realised there was no time to work out what her reaction should be. The two of them were almost upon her. A lifetime of self-control came to her rescue. She stood up very straight, braced herself with understanding, quickly calculated that they should drink tea from the best china. She would not have Henry accuse her of indignity or lack of hospitality, even in such a crisis. Automatically she arranged her smile. She was determined their first view of her should be a brave and smiling one, full of the kind of welcome that Henry would expect of her in any circumstances.

Much later that night Rosie was rewarded for her stoicism. Bustling about with plates of dumpling stew, having enjoyed entertaining Lark to a huge tea, she felt bold enough to admit to Henry the foolishness of her earlier supposition.

'You know for one minute, silly old me, I really thought you were bringing in a fancy lady,' she said. 'I said to myself, why, after all these years, Henry Evans has found himself a girl, and has come to tell me.'

For the first time in more weeks than Rosie could remember, Henry laughed.

'You women, daft notions you do have,' he said, before falling back into his customary silence. But the lightness of his tone was enough for Rosie. She went happily to the larder, unable to resist a spoonful of the cold baked custard she had made for lunch, sweet in its congealed sauce of golden caramel.

The house was on fire. Flames sprouted from the roof and every window, lighting the night sky. Their flickering was doubled in the water of the pond. Augusta, trapped in the branches of the weeping willow, struggled to get near the house. Her help was essential. Buckets of water. Alone she would put out the flames because there was no one else there. But the branches of the tree held her back. The more wildly she struggled, the more firmly they entangled her.

She screamed, waking herself. The house burning down had become a recurring nightmare. She was sweating, as she always was when she woke, very cold. Through the blinds she could see the beginnings of light.

Augusta got out of bed and went to the window. She raised one of the blinds. Mists of a winter dawn disguised the shapes of the garden, but the intensity of yesterday's fog had gone. The willow was a faint imprint, grey tracing against paler grey. Augusta looked to see herself fighting against its branches, but they were quite still. The pair of swans stood on the bank of the pond, heads tucked into puffed-up breasts. After a while, with one accord, they lifted their heads, stretched their long necks. Luminous white in the mist, they raised their wings, testing sleepy feathers. Then, grotesque ballet dancers, they launched themselves into the air. In a moment they were high above the garden, moving in the direction of the brickworks. Augusta, listening to the creak of their wings, watched them flying side by side till they vanished in the distance. Then she remembered that in a few hours' time a lorry would be arriving full of packing cases, and it was her job to start to fill them.

On the evening of the old people's party it began to snow. Not thickly, but enough to crust the ground with translucent white. Augusta prepared for her solitary return. She put four mince pies in a low oven and piled logs on the hall fire. She also lit the Christmas tree, which she had decorated that afternoon. Its firefly lights cast starry shadows on the ceiling and flagstone floor, and made tiny flames in the multi-coloured glass balls. Augusta left it with reluctance. Her feet crunched over the cobbles of the back drive, and the cold made her clutch her arms under her breasts. It was a pale night for December, clear stars.

In the village hall all was merriment and light. Augusta slipped in unnoticed. She stood looking around at the bustle of elderly people, listening.

'There were five or six of them up here all day, doing it.'

'They've made the crackers nice.'

'And Ellen had a stroke this morning. Did you hear? I popped round. Doubt if she'll get over it.'

'She was looking forward to it so much, too. She'd had her hair done, and all.'

There had been so much effort. A flurry of cottonwool snowflakes on every window, much thicker than the real stuff outside. Crackers stuck at sword angles on the walls. Streamers and balloons. Long trestle tables set with white cloths and primrose china, a funny hat at each place. Poinsettias on the stage.

She was welcomed by Lily Beal and Mr Roper, the chairman of the club, golden wedding a few days behind him. They were apologetic when they realised she must have been standing there awhile unnoticed. They led her to the place of honour at the top table beneath the stage. She sat between Mr Roper on her right, and a fat lady in a beige jersey dress and jacket, intricate piping on collar and cuffs. Augusta, judging by her expensive handbag, guessed she must be someone with benevolent interest in the village, who would no doubt replace Hugh as President when the Brownes finally left.

There was a sit-down hot meal for 75p a head. This had been provided by an up-and-coming caterer who chafed at the back of the hall, casting a bossy eye on his team of waiters. His moustache was the same shape as his bow-tie, wide at the edges, thin in the middle, and he smiled without rest. Mr Roper informed Augusta he was new to the area and at this, his debut, he naturally wanted to make a good impression. There was no doubt the members of the Darby and Joan Club were much delighted by his efforts: tomato soup, turkey, package-fresh balls of stuffing, peas, potatoes boiled and roast, tinned fruit salad with a puff of cream, cheese and coffee, candelabras and paper napkins thrown in. Augusta did her best to eat, but had little appetite. She noticed the ratio of women to men was ten to one, and wondered when it came to the aloneness of old age which it was least desirable to be, man or woman. The old ladies had paid a lot of attention to their party clothes and hair. There was a preponderance of pink diamanté brooches, sometimes a whole collection on one bosom, and crystal beads clustered in withered dewlaps. There was much laughter and the few old gentlemen, scattered with great fairness among the tables, were subjected to an abundance of nudges from their lucky companions. It seemed to be going, as Mr Roper pointed out, with quite a swing.

Supper finished, he tried to stand up. But his chair was too near the stage. It cut into the backs of his knees, causing him to topple over the table. Regaining his balance, with infirm voice he drew attention to the small brown envelopes by each place. He asked that everyone should give a big hand to the kind lady who had provided them – 25 pence in each one. Perhaps she might like to say a few words?

The good lady in matching beige tried to rise, a little flushed now her gesture had been exposed. She, too, had trouble with her chair and the stage, but she had learnt from Mr Roper. She gripped the chair's back rail with one hand, so that it should not butt her from behind, and clutched the table, screwing up the cloth, with the other.

'I'd just like to say thank you all very much,' she said, 'and as for the little envelopes – well, they come from the heart.' She sat down again, to applause. 'I've never spoken in public before,' she whispered to Augusta. She was shaking.

Augusta's own speech was brief. She read a telegram from Hugh, and said how sorry they were to be leaving the village. They would miss everybody, and remember all the good times. But soon she would come back and visit them. That was the only lie. By the time she felt capable of returning to the village, most of them would be dead.

As the hall was cleared the old ladies scraped back their

chairs and pulled their cardigans more tightly over their party dresses. One old man, knees apart, pulled a bowler hat down over his ears. He got a big, pent-up laugh. Encouraged by his success, he waved a walking stick in the air and sang the first line of *My Bonnie Lies Over the Ocean*. Several of the old people talked round Augusta, and reassured themselves.

'You like our new stage curtains? We got them from the WI for £5.'

'That was a lovely meal.'

'They say a professional compere's coming.'

'And professional dancers.'

'And professional singers.'

'My.'

'Anyone know if the milk for the tea is in the gents?'

Dancers first. The fluorescent bars of light went out and a blue spotlight shone on to the stage. A composed twelve-year-old fluttered out from behind the bargain curtains, her pubescent breasts flattened by a tight satin bodice. Scraped-back hair made her face very old. She danced to the thud of an upright piano played by the local music teacher. Sometimes her rhythm and the child's movements were not synchronised, but their concern to please was quite in harmony. Then came two eight-year-olds in huge ears, long tails and pink noses, pulling behind them a large cardboard box. Their teacher, a pink flower pinned like a beacon to her vast bosom, followed them.

'In case you didn't realise,' she said, 'these are two mice with a piece of cheese.'

There were a number of acts throughout the evening, smoothed on their way by the professional compere, who was also a policeman. There were Italian teenage twins with long wavy Drene hair, like 1940 stars, who sang *Puppet on a String*, and a semi-retired conjurer who moved away from the exposure of the spotlight to pull tangerines unconvincingly out of thin air. Augusta, looking round at the audience, saw their bodies had become slack with appreciation: knees slung apart, hands resting upon them with palms turned upwards.

Mouths hung open, some eyelids drooped a little. At the back of the hall, Augusta saw with surprise, stood Brenda and Evans, coats still on, collars turned up. She wondered why they had come. They had the air of people who don't intend to stay a long time.

'And now,' said the compere, clashing his knuckles like cymbals, 'and now, ladies and gentlemen, it is time for our star. And our star tonight is a little lady whose name may not be very familiar to your ears. But, believe me, ladies and gentlemen, she's a very big singer with a very big future.' He paused, pleased by his own sense of timing. 'Her name? Well, her name is very simple. As she sings like a bird it is, appropriately enough, just Lark. *Lark*, ladies and gentlemen. I ask you to give her a big hand.'

They clapped quite hard as Lark came on to the stage. The compere went away, having squeezed her shoulders and banged his big hands right under her nose. She placed herself in the middle of the circle of blue light, let her hands fall to her sides. She wore Augusta's Peaseblossom dress, its silvery folds limp against her bones, its jagged hem making shadows on her stick legs and silver shoes. She had painted her eyelids leaf green, to match her eyes: they shone with a strange light from out of the huge shadows beneath them, and the skin under her cheek bones was drawn back into angular hollows. Her hair had been washed and ruffled, and pinned with a Christmas-tree star. Lark swallowed and, just once, fluttered the scarlet nails of both hands on her skirt.

There was absolute silence in the hall. A sense of surprising awe. Lark's aloneness reminded them. In that moment of quiet there was almost fear, Augusta thought: in revealing the solitary nature of her own being, Lark might expose theirs, too. Then she smiled, to reassure them, and breathing could be heard again.

The pianist scratched a lump of suspender that was troubling her thigh, and began to play. She was an incompetent musician, but had the sense to remain *pianissimo*.

'I'm just going to sing a few songs I've always liked,' said

Lark. 'Nothing to do with Christmas, especially, but I hope you like them, too.'

She started with *Linden Lea*. One or two of the elderly people stifled gasps of admiration, as they might at beautiful music in church. For Lark's voice was so pure, so sweet, so sad, as to clear the most confused mind with the beauty of truth. No larger than a child, unmoving, the notes that soared from her pierced to those dormant areas of regret, or love, or distant pleasure that are from time to time rekindled by the workings of art. She sang a Welsh folk song, *Yesterday*, and *Silent Night*. Finally the theme tune from *The Threepenny Opera*, most melancholy of all. There was no one who did not recognise her quality. They applauded as hard as they were able, but it was the applause of those who have been ungrounded, rather than the riotous clapping accorded to lesser talents. In between songs Lark bowed her head and barely smiled. When it was all over she came to the front of the stage, but looked beyond the audience, overwhelmed, not seeing them. She could not be more than six stone, Augusta thought. Her shoulder bones pierced sharply through her skin, her arms were skeletal. She gave three small bows, bringing the dress briefly to life, making it flutter in imitation of its vivacious days, when Augusta had danced in it all night for Hugh.

Lark said thank you and left the stage. The applause continued, although not everybody could join in.

'I can't clap,' whispered an old man near Augusta, 'in case I break my hands.' They lay clasped together on his lap, rigid blue.

After Lark there were to be games and dancing to cover the anti-climax. Evans and Brenda, Augusta saw, had already slipped away. She thought that she, too, might leave. She said her farewells to Mr Roper and the others, and suggested she might drive Lark home. This was a welcome idea, for it would spare the club the price of a taxi.

Outside the snow was falling more thickly, sticking to the windows of the hall. The cottonwool flakes inside became caricature reflections. Lark was huddled into a coat of shaggy fur, her bony hands clutching at the collar, and at a Cellophane parcel of chrysanthemums. Her face was quite exhausted, but she smiled, incredulous. Augusta suggested that first they should go back to the house and get warm by the fire. She agreed eagerly. Simultaneously they turned for a last look through the snowy windows and saw the old people dancing with much abandon, skirts held above their knees, paper hats all crooked on their heads.

'Do you think they liked it all right?' asked Lark. 'I couldn't see any of them smiling.'

'I think they were too amazed,' said Augusta. 'You sang too well for any of us to smile.'

Lark had never been to the house before. Through the glass panes of the front door they could see the coloured lights smudged among the boughs of the Christmas tree, and the flames still burning brightly in the fire. Inside, Lark stood quietly in the hall, still clinging to her coat.

'What a tree,' she said at last. 'Is that all for you? Or are you having a party?'

'I leave in three weeks,' said Augusta. 'No party. But I thought I might as well . . . have a tree. We have one every year. Now, take off your coat and sit yourself by the fire. I've got some warm mince pies. Let's have them, shall we? And champagne. We must have champagne. Singers always do, you know, after successful first nights like that.'

'Do they, do they really? Oh Lordy, what a night.' Lark was laughing, throwing her fur coat on the golden flagstones in front of the fire, making it into a rug. She sat down, drew up her knees to her arms, so that the dress fell about in tatters, Cinderella's rags. 'I've never been to a place like this before,' she said. 'Champagne and Christmas trees and ceilings high as the sky. It must be funny, all alone. Brenda and Evans told me all about it. They love it here, you know.'

They sat for a long time in front of the fire, eating the mince pies and drinking the champagne. Augusta was anxious to convince Lark how remarkable her performance had been – how it had shaken them all. But she felt inadequate.

'You're a really marvellous singer, you know,' she said. 'I mean it. I don't understand why you never trained.'

Lark shrugged.

'Well, I wanted to. But it never worked out like that. I had to earn my living, didn't I? I had to help out my mother once my father died. Besides, I had these weak lungs. They said I'd never have the strength.' The firelight and the champagne had brought a flush to her face. 'Still, I enjoyed tonight. I might do more, if anyone would have me.'

'Maybe I could help,' said Augusta. 'I know people who might be able to help you.'

'That would be kind, though I don't expect you'd have much time with all this moving. Here,' she added, picking at a chiffon wisp on the skirt of the dress, 'I know where this came from, you know. Soon as Brenda brought it home for me I knew it couldn't have come from a shop round here. I knew it came from you – the quality.' They both laughed. 'It's the most beautiful dress I've ever seen. Did you wear it a lot?'

'Sometimes,' said Augusta. 'Hugh liked it.'

'He's gone, has he?' Augusta nodded. 'Swines, men are, aren't they? Always going. Still, I suppose that's the risk you take if you marry. Can't say I'd mind taking the risk, though. 'I'm always looking out for my chance. There's a man at my office, a drip always on the end of his nose and smelly breath. He says he fancies me, the silly sod, and he'd give me security if that's what I'd like. I say that's not what I want. Not just security. I wouldn't mind a bit of love thrown in, I say, and he says, poo, that comes. But you can see so often it wouldn't, ever, can't you?' Augusta nodded again. 'So you go on dreaming about Robert Redford and having the odd screw behind the filing cabinets. But what they don't realise, those sods who get your knickers down, is how little they're getting. They like to think you're all swoony about them. Grateful. Huh! One day I shall say what's really filling my mind. The dreadful price of tea, or something, just as they're huffing and puffing. Lordy, this champagne isn't half going to my head. I am going on, aren't I?'

She looked up at the lighted tree, twirled her glass in her hand so that the flames from the fire spun among the bubbles.

'I can imagine the parties you must have had in this house,' she said. 'I can imagine the rooms all full of people.'

'They used to come,' said Augusta.

'Still, it's nice, the quiet. Though it must be sad selling it. What are you going to do?'

'I don't know really. Go to London. Live in a flat. Try to forget about this.'

'Impossible, that,' said Lark. 'I'm telling you. How could you ever get a place like this out of your blood? Here, you know what? Whoever comes next, you'll haunt them. They'll see your ghost coming down the stairs, opening the door for them to go away. They'll feel the draught on their legs, the bastards. They'll be so shit-scared they'll leave and you can come back. Don't you think?'

Augusta laughed and raised her glass to meet Lark's.

'Here's to your ghost,' Lark said. 'Now, I must be going. But Evans told me you had a lovely piano. Before I go, would you let me see it? Don't know what it is, but I love pianos, the great big ones. I've always fancied myself leaning in that curved bit of a grand piano, you know, singing at the Albert Hall. Daft as a brush I am, aren't I?'

Augusta led the way to the drawing-room. She left the door open but did not turn on the lights because she did not want Lark to remark upon the packing cases. So the room was quite dark, the shadows scarcely broken by the glow from the Christmas tree. Lark went at once to the piano and ran her hand along its mahogany lid.

'Do you play?' she asked.

'Well, I used to. Not now.'

'Go on, try. I can't play a note.'

'I'm completely out of practice.'

'Doesn't matter. Just something. Please. Here I am,

aren't I? Leaning up against a grand piano after all this time. My mother'll die when I write to her about tonight. She won't believe it.'

Augusta sat down on the fat velvet stool. The champagne had mellowed her, and Lark made her want to laugh, or cry, she wasn't sure which. She felt for the notes, sounding them gently, chords coming back to her. She began a carol.

'I know that,' said Lark. 'I sang that when I was a child. I sang in the choir, solo, when I was ten. My Dad, he nearly bust himself with pride.'

She nestled into the crook of the piano and stretched one arm right across its lid. She hummed for a moment or two, then remembered the words.

> *Three kings from Persian lands afar*
> *To Jordan follow the shining star . . .*

She broke off to sip at her champagne.

'Lordy, I'm drunk as anything, aren't I? Gin never does this to me. Still, it's nearly Christmas, isn't it? Who said you couldn't play? Now, hang on a tick, it's coming back . . .'

> *And this the quest of the travellers three*
> *Where the new born king of the Jews may be,*
> *Full royal gifts they bear for the King,*
> *Gold, incense, myrrh are their offering.*

Her voice was remindful of a flute played by a hillside shepherd. Accustomed to the semi-darkness by now, Augusta could see that for all her claims to intoxication, Lark's eyes shone quite soberly. She had confused drunkenness with the happiness of singing by a grand piano. Perhaps they were almost the same. She ran both hands through her hair, dislodging the Christmas tree star, and laughing. Against the moon panes of the huge windows snow lodged in swooping curves. The church clock struck two. With the confidence of old partners by now, Augusta and Lark began the second verse.

Augusta refused all invitations to go out on Christmas Day. She stayed quietly in her study packing letters into boxes. It took her a long time because she read each one before putting it away. She hoped Hugh might ring, but the telephone remained silent: he had said he would be abroad with friends. In the old days he would ring from all parts of the world. She ate two kippers and two mince pies for lunch, and watched the snow fall in the garden, and swallowed several pills with a glass of Hugh's best port to kill the pain in her jaw. She went to bed at half-past four in the afternoon, made drowsy by the pills. Drawing the blinds of her windows, she saw a pattern of coloured lights on the snow in the drive: she had forgotten to turn off the Christmas tree. But she had no further energy to go downstairs again, and besides, she liked the idea of their colouring the snow all night.

If it had not been for the worry at the back of Rosie's mind about the extent of Henry's Christmas celebrations, she would have enjoyed the day very much. As it was, she had to steer the delicate course between remaining on her guard, and at the same time appearing to be full of the Christmas spirit. After church she was overwhelmingly congratulated on the state of the altar, which had taken many days to deck with holly sprayed with gold. She had refused all offers of help, knowing only too well the downfalls caused by inferior artistic effort: and in spite of all the work she had had to do herself, she had managed to find time to advise Mrs Tuffin about how best to decorate the tree, and the vicar's wife on how to gird the pillars with ivy. Warm with success she returned home to find the turkey cooked to perfection, and Henry sitting in his chair by the fire. He had been to the Star, he said, and treated himself to a couple of cherry brandies, seeing it was Christmas, and had come home early to open the sherry. Rosie swelled with relief. Henry had not remembered to give her a present, but this gesture more than compensated for the omission. To have him sober on Christmas Day was something she had not dared to hope for. In high spirits she set about laying the table, most of which was taken up by a landscape of cottonwool snow and mirror lakes, dotted with small plastic deer and nylon Christmas trees – a little surprise she had been planning for weeks.

Evans and Brenda and Lark came to lunch. Lark had knitted everybody long scarlet scarves. Brenda, of less imagination, had brought different-coloured tablets of soap from Boots. It occurred to Rosie, as she made her polite thanks, how happy she would have been if Evans had fallen in love with Lark instead of Brenda . . . But it was a disloyal thought and she quickly put it from her mind. She had to admit that when it came to looks there was not much competition between the girls. Lark was a mere scrap of a thing, painfully thin these days, while Brenda was a big strapping girl, well made. And Evans seemed happy enough, full of talk about the new house. She could only hope the marriage would be a happy one: for her part, she would do all she could to help and advise them.

In the afternoon Evans and Brenda went off for a walk. She overheard Brenda saying something to Evans about always having wanted to have a bash in the snow, and the remark caused Rosie to blush so hard she had to slip away into the larder and pick at the cold Christmas pudding while she awaited the return of her normal colour. Lark stayed with them by the fire, talking to Rosie, because Henry soon fell asleep. Rosie was able to pass on the news that the whole village had been talking about her performance at the old people's club, and it was certain she would now get many more professional offers. Lark seemed pleased. She ate a lot of Rosie's cake, the top decorated with a miniature ski-resort fashioned in icing, but declined to stay for supper. She left at six, saying how much she had enjoyed her day, but now felt a little tired and would go home for an early night. Rosie privately thought one of her attacks of indigestion was coming on, and suggested some tablets. But Lark shook her head, declining. She left to walk home, well wrapped up in her yellow scarf, saying it wouldn't take her long and she could do with the air.

Henry's good resolutions did not last quite the whole day.

At opening time in the Star he woke up and said he was going for a quick one. He then remembered that by some daft tradition he always invited Rosie to come with him on Christmas Day. He issued the invitation with little grace, and Rosie declined. She could not face watching him downing drink after drink, as on the evening of the car crash, and then having to help him home. No, she said, she would stay at home and prepare a cold supper and watch the Spectacular on television. Brenda and Evans were going to a party, but she would be quite happy by herself until he came back.

He returned earlier than she expected, a little unsteady, but not half as bad as he had been on so many occasions in the last few weeks. For the second time that day Rosie was elated by relief. She hummed to herself as she fried slices of Christmas pudding – which would sober him up completely – and couldn't resist observing, many times, what a nice family day it had been. To show her appreciation further, she went so far as to suggest they have a glass of sherry before they went to bed. This Henry refused, and took a swig of whisky from the bottle instead – a reaction to her offer which Rosie had failed to anticipate. Her own glass of sherry had the happy effect of making the day in retrospect even brighter than it might have been in reality. And then, in bed, it was her turn to remember a Christmas tradition.

Due to Henry's behaviour in the last few months Rosie had decided to postpone making any overture to him in bed, with or without her mittens. Tonight, although the sherry had made her a little carefree, and she would have done any-thing to rip the wretched mittens off and curl into his back, naked hands wandering his shoulders, she managed to remember resistance would be the wise thing. She prayed to God for strength, having thanked Him for such a nice day, and kept her hands to herself. But after an hour of wakeful-ness, sensing from Henry's slight shifting that he was awake too, Rosie gave in to the weakness of the flesh. Overpowered by the thought that Henry should be rewarded for having made today easy, and wanting to indicate a small part of the great love for him that welled chokingly inside her, she stretched out a mittened hand and laid it on his shoulder.

The only way that Henry had been able to get through Christmas Day with some semblance of civility was to remind himself every hour that it would, at least, be the last ever such day. He knew this without any doubt. He could not be sure precisely when it had come to him, but some time during the last few weeks a conviction had grown that the New Year was going to bring a change in his fate. This was fortunate, because once the Boy was married, the house without him would be intolerable. Whatever happened Henry would be forced to leave home. But the strength of his new instinct protected him from any qualms on this matter. He was sure Fate would plunge in with nice timing and produce the Leopard – who would, of course, go with him.

Henry had resisted going to the Star for more than two short visits not as a goodwill gesture towards Rosie, but because he guessed that on Christmas Day, drat it, it was unlikely the Leopard would be visiting a pub some distance from where she lived. Exactly what she *was* doing he didn't like to imagine. When pictures of her by a tree with children, a possible husband in the background, came to his mind, he fought against them. By evening he had managed to replace them with images of her, still in leopard coat, swopping presents by some vague fire with her parents.

But it wasn't till the clatter of the whole dreadful day was over, and he was in bed, could Henry finally indulge in his fantasies undisturbed. These were of next Christmas. Very clear, they were, too. He and the Leopard would be on a cruise – an inspiration that had come to him from an ad on the telly. Sunny days and balmy nights. Walking the decks under a tropical moon. Palm trees and white beaches, coconuts, deck chairs – did they have deck chairs in the tropics, Henry wondered? And the Leopard would be the toast of the ship, of course. All the men would want to flirt with her and buy her rum punches. But he'd take good care of her, not let her too far out of his sight. If a respectable gentleman asked her to dance (small orchestra in dinner jackets playing *The Nearness of You* over the Sargasso Sea) – well, he'd probably give his permission. Provided the fellow didn't look as if he'd be up to any hanky panky, and promised to keep a respectable distance in his waltzing. They'd have a top deck outside cabin, of course: and considering Henry's naval past he had no doubt he'd be able to pull a few strings when it came to who should sit at the Captain's table. Ah, it would be the hell of a good time. Something he'd been waiting for all his life, it occurred to him now, though in the past he had imagined no clear details, just a general hankering for something different. They would be drunk on love, he and the Leopard. Age was no barrier to passion. Time would stand still. Though if and when it did start up again, and Southampton appeared on the horizon – why, then would be the moment to go to Cambridge. In fact, if he calculated it all with naval precision, they would time their return for the daffodils by the Cam.

Henry gave no thought to the money necessary to finance his tropical future. He was of the opinion that if dreams were strong enough to become true, then Fate would play its hand again, and provide. Anything could happen on the Pools in the next few weeks, or – another thought – the Leopard herself might be the daughter of a millionaire. Judging by the coat, this was very likely. *Oh, my dearest Leopard, I hope you've had a better Christmas Day than me. What wouldn't I give to have you here with me now, your arms about me, your hands gentle on my skin . . .*

Henry shifted violently. For one delirious moment he imagined his wish had been granted. There was a scratching at his shoulder, soft as he required from the Leopard. Then the terrible unfairness of life twisted him into a position of physical agony. He groaned out loud and his pillow fell to the floor. Rosie's repellant foot, icy cold and scaly skinned, rubbed at his leg. She whimpered, pressing her vile hand deeper into the flesh of his shoulder.

'What's the matter, love?' she cried.

'Bugger off, woman,' he shouted back. 'And don't ever lay your hands on me again.'

He rolled as far as he could to his side of the bed, pulling the sheet and blankets with him. When Rosie began to sob he blocked his ears with a pillow, and decided to send off for travel brochures tomorrow. Soon as he got details of tropical cruises he'd set about making his arrangements.

My Leopard, we're nearly there. Leave it to me.

He fell asleep and dreamed that he went with a works outing from the brickworks on a cruise to the Caribbean. Just one condition had to be adhered to: all men should bring the ladies of their dreams, and leave their wives at home.

With some peculiar deference to Christmas, Evans decided to go back to his parents' house when the party was over. He dropped Brenda back at the flat first. She made no objection. A mixture of ginger wine and whisky had made her sleepy.

Brenda would have liked to have gone into Lark's room and told her about the party, as she used to in the old days before the room at Wroughton House, but there was no light under Lark's door and Brenda imagined she was asleep. She herself got into bed quickly, and slept at once.

She was woken by the sound of moaning from Lark's room. Hurrying there, icy floor beneath her feet, she found Lark on top of the bedclothes, doubled up, both arms clutched round her ribs. Her face was blanched, and shone with sweat. When Brenda, alarmed, asked if this was a bad attack of indigestion, Lark could only groan in reply.

It didn't look like indigestion to Brenda. She ran to the coin box on the landing and dialled the ambulance. Then she pulled on some clothes and returned to Lark's room. She sat on her bed dabbing at her forehead with a wet sponge. Lark's groaning was horrible. She kept opening her mouth so wide Brenda could see all her back teeth, black with fillings. Through the curtains loomed a foggy dawn.

The ambulance men took one look at Lark and returned

for their stretcher. With great skill and speed they carried her downstairs. In her terror, Brenda felt their efficiency to be the only thing she could count upon as reality. She had never witnessed a real crisis before, and found to her shame she trembled.

'I'm coming too,' she said, when they had put Lark into the ambulance.

'You a relation?'

'No, but she's my friend.'

She and one of the men sat on the bunk opposite Lark, who groaned more loudly when the vehicle moved. Her body made a small ripple under the scarlet blanket, no larger than a child's. Pity she can't see the colour of the blanket, thought Brenda. She would have liked that. Then the ambulance siren gave a great scream, making her own heart jump. It wailed continually as they drove fast down the roads. Brenda longed to ask the man what was the matter with Lark, but he was holding Lark's hand, letting her clutch it with her bony fingers, and Brenda's voice failed her. She reached into her pocket for a packet of Woodbines, but when she brough them out the man shook his head and she put them back again.

At the hospital Lark was rushed on a trolley along green passages rank with disinfectant and lit by strips of neon. She was pushed into a cubicle. There, someone pulled a curtain, barring Brenda's entrance. She stood for a moment, helpless, listening to Lark's noise through the curtain. The material was covered with sunflowers, larger than life, a hideous yellow in the neon lighting. Brenda had never seen such ugly flowers. She sat on an upright plastic chair, one of a small row against a wall, and wondered how many people had sat on that very chair waiting for verdicts from behind the sunflowers. She was aware of the smell of her own nervous sweat.

Two nurses appeared. They took no notice of her. Their faces were brightly made up, as if they were going to a party. The wall clock said five to four. Who were their made-up faces for? Night-time casualties, or the puny doctor who followed them into the cubicle? Brenda listened to their voices but could decipher nothing against the torrent of Lark's groans. Then, suddenly, silence. The small starched noises of hands against aprons, the dull tap of shoes on muted linoleum. The doctor's voice, quite clear.

'Riddled with it, if you ask me,' he said. 'Tests in the morning.'

The words meant nothing to Brenda, though she felt her heart turn wild with instinctive fear. The foul sunflowers were snapped back, shrinking their petals into ugly folds. The white-coated doctor held a clipboard. Brenda stood up. She could see Lark lying on her side, apparently asleep.

'I'm her friend,' she said. 'Is she all right?'

The doctor was suspicious.

'No relation?'

'Just her friend.' Friends, in a crisis, were apparently of little use. The doctor licked his pencil. Ominously, Brenda thought. 'We share a flat. I rang for the ambulance.'

'Can you tell me her name?'

'Lark.'

'What was that?'

'Lark.' She spelt it. The doctor looked impatient. His pencil hovered, incredulous, above the clipboard.

'I mean her real name.'

'That is her real name.'

'Funny sort of name.' It had never occurred to Brenda before that Lark was a funny sort of name. The idea seeped across her mind now, sluggish as oil. She felt the weakness of disloyalty. Behind the doctor the two nurses stood like a small chorus each side of Lark's bed, their party faces smeared with patience. 'Lark what?'

Brenda paused.

'Jackson,' she said eventually.

'And her nearest relative? Where can her nearest relative be contacted?'

As Lark rang her mother in Westgate-on-Sea twice a week Brenda knew the number by heart. She answered the rest of the doctor's questions, sensing the hostility between them. Then, he wanted to get rid of her. But Brenda stood her ground.

'What's the matter with her?' she asked. 'Will she be all right?'

The doctor chewed the pink worm of his bottom lip, denting it. Tact was a reflex action.

'We've given her something to make her comfortable,' he said. 'If you like to come back later on in the day we should have more news. We'll be doing tests in the morning.' He hurried away, clipboard under his arm, no kind words about not worrying.

Brenda returned along the green corridors without looking back at Lark. She had wanted to touch her, the small mound of a foot under the blanket, but had not liked to in front of the nurses. She walked through the swing doors into an opal dawn. The hospital grounds were divided by tarmac drives. A suspicion of disinfectant in the smell of wet earth from the mean flower beds. Dead plants, mournful laurels. Two bicycles propped up against a pavement with that ludicrous, urgent look that waiting bicycles have, as if charging themselves for a race. A long time ago Lark had suggested they might follow the Tour de France for their holiday. Brenda had been very scathing and Lark had not mentioned it again.

Infirm of purpose, Brenda found herself walking through the town towards Wroughton. She had no clear idea what best to do, or how to pass the hours until she could return to Lark. She walked the three miles fast, hot and sweating, uncooled by the dankness of the air. She reached the farm, went to the chicken shed. Unlocked the padlock on the door. It seemed natural to her the birds should be the first to know.

They were surprised by her early arrival, started a speculative clucking. They were not due to be fed until tomorrow but Brenda decided on a premature meal: it would give her something to do and her hands, running through the mash, would be forced to stop trembling.

It was almost dark in the shed but Brenda had no heart to turn on the light. She emptied a bag of mash into a mixing trough, then added three scoops of maize. She mixed the stuff with her hands, slowly, even in her fear liking the familiar sensation of fine grain scurrying through her fingers. Some time ago Wilberforce had come to her with a fancy idea about adding a new-fangled chemical to the mash, which deepened the colour of the egg yolks. But she had been adamant. No, Wilberforce, she had said: we're just a small farm here. Only three hundred hens. For God's sake, let's stick to the maize and paler yolks. The birds have a bloody enough life as it is. Don't take away what might be their only pleasure. Wilberforce had agreed, not really interested.

Brenda fed the birds. In the half-light their eyes were indignant at the shift in their routine. They conveyed no sympathy, only irritation. Hard-hearted buggers. 'Lark's ill,' Brenda suddenly shouted out loud, startling them: but immediately they continued their impervious chatter. For the first time, this morning, she hated them. She noticed that Priscilla, a bossy bird, had something wrong with her comb: it hung to one side, pale and swollen, the obscene shape of the hand of a foetus. Brenda didn't care. It reminded her that all the birds were fifteen months old. Six weeks, two months perhaps, and they'd be killed, their use over. Within hours they'd be replaced by the birds now in the rearing pens. But Brenda knew quite clearly she could not face a new generation, all the bother of finding a new queen, and new names. No. When this lot went – sold off cheaply as boiling fowls – she would go too. Her notice, this time, would be final.

Through the skylight the paling light indicated real morning. At seven Brenda would go to the Evanses' house and break the news. Meantime she began to collect the eggs: not in her usual manner, walking down the rows putting them in a basket, but one at a time. She picked up a single egg, weighed it in her hand and walked with it slowly to the box

253

at the end of the shed where it would lie prior to sorting. Thus she strung out the job to last a long time, forcing herself to concentrate wholly on the shape of each egg, perfect in her hand, so that there should be no room in her mind for the vision of Lark twisted and screaming under the scarlet blanket.

Within a few days Lark was quite absumed by her illness. She lay back on the pillows, too weak to sit up, geranium nails spread out on the white sheet, unmoving. They had given her many pills and injections, and the pain now was a faraway thing like the shuffle of a distant train. She could see it rather than feel it, sense its approach. When its rattle became noisier she would tell a passing nurse and they would bring her more pills. She was allowed her gin: Brenda had made sure of that. A bottle of Gordon's and a glass stood on a tray at her bedside. Sometimes she swallowed the pills with the gin and for a few moments felt quite energetic as if, given the chance, she could stand up and sing.

The ward was a cheerful place: walls and high ceilings the colour of sand dunes, all strung about with streamers and balloons. For stretches of time Lark observed the other inmates clearly – mostly old people with moussy arms hanging from bright nightdresses: early daffodils and Get Better Soon cards by their bed. Sometimes they forgot to put their teeth in before they smiled, and clapped their hands over their gums in shame. They slept a lot, their skin less yellow in sleep. There was one younger one, long red hair, who thrashed about and moaned one night, and whose sunflower curtains were quickly drawn round her bed. She was no longer there next morning. Then there was a night when a few of the patients, great burly visitors round their beds, had struck up a chorus of *Auld Lang Syne*. New Year's Eve, they said it was, and the dreadful singing made Lark sad. All out of tune. She wanted to lead them: the notes were clear in her head waiting to be struck, but when she opened her mouth the strangest whimper emerged, far from the sound she aimed for. She felt tears on her cheeks and reached for her glass of gin. A nurse, hurrying by, said there, there, dear, don't upset yourself: everyone cries on New Year's Eve.

At other times a mist seemed to separate Lark from reality. Whether it was a mist of sleep, or some kind of actual vapour, she could never be sure: but it confused time, bringing cocoa and darkness when she had expected morning, or visitors when she thought it to be night. The Christmas decorations seemed to hang unsupported. Lark would move her eyes to see where they were fixed, but could see no place on the walls. There was a feeling of underwater living, dreamlike, never still. Everything was insubstantial. Solid forms melted. Faces became misshapen, voices obscure. Then the mist would clear, and the line of a window or the iron end of her bed would freeze into such sharpness that it hurt her eyes.

One thing Lark was clearly aware of: her illness had, curiously, brought good luck to her friends. A strange irony that she could not fathom, but a positive fact. They had all come to her with good news, and while they spoke their pleasure caused tangible happiness to seep through her veins, giving strength.

Mrs Browne, for instance, who brought mince pies, seemed no longer sad at leaving Wroughton House. With amazing cheerfulness she spoke of her new life in London: how she was looking forward to it, how she intended to start work again. She also said, when Lark was better, she would arrange for her to record a tape of her songs, and she then would take it to a friend in the music world. With a voice like hers, there was no reason Lark could not become famous overnight. Lark felt infinite faith in Mrs Browne's influence. She imagined a picture of herself, in the fluttery grey dress, on the sleeve of a record. She tried to smile. But her mouth was without saliva, and her lips tight as an elastic band across her teeth. Later, she dreamed the record had reached the charts.

Rosie Evans, who took off her meringue-like hat but kept

on her woolly gloves, had news that the damaged Morris Minor had been sold. She and Henry had decided – after a long discussion, she said – they no longer needed a car and could do with the money instead. Only yesterday they had received £75 in cash, which Rosie had hidden under a tin of apricots in the larder.

'I wouldn't tell that to anyone else, Lark dear, but you,' she said, and Lark, who was aware of the distant hum of the train, felt a small sense of honour. 'You're a person anyone can trust, so I'll tell you another thing. I'm saving up that money for a holiday. France. The French. Just Henry and me, first time for years. We went to a French restaurant, the other night, you know, and that's what gave me the inspiration. Only you mustn't say anything to Henry because I don't want him to know till it's all arranged. So you won't say a word, will you?' Lark shook her head. 'Well, I must be off. Don't want to tire you with all my silly plans, do I? Silly old romantic me, you know. Always have been. Anyhow, dear, you've got a lovely colour in your cheeks today. Much better. You'll be up and about in no time, and I'll feed you up with some of my puddings.'

She replaced her summery hat, patted Lark's knee and walked back down the ward, sniffing slightly at every bed as if each patient was some kind of food.

Her visit tired Lark. She slept awhile, and woke to find Henry Evans by her side. There seemed to be no visiting hours in this ward: people came and went as they pleased, even in the middle of the night, sometimes. Lark felt herself lucky to be in such a hospital.

Henry Evans looked awkward, ill-placed on the upright chair. His face was drawn, the skin of his nose and cheeks purple with broken veins. Lark had not remembered his hair to be so white, or his hands so shaky.

'Just on my way back from the Star,' he said. 'Thought I might as well pop in. The others told me you were better.' Lark tried to smile at him and he quickly looked away from her face. 'Anyhow, there's one bit of good news, that I will say.

You remember I told you, that time we were coming down from the woods, I was planning this visit to Cambridge? Well, it's all fixed up. Spring. Definite. Down to the last detail.' He moved his lips in a way that indicated the beginnings of a smile. But realising the rashness of this, he quickly dropped them back into their customary downward curve. 'There are also indications,' he went on, so low Lark could scarcely hear, 'the Cambridge trip might be preceded by a visit of a more adventurous nature – namely, to tropical places. I have in mind a cruise. The South Seas.' He paused, then added: 'With a companion, of course. Don't know why, but I thought you might like to know that.'

Lark moved her head on the pillow. She had never heard Henry Evans speak so many words at one time. They had exhausted her, so many confidences, flattering though they were: and they looked as if they had exhausted him, too. He stood up, one foot sliding on the floor, cap in hands, eyes full of hope.

'Well,' he said, 'there's the good news, Miss Lark, and you'll be riding out the storm, I've no doubt.' He turned from her and left. Unlike his wife he looked neither right nor left as he drifted uncertainly down the aisle between the beds, head hung between hunched shoulders.

Brenda came often. Lark lost count of the times. She would frequently wake to find her friend sitting there, staring at Lark's nails rather than her face. Several times she re-painted the nails, apologising for her lack of skill, and she brought constant half-bottles of gin. One day, a clear time, Lark noticed Brenda looked tearful: eyes swollen, lashes damp.

'What's the matter?' she whispered. Definite tears came to Brenda's eyes. She remained silent for a long time. Then she said, 'Oh, Lark. It's my father. The good news, it's too much for me. He is an Admiral, you know. I always knew he was, didn't I? I saw his picture in the paper, shaking hands with the Duke of Edinburgh. I know it was him. No doubt.' Lark felt her own tears reflect Brenda's pleasure. She wanted to ask many questions, but could only muster strength for one.

'The paper?' she whispered.

Again Brenda paused. Then she said:

'The *Daily Telegraph*.'

Lark nodded. If the picture was in the *Telegraph* that somehow confirmed everything. That was the paper Lark liked to read on the days she felt like reading at all. That was the sort of paper that would be helpful at tracing the admiral in the photograph, and Brenda's joy would be complete. She had no energy left to say all these things, but reached for Brenda's hand, and grasped it. Then she indicated that they should share the gin in the glass by the bed: with so much good news she knew without saying that Brenda would understand it to be a celebration drink.

Evans came often, too. Each time he brought scarlet flowers – geraniums, poinsettias, carnations. He arranged them with great care on the small bedside locker, and when there was no more room he'd put some on the table that bridged the foot of her bed. They were always the first thing she saw on waking, a flurry of scarlet petals which made a confetti of pink shadows on the white blanket, reminding Lark of her own room. Evans spoke much of the progress of the house: it was nearly finished, now. They'd be moving in a few weeks and would combine their house-warming party with celebrating Lark's recovery. She better not drink too much gin that night, he said, because he didn't want anyone being sick over their new carpets. Lark at once pictured herself in her grey dress, fluttering among the guests. They'd be bound to ask her to sing. She looked forward to it.

One evening Evans arrived solemn-faced. Lark's mother, he said, was unable to visit her because her arthritis had taken a turn for the worse. She was in bed, unable to move, but sent Lark much love and would dictate a letter. It was nothing to worry about, Evans added: just a little extra discomfort brought about by the bad weather, bound to clear up in the spring. Lark had scarcely thought about her mother since she had been in hospital. With Evans's news she now imagined her – not with twisted joints lying in bed, but sitting on a shingle beach, dark hair blowing in a sea breeze, unwrapping egg sandwiches. Later they had held their skirts above their knees and paddled, and Lark had remembered it to be the nicest day of her childhood until, in the evening, eating ices on the pier, her mother had said that her Dad had gone off with a new lady and wouldn't be back any more. Now, she felt a small flicker of worry, but the worry slid about, eluding her concentration. But she knew Evans was right: arthritis was less bad in the spring, and when she was better she would go herself to Westgate-on-Sea. She hadn't been for months, and her mother never complained.

Lark felt more tired than usual that evening. She strummed her fingers on the sheet and Evans pulled up a chair to sit close beside her. He still clutched a new pot of poinsettias, burning red. Their colour reflected into his face, making Lark want to laugh.

'Lovely, thank you,' she said.

'Just adding to the collection.' Evans put them on the locker by her bed. 'Roses, tomorrow, if I can get them.' He lifted her hand, waggled it about as if it was a thing independent of her body. 'Not much flesh on this, then, is there?' he said. 'It's all that living off gin and eggs, you know. Not a healthy diet at all. We'll have to be fattening you up – and we don't want any complaints.' He was smiling and frowning at the same time. Lark could smell him: some kind of leathery after-shave, rather sweet. Familiar. His face so handsome, so gentle. The funny eye twitching. His big hand heavy on hers on the sheet. *Dear God, I love you Evans Evans,* she wanted to say: *you're the only one I've ever loved.* She opened her mouth, but no words came. Perhaps a good thing: misplaced love should be kept secret, for fear of encumbering. But, tonight, Evans so close and quiet, she wouldn't have minded risking . . . She opened her mouth again. It was quite dry.

259

'You remember that night . . . ?' she whispered. The sound was like a scraping of leaves, far away. Evans nodded, blushing. His eyes were full of horror. 'Well, that night, Evans . . . That night was . . .' But she could not think what it was. She could not think what it was she had to tell him, except that she loved him, and he must be able to see that, this close.

The details of his face began to recede, then. She felt his arm behind her head, and she felt him holding the glass against her mouth. She swallowed a lot of gin: some of it ran down her chin and fell in cold spots on her chest.

'Reckon you needed a swig of that,' Evans was saying, and sat down again. He talked to her for a while, house news, and saying that she was the belle of the ward, mind she didn't let the doctors take any liberties or he'd be right jealous. Then he got up to go, promising to be back before work next morning. Lark would have liked him to bend over her and kiss her cheek: instead she watched him pick up her hands and kiss each scarlet nail, slowly, one by one.

When he had gone she reached for the glass of gin. It was empty. She picked up the half-bottle, surprisingly heavy, and drank directly from it. Soon, as she knew it would, her mind became beautifully silvered. Later that night she died.

Lark's mother requested that she should be buried near her friends. She herself, bedridden, was unable to attend the funeral.

It took place on a bitter day in early January. The sky was swollen with snow waiting to fall. The churchyard yews stood dense black shapes against it, and the elms quivered in an easterly wind. There were few mourners: Augusta Browne, Henry and Rosie, Brenda and Evans, and Lark's boss, a balding man with a permanent drip on the end of his nose. Now, he would have to offer his security elsewhere.

They stood by the grave listening to the monotonous threats of the vicar. Dust to dust, in his voice, lacked reso-nance. Everyone had sent scarlet flowers. They littered the coffin, and the ground near the grave, only brightness in the landscape. Augusta stroked her cheek with a bare hand. The cold hurt. Her skin was hard and icy as slate. She was thinking this sort of finality was in some ways easier to accept than the smaller deaths, the lesser endings, which life itself distributes. At least, after this kind of death, according to her own belief, there was no proven going on. In life, an era over, to continue with some measure of normality is the battle. To acquire optimism. To re-pursue. To believe in the possibility of further chances. When it came to such matters, and the time had come, Augusta was aware of her own helplessness. Her weakness. She shivered in a blast of wind, despising herself: here she was at Lark's funeral thinking about herself. Though perhaps that is the secret of most mourners. The death of another is the strongest reminder of one's own transience: one's own frailty: the body in the coffin narrowly thought of only in relation to oneself. Augusta tried to visualise Lark – not as she had last seen her, prematurely geriatric in hospital, but the night of the concert: enchanting the pensioners with her voice, drinking champagne by the fire, singing of Persian kings. But Lark's face had gone for the moment. Had it eluded them all so soon? How long did it take for buried flesh to relume itself in the memory? Augusta looked round.

Brenda could see Lark lying in the coffin clearly as if the wooden lid was transparent: white wax face, hands with scarlet nails crossed over her breasts, fluttery grey dress motionless now round her ankles. She had insisted Lark should be buried in that dress though she had refused to look at her, as Evans and Rosie had done, in the undertaker's chapel. Which, she wondered, would turn to dust first? The silvery materials, or Lark? At the thought of such decay Brenda let the tears run uncontrolled down her cheeks, to be dried by the wind. The bloody unfairness of it all. Lark so good, and dead. Ill for years and no one noticing. No one caring. Brenda blamed herself. She would never get over it. Never, never. She'd never be able to look at another gera-

nium without thinking . . . and she hadn't even said to Lark,
ever, how good she was. How much she loved her. Why
didn't people take chances instead of spurning them for fear
of looking foolish? Well, with Lark gone, there was one
chance *she* wasn't going to lose, now: Evans. In the void
caused by Lark's death his living presence had become
desirable in a way Brenda had not experienced before. Not
exciting, mind: just precious because it was alive, and firm,
and steadfast. Worth clinging to, worth appreciating. Poor
Lark: she had had a mean life, known nothing of the luxury
of a man's fidelity. Just a few screws behind the filing
cabinets. Remembering such indignities, given in generosity,
Brenda sobbed more loudly, and got a look from the vicar.
Silly old bugger. He ought to know people were entitled to
cry at funerals. Evans pressed her arm.

He let his fingers twirl through the beaver fur of her coat, a
clumsy but soft old thing she'd picked up at a jumble sale.
Through its skin he could feel the warmth of her flesh: a
strange sensation, out here: as if he was experiencing both
the warmth of indoors and the harshness of the elements at
the same time. There was comfort in the warmth beneath the
cold. There was no comfort in the memory of Lark's bones,
covered by a scant white sheen with little resemblance to
flesh, that would haunt him always. He remembered with
loathesome clarity the way that maddened night she had
crumbled beneath him like paper, whimpering. He must
have hurt her badly. Dear God, that she might have forgiven
him. Poor little wretch: kind and lonely and uncomplaining,
all her pleasures vicarious. Yellow kitchen walls, she'd said.
Well, they'd have yellow kitchen walls all right, the last
tribute he could pay her. When he had left her, that last time
in hospital, she had tried to smile, dragging back her lips
from teeth which had protruded more cruelly each day. He
had meant to kiss her on the cheek, but had not the courage.
Thinking only of his own horror and repulsion, his final
gesture had been the formal kissing of her hands, a thing he
had never done in his life before. He was sorry. Christ, when

he heard she had died that night, how sorry he was. He hoped she had not thought too badly of him before death reached her. He hoped the gin had nicely silvered her mind (he remembered her description with a renewed pang) and brought her peace. On the coffin lay his huge bunch of scarlet roses, too late for her to enjoy, but symbol of his affection. Blasted by regret, his cold hand felt for Brenda's warm one. The vicar's intonations blurred in his ears with the wind as privately he thanked God, upon whom he rarely called, for the warmth of a girl he loved. Brenda, beaver-coated, breathing near him, who must not die for many years.

On his other side Rosie, in black mackintosh and velours hat and red scarf knitted by Lark, was beset by fatigue as well as sadness. She had been up much of the night before arranging flowers in the church in a way she thought Lark would have appreciated, and making a wreath of carnations from herself and Henry. The days preceding Lark's death had taken their toll: visits every day to the hospital, and Henry more difficult than ever at home – snappish one moment, morose the next. Almost constantly intoxicated. Scarcely eating, restless in bed every night. Rosie planned a secret meeting with the doctor, though the very idea of this caused a battle within her conscience. On the one hand she felt it would be disloyal, on the other she badly needed help and advice. Cheerfulness and tolerance, it seemed, were some-times not enough. She still had not made up her mind what to do, and the problem battered her resistance.

Sudden tolling of the churchbells brought Rosie's attention back to the present. Poor dear Lark. Always such a scrap of a thing. Quite undeserving of so horrible an end. Of course, Rosie could have told anyone it wasn't indigestion Lark suffered from: but no one had asked her, and it wasn't her place to interfere. In the circumstances, it was a good thing Evans had chosen a healthy girl. She wouldn't wish any son of hers an instant widower: but she did wish Brenda would control her sobbing. The sound brought tears to Rosie's eyes as she remembered Lark's appreciation of her Christmas cake. In the end, *Henry* hadn't touched a slice. He didn't know how he hurt, Henry. Like this morning: it was only good sense to advise him to put on his overcoat for the funeral. Standing about in an east wind, Rosie had said, anyone could catch their death. But he had defied her, told her to mind her own bloody business. He could look after himself, didn't feel the cold. Afraid of the note in his voice, Rosie had said no more and had set about peeling the potatoes with inflamed hands that shook quite hard. She had silently prayed to God to make him change his mind, and put on the coat at the last minute. But God was evidently too busy welcoming Lark to heaven – where she was entitled to rest in peace, poor lass – to hear Rosie's prayer. And when they left the cottage for the church, Henry at her side, he was not only coatless, but undid the buttons of his jacket. Rosie had struggled hard and forced herself to say nothing. As the bell continued its melancholy tolling she glanced sideways and saw the wind bubbling under his shirt. She looked quickly back at the coffin. Lark, she knew, was safe. It was Henry she feared for now.

To catch his own death at Lark's funeral was precisely the idea that appealed to Henry very much, and once he had decided not to wear his overcoat nothing could alter his plan. He knew it would worry Rosie, but her concern was nothing to him. He also knew, should he actually catch pneumonia and die – pretty likely in his frail condition – he might risk missing the cruise and life with the Leopard. But cruising plans, since he had told them to Lark, had gone a little sour on him. The brochures had arrived in plain brown envelopes, and he had studied them many times in the lavatory at the Star. After several drinks, the white-shored, palmy islands tempted in their original fashion: but at other times, sober, they seemed very remote. Besides, where was the money to come from? Henry had reluctantly agreed to selling the car and Rosie had stored away the £75 in a secret place. To request it would mean her asking why. What convincing story could he tell? And anyhow, £75 wouldn't go far towards the kind of luxury cruise he planned.

While Henry's mind, at the graveside, was tormented by such problems, his body was happily wracked by the savage wind. He liked the feeling of it razoring through his bones, between his ribs, freezing his blood, numbing his face and hands. At this rate, it was almost certain he would become the next admittance to the graveyard. In the unlikely event of survival – ah, well, that surely would be an omen. That would mean that Fate endorsed his life with the Leopard, and he would re-encounter her quite soon.

Henry looked down to the coffin, encrusted with pillar-box-coloured flowers, vulgar as a hat, and longed for a drink. He couldn't say with any honesty he was that upset by Lark's death: she had been a nice enough little thing – pretty voice giving him a nasty turn that day in the woods – but he had not known her well. He would remember her, should he live, as the girl who had taken part of his secret to her grave. And due to the vicar's sense of self-importance, by God, she was taking a long time getting there. He must remember to tell Rosie he wished to be cremated, and none of this mumble-jumble over the scattering of the ashes. It required all his strength, now, not to protect his chest from the wind with his arms, but that would cause too much gladness in Rosie's heart. So he remained upright, frozen hands at his sides, and listened to the church clock strike four. Two hours till opening time. Jesus Christ. Bloody hell. He noticed all the others had their heads bowed, pinched faces, eyes shut. Could be they were coming up to the finale at last.

'Amen,' they all said, together.

Too late to join the chorus, Henry would not have liked it said of him he had failed to salute poor Lark. He looked up at the billowing sky and his heart ached for the rougher grave of a naval man. Burials at sea had always moved him to a tear: Lark's cage of earth left him without feeling.

'Amen,' he said, alone.

When the ceremony was over Augusta Browne invited everyone for a drink in Wroughton House. Henry was the only one to accept with reluctance, but decided it would be as good a way as any to pass the time till his visit to the Star.

They sat about, a disparate group, on odd chairs and upturned packing cases, in the hall. Rosie, always nervous on social occasions, immediately spilt sherry down her scarlet scarf, causing Henry unspeakable irritation. Mrs Browne filtered about in a long black coat and a black Stetson hat. She looked like a young widow, Henry thought, sad eyes bearing no relation to her kind smile as she poured large glasses of strong drinks. The heat of the fire and the strength of the alcohol induced the kind of post-burial conversation that is the final part of the mourners' duty. The sniffing boss took upon himself recollections the others could not dispute.

'Best little secretary of my experience. Not a natural one with figures, I will say that, but always humming away, always pleasant, always concerned I should have a nice selection of gâteaux with my afternoon tea.'

'Ah, God bless her soul,' said the vicar, who had never met Lark.

'Just a small one,' said his wife, to the offer of more sherry.

'You'll be leaving these curtains, will you, Mrs Browne, to the executives?' asked Rosie, who liked to think all business-men were executives. 'I expect they'll be glad of them, such lovely stuff.'

Henry, too cold to speak, sat huddled by the fire. The decrees of convention seemed to him most unreasonable: why should people who had nothing in common except the death of a friend bother to gather uneasily together? In low spirits already, why tax themselves further? It all seemed daft to him. Only compensation was Mrs Browne's fine whisky. He drank three large glasses before leaving. She was a generous lady, ever alert to his empty glass, and he blessed her for that.

He accompanied Rosie down the drive and to the cottage, very steady, the depression of the day slightly lifted. He told

Rosie he would be back later for supper, and when she had gone upstairs to relieve herself of her gloomy hat, he quietly took down his overcoat. Melted by Mrs Browne's fire, he did not relish a second freezing.

Henry walked briskly to the pub. Though bitterly cold, it was a fine, clear evening, the sky full of stars. His footsteps, cracking like shots on the road, signalled the frost that would come later. Henry envisaged the warmth inside the Star: the lights and low voices, the small fire and thud of darts. There, at his corner table, – of late, he noticed, the others had given up trying to draw him into conversation – he could sit and think of the Leopard undisturbed. Drink his six or seven whiskies, and keep his eye on the door. An evening identical to countless others, only escape from the stifling life at home.

Soon as he went through the door into the lounge Henry smelt the gust of warm familiar smells: rubber flooring and hot pies and smoke, dearer to his senses than the more sophisticated scents of Mrs Browne's hall. He hung up his overcoat, rubbed his hands to scrape away the chill they had acquired on the journey, and looked round. A few of the regulars were already at their tables. A single figure, back to him, was on a high stool at the bar.

Henry blinked. He had only had three drinks with Mrs Browne. They had fractionally lifted his spirits, but that recognisable state of confusion, brought about by a heavy night's drinking, was far from him. He could see quite clearly. He could see quite clearly that the figure at the bar was a woman. She had blonde hair and wore a leopard skin coat. Beside her on the bar was a small glass of ruby-coloured liquid: snaking through it, among cubes of ice, a twist of lemon.

Henry experienced the timelessness of shock. He felt a spasm in his bowels and lethargy, rather than weakness, in his knees. Such ineluctable confusion, shrinking his skin as well as his reason, caused him to sway gently on his feet, as if already inebriated, and he noticed old Joe gave him a funny look. Then his head cleared, though the pounding of his heart had sent the blood to his face, and he felt himself to be as scarlet as Lark's horrible flowers. He moved slowly, thoughts trailing some paces behind his movements. In a way that sometimes happens in times of crisis, a plan came easily to him. He would go the bar, order his first drink, and take it to his table. He would consume it quickly, but give himself time enough to gather courage and gallantry. Then he would return to the bar and offer to buy the Leopard a drink, at last making real the moment he had imagined so many thousand times that the picture was part of the tissue of his mind.

The bar was suddenly before him, supportive. Bill was pouring his drink, muttering about the weather. The Leopard, his Leopard, was not two feet from him. He dared not look at her, but could smell her powerful scent. He was aware of her small movements: glances at her watch, the crossing and recrossing of her legs. Then, as he turned, drink in hand, to go to his table, the whole picture of her, three-dimensional, life-size, billowed into his vision. It filled in small blanks that had confounded his memory: her nose tipped upwards, delicate, in a way he had never recalled. Her hair fell in chunks, rather than curls, on her forehead. Her wrist, thicker than he remembered, was cut by the thin gold strap of her watch in a way that must have been painful. Pushed back from her poor wrist was the cuff of her fur coat. Its beautiful spots, which had patterned Henry's sleeping and waking hours for nine months, dazzled him now in reality. Incredible. Henry's eyes remained on the cuff. He could not drag them away. There was something about it he had not expected, a thinness of quality. As he stared harder, he realised the edge of the cuff was worn to a thread of baldness, and he bit his lip to stifle an amazed cry. For here, under the cruel lights of the bar, the fabric of the coat was exposed, the illusion broken. *Nylon*. Henry said the ghastly word to himself several times, weak with disbelief. But he knew his eyes were not mistaken. No one, then, had hunted a wild animal in the jungles and had its skins fashioned for his Leopard. She was but the possessor of a cheap nylon coat, the kind of thing thousands of women, of lesser breed than her, fancy will upgrade them in the esteem of men. How could she have deceived him so?

'Good evening,' she said, head turning to him, eyes wide, shadows from clotted eyelashes fluttering on her cheeks. A low voice, she had, and plum-coloured lips that shone as if with grease. One of her front teeth protruded a little, and rested on the cushion of her lower lip. It was a dark, inky colour Henry had not remembered.

'Evening.' His face burned. Should he apologise for having stared at her? Even as he contemplated the question Henry felt himself moving away towards the safety of his table. He sat down with relief and took a long gulp of whisky, determined to look no more in the direction of the Leopard until it was time to put his plan into action. Only two things crowded his mind: the thought that the Leopard's smile and greeting had been an invitation – she was making it easy for him. And, less good, that she had tricked him with her coat. However, he could forgive her for that. Christ, it wasn't even a case of forgiveness: simply a matter of overcoming his own foolish shock. He would love her whatever she chose to wear, whatever illusions she chose to employ. It was a woman's prerogative, after all, to attract by any means: the fact that the Leopard had turned out to be as weak as any other woman was suddenly more endearing than Henry could bear. Dizzy with love for her, he finished his whisky with shaking hand and wondered at the scorching sensation that scoured his body. Was he feverish? Had his death plan worked too well? Was he already struck by pneumonia? At the thought of such irony tears grazed Henry's eyes, and he had to dry them with his handkerchief.

In that moment when they were shut painfully behind a blur of cotton, smelling of Rosie's horrible lavender bags, Henry missed the entrance of a man into the lounge. By the time the handkerchief was back in his pocket, eyes and cheeks still burning, but dry, a new scene was taking place at the bar. A scene Henry could not resist observing (indeed, none of the regulars made any pretence of ignoring what was going on). The Leopard was laughing, *laughing* up at the great swarthy brute of a man beside her. He was unkempt, unshaven, cocksure – Henry could see that just from the mould of his back. One of his hands was over the Leopard's wrist on the bar, digging into the flesh in so familiar a manner that Henry felt a sour flame of nausea in his throat. The man, who then Henry recognised to be that vile brute Wilberforce (crooked bastard, shady past), was tugging at the Leopard's hair with his other hand, making her laugh more loudly: a sharp, frosty laugh, whereas Henry had always supposed it would have been musical as sleigh bells (at least, how he imagined sleigh bells would sound). As he tugged at her hair Wilberforce parted it and thus exposed areas of dark root. From where Henry sat, some yards away, he could see them quite clearly. It was perhaps a trick of those confounded bar lights. Was the Leopard's hair not pure gold, as he had remembered? But Henry had little time to contemplate such matters: stunned, he concentrated on the actions at the bar. Wilberforce was giving a handful of silver to Bill. Then, with the same hand that he had groped through the Leopard's hair, he wiped his glossy mouth, but failed to clean it of a long string of beer froth that ran down to his chin. The Leopard, with a spring of impatience, left her high stool, and stood beside him. She put her hand through his arm. Henry noticed the extraordinary smallness of her waist, gripped in its leather belt, and a spray of dried mud on one of her legs. He saw her smile at Wilberforce, and knew she was going for ever. He stood up, raised his arm, noticed the pattern of pulsing veins on the back of his hand: all he had to do was to stretch out to her, and take her, and protect her, and save her.

'My Leopard!' he cried, and no one heard. But she looked at him, eyes still for a fraction of a second, and for the same amount of time Henry saw himself as he appeared in her vision: a drunken old man, swaying by his table, indeterminate hand raised to indicate some kind of muddled idea that he could not hope to articulate.

Then she and Wilberforce were gone, together. They swooshed through the lounge, arms linked, exuding that peculiar heat and energy that a man and woman, sexually or emotionally enflamed, have no interest in hiding.

Henry lowered his hand very slowly. The pulsing veins reminded him of a dying animal. He picked up his empty glass and took it to the bar. Bill grinned at him.

'There's a pair that'll come to no good,' he said, but Henry did not answer. He stood at the bar, drank several more whiskies – he did not count how many. His left hand rested on the leather seat of the Leopard's stool. At first it still retained her warmth, but soon cooled. Her scent was strong in the air. Her sharp laugh, her bald cuff, and her puffy wrist cut by the gold watch strap – the visions ebbed and flowed in Henry's mind, flotsam against the nobler memories, unstable, giddying. Only the bar stool was firm beneath his hand.

When he left the Star Bill warned him to take care. He even offered to go with him. But Henry shook his head. He needed no help. There was a full moon: he was quite capable of navigation. He steered himself along the sharp roads, pausing only at a hedge to be sick. There, in the bitter retching, he rid himself of every living organism in his body, and with them he spewed out the illusions that had bred and festered within him for so long. So when he stood up again, pushing a hand into a mass of brambles for support, he could feel no pain, for there were no nerve ends left with which to feel.

Much later he arrived at the cottage and knocked at his own front door. He listened to the twittering of the elms, and watched the cracked image of the moon in the kitchen window. Then the door was opened, cautiously. Rosie's face, ridiculous with concern, but it no longer irritated him.

'I'm a dead man,' he said.

Rosie's mouth, feeble, shaking, fell open.

'Oh, dear, there you are, Henry,' she said. 'What on earth do you think you're doing, knocking like that? Come on in.' She dragged the door wider open. Henry staggered into the husky lights and shapes of a room he recognised to be his own kitchen.

'I'm a dead man,' he said again, and fell into his chair.

Rosie smiled, controlling her mouth.

'There, there, my love,' she said, bustling, somewhere. 'You're so cold, too. Chilled to the bone.' She stoked the fire. 'The kettle's on. We'll soon have you warm, won't we? Lark's death, it's given all of us a bit of a turn, hasn't it?'

'Lark?' said Henry. He had forgotten she was dead, too. Rosie handed him a mug of tea.

'Here, drink that up,' she said, still smiling.

'Dead,' said Henry.

'Buried this afternoon.'

'Was I?'

'Now, come *along*, love. You're all confused. Your tea.'

Henry let a dribble of the strong liquid spread over his tongue, dulling the bitter after-taste of vomit. He had never been less confused in his life, but the clarity of his new state could not be explained to Rosie, or to anyone on earth.

Augusta did not sleep the night before the move, but she felt no tiredness in the morning. She was glad, at dawn, to see the sky still gravid with unfallen snow. Winter sun would have been unkind.

She lit the fire in the hall, trying to pretend it was a normal day. She made coffee, and cupped the mug in both hands, hoping for warmth. There was a chill within her, there now for many days, that the brightest fire had not been able to melt. Since Christmas she had given up taking pills of any sort, tranquillisers or pain killers, thus leaving her senses exposed to each raw hour of every day. This, the last day, she was light-headed from lack of sleep, and still cold, but for the moment sensations more difficult to cope with had left her, a thin tide on the horizon, ready to encroach at some later hour.

The removal men arrived early. She recognised some of them from the day they had moved in. They were strong, elderly men in starched white coats. Their handling of the furniture was systematic and careful. When it came to the grand piano they acted with particular reverence, swathing its various pieces in blankets, and carrying it to the van in more respectful fashion than the coffin bearers had borne Lark on her journey through the graveyard.

Rosie and Brenda arrived later. They packed china and glass into packing cases in the kitchen and the dining-room. They carried piles of bright towels from the linen cupboard. They drank many cups of tea. Rosie's face was drawn and tired. She worked with a nervous energy, making two journeys where one would have been necessary. Brenda was in a dreamy state, hands moving slowly, pausing to comment on each thing as she wrapped it. She seemed sated in some private way, mind elsewhere. Augusta herself made an effort to be useful, but no sooner than she began to clear a shelf of books or china, she felt it imperative to leave the room she was in to observe the emptying of another one.

By half-past two the last van had gone. The house was quite cleared. Augusta, Rosie and Brenda stood in the kitchen, drinking yet more tea, in cups thoughtfully provided by Rosie. Crumpled newspapers made a choppy sea of the floor. Devoid of the bright colours made by pots and china, the empty room was unrecognisable.

'Henry's badly got down by Lark's passing,' Rosie was saying. 'He keeps speaking of dying.' Augusta noticed that her hands, clumsy on her cup, were mottled as snakeskin, an unhealthy mole colour.

'He'll get over it,' said Brenda, blowing her tea. 'We'll all get over it, I daresay, one day.'

Rosie found it difficult ever to agree with Brenda.

'Hasn't been a good beginning to the year, if you ask me,' she said. 'Lark going one way, Mrs Browne the other. Won't you have a biscuit, Mrs Browne? You're thin as a rake. You need the strength.'

Augusta shook her head. Evans arrived a few moments later. He and Brenda kissed, clinging to each other as if they had been parted for a long time. Arms linked round each other's waists, they leaned against the sink, warm and awkward in their protection of each other against the elements they had been subjected to of late: anger, jealousy, and finally death.

There was no further reason for any of them to stay, but to leave was not easy. Rosie kissed Augusta on both cheeks, sniffing back tears, and said the village would miss her. Augusta doubted this, but acknowledged the compliment with a smile. She shook hands with Brenda and Evans, who thanked her for the use of the attic room. It had made all the difference to their lives, they said. They wished her well in London, and left holding hands. Rosie had to be on her way, too, she said. She had an appointment with the doctor to see if he could give her anything new for her hands. Once they had cleared up, why, she'd feel a different woman, up to anything.

When they had gone Augusta made a final pilgrimage round the garden. It was dank and gloomy, quiet but for the dripping leaves of evergreens. She picked a small bunch of winter jasmine from the wall outside her study, brief reminder of sun, and put it in her car. Then she toured the house, room by room, banishing the unfamiliar shapes of emptiness from her mind even as she observed them: carpets dented by the feet of parted furniture, walls patterned with dark shapes left by pictures, bare shelves. She would never remember it like this. The rooms would remain in her memory furnished as they had always been.

When the church clock struck five she lay on the floor of her study, where the telephone now stood, and rang Hugh.

'I'm ringing you from Wroughton for the last time,' she said, knowing she should have forced herself not to have rung at all.

'Did it all go well?'

'Oh, yes. There's no news, really.'

'No, I don't suppose there is.'

'Sorry . . . to disturb you,' she said.

There was a pause.

'That's all right,' Hugh answered, more gently than in the past months. 'Drive carefully when you leave. There's fog on the motorway.'

They said goodbye. Augusta went to the hall. It was already almost dark. She put more logs on the fire, giving in to final weakness – carrying out her plan which was to wait until the fire went out before she left. She sat down on the flagstones beside it.

Some hours later, coming downstairs for the last time, she paused to listen to the comfortable crackle of the fire. Shutting her eyes, she imagined it was an ordinary night of a few years ago: one of the many times she had descended the stairs to the warmth of the hall. The sounds of shifting logs were the same – the dim, summery smell of apple boughs, preserved out of season in this winter house, unchanged. The polished wood of the banister beneath her hand, its familiar hump arching in her palm, the creak of a stair beneath her feet – if all was still tangibly the same, which it was, then the destruction that had taken place today was surely no more than a nightmare?

The illusion lasted only while Augusta kept shut her eyes. When she opened them, and returned to the bare hall, she smiled at her own absurdity. The emptiness of reality was all about her, intumulating that sudden, last, pathetic hope with a force that flayed the strength she had relied upon all day. She sat down by the fire again, to keep watch over the flames for a few more hours.

Much later that night Henry walked slowly home, agreeably surprised by occasional flakes of snow that melted against his face. Coming up the road to the cottage, he noticed a dim glow from the hall windows of Wroughton

House. Firelight rather than lamplight, he thought, and without determining upon any plan found himself approaching the house.

Reaching the front door, he saw the empty hall through its glass panes, and remembered today was the day Mrs Browne was leaving. Then he saw her sitting on the floor by the fire, which was little more than a frill of small flames among red ash. Her knees were drawn up, her head upon them, the whole structure bound together by her arms. She seemed becalmed. For a moment Henry thought of going to her, then decided against it. There is unwitting mockery in consolation. There are areas of despair no outsider should intrude upon, lest they are rekindled by well-intentioned kindness. Henry turned away. He was shocked at having witnessed another's private anguish, and at the same time consoled.

As he made his way back down the drive the snow began to fall more thickly, sticking to his clothes. He did not feel drunk tonight, though he knew by rights he should be. As far as he could tell, he walked quite steadily.

At home, Rosie was knitting.

'Mrs Browne's dead,' he said. 'I've just seen her. I looked through the window and saw her by the fire.'

A look of horror flared in Rosie's face, quickly replaced by one of understanding.

'Don't be silly, love,' she said. 'I was with Mrs Browne most of the day, helping her pack up. I expect she's just upset. She loves the house.'

'She's dead, I tell you.' Henry sat heavily in his chair. 'You may not know it, Rosie, but there are a lot of dead people walking about. You run into them everywhere.'

'Yes, yes, love,' Rosie replied in her patient cooing voice. He could see her gather her most welcoming smile, which she turned upon him, striking him as it always did with profound irritation. The uncomprehending busybodying old cow. Not that her welcomes mattered, really, any more. He could pass through their smothering as a ghost pierces solid substance. So she could carry on her smiling, much as she liked – he would have no care. One day, perhaps, she would learn that welcomes are nothing to the dead.

Brenda and Evans were married a few days after Augusta Browne had gone. Happily confused by the blurring of snow and confetti in their eyes, they left for a honeymoon in Brighton.

When they returned they found that Wroughton House was already being transferred into offices, and the elms were cut down. But they weren't very interested. They had their own home, now, and much to do to complete it. Often the convenience of the chickens – free-range birds at the bottom of the garden – seemed to come first. Bloody chickens, as Evans still thought of them, privately. They took up so much of Brenda's time and thoughts.

Gradually they acquired furniture and curtains and potted plants all of which, Evans liked to think, Lark would have approved. Augusta Browne had given them the brass bed as a wedding present, which reminded them occasionally of their attic nights, and sometimes they wondered what had become of her. But, their long wait over, its frustrations were almost forgotten. The room at Wroughton House had been merely a part of that time of waiting, and was banished now from their minds by the present interests of their new life.

LAND GIRLS

Angela Huth

'Piquant, witty and entertaining'
Tatler

The West Country in wartime, and the land girls are gathering on
the farm of John and Faith Lawrence.

Prue, a man-eating hairdresser from Manchester; Ag, a cerebral
Cambridge undergraduate; and Stella, a dreamy Surrey girl stunted
by love: three very different women, from very different
backgrounds, who find themselves thrown together, sharing an
attic bedroom and laying the foundations for a friendship that
will last a lifetime.

'Angela Huth's riveting novel ... is evocative and entertaining'
Mail on Sunday

'It had me in its grip and I couldn't rest until the final page ... It is
satisfying and rare to read a book whose characters are dealt the
fates we feel they deserve ... A beautifully spun tale that absorbs
without the need to address "issues"'
Literary Review

'A good story, told with wit and a keen observation of detail'
Times Literary Supplement

Abacus
0 349 10601 0

NOWHERE GIRL

Angela Huth

'A first-class writer'
Sunday Telegraph

Estranged from her second husband Jonathan, Clare Lyall is less sure than ever about the role men should play in her life.

Her first husband, Richard, was much older than her, and his casual disregard for youth gradually hardened into indifference. And Jonathan, if anything, was too easy - too attentive, too concerned, and just a little too pedantic.

So when she meets Joshua Heron at a party, the offbeat Clare isn't exactly thirsting for love. But she *is* mildly impressed when Joshua stubs his cigarette out on his thumb, and swayed still further by the advice of her new friend, the indomitable Mrs Fox. 'Take a lover,' she says, 'it's better to have a lover when you're young than neurosis when you're old ...'

Gentle, wistful and wry, *Nowhere Girl* is a beautifully controlled love story from the acclaimed author of *Invitation to the Married Life*.

'There is a very strong case for Huth replacing Jane Austen on the school syllabus'
Sunday Times

Abacus
0 349 10630 4

☐ Invitation to the Married Life	Angela Huth	£6.99
☐ Land Girls	Angela Huth	£6.99
☐ Nowhere Girl	Angela Huth	£6.99
☐ Virginia Fly is Drowning	Angela Huth	£6.99

Abacus now offers an exciting range of quality titles by both established and new authors which can be ordered from the following address:

> Little, Brown & Company (UK),
> P.O. Box 11,
> Falmouth,
> Cornwall TR10 9EN.

Fax No: 01326 317444.
Telephone No: 01326 317200
E-mail: books@barni.avel.co.uk

Payments can be made as follows: cheque, postal order (payable to Little, Brown and Company) or by credit cards, Visa/Access. Do not send cash or currency. UK customers and B.F.P.O. please allow £1.00 for postage and packing for the first book, plus 50p for the second book, plus 30p for each additional book up to a maximum charge of £3.00 (7 books plus). Overseas customers including Ireland, please allow £2.00 for the first book plus £1.00 for the second book, plus 50p for each additional book.

NAME (Block Letters) _____

ADDRESS _____

_____

_____

☐ I enclose my remittance for £ _____
☐ I wish to pay by Access/Visa Card

Number ☐☐☐☐☐☐☐☐☐☐☐☐☐☐☐☐

Card Expiry Date _____